African Cookboy

African Cookboy

David Dinwoodie Irving

First published by Jacana Media (Pty) Ltd in 2010

10 Orange Street
Sunnyside
Auckland Park 2092
South Africa
+2711 628 3200
www.jacana.co.za

ISBN 978-1-77009-869-5

Cover design by Joey Hi-Fi
Set in Sabon 10.5/14pt
Job No. 001242
Printed and bound by CTP Book Printers, Cape Town

ISO 12647 compliant

See a complete list of Jacana titles at www.jacana.co.za

this novel is for you, the reader,
whoever you are,
wherever you may be,
however you obtain your reading pleasure –
from bookstores, from friends, from second-hand charity
    sales,
even from discarded but still legible literary treasure
found fortuitously lying in a rubbish bin
without you,
writers would not, could not
exist,
and the world would be a world
bereft of shared experiences
and shared flights of soaring imagination;
of knowledge and laughter and . . .
. . . and all those other wonderfully precious things

PROLOGUE
The Present

'The Minister is very, very busy, young man.'

'Let him in, Miss Khubeka. He's been pestering me for months. That's right, grab a chair, young man.'

'But, Minister, you have urgent – '

'That will be all, Miss Khubeka. Close the door behind you. Now, what can I do for you, young man?'

'Minister, sir, I'm researching early township gangsterism for my thesis at university and –'

'And what on earth makes you think I can help you?'

'Sir, my great-uncle said to mention the name "Shatterproof" to you and you might help.'

'Shatterproof, eh?'

'Yes, sir, he said that nickname would be the key to unlocking a flood of memories, sir.'

'Do you know how old I am, young man?'

'Yes, sir, yes I do, sir.'

'I don't have that much longer to live. No, no, please don't think I'm being overly melodramatic. That's just the way things are. We only make ourselves unhappy by not accepting the fact that all roads come to an end. It is the way of our time here on this earth. What is meant to be, young man, is meant to be. Perhaps it is time to tell my story.'

1

'I would be very grateful, sir.'

'The possibility exists that I am the one who should be grateful. Here, take this.'

'What is it, sir?'

'A pass to get you past my security guards this weekend.'

'But why, sir?'

'Because circumstance and protocol prohibit the use of this office as a confessional. What I have to tell you will take many weekends of your time and much patience. Be at my residence this Saturday morning, ten sharp.'

'At your house, sir?'

'Are you hard of hearing, young man? Miss Khubeka! Miss Khubeka! Show our visitor the way out, if you please.'

'Sir, do you mean it, sir?'

'Ten sharp, young man. Don't be late.'

Black And
White Bioscope

Before the Nigerian crime-cartels took over.

Before the democratic slayings for staked-out territory and the permanent arrival of the lucrative smack and crack trade.

Long before ubiquitous computers and electronic hacking-scams.

Oh yes, *mfowethu*, way back then there was another way of life in the vast and sprawling black townships of South Africa that were springing up like mushrooms after heavy rainfall once the insanity of the Second World War's worldwide bloodshed had petered out and the White Nationalist Government had waltzed into power.

Born there, your subsistence destiny was preordained:

You were birthed from your mother's heavings straight into a mould made of something far stronger than steel or concrete, more rigid than the mightiest of immovable mountains.

You were born into the world of doormats:

Your life was a doormat's life, something so unnaturally low it could only be meant for somebody else to use to scrape the shit right off their shoes.

Unless you chose the only alternative.

The life of a *tsotsi*.

Often short-lived, agreed.

Brutal perhaps.

Pointless perhaps.

But the air you breathed was your own. It was not farmed out to you on the basis of begging the Nazi *amaboere* for every oxygen inhalation.

The first money I ever remember making was running KB for the thirsty brothers at the local soccer club in our section of Soweto.

Come again?

What's KB?

Kaffir beer, *bra*. Those days even we darkies used to call it that. Home-brewed illegal intoxication of magnificent renown.

Most favoured was the highly potent concoction *sebapa le masenge*, meaning roughly 'that which creeps under the sink', referring to the disorientation it gave to the legs of those careless and often over-enthusiastic drinkers with proudly alcoholic egos. Pride *always* goes before a fall.

My uncle Phuza '*Babalaza*' Mthembu, his township name meaning '*bad* hangover', the *worst* kind, was unofficial head of the club. He used to give me and my brother Vilakazi ten cents every time we fetched and delivered a five-gallon paraffin tin of either *skokiaan* or beer for his sideline business. When filled, this tin was so heavy that together we staggered for balance, barely able to carry it.

At the end of a blisteringly hot, dusty day, our labour would earn us up to maybe fifty, sixty or even seventy cents, which was a lot more cash than most of the *abantwana* in our neighbourhood of jerry-built shacks had.

Come to dwell on it, it was just about the only semi-legitimate earnings I ever made in my life. Every other wage I ever made came out of something the *amapolisi* would call criminal in one way or another.

My uncle Babalaza was a big *indoda* in the neighbourhood. This, by association, gave me and Vilakazi a certain standing even when we were pipsqueak *mfaans*.

My father never liked Uncle Babalaza. He used to thrash us bleeding brown-and-blue whenever he discovered we were hanging around my mother's brother. My father would tell my *mame* that Uncle Babalaza was a *skebberesh* and a thief and a *skebengu*-gangster, but he never said it loud enough for anyone else within eavesdropping distance to hear him.

Everybody in the neighbourhood, apart from my holier-than-thou father, called my uncle '*Baba*' Babalaza, or 'Father' Babalaza, a term of enormous respect, and moved aside whenever and wherever he walked his singular path along the interconnecting dirt streets.

My father's principles were a lot more important to him than they were to Vilakazi and me. By the time my father died from a wracking lung disease that originated in the cement-products factory he worked at six days a week, Vilakazi and I were running a lot more than KB for Uncle Babalaza. When I was twelve and Vilakazi was thirteen we were selling *dagga* parcels for him and earning as much as twenty *amarands* a week, sometimes double that amount.

I usually had to wait for Vilakazi long after school was out because he was punished by after-class detention with monotonous regularity. Me, I liked school, and Vilakazi, of course, hated it. Even though he was a year older than I was, he was a whole standard behind. I don't like to talk bad-breath about my own brother this way, but it must be said: Vilakazi was not a recipient of overmuch in the brains department.

It was like that all our lives. Me, I've never stopped

learning – and I never will, until *tshelete ya matsidiso*, or 'mourners' money', is collected for my funeral. See, *mfowethu*, when Vilakazi got so he could read the newspaper, he judged that was enough. I never saw him read anything else.

We used to meet Uncle Babalaza in the back room of our *apartheid*-granted White Social Services-sanctioned *Bantustan* soccer club. Famous guys like Syd 'Shortex' Kitsa and Solly 'Buya Msuthu' Nkutha had their beginnings there. Uncle Babalaza would give us each about ten of those giant-sized Lion matchboxes packed with weed and a list of places where we would 'meet' paying customers.

Usually we were to stand on a certain corner, or in front of a camouflaged *shebeen*, and wait until the right target came up and asked if we had anything for him. We were taught to ask for '*dollars*' first and to count every grubby note and tarnished coin before we handed over the compacted *insangu*.

That was all there was to it.

Even then, it ate at me like starving rats with needle-sharp teeth to carry around all that spending credit and know that I was only getting a pauper's measly share for taking all the risks.

Vilakazi and I talked this over quite seriously in our own grandiose pubescent way, but we knew Uncle Babalaza was the wrong *geeza* to cross so we never did anything about it. He was a real '*axeman*' from the old school of an eye for an eye, and then the teeth plus broken arms and legs for good measure. He had been arrested by the *amapolisi* for everything from rape to murder, but had only once been in prison for six months for being a passenger in a car that he claimed he didn't know was stolen.

One of his favourite oft-repeated stories was about a flash boy called Spokes Wheel, who'd been a delivery messenger for him. Uncle Babalaza would pause there, and at that point we were supposed to ask for the umpteenth time, 'What happened?'

'Spokes Wheel finally showed up. It turned out he had an appointment with the grave!' Uncle Babalaza would laugh, slapping his thighs with merriment.

There never was any doubt in my or Vilakazi's mind about what happened to Spokes Wheel. Uncle Babalaza never let us forget that the same appointment could be kept by us.

The year Vilakazi was fourteen, he turned his back on school and started to work for Uncle Babalaza full-time. He rented an added-on outside room of cardboard and plastic sheeting from a respectable family next door to the soccer club, saying he couldn't stand the noise around our house. I had three baby sisters and with my *mame* out working her domestic jobs most of the time, I had to take care of them. It nearly drove me crazy, *mfowethu*, I can tell you.

After two months of playing milksop nursemaid I moved in with Vilakazi.

I never went back home except to drop off some spare cash once in a while.

Vilakazi and I deviously began to spread our own acquisitive searching tentacles as time passed. There was a lot of stuff to be picked up if you were audacious, bold and as fast as a professional illusionist at using the obvious to hide the surreptitious – especially from parked cars and unattended white houses on the outskirts of Jo'burg, away from the *amapolisi* checkpoints. That stuff would bring in plenty of dollars if you knew where to sell it. And there were numerous other *rwa* methods to pick up some cash if you had the right connections.

At that time there was a wild bunch of young *amacrazies*,

seriously dedicated macho maniacs who called themselves the Lone Rangers. They hung out on the Dube side, what we called 'Darkie Houghton' in those days. Nearly all of them are dead now, or else scattered across the length and breadth of South Africa rotting in jails on multiple life-sentences. A few of the best, years older than me, are still around. No names, but we have stayed in touch ever since we were laaitjies. Vilakazi and I used to pick up extra dollars from the biggest survivor of that group by selling their hit-or-miss hot merchandise.

Around this time, Vilakazi began to hang around with a mad hulking skebengu from Sophiatown – the hub of black art and music, later destroyed, annihilated, laid to waste by the white amaboere government Nazis in control. They had the guns, we didn't; but leave that. Political analysis is beneath my notice, mfowethu. Black, white, they're all the same scumbags beneath the skin. Aren't we all?

This guy Vilakazi chummed up to was called Big Bang Bongani. He was about three or four years older than we were, and he was a real psycho-case. There wasn't anything he wouldn't go for. He and Vilakazi attempted a couple of muggings, botched them, and nearly got wasted themselves in the Neanderthal wasteland of absent intelligence the process required.

I had to explain patiently to Vilakazi that for the few lousy dollars you got from some poor working bastard's weekly pay-packet, it simply wasn't worth it. Not when he was prepared to die for it; die, or make you dead. If the victim resisted, there was no ways you could bluff – you had to go all the way. That is, if you wanted the job completed. I finally got it through Vilakazi's thick, woolly head that strong-arm violence aiming indirectly at the permanent cessation of life was for mampara birdbrains. All it could do was land you so deep in the uthuvi you'd need crayfish filtration gills to survive.

Big Bang Bongani lived in Sophiatown, as I said, but every weekend his mother would send him to stay with his elder sister Sweet Cherry, who lived a few streets away from our soccer club. Sweet Cherry was a slim, long-legged doll who worked nights in a busy *shebeen*, her enormous unharnessed breasts a huge repeat business drawcard. She slept most of the day.

That's how I first saw her.

I was looking for Big Bang and Vilakazi on a Saturday morning when I walked into the cramped room and saw her lying asleep on the bed.

She was on her stomach and had taken off her flimsy nightgown because of the heat seeping through the cinder-block walls and corrugated iron roof. Her head was turned sideways, resting pillowed on an outflung arm. There were sparkling beads woven into her hair and she seemed to glow lustrously in sleep from the crown down. Me, Dhlamini Bhekuzulu, I tell you no lies, *mfowethu*.

I closed the door of ill-fitting cross-latticed wooden planks as carefully as I could so as not to make any noise.

I must have stood there for ten minutes easy, just eating her inch by inch with my eyes.

It was the first time I'd ever been alone so close to a naked, blossomed-out young woman at such tight proximity. Watching groups of nude girls bathe didn't count. I was imprisoned by her sensuality. A hopelessly chained willing slave to my nerve-tingling tumescent captivity. I couldn't get enough of it: my eyeballs felt her beauty inflating them like kids' balloons.

Finally I walked the sort distance separating us and sat down on the bed beside her. She turned over and opened her big almond-shaped lazy eyes. She reached for the sheet, but it was down around the end of the packing-case bed with its horsehair mattress. Then she began to smile, her big lips and white teeth of pure eroticism beautifully displayed.

'You must be Dhlamini,' she said. 'Bongani said you might come around looking for him.'

I put my hand on one enchanted globe of a silken world-encompassing breast and she went still as a cat halting its stalk of a suddenly nervous feeding pigeon. Then she smiled again.

'You like that?' she purred. 'I thought sweets would still be your main attraction.'

My mouth was dry, but she didn't stop me doing what I was doing. Just threw out her arms, stretched in the bed luxuriously and unselfconsciously, looking more like a cat with every passing second.

Then I see her eyes are feasting on the tent made by my *umthondo*, which is throbbing and pointing skywards, the rough cloth of my *gangsta* Jewish hopsack trousers restrictive and scratchy.

I'm unbuttoned before I know it, then I'm naked, and she's pulling at it gently, but I shiver and tense from the contact. Nobody has ever touched my *umthondo* before.

Then I let myself relax, *mfowethu*, and I feel rigidly nervous but opulently sumptuous at the same time, a pivot upon which all riches balance.

Then I'm on her creaking bed, pulling her to me, my hard *umthondo* pushing up against her soft thigh.

We play for a while, me fumbling like crazy. A wrestling *laaitjie* who knows only how to look for an opening advantage in order to hold his opponent down for the count of three.

Then she slowly opens her legs.

I gasp to myself. Her soft womanhood highlighted by those vee-shaped tight black springcurls looks so beautiful to me, strange but familiar; my vision is riveted.

Next I'm between those spread legs and on top of her, feeling her groin against mine. I try to get it in the place *where the liquid heat of her secret passage must be*, but I'm pushing uselessly against dense, wiry pubic hair and dry flaps of flesh *and I'm going soft and I can't find it!* I start kissing her furiously and I'm immoderately pleased to find I'm hard as ironwood again, running my hands over the mounds of her voluptuous breasts, teasing her big hard nipples.

Once again, I try to get my swollen *umthondo* in, but *ayikhona, ayikhona wena*, I'm just rubbing it in a forwards motion against the frustrating flaps, hoping it will somehow slide into that elusive slippery dreamworld, *but there's nothing there!*

There's nothing there!!!!!

I'm beginning to panic, *mfowethu*, but now she firmly grasps my hand and places it down there on her spiral *nguni*-goldilox, eases my forefinger free and begins a movement with it that I'm uncertain how to follow. Then she lets go.

What does she want me to do?

I'm touching her blindly, rubbing all my fingers in and around her dry, shockingly uncooperative labia lips, still trying to find that place that I know *must be there*.

Then came the breakthrough!

I found it!

Much further down than I had assumed and so close to her anus I was startled and terribly afraid of offending her.

Too small for me – no ways, *mfowethu*, would my *umthondo* go in that tiny mouse-hole.

I worked my forefinger, trying to enlarge the gap I'd found and I could feel Sweet Cherry's lack of participating enthusiasm. With a sigh like a kettle boiling over, she reached down, pulled my finger up and placed it on what felt like a fleshy hard-soft button.

As I laboured at this little gecko-head Sweet Cherry started relaxing as if she'd been melted like hot candlewax. She was writhing and twisting, *squirming* actually, emitting sounds like she was short of breath. She became a snake entwined around my vibrating finger. My wrist was grasped and she tugged my hand down.

Her miniature mouse-hole aperture had changed!

It was moist and wide and my forefinger slid in as easily as if it had been greased, *mfowethu*!

Now I comprehend, at long last I comprehend!

Press the lightswitch at the top and the witchdoctor's secret seduction spell of sex will be magically illuminated.

Now I'm no longer in a hurry.

Neither was Sweet Cherry.

My virginity was encased in walls of sensation about to devour it forever.

After that, I used to see a lot of Sweet Cherry when she wasn't working, even though she was seven years older than me. She was the only reason I saw so repetitive much of her brother Big Bang.

He was strictly poison to me, understand, because he was a real *amacrazy* – you could never tell what he was going to do next. You could change from friend to foe in the blink of an eye and just as fast become the pulped object of his vacillating, destructive judgement's pointless violence. That guy was missing all his marbles, I kid you not. A *geeza* like that is virulently dangerous to everybody around him. I kept trying to tell Vilakazi this, but nobody could ever tell Vilakazi anything. Something in Big Bang got to

Vilakazi – maybe the attraction was his lunatic bravado, careless of the consequences, that Vilakazi didn't have. It made Vilakazi feel big and dangerous just to be around the short-fuse, maverick, glycerine-unstable firecracker that was Big Bang, and it was finally what screwed us up with my uncle Babalaza.

The first I knew of it was when I strolled casually unaware into the back room of our soccer club, jiving loosely to a lively *mbaqanga* tune filling my head.

Uncle Babalaza was sitting at the Formica table, a naked lightbulb overhead spotlighting the machete-made scars from an early gangland confrontation on his shaven skull, and Vilakazi was standing in front of him. I could see right away that Vilakazi was nervous – defecating his pants, in fact. He looked fantastically glad that I had walked in and he began sprouting a crop of babble-words fast as weeds multiplying on an overdose of rapid-growth fertiliser.

'It's just like I said, *umnumzana* [important one]. I made the drop in the bioscope, just the same as you ordered me, *umnumzana*. The mark sitting there gave me the pink dollars and I handed over the merchandise. Then all of a sudden, the *skebberesh* grabbed the cash and started to run. There was plenty noise, a big row, *umnumzana*, people. . . yelling. . . and shouting. . . ' Vilakazi's words tailed off into an inaudible whisper. He looked at me pleadingly, expecting me to back him up. 'I went scared out the fire-exit, *umnumzana*. . . I *ran*, *umnumzana*, I came straight here to you. . . *umnumzana*?'

Uncle Babalaza just sat there motionless staring at him, and Vilakazi began licking his lips with a tongue so stiff it looked like they were covered with glue.

'This is a simple matter for me to judge, *ntwana*,' Uncle Babalaza said formally but sounding peculiarly raw-edged, his voice pitched low and gravelly, yet amplified to my ears

13

as loud as a fire-and-brimstone preacher's scathing sermon. 'You are a liar. I know that customer for years.'

Uncle Babalaza stood up and took off his belt, moving intently forward like a vengeful dominant male leopard, and began banging Vilakazi viciously hard with the heavy buckle end of it. Vilakazi's lips, nose and forehead began spraying blood.

'*Hawu!* I speak truth!' Vilakazi *screamed* loud enough to deafen you. He kept yelling '*Hawu! Hawu!*' while Uncle Babalaza cut at him with the buckle, but he didn't do anything to stop it, even though he was twice Uncle Babalaza's size.

Now me, *I could tell Vilakazi was lying*, but I didn't see how Uncle Babalaza could know that. My brainbox was so shatter-thought disorientated, I didn't know what move to make.

Uncle Babalaza missed with a lunging swing of his improvised weapon and it flew out of his whitened brown fingers flecked with slippery dribbles of red. He stood there for a moment, malevolent and breathing hard. Then he reached into the pocket of his Jewish stylish-cut trousers for his switchblade and clicked the spear-size weapon open.

That was when I judged Uncle Babalaza was truly on some chemically mind-corrosive substance. He was sparking unearthed electricity from his toes right up to his voltage-overcharged ears. He began to move towards a fossilised Vilakazi and I knew with certainty what was going to happen next.

I grabbed up the tubular steel chair he'd been sitting on and bent it over his shaven, scarred skull with everything I had.

Then I grabbed Vilakazi and we footed it out of there quickstyle.

I took Vilakazi to an old warehouse that smelled of

stale animal droppings. By the time we got there the blood from his cuts had congealed, but he was still a mess.

When I got him backed into a corner, I slammed him hard up against the neglect of a filthy wall.

'Listen, you *gal pil mampara*! What did you do? Spill the beans, you *fokken moegoe*, or I cut you bad myself!'

Vilakazi was so surprised by my shrapnel vehemence that it all came pouring out at once.

It seems he'd let Big Bang Bongani talk him into a double-cross, *mfowethu*. Big Bang was supposed to jump Vilakazi after he'd got the money, but he'd jumped the *client* instead, his head vortexing on purple hearts, booze and *insangu*, before Vilakazi had a chance to hand over the merchandise. Big Bang figured loony-tunes-style they'd have the goods as well as the pink dollars, and they could sell it somewhere else.

Of all the dead-brain scams I ever heard of, this one topped them all. Neither of them ever considered that if the customer got his goods, the chances were he would mind his own business at the end of the day. *And* if he didn't get his goods, he was going to cry so loud you could've heard him all the way down in distant Cape Town.

Also, halfwit moves like this *mampara* manoeuvre could ruin business if it got around, worse than wildfire making a meal of combustible thatch.

'Listen, *ntwana*,' I said, easing off on Vilakazi. 'You're going to find that customer and you're going to give him back his purchase, you sweet with that? Then you going to pay back Uncle Babalaza, just like it really happened the way you fabricate it did. You with me, *ntwana*?'

I was so white-spots-in-front-of-my-eyes mad I drew back and punched my brother hard on the side of his mouth. A white tooth flew out from the back somewhere and skittered away out of sight as his head was flung back.

'Vilakazi, you don't do what I tell you, *ntwana*, I give you back to Uncle Babalaza. You got me straight?'

He must have taken me serious like, because that's just what he eventually did.

The next day I went around to see Uncle Babalaza at his barbed-wire fenced, cement-brick two-roomed house with the big flash American convertible parked out front. He was sitting up in a chair with an overlapping big stained bandage wound around his shaved dome. Before he could say anything, I told him in my best obsequious manner that he had no business going for Vilakazi like that, not when he was thrumming on a misjudgement high.

He knew I was right about that, no *indaba* necessary.

Then I told him I believed Vilakazi, and since the customer had vanished like everybody else from the improvised township bioscope when the *amapolisi* came, there was no ways to prove nothing. And so what if the customer had no goods at the end of it all? Why should he have more than his original *pink dollars* which he hadn't parted with anyway? And besides, Vilakazi was additionally going to pay back Uncle Babalaza every cent of his, Uncle Babalaza's, calamitously lost income just to show gratitude and goodwill. Sweet or what, Uncle Babalaza?

Uncle Babalaza looked at me a long time.

'Keep that piece-of-dog-shit brother of yours away from me,' was all he said, and then ignored me.

So I judged Vilakazi was safe for a while, but I also sussed we could kiss our soft little delivery racket goodbye for keeps.

Cash Crabs

In our neighbourhood, all of the young bloods made a blackboy version of whiteboy reformatory sooner or later.

Mainly because I was always so hyper-careful, Vilakazi and I made that graduation fairly late.

I was midway fifteen and Vilakazi going on for seventeen, when, following our termination in Uncle Babalaza's employ, I engineered a survival scam which at the time seemed pretty foolproof to both him and me. Though Vilakazi moaned about leaving out a 'brother', this time I made sure Big Bang Bongani stayed on the ignorant outside of my scheme.

My improvised plan was simple in the extreme. It was lacking only in foresight.

We'd pick up three or four willing *picannins* from our area and take them up around one or another of the drinkers' *shebeen* districts at about ten or eleven o'clock at night. We'd select a corner heavy with going-home human traffic.

Now when a man heads for home with warm alcohol singing *muhle* songs in his belly and he pauses to evaluate the possibility of any oncoming vehicles before crossing a road, he's likely to have his hands in his pants pockets. The

17

odds are even better that his fingers will be curled around his change and maybe even some nice-denomination paper money.

It was my job to grab the target's arms and violently jerk his hands out of his pockets, before he had a chance to uncurl his fingers.

Then I'd run as if the wind possessed my heels.

Vilakazi and the *picannins* would swiftly take over.

They scrambled like hyperactive, scuttling crabs for the coins and notes which spilled every-which-where on the ground. The boozed-up target would usually just stand there with his mouth slackly open, while Vilakazi provided more confusion by screaming imprecations at the miniature money-mongrels, all the while ready to lurch hard as a rugby tackle into the sucker if he showed any signs of retaliation. But no worries, *mfowethu*, the target was always too bombed out to make the slightest move. Even if he did crow like a violated rooster it never got him anywhere. There's something flawlessly ridiculous about a grown man who's been taken out by a bunch of babies.

With a good night's score, we'd make maybe thirty or forty *amarands*. The *picannins* got their favourite sniffing glue and a few coins as their reward, and Vilakazi and I split the rest.

We hit a different 'hood every night and in the sprawling ghetto that was Soweto, it looked like it would last forever.

Then I picked a target who turned out to be a sober black cop undercover in civilian glad-rags. I guess I'd become greedy: his shoes alone should have given me every clue I needed to spot him a mile away and back off.

To cut a long story short, we were all caught.

They layered '*Contributing To Juvenile Delinquency*' in legalese Afrikaans all over Vilakazi and me because of the *picannins* working alongside us. The white judge threw his heaviest book at us. It was the first but not the last time I've been called an 'evil monster'. I'll never forget it though. The judge gave us as much as he could – a one-way ticket to years in reformatory.

I only knew one thing when I got out. I was never going back.

The less said about the drawn-out indignities experienced there, the better – mental, sexual, physical, incessant torture that went beyond beyond. Bad as it was, I suppose it was no worse than any other segregated reformatory hell.

Vilakazi did his time standing on his head, but for me it was degrading, humiliatingly out of the reach of words to describe – and as I said, I didn't want it to happen ever again, *mfowethu*.

A few of the *guluvas*, jobless but flush *geezas*, I know never did any time at all. They're the smart ones, the ones who suss the geometry of society's angles. When I left that festering, diseased hole, I knew that the only way to stay out of it was to get super-smart myself. Pick something where the risk is small and always have the fixed game going for you. That's the only game to play.

When I got back to Soweto, things had changed, *mfowethu*.

I met Shadrack Matthews, a genial shopkeeper originating in Alexandra who was determined to rid the township of the Spoilers, a sadistic gang of murdering thugs who thrived on 'protection' money extorted from defenceless businessmen, taxi drivers and even private residents. He, Shadrack Matthews, had formed a large civic guard (later to be named the Msomis, after the KwaZulu-Natal mass murderer Elifas Msomi) and moved into equally vicious and murderous wide-spectrum retributive action. He and his *amadoda* worked in close collaboration with the *amapolisi,* and soon the terrorising Spoilers were brought to their knees.

Barely had the gun-smoke cleared away and the knife blades been wiped clean than the Msomis themselves switched their moral allegiance and became better-equipped and more organised *rawurawu* gangsters in the Spoilers mould.

They set out on a rampage of extortion, robbery and wholesale killing.

Eventually, after a series of fierce street battles with the Brixton Murder and Robbery Squad, most of the gang was cornered and brought to justice. But the wave of gangsterism continued, notwithstanding the fact that by the late 1960s Sophiatown and similar breeding grounds of *amacriminals* had been broken down to empty acres of uninhabitable rubble.

In actual fact, seasoned *rawurawus* and *guluvas* now found themselves in the very heart of Soweto, KwaMashu, Umlazi and other residential complexes. They could not have been more strategically placed to expand their ongoing influence, *mfowethu*!

Shadrack Matthews told me that 'Potato Crisp' Nxumalo was the top man; he had the white police in his pocket and was dreaming up more ways of making illegal money than politicians had guilt-free consciences. Their sphere of operation had expanded – liquor, many new variations of blim-blam dope, whores, gambling, extortion, and what the American *amacriminals* call 'loan-sharking'.

A man known as The General was in charge overall. We heard via the grapevine that he was even a welcome guest in the homes of some *white* officials and ate off *white* plates with *white* knives and forks, even drinking brandy out of *white* crystal snifters. Sol Plaatje might have been impressed, but not me, for definite sure – you think *white* saliva got fewer germs than *black* saliva?

To continue, after The General in the big-boss pecking order came George 'Potato Crisp' Nxumalo, not only in Soweto, but in all the surrounding townships as well.

Shadrack Matthews told me how George Nxumalo had got his nickname.

Some money-hungry *amafreaks* who had pulled off a few grocery-store cashpoint robberies had snatched him to make him tell where he had stashed a batch of 'black bombs', superior-quality amphetamine smuggled in from India. Back then his stuff was big anywhere kids, black or white, fancied dancing the night away without any weariness to interrupt their frenetic fun.

Those *umdidi we mpisi*, hyena's anus upstarts, didn't realise you had to be connected to distribute both wholesale and retail; they just saw the big, fat pot of gold at the end of the pretty rainbow.

They hung up Potato Crisp Nxumalo by his thumbs after thrashing him into a bloody pulp for a couple of hours. Then they went to work on his face with burning cigarette coals followed by lighted matches wherever they fancied. They fried the brother with more dedicated enthusiasm than Colonel Saunders trying out a human alternative to crispy chicken and left him there for dead.

It must have been quite a surprise when he showed up again.

One by one, with The General's strong-arm *amadoda* making sure he was obeyed, Potato Crisp Nxumalo gave them the choice of eating a whole pack of rat-poison beautifully sealed in a packet of regular Messaris Salted Potato Crisps, or eating their own amputated genitals.

That then was how Potato Crisp got the myriad white crater-scars on his face and the dead-nerve hanging droop in his right eye, inclusive of his nickname. I've seen him plenty times stripped down to a pair of shorts, and it's a good bet he's got more scars than he's got birthdays.

Vilakazi and I were dossing like stray alley-cats in the furnace basement of a seedy block of white-occupants-only flats near the Jo'burg railway station when I went to see Uncle Babalaza. We needed a stake. Desperate-style, *mfowethu*.

He hadn't changed, and he didn't splinter into shards of joy at seeing me. He didn't say anything about me coming back to work for him either.

I borrowed two *pink dollars*, two fifty-rand notes, from him and I could tell he never expected to see the money again, which was alright with me because I had decided that his sphere of influence was no place for me to be.

So I shook his hand, cool brotherhood fashion, and walked out.

I never saw him again, but later I did see a newspaper photograph of what they claimed was him, when they exhumed his body from somebody else's grave near Pretoria. It must have been a unique experience for him if they took him there before hacksawing off both feet at the ankles and letting him slowly bleed to death while encouraging him to flee – Uncle Babalaza had never been further than Jo'burg city-centre his entire life.

Years later, Potato Crisp Nxumalo told me he was sorry this had to happen. Uncle Babalaza was one of the *ngonyama madalas*, lionmen old-timers, who had to go when Potato Crisp introduced sales targets and accountancy and upped the level of operations into an organisation with an unwavering eye implacably fixed on visible profit and loss. In less than a week, about fifty established big frogs in small ponds were mysteriously and violently killed in every major black township in what was then called the Transvaal. They were all of the *ngonyama madala* mould, the loners, the savage old surviving individuals steeped in blood and battering who wouldn't take to modern methods or ideas, and they had to go.

Uncle Babalaza was way up on the list of priorities.

Things were pretty unsettled, to say the least.

Though The General was still the top man and though he had every lucrative activity pretty well organised, he still had a lot of rivals. People kept bumping heads and fracturing skulls all the time. Every few days you'd read about somebody being filled full of bullet holes or chopped into roast-beef-size chunks of raw meat.

The longer I looked at it, the more it seemed to me there were healthier places to be. No matter who my brother Vilakazi and I hooked up with, we could never be sure we weren't going to tangle wires with somebody who would use those same wires as both an excuse *and* a method to strangle us dead. *Garrotte*, as the Frogs so delicately put it, an abysmally refined word for such an ugly burst-windpipe death.

Not that there wasn't plenty we could do.

I talked to Shadrack Matthews and he told us he could fix it with Potato Crisp Nxumalo to hook us up in the illegal substances business again, or we could work on Shadrack's own collection payroll handling beer and whores.

Additionally, there was plenty of strong-arm enforcer work, and *amadoda* were always needed for the various robberies around the affluent white suburbs, appliance-producing factories and similar retail outlets.

But the day after Shadrack told me what he could do for us, he was hit bad himself. He got betrayed, plus getting three broken ribs, a bullet-shattered arm and a ruptured spleen out of it where the boys had put in the boot and the pickaxe handles. He was lucky he was a class sprinter or else he would have received much more permanent

23

damage.

One didn't need to be an Einstein at calculus to figure out that there wasn't any percentage in this kind of work.

What Vilakazi and I needed was a sweet spot in some outfit with an angle where you weren't just sitting around waiting for some avaricious *skebberesh* to move in and annihilate you.

A few days later Vilakazi came bouncing in like an effervescent yo-yo on a fail-safe string, with a grin wide, white and sparklingly enthusiastic enough to send a dozen dentists into manic depression.

Big Bang Bongani was behind him.

For once I was glad to see that Brobdingnagian lunatic of plant-life intelligence, the Oversize Human Venus Flytrap. He had a hold on what sounded like just the thing we were looking for.

To be frank, it didn't seem so to me at first, but after I grilled him, *mfowethu*, the business-business appeared better and better to yours truly.

Big Bang was now a protection heavy for a group that handled nothing but *amaliquor*. They had disguised warehouses in government-allocated, rent-controlled *khayas* for white Railway and Post Office employees, and these houses were clustered in architecturally offensive eyesores that seemed to attract an influx of 'Poor Whites' – those of pale skin as low down the poverty line as most blacks were, and just as desperate for money. From these 'warehouses' *amaliquor* was transported to any *shebeen* willing to buy.

'Safe as houses,' Vilakazi said, without realising that he had just made one of his few-and-far-between original jokes.

Big Bang's job was to safeguard against hijacking at the collection points.

Once the *bakkies* and taxis had moved out, he was usually free for the rest of that day. And for this he was sucking out hundreds of *amarand* dollars every week! But he carried an *isibhamu*, a gun, a weapon no black man was allowed to possess in draconian *apartheid* South Africa. This act of defiance by ownership carried a ten-year-minimum jail sentence – if you weren't first given free 'flying lessons' out of an upper-storey window at John Vorster Square.

From what I already knew and from what Big Bang had told me, there was very little major competition. The General made pay-offs to the officer hierarchy at police stations via street-patrolling young white constables blood-related to powerful captains and majors.

Such is the disparaging truth of life, *mfowethu*.

Of course, there was plenty of 'opposition' from hijacked SAB and high-octane booze-merchants' trucks – hit them hard and quick and take it away from them was a popular *modus operandi*. But nine times out of ten, the gung-ho bandits responsible would approach The General to take the entire score in bulk off their hands anyway, so nobody's feathers got ruffled.

At that time, stills were just beginning.

We darkies were catching on fast to making our own firewater alcohol.

It was simple.

We just copied the *amaboere* farmers who'd been making their own illegal ninety-proof *mampoer*, or peach brandy, for centuries – those same *amaboere* who claimed strong booze exploded in a black man's skull because the bones were too tight for a brain squeezed even smaller by our constrictive woolly caps of tight head-curls. Did I *forget* to tell you consumption of *amaliquor* was *against the law* for an indigenous biped back in those not-so-long-ago days? How careless of me. Oh yes, *mfowethu*! Oh y*ebo yes*! This myth was propagated relentlessly from public speakers' podiums by big-wheel white Afrikaans university academics no less – booze made *kaffirs* go *kaffir-crazy*, man!

Well, give us a gap and we'll go for it, same as you pale-skinned *abelungu* with big-enough balls.

The new stills were generally quiet places. And if you were running a still yourself, you could make plenty – enough for everyone – with very little risk.

Big Bang told us he could take us to a *geeza* who might be able to give us jobs.

It was on a bright African summer morning that we drove out in Big Bang's limousine, a monster red Ford Galaxie with chrome wheels and white sidewall tyres. He took us to an upgrade *shebeen* just off the humming highway and turned us over to an old Kraut, an ex-*übermensch* white wreck named Oom Kaffirboetie, or *Uncle Niggerbrother*. He had earned this, to some, derogatory nickname because he was crazy for black pussy and was therefore shunned by the majority of his own skin-colour South Africans. Oom Kaffirboetie had built the first prototype of black-financed alcohol-producing stills. That's where we were going to work.

It was as easy as that.

We would work, under his excellent tutelage, at producing high-octane booze.

But most important were our side-duties to keep up a plentiful supply of young, willing black girls, and the budget we were given covered that admirably with a plenitude of spare change.

That was how I got into the *amaliquor* trade.

I've been in it at one end or another, until democracy arrived like a virgin ballerina mistakenly booked to perform in a pornographic version of *Swan Lake*.

Sourcing
The Source

I was nineteen years old and I started at the bottom.

We ran everything from blindness-inducing rotgut to copies of whisky, gin, vodka, cane and brandy – Oom Kaffirboetie knew how to give a passable flavour to any raw product. I learned how to build from scratch a still that could turn out dynamite-proof alcohol as good as any in the country. I learned how to keep that illegal home-made still supplied and working without a hitch. We didn't call it a 'still' like they did overseas, of course. We called it simply *umPheki*, the Cookboy.

I learned how to camouflage an *umPheki* so that with any luck it wouldn't be found for years. If the luck ran out and the *amapolisi* smelled it, I learned how to take care of that too. The same old way it's been done for a thousand years, *mfowethu*.

There was a fortune a minute to be made, I kid you not.

Man's appetite for booze, especially if it's *forbidden by law* (and that law exacerbated for every black man with a thirst by the grog-swilling *amaboere* themselves), will be forever unquenched.

It wasn't long before the competition suddenly became the toughest imaginable. Every *tsotsi* wanted a piece of the big rising dough and a lot of mega-players wanted it *all*. I played it as safe and smart as I could from the very beginning and I *made* Vilakazi play it that way too.

Oom Kaffirboetie took a liking to me and he encouraged my infant education with a steady provision of a huge variety of paperback literature. Reading books was steadily improving my ignorant *mampara mfaan* English to be on a par with his. He had a lot to do with most of what's happened to my future. He was a chemist in Hitlerland before he got to South Africa, and in the beginning, before the first liquor-sweating Cookboy, The General had given him a really special job. It was an unusual job that those of us he called, somehow without being insulting, 'uneducated hairless brown monkeys' knew zero of or even how to begin carrying out.

Before Cookboys, you see, *mfowethu*, a lot of *shebeen amaliquor* came from your average commercial household-cleaning products. There were various adulterants put in the largely alcohol-based liquids to make them poisonous for drinking purposes; you've all seen what happens when a booze junkie drinks methylated spirits. Bad news, *mfowethu*, bad news indeed. It was Oom Kaffirboetie's very first job to analyse the formulas and then *crack* the alcohol to take out the impurities so that you could drink it with no greater ill effect than a crackerjack brain-busting hangover. The big commercial firms and the *swart-gevaar*-paranoid Nationalist Party government would regularly change the formulas – just to make us illegal-booze merchants cross-eyed. None of their machinations bothered lascivious old Oom Kaffirboetie. He claimed the formula wasn't made that he couldn't bombard out of existence with what he described as '*advance through technology*', though I forget now the German words used for that phrase.

The trouble was that when I met him, Oom Kaffirboetie

himself was a few bricks short of his own flawed building. He was okay, *mfowethu*, about ninety per cent of the time, but the other ten per cent he was a serious liability, and unchecked he could get us all arrested.

Example?

You want an example, *mfowethu*?

How's this?

Bombed out of his box, slewing his big black Mercedes right through the elite master-race suburbs of Saxonwold and Houghton and, at the finest white Rosebank restaurants he could only blurringly focus upon, *demanding* a table for himself *and his three slatternly dressed teenage black female companions.*

Ayikhona, wena! Eish, mfowethu!

The worst kind of unwanted publicity!

Fortunately, you could see the thunderclouds of temporary insanity gathering over him ahead of time.

The first clue was infallible.

'*Fooking fascists! I haff hatt fooking more zan enuff uff fooking fascists!*' Oom Kaffirboetie would start muttering away, his long white hair flying sideways as he flung his head about in a surfacing rage. Forewarned is forearmed, *mfowethu*. We'd lock him up in his room with a couple of naked girls for company until he was over his spell.

We were staked out in tree-filled farmhouse grounds between Jo'burg and Vereeniging – Oom Kaffirboetie, Vilakazi and me. Plus a small bow-legged guy named Black Chimp and another *geeza* named Eight Cylinder, who drove the delivery truck. Then there was the white Portuguese farmer, also addicted to breaking the *Immorality Act* through sexual congress with black women, who was the legitimate owner, legitimately growing vegetables on the place.

Our *umPheki* was a half-mile back from the farmhouse in the woods on a dribble of a stream that was the necessary water supply. It was a medium-size cooking contraption, averaging many gallons of booze a day. One of us had to watch it every second, but the rest of us had plenty of time to spare on our hands.

Eight Cylinder hauled away the alcohol and brought back sacks of sugar, empty five-gallon paraffin tins, newspapers, cigarettes and other basic supplies, good food included. Aside from smoking and listening to the radio, there wasn't much else for us to do.

This was tough on Vilakazi and Black Chimp, who was also a part-time *shebeen*-nightclub comedian, but it suited me fine because Oom Kaffirboetie was teaching me things I could never have learned any other way, *mfowethu*.

First of all, he taught me to read.

How to read says it better.

I already knew how, *mfowethu*, but I mean *how* to read by getting it into your head *what you are reading*. He also taught me *what to read*, and a whole lot about ground-level chemistry that you would never learn at university. That old Kraut could make bombs out of playing cards and pigeon shit, I kid you not – give Oom Kaffirboetie a glass gallon winejar and a few domestic products, and he could blow the side of a stone-block jail into powdered dust.

Most important of all, Oom Kaffirboetie taught me just about everything there was to know about distilling. Booze was going to keep *'pap en vleis'* on my table for a long time, *mfowethu*.

Distilling may sound fairly simple.

Just a matter of combining sugar, water and fermented crushed grain, and 'cooking' it until the end essence distils off through your end-of-the-line exit pipe.

But there are secrets to it without which you'll be lost, guaranteed.

I can make any kind of glug-glug *ugologo* you can name, most of it better than you can buy on any budget shelf in the big, legitimate liquor outlets. I can also make base-booze out of almost anything you can think of that will distil – mielie meal, white flour, laundry starch, chicken feed, fruit, tapioca, potatoes, cabbage, rice, Aqua Velva and Old Spice, to name a few. Just give me enough of any one of them and I'll turn out the finished product.

You'll look a long time before you find a hundred-percent-proof magician who can turn out a top-class product every time for the least possible outlay. A *tsotsi* magician like me who knows how and where to buy raw materials, how to distribute to his markets and how to get the best price possible for his merchandise. When you have to do all this with the fire-snorting bigoted dragon of *apartheid* plus jealous gangsters and the ever-present Van der Merwe mentality law breathing hot down your neck, it gets to be quite a problem. *Yebo*, a problem you need *ngxamile hlakanphile*, the serious smarts, to overcome, *mfowethu*.

For the next couple of years Vilakazi and I worked in four or five different branches of the booze business. We played nursemaid to multiplying Cookboys, drove supply and delivery vehicles, did a little selling; we got to know how things were done.

I'd like to give a little detail here on selling.

The white man's world was the white man's world.

The black man's world was the black man's world.

Shebeens were where black men and women drank.

Shebeens had become so much an integral part – in fact, the very foundation – of the township scene because of short-sighted white idiots like Verwoerd and Vorster, Prime Ministers who had no prime clue as to the rules they'd made that actually turned the wheels of commercialism.

Queens mostly ran them, *mfowethu*.

And when I say 'Queens', I mean Royalty with a capital *R* and Queens with a capital *Q*.

There were three classes of *shebeens* in our larger township areas – lower, middle and upper. These were categorised according to the kind of persons who frequented and ran them, including the all-important standard of service they offered.

All *shebeens* at that time were to be found in private homes, often with large, accommodating but camouflaged extensions at the back hidden by high split-pole fencing.

The best *shebeens* were usually, but not always, in the 'better' areas. Nevertheless, that did not guarantee that the worst were on the 'wrong side of the tracks'. There were *shebeens* for the well-to-do and *shebeens* for the desperately poor, fashionable *shebeens* and *shebeens* so grungy you needed to wash your clothes after a visit, but all thrived in their own way.

Shebeens have to be counted for posterity as among the most fascinating aspects of entrepreneurial township life. Besides being the big money-spinners they were, they bubbled with the foam of frothy beer; they throbbed with the rhythm of unique down-south jazz and hardtack-fuelled, many-voiced laughter; their undercurrent of volcanic sexuality would have brought a frozen samovar of coffee to the boil faster than liquid lava; and they could also resound with the bloody discord of quarrelling men for whom any argument could be settled only by decisive and pointless violence.

The lowest class of *shebeens* were called 'Small Time Joints'. These were patronised by real roughnecks and petty swindlers, ratbag thieves, up-and-coming young *tsotsi* gangs, wanted fugitives from the law, and the notorious and often diseased 'Fresh Girls' – degenerate booze- and drug-soaked prostitutes who'd *phatha-phatha* you standing up quickstyle, sometimes for the price of a single drink. Their habitual prey was youthful thugs and an endless stream of lonely, dirt-poor, hopeless adult drunks.

'Small Time Joints' bought their unsophisticated imbibement only from me – any label would do, as long as it said BRANDY, WHISKY, GIN or whatever. 'Small Time Joints' were renowned for the *'special intoxicators'* they served, these being my cheap-end speciality. Best-known among them were *miza* and the *sebapa le masenge* I mentioned earlier.

The better type *shebeen* was where 'Bangies' hung out, a *tsotsi* term referring to the customers who went there in groups for fear of clashing with the ubiquitous gangs of rabid teenage thugs. This was the 'working man's' rendezvous, where female company was not unrespectable and where 'Whitewash', traditional sorghum beer minimally spiked by yours truly, was plentiful and affordable. If you preferred the White Man's liquors, they were also plentifully supplied by me and at huge White Man's *'Black-Market'* prices, *mfowethu*!

It was at the top-class *shebeens* like Old Mathoko's that the 'Big Guns' drank and mingled. Big-time expansive personalities from boxing, soccer, retail and show-business, as well as smooth-tongued, expensively dressed spivs and hail-fellows-well-met – the kind who expected you to shovel your nose up their rectums to inhale their anal perfume and who delighted in abruptly yelling, *'Drinks on me all round!'* Copycats from American films seen in the bioscope, *mfowethu*, the thought in their self-inflated *uthuvi-amakhanda* as original as the urine they piss like anybody else. Shitheads, one and all: some pleasant, some unpleasant, but shitheads all the same.

Good music, fine glassware, modern furniture, sexy

serving girls like Sweet Cherry – all neat, classy and clean with flattering lighting and any price asked was the price paid without a quibble. You had to show style. And that need was lining my pockets just fine, thank you. No nonsense either in these posh *shebeens* that stayed open until dawn, no abrasively loud arguments, no fights, or else you got spoken to by methodical top-line bouncers, brawn who didn't accept favouritism bribes.

So much for illegal *shebeens*, the thousands and thousands of them from which alcohol poured out and money poured in.

In addition to the booze trade, The General had things sewed up so well that it was hard to operate any kind of line without his okay. He made all the necessary pay-offs, so he had most of the brass who pulled the strings in White-Controlled Law Enforcement working indirectly for him. If he didn't want you around, he just passed on the word to his *amapolisi* connections and you were out, usually with a rubber-truncheon beating that incapacitated you for weeks thrown in for good measure.

Three or four carloads now went out from my *umPheki* steam-engine each and every day of the week, and I knew of another three Cookboys that The General had going for him locally.

All of this was only The General's personal business. In addition, there were a lot of smaller gangsters paying him off in one way or another. All in all, he had the closest thing to a democratic organisation South Africa had ever seen. He wasn't totally invulnerable though – much later, because some somebody was getting more pay-off than some somebody else, The General was found guilty on a trumped-up charge and jailed for a few months, but that was the only time he ever did time.

Before that, however, a catalyst took place that changed

my whole life, *mfowethu*.

It didn't seem much when it happened, but it allowed me to get to know The General. I was with him for a long time, and I still think he was the best business *amigo* luck ever allowed me to have.

You probably never heard of The General.

The reason is that he never stuck his neck out. He never did anything to get his name in the *amanewspapers*, and he never was greedy. He's quite incredibly old now, but still powerful, believe me, and nothing ever happens that he doesn't have the inside information on, including this great mirage called politics.

I was working a brand-new *umPheki*, a copper and iron booze-baby that gurgled with joy when you tickled it.

We hadn't been there more than a few days.

Vilakazi was off with our minibus called Woof-Woof because its windowless sides were abundantly painted featuring blissfully happy and nauseatingly 'groomed' canine representatives of the dog-parlour trade.

Meanwhile, me and a true-blue *skellum* named Ding-Dong Dingane and another guy whose name I don't remember were loading the vats for a fresh batch.

This Ding-Dong was a surly *skebberesh* who'd charge you for the time of day. He always carried a chromium-plated, pearl-handled automatic strapped to his ankle: I think he even slept with it. He was as nervous and jumpy as a grounded grasshopper among a herd of flat-footed elephants on the move, and being around him made me nervous and jumpy too. I've never liked guns – if you're going to carry an *isibhamu*, you're going to have to use it sooner or later. Vilakazi would carry a thirty-eight revolver when he was driving, but I've never carried a firearm in my life. For me, an *isibhamu* spells nothing but grief.

It was about dusk and we'd just finished priming our

umPheki when a shadowy figure with a rifle steps out from behind a tree and says something like, '*Staan stil, vokken kaffirs, of ek skiet! Ons het julle nou vas!*'

Then three or four other figures stepped out of the bushes and closed in on us.

'*Bulongwe!* Bullshit! These *geezas* are hijackers!' This Ding-Dong screeched out like a scalded cat.

I had put my hands up, like I would have done anyway in the face of threatening opposition *or* the threatening law, when our trigger-happy Ding-Dong bends and makes a grab for his fancy *isibhamu* and starts blasting away.

There's nothing to be gained by doing this at any time, but that was truly the vacant grey-matter reaction of a village idiot to a situation where it's five-to-one against in firepower.

At that precise moment all I could think of was that if law enforcers get shot at, *they* can shoot back, and any illegal act of participation, such as merely being present, condones your becoming a corpse by association. You're guilty because you're guilty, *no matter who set things off*, the afterlife your only chance of redemption.

So I jumped Ding-Dong Dingane.

I ripped the chromium *isibhamu* away from him after an abruptly fierce and intensely violent atavistic struggle.

I got a bullet clean through my lower calf for my troubles and a long flesh-slice down the side of my face where Ding-Dong raked me with the gun barrel. The scar is still there today, as you can see, *mfowethu*.

By then there were so many triggers being pulled and such a cacophony of mind-numbing explosions going off all at once that I don't know who gave me my gunshot wound.

I dropped Ding-Dong's shiny glitter-weapon and fled with rocket-speed adrenalin propulsion long before the haze of cordite smoke cleared.

From behind the cover of a stout and friendly tree, I glanced back like a spooked jackrabbit unaware of its own rapid loss of blood and saw our 'attackers' were indeed the *gattes amapolisi*. There was no mistaking those inelegant uniforms that only a regular salary and a guaranteed pension could coerce you into wearing.

I also saw that Ding-Dong and the other guy whose name I don't remember were stone-cold dead; even at that distance in the settling dusk I could register the shrouds of glutinous wet redness that oozed from their prone unmoving bodies.

I reached Vilakazi's township pad safely.

He was waiting for me.

He laughed at my hurt, making it negligible, and squeezed my arm.

He made me feel alive again.

A few days later, me stitched with a dressmaker's sewing needle and bandaged up, we had a caller.

'Looks like you did alright, Dhlamini,' a big fat guy with a big fat baby face made even fatter and rounder by tractor-tyre lips and a zoot Panama hat like an umbrella overhead said to me. 'The General wants to see you.' He glanced at Vilakazi and grinned like a rotund crocodile. 'You stay here, Vilakazi. The General don't want to see small fry, *ntwana*.'

He pissed me off, that blubber reptile, but Vilakazi winked, slapped me on the back, and footed it out the door and disappeared down the dusty street.

Then, in the cramped seats of a plain, very inconspicuous Volkswagen Beetle with blacked-out windows, Baby Face drove me to meet The General.

General Advancement

The General lived not in a sumptuous home but in an ordinary face-brick unit that was called the Glass House. This was because it was full of big, wide windows with the curtains always drawn open so that you, or anybody else for that matter, could see everything going on inside.

Underneath, in an air-conditioned basement nearly as big as the house itself, The General had his offices, playroom, bar, and his very own exclusively appointed bioscope, with a projector, big screen, tiered seats, the works.

I was led to a huge, ornate desk covered with telephones and piles of paperwork behind which sat a short, extremely skinny black man, his face dignified by an old-fashioned chin projectile of a spade beard. I could tell he was The General because I could almost feel Baby Face's dramatic change of demeanour in the man's presence.

For me the tangible effect of The General's presence was different. All of a sudden, in the time it took me to walk the length of floor that separated us, The General went from being a big bad giant of a *geeza* in my awed perception to being a normal, much-respected person, and he was never a big bad giant of a guy to me ever again.

'Boss General, sir, meet Dhlamini Bhekuzulu.'

The man behind the desk motioned me to sit down.

I pulled out a chair.

Baby Face stood there for a minute. Then he wallowed away towards the full-size bar and sat his monstrous *ezzies* on a high stool, the seat of which vanished instantly under the fleshy lard-mountains of overlapping *glutei maximus*.

The General – it was quite a while before I ever called him The General – had a smooth, unlined face, and there was only a hint of grey in his pomaded ebony-bright hair and stiff spade-cut beard. It was impossible to tell how old he was – he might have been thirty-five or sixty. He looks almost the same today except his hair and beard are overall a legendary silver.

When he looked at you and you saw his eyes, he wasn't little and he wasn't skinny anymore. He was a Big Man and he would always be a Big Man, anywhere, anytime, anyplace.

He had a real deep voice, very soft, but his words came out clearly and concisely.

'How long do you think you will survive? If you keep jumping lunatics with loaded guns?' was the first thing that he, speaking Zulu, ever said to me.

I didn't have any answer to that one, *mfowethu*, so I just grinned at him.

He didn't smile back, just sat there looking at me seriously with those penetrating raptor's eyes of his, until I began to feel like an obsolete spare part for a discontinued appliance. He could do the same thing to me today at a whim – make me feel the same inconsequential way anytime he felt like it.

'Why did you do it?' The General asked me.

I tried to figure out what he wanted me to say. I couldn't, so I decided to tell the truth.

'I judged I'd take my chances, *umnumzana*.'

'You did the right thing, young man. That fool Ding-Dong could have put us all in deep trouble if he had killed a white policeman. Sheer folly. You, Dhlamini, are you always such a sensible, if volatile, person?'

For no reason at all I began to get annoyed.

The General made me feel as if I'd done something stupid, and I knew in my bones that I had not.

'Hear me, *umnumzana*,' came carelessly fast out of my mouth as if another person was operating it. 'I've been taking care of me, number one, for quite a while, and up to now I've never had any complications, understand? I wasn't going to let any kill-crazy baboon waste my life for me.'

'You spent two years rotting in juvenile purgatory. Is that taking care of number one? I believe your brother unfortunately shared the miserable fate you decided upon?'

Where had he picked up *that* juicy little titbit?

He burnt away my cool faster than a blowtorch on full flame roasting a chocolate ice-cream and left me cindered brown-fool legless, *mfowethu*. There wasn't much I could say to that verbal assegai thrust. I sat there with my fists clenched under the desk until I heard a disembodied voice that sounded like mine say, 'That was a mistake I don't plan to make ever again.'

The General looked at me steadily once more for a long moment. I felt I was under a microscope, a germ frozen into unmoving obedience.

Then he smiled.

A wonderful smile, a smile that made you weightless.

'You are not a warrior, young man. Warriors are a dispensable necessity. They no longer spearhead the race for survival. I need men with *ikhanda*. My instincts tell me you are one of that new breed. You are a young man of possibilities, Dhlamini.'

Over the years I've seen The General smile fewer times in total than I have fingers and toes. When he does smile that lovely smile, *everybody* around him smiles automatically too, no matter who they are, butcher, baker, candlestick maker, even the biggest of big cheeses. All of a sudden I began to feel like a millionaire.

The next day I went to work for The General. A direct, personal-staff sort of appointment, an unofficial link to the main man himself, no longer just a useful number.

That was decades ago.

I've been working on and off for him in one way or another ever since.

There have been times when I've been like a divorcée out of touch with her alimony, sure. But it seems to me now that most of the times I've been in bad trouble I make a beeline back to him. He was a friend to me when I needed a good friend, and I can count my true *bra compadres* on fewer digits than make up the extensions of my left hand.

My first real job for The General was as a dispatcher in one of our camouflaged warehouses, or 'drunk man's drops' as we called them.

I already knew the manufacture set-up pretty much forwards and backwards. My new task was to see that the raw material from various sources was delivered to the warehouses on schedule. Next it was processed according to pre-ordered demand and reloaded for delivery east, west, north and south, out to Meadowlands, Diepkloof, Phiri, Senoane and other townships, all of which fell within our immediate sphere of influence.

It was a regular delivery schedule, requiring spot-on

maintenance. We had a veritable mini-fleet of everything from VW Kombis with false floors to Red Cross marked ambulances complete with sirens and uniformed drivers. You see, *mfowethu*, ambulances too were rigidly segregated by *apartheid*. There weren't many white cops keen on eyeballing any blood-and-spilled-guts *vokken kaffirs*, who, in dying, were reducing the imbalance of population numbers anyway.

We had a regular garage owned by a blowtorch-blue-eyed Aryan compatriot of Oom Kaffirboetie's who looked after servicing. He kept our wheels rolling like Swiss clockwork. In that business, breakdowns along the road spelled multiple disaster, *mfowethu*.

We never had any breakdowns.

I also had to work out the complex routes and the all-important time-schedules with two sussed brothers called Ace and Joker Makanda. They were Tsonga boys who had worked previously in Post Office Transport and took care of 'honeypots' along the way. Honeypots were the places where you had to sweeten the local law to make sure your load got through hassle free. For safety's sake, we kept spontaneously changing the various routes to give gun-happy hijackers maximum tangled confusion, so Ace and Joker spent most of their time on the road.

Before three months had passed, I had that delivery schedule running as smooth as cream blended with imported Chivas Regal.

I knew this was my big chance.

If I could excel in the job, it wouldn't be long before The General would give me a helping hand up the ladder to success and riches.

I brought in my brother Vilakazi to drive one of the overburdened routes for me. He was partnered by a tough hombre called 'Guy Fawkes' Rakhajane, a wild-haired six-foot-five Sotho immigrant so named because of the pyrotechnic way he exploded when the magnesium threads of his temper ignited. Assiduously I made sure to *prepare* Vilakazi to learn *everything* he could about how Ace and Joker Makanda operated. This was hands-on knowledge and I had to know every detail of the operation. Meanwhile I spent my own time learning how to perfectly boss a clandestine warehouse.

Bottles which matched the contents of what we were selling were hard to come by.

Ever wondered what those crazy old black men traipsing up and down every white suburb in those days with a donkey and rubber-wheeled cart yelling 'EMPTY BORRELS! EMPTY BORRELS!' were about? Now you know.

Later on we managed to gain access to a legitimate glass-bottle manufacturing firm who weren't particular about the account details on company invoices if cash was paid upfront. But at that earlier time, besides the donkey carts, we also had droves of *picannins* spread out like hungry locusts, searching just as rapaciously as any devouring *izikhonyane* swarm for undamaged, refillable items for which we paid them five cents each.

You might as well know how it worked.

The various flavours and colourants were added to the big drawn-off vats, before we bottled the stuff. We got our labels from a stereotypical upper-class *mlungu* who spoke with a mouth so full of puffed-up starchy vowels you could hardly understand his own mother-tongue English.

His name was Teddy Huffington.

He had a printing business and in the right circles was vocally committed to the overthrow of *apartheid*, besides being an alcoholic sympathetically committed to his own addiction. He wouldn't raise his voice too loud in the company of African National Congress radicals, nor would he add more than acquiescence when surrounded by tuxedo-clad clones of Prime *Umdidi* Minister Malan, the one who began all this *Blankes Alleenlik*-labelled strife back after the first Nationalist Party government's 'landslide' victory through isolated 'majority' voting polls. But enough of that dreary history, *mfowethu*.

After the consignment was all packaged and cased, we'd load it for delivery to the destination points I had assigned.

I had Big Bang Bongani and another *tsotsi*, named 'Two Bulls' Kekana because of his renowned sexual prowess, doing security at the drop point. From the moment the back door of the 'warehouse' opened and vehicles started rolling out until the last one was making exhaust-fume tracks, the whole delivery operation had two twelve-gauge shotguns loaded with Triple-A buckshot covering every move to discourage hijackers. I made it clear to Big Bang and Two Bulls that hijackers were their *only* target. A careless bloodfest of unwarranted manslaughter would put us on The General's list of those not intended to live long lives.

In six months I had become a sort of general manager.

I was handling some of the pay-offs too, local ones, which meant I was really in, *mfowethu*, with my backside in the butter.

An entirely black-patronised, wholesale butcher shop by downtown Jo'burg's Kort Street, always crowded to distraction, was our pay-off 'central office'.

Every Monday morning more than thirty thousand *amarands* was passed out to the various bloodsucking vampires on the take.

The local law, almost exclusively Afrikaans *apartheid* policemen, were the *easiest* to bribe, believe it or not. Our own uniformed darkie brothers were too often the incorruptible ones who gave trouble by sticking to the letter of their job descriptions.

Politicians, magistrates, railway officials, government inspectors and everybody else you could think of would be in the Monday-morning queue with his greedy, voracious hand spread wide.

If a strange car was seen driving around the vicinity of that butcher shop on a Monday morning, the *amapolisi* would pick it up in minutes and take it and the occupants to the nearest charge office. Then *Nkulunkulu* help you if you didn't have a valid reason for being there. If you were black, the cops turned their best blue-eyed sadists loose to hand out a ferocious panelbeating just for the sheer hell of it.

I also began seeing more of The General.

I used to do little errands for him. Sometimes, just after dawn on a Sunday, I would drive him in his inconspicuous but bulletproof Ford Cortina to see family living just inside the Natal border, only three hours there and three hours back, no sweat. I also spent one or two evenings a week as a guest in his Glass House. There I met a variety of people, men from the undercover ANC, white activists labouring for Human Rights, and, of course, some of the heaviest connected gangsters you can let your imagination run riot conjuring up.

At the Glass House I also met a burly, slow-talking Lebanese businessman with a pronounced lisp who owned a string of outlets with legitimate access to *denatured alcohol*. There are two kinds: *special denatured alcohol*, which is used in such things as pharmacological tonics, and *completely denatured alcohol*, usually used in solvents in paint manufacturing, for example. The firms that are licensed to make this commercial alcohol put everything they can dream up into their product to make it impossible for thirsty people like us excluded-from-*Homo-sapiens*-darkies to drink.

The trick here is to analyse the adulterant used, identify it and then apply yourself to removing it. As I said before, the manufacturers kept changing formulas, but who said life was meant to be a soft and easy marshmallow ride? That's where geniuses like Oom Kaffirboetie came in.

That black-pussy-motivated old German jackboot could crack any commercial formula I ever came across and end up with a result you'd feed good Father Trevor Huddleston as an *aperitif* preliminary to handing him a hefty church donation.

Breaking down most *special denatured alcohol* is child's play. For each gallon you add about a pound of charcoal, charcoal you can make easy yourself if you have enough base intelligence to strike a match. You mix this thoroughly, *mfowethu*, let it stand and settle for a few hours, and then filter off the pure alcohol. European filter-paper pods designed for caterering-volume use with exclusive imported coffees do a superlative job in this regard. What you get is a dynamite-proof result – the only setback being that you can never guarantee either a fair or foul aftertaste.

Completely denatured alcohol is another kettle of belligerent fish altogether, a harder, tougher job – you with me? But it gives the best results, superior in every way. You dilute it down to about seventy-five per cent of the original and then add caustic soda and mineral oil to separate the mixture. Then you pump the lower layer into your *umPheki* and run it off. From this you get alcohol that you can dilute by half with a free conscience before bottling, but it does contain up to thirty-five per cent subtly poisonous wood alcohol.

Not so bad, *mfowethu*, if you think about it rationally. It'll take years of steady imbibing before it kills you.

Fighting Fit

The General had an interest in the many brand-name fast-food outlets that were beginning to spring up and proliferate on South African soil like mushrooms after a heavy rainfall, an interest that was about to become active. So every once in a while I would drive him to an investigative meet with his white lawyer, Greg Morris, in tow, a four-eyes easy-going *bra mlungu* guy who shared The General's passionate love of soccer and boxing. The only way those putty-faced franchise folk would deal with The General was if he could get a famous black sports personality to front for him.

Was this a problem?

Look around you, *mfowethu*, and tell me how many takeaway chicken outlets you can spot?

End of *indaba*.

I was taking in a tremendous accumulation of treasured knowledge about the way things were. I learned that *nothing* would work for you if the *sonta*, or the 'twist', hadn't been prearranged in your favour. If you go for it on your own, the odds are fifty-fifty you'll slip a vertebrae and come away stunted-spine short. Even if you get a *muhle inkalakatha* thing going and you manage to keep out of the way of the law, somebody with saurian predator's grey matter is sure to eagle-eye your good thing and barge in with bared fangs to wrest it away from you.

You have to be on the right side, not morally, but physically.

Also, everybody and anybody will take a bribe if you yourself 'twist' it *just so*: the *amapolisi*, the courts, the politicians, the clerks with the 'vanished' criminal dockets, the taxmen in charge of overdue revenue. I've never seen one of them who wouldn't take the offer if the price and the phrasing were right.

I'll give you a perfect example.

I remember it clearly because many things came together at the same time.

The night I'm mouthing about, The General had best seats to see the big championship fight between Tony 'Blue Jaguar' Morodi and odds-on popular challenger Moses 'Easter Monday' Mthembu down at Durban's Currie's Fountain. Potato Crisp Nxumalo was in his entourage and he had invited me to go along.

After arriving in convoy and personally dropping off The General and Potato Crisp at the biggest pink and white mansion you ever saw in the segregated Indian suburb of Chatsworth, I took care of my own *amadoda*'s accommodation, returning at about seven. We were to go from there to the fight with Desai 'Bengal Tiger' Mohammed, the pink palace's megabucks owner.

I could see right away that something was wrong.

Potato Crisp was at the darkwood solid-mahogany and polished-brass bar (who said Muslims don't drink?) and fragrant incense perfumed the air. The General and Bengal Tiger were hanging onto Potato Crisp's arms, imprisoning them at his sides. He was so enraged, his pitted, white, facial burn-scars flaming, that he could barely speak. I stayed out of the way and, after a while, keeping my ears tuned, found out what was wrong.

It seems that Potato Crisp had just opened an innovative and luxurious state-of-the-art *shebeen* and it hadn't run forty-eight hours before the *amapolisi* had knocked it off. What was a mystery was that the close-down mercenaries were *the local cops* and the 'twist' was firmly in place. That meant somebody had double-crossed Potato Crisp Nxumalo and for fifty thousand *amarands*, because that's what the bribe price had been.

Potato Crisp put in a long-distance telephone call to find out what had happened, but nobody could find his go-between.

When we entered the front area of the stadium prior to being led to our seats, there was a big party mingling alongside of us, including gorgeous dusky women dolled up in furs and jangling jewellery in spite of the humid coastal heat.

A guy separated from the party and walked over to Potato Crisp and slapped him on the back.

It was Samuel 'Shakedown' Tuli, a black lawyer who was the white mayor of Johannesburg's personal assistant. This was a clever move on the wide-awake mayor's part. Kept him sweet with those who could vote *and* those with influence hoping for better days.

'Good evening, Mister Nxumalo. What's the word on the big fight tonight?' he said, giving everybody within range a toothpaste-advert grin.

Bengal Tiger started to say something, and got kicked sharply on the shin for his pains.

'Don't know a thing, Shakedown,' Potato Crisp answered in a voice as deadpan as his drooping eye.

Shakedown Tuli made small talk for a while and then filed in with the rest of his crowd.

I judged Potato Crisp was just wired-up in general because we all of us had small fortunes wagered on Tony 'Blue Jaguar' Morodi. The word was that the result would be a knockout in the eleventh round, and as far as I could see, there was no reason not to let Shakedown Tuli also get down a few pink dollars and improve his bank balance.

During the preliminaries Shakedown and his party were sitting in the first row, in front of us at the ringside, all of them laughing and talking with canon-size cigars blazing away, having a good time.

About midway during a hard-fought, classy semifinal, a young Zulu guy with traditionally stretched ear-lobes filled with stamped gold rather than ethnic artwork sidled across and handed a folded note to Potato Crisp Nxumalo. He read it carefully and then leaned over towards The General.

'That *umdidi we mpisi* got his fifty grand twist-money spot on time!' Potato Crisp said vehemently, nearly vomiting out his words like barbed projectiles. 'But the bastard, shit-eating *inja*-bitch did nothing for us!'

He then leaned the other way and those white crater-indentations on his scarred face were turning luminous again. He tapped Shakedown Tuli on the shoulder and spat out something I couldn't hear.

Shakedown turned in his seat, went sort of an instant-coffee-with-condensed-milk colour, and raised both hands as if to protect himself.

'*Jesus Christ, Mister Nxumalo!*' he almost screamed. '*I forgot about it completely! I'll make it right! I swear I'll make –* ' and then his words were guillotined as Potato Crisp got him by the throat and started to throttle him with dedication, his face transfigured into a mottled mask of demonic, righteous anger.

Shakedown's upwardly mobile friends must have thought it was a joke.

I didn't.

I could see Potato Crisp's thumbnails digging into Shakedown's soft throat and blood starting to leak out around the edge of the fierce, digging pressure concentrated there. After a convulsive, centuries-long minute, The General and Bengal Tiger, who were sitting on either side, pried him loose. Quick as a flash, Potato Crisp gouged out one of Shakedown's eyeballs and Bengal Tiger wrapped his long, blue silk boxing-fan's scarf around the victim's damaged head to hide the horror it displayed.

We got out of there quickstyle with our *amadoda* running interference before the cops came and charged Potato Crisp with attempted murder.

I never did get to see Tony 'Blue Jaguar' Morodi win by a knockout in the eleventh round, a monumental sporting event that took place towards the close of the 1950s.

Shakedown's eyeball was apparently still hanging attached by its optical nerve. I later heard that it and his sight were somehow miraculously saved.

At any rate, what this boils down to is that you can see the 'twist' went right to the top. You think the white mayor of the City of Gold didn't get his slice of the pie? When did you leave kindergarten, last week or last month?

Without the 'twist' you were out of business, *mfowethu*: take that as gospel.

Vibrating With Vilakazi

The next few years were good for me.

Things went the way I wanted them to go: an *ingelozi* was sitting on my shoulder.

First of all, Vilakazi got an improvised route going that doubled our personal income.

The day came when I put a proposition to The General that he should let me run a few transport vehicles of my own to tie in with his routes and share thirty-seventy after expenses, with him getting the seventy.

I'll never forget what he said, speaking in his usual staccato-short sentences.

'Why should you offer me seventy per cent, Dhlamini? When you do the work and take the risks? Even though I ensure the protection organised for you? Did you think I would answer "no" if I did not have the lion's share?' He paused, not expecting an answer from me. 'Listen to me, young man. It is only greedy human baboons who get their clenched hands stuck in the dried pumpkin-gourd trap. There is plenty for everybody. There is no need to hurt others with your ambition either. The people who work for you should be happy with you, understand? You have to let them eat well at your table. Otherwise they will think of nothing else but how to take *your* place. I am talking about them making themselves a seat at the head of that *very* table that belongs to you. It costs me nothing to let you in with two transporters. They make me money without my doing any work. Can I refuse such a magnanimous offer?' He looked at me with those raptor's eyes twinkling. 'All I ask is that you provide clean vehicles. Stolen wheels are bad for business.'

Big Bang raided two high-canopy *bakkies* quickstyle while The General's words were still hanging in my head like an executioner's noose. Between dusk and dawn both were branded with the famous logo of 'FATTI'S & MONI'S / DURHAM WHEAT PASTA' in bright, visible, guiltless blue and red. Inside of a week the new paint jobs, fresh upholstery, engine and chassis number changes, and forged ownership papers were all in order. By that time the original owners wouldn't have known their own vehicles even if in a spell of indulgence they'd been invited to test-drive them.

I got a *tsotsi* named 'Honest' Hlapane, who had two brothers – both black cops in his area – to take over my old routes. My focus was entirely on my first solo capitalist venture, my first approved, autonomous selling route. I was aiming high. We were catering almost entirely to a herd of two-legged upper-income consumer cattle who could afford the good stuff: imported but profit-enhanced and therefore necessarily adulterated brandies, gins, whiskies and snob-branded aerated mixes. I cut Vilakazi and Big Bang Bongani in on the whole operation with equal shares. Vilakazi supplied the drivers and the hijacked or siphoned-off stuff, Big Bang the necessary warrior's muscle, and me the connected protection.

Now was when all the accountancy lascivious old Oom Kaffirboetie had drilled into my head started to come in handy, *mfowethu*.

You can sweat blood and tears all your life, but if you don't know how to handle figures and make numbers bend for you, you might as well whine, roll over and play dead. You don't get anywhere unless you know how to judge the percentages of your bets.

About this time I got The General to advance me half of what I needed to set up my own alcohol-spouting *umPheki* plant. He made me sign legal promissory notes for every cent, with a virulently healthy interest added for good measure, which was okay with me because I was going to pay it all back in record time. I learned that your personal economy doesn't need to be bolstered by *cash* as long as you have that sometimes-elusive line of *credit* laid on for you.

Before twenty days of operations had passed, I had my *umPheki* paid for, Oom Kaffirboetie on my payroll and a juggernaut profit rolling in.

I was really and truly on my way.

I was clearing close to forty thousand *amarands* every calendar month – and remember, in those days, a brand-new set of luxury wheels set you back less than ten thousand. My delivery vans were averaging twenty-three working days on the road every thirty, and all I had to do was keep them and my Cookboy running. I was putting money in the bank so fast I couldn't count it, *mfowethu*. Admittedly, heavy sums were going out in protection and overheads, but what stuck to my sticky fingers was enough to take your breath away.

Things were going smoothly.

So smoothly, I started to worry that the benevolent angel perched on my shoulder might vanish.

All my life it's been that way.

Every time things are running like clockwork – blue

skies with no thunderclouds in sight – I *have* to start worrying.

I'm usually right.

Another notch on the handle for that hired gun called pessimism.

One night I got a message from my 'warehouse' to return a long-distance call urgently.

I knew it could mean only one thing.

Vilakazi.

I could tell he was drunk when I heard his familiar voice on the line.

'The *gattes* got a description out on me yet, *bra*?'

I could *feel* the fear that was lashing from his sweating pores like salt-and-acid rainfall.

'Calm down, Vilakazi,' I said. What're you talking about?'

'Fuckssakes, you mean you haven't heard nothing?'

My innards turned over.

'Jesus Christ, what have you got yourself into?' I found myself yelling at him. 'Cut the fucking *bulongwe* and spit it out, *bra*!'

Vilakazi sounded really scared, freaked out.

'Just outside the number eight drop, a big yank tank going fast starts to crowd Big Bang and me. It squeezes right over in front of us like the aim is to drive us off the road. Big Bang yells, "*It's got to be a fucking hijack!*" and grabs for his twelve-gauge *isibhamu*. He must have blasted one of the tyres, because the yank tank suddenly flips right over on one side and fucking crashes out of control down the embankment. We got down there quickstyle, *bra*, to make sure nobody's gonna see no living witness. Only when we get down to the wreck, it's on its back with the wheels spinning in the air, there's no hijacker-gangsters, only two dead *abelungu* in respectable suits with crushed skulls and a blond white girl full of windscreen-glass cuts on her face – and – and – and she's crawling out from under the back seat, *bra*! Fucking madness! She keeps shrieking, "*You shot us! You shot us!*" loud enough to waken the two dead *geezas* – and – and so Big Bang clubs her unconscious! He wanted to fucking kill her, *bra*, but I said no, we're deep enough in the shit already, know what I mean, *bra*?'

'Go slowly, Vilakazi, but don't stop,' I said, drawing a deep breath.

'We vamoosed, *bra*, fucking quickstyle, no jokes. We sitting *vas* here by the number eight drop. What we gonna do, *bra*?'

I cursed Vilakazi until I had to pause to replenish my lungs with air. Of all the *mampara* luck. My luck. My luck that I had to be mixed up with that trigger-happy moron Big Bang Bongani.

I heard Vilakazi screech thinly like a transparent ghost:

'Jesus, fuck it, Dhlamini! How could we know? That fucking yank tank looked like a fucking hungry metal shark, *bra*!'

'Listen, Vilakazi, you stay right where you are until you hear from me. And keep that mad bastard baboon Big Bang out of trouble. Give the *shebeen* Queen her whole delivery free of charge and tell her she's never seen you when you're gone. You sweet with that?'

'Like a lemon, Dhlamini. Sweet like a lemon, *bra*.'

'Good. I'm going to call The General and see what can be done.'

'Okay, *bra*, I'll stay put.' Vilakazi sounded relieved, confidence surfacing in his voice like a drowning swimmer being freed from the grasp of a treacherous undertow. 'I like it here. Classy babes, *bra*, good booze, ha-ha. Fuckssakes, I'll stay here a week, *bra*, if I have to. No sweat, you can rely on me.'

I hung up on him before I burst a blood vessel.

I tried The General every place I could think of and I couldn't get a trace. Finally I called Honest Hlapane, my salesman, and, without spilling who wanted the information or why it was wanted, told him to find out from his *amapolisi* brothers if the cops had any witnesses. I sat there chewing my fingernails down to the quick before Honest called me back.

I couldn't judge what he was telling me.

According to him, the young white woman was in hospital and hadn't talked to the cops . . . yet. As far as he could tell, the traffic *gattes* were treating it like a routine road accident with an unfortunate death toll. Nobody was breaking his back in the *amapolisi* ranks with any unwarranted investigation. I got this sneaky feeling there must be a wild joker-card hidden in that hand somewhere, *mfowethu*: I couldn't get *that* lucky.

'How about the car?' I grilled him. 'The yank tank?'

'Shit, Dhlamini, I don't know, *bra*. In the *amapolisi* garage there, I suppose.'

'Hear me too good now, Honest. You get over there as fast as you can. According to Vilakazi, one of those tyres is full of buckshot. If anybody spots it, we're fucked. You get that tyre changed – call in your brothers, whatever it takes, but *get it* and bury it deep somewhere. I don't care how you do it, *just get it done*. I'll get to the white girl in the hospital.'

I gathered up all the cash I could lay my hands on. The best I could do was four thousand *amarands*. I didn't know how much I was going to need. For all I could tell, my liability might include paying off an entire police station.

I had no more time.

I took off.

I must hold a speed record for that road trip. If I'd been a fraction of a minute later I would have missed her.

I have to accentuate the positively obvious here again, *mfowethu.*

Hospitals in South Africa were just as rigidly segregated as hotels, bars, toilets, schools and suburbs. *Apartheid* said white patients got white hospitals and black patients got black hospitals. Tough luck if you were a professor of philosophy in need of an urgent blood transfusion with your own colour-bar medical service too far away to make it in time for your survival. Tough titty, as they say; suck on that dried-up hag's hanging dug philosophy and suck off.

I ate humble pie and told the three-hundred-pound lesbian nurse at reception that I was a big-cheese insurance investigator's driver. Just then, the young blond woman came down in the lift – it *had* to be her, the superficial glass-grazes on her face covered with patchy gauze bandages. A barely adult, leather-lumberjacketed, *skollie*-type white-trash ducktail was holding her by the arm, a greaser guide dog no less.

I took a good look at her and judged my luck was holding.

Black or white, you could find ten like her anywhere they sold booze.

I knew how to talk to this kind of woman.

I talked to her one thousand *amarands* worth, still playing the bogus insurance company driver. I was right. Those two brain-mashed corpses were nothing to her, drunks she'd picked up in a bar. The one thing she didn't want was trouble. The second thing she didn't want was more of my upstart darkie presence. She snatched the cash and that was that.

When I got to the unlit, open-lot *amapolisi* garage, Honest Hlapane was waiting for me, squatting nonchalantly on the curb like he owned it, white suburb and all. He gave me a thumbs-up sign, came over and leaned in my driver's window.

'I got it off, Dhlamini, no problems. You were right, buckshot made it look like a rubber sieve filled with lead ballbearings. I put the spare tyre on.'

'Where is it?'

'On the car, like I said.'

'I'm talking the tyre full of buckshot, *mampara*.'

'Three blocks away, *bra*. I'm not stupid. I was waiting for you.'

'Let's get it in the back seat and get out of here. The quicker the better.'

I burnt rubber flying the short-distance gap.

Honest had thrown a tarpaulin over the mangled tyre, just like that, without any pretence of intelligent camouflage. There it sat right next to a red postbox. Now I was the one who was sweating.

When we examined it, the rim was all bent in and buckled skew. The rubber hanging from it was in shreds, spherical lead pellets in clear evidence. You didn't have to be a genius to see that something besides a 'natural' accident had happened. I held the back door open without getting out while Honest was pushing the mangled wheel through onto the rear seat, when an apparition materialised out of nowhere and stuck its head in the opposite window – a big, ugly, black bastard of an apparition in a lawman's horrendously unfashionable apparel.

'*Sawubona*, Honest, *bra*,' he said to my trustworthy salesman. 'Thought I'd drop by to make sure you got what you wanted.' He was looking steadfastly at our tyre and I could see his mean, feral little hippopotamus eyes go bright with avarice. He hadn't finished with his verbal enlightenment just yet, however. 'Looks like somebody shot up that tyre of yours with a twelve-gauge shotgun.'

'*Sawubona*, Hlati, *bra*,' Honest lightly returned the *bulongwe* greeting in a fair imitation of being cool. 'Dhlamini, this is my brother, Hlati.'

I stabbed Honest real hard with my eyes and I could register it was his turn to break out in a sweat. He closed the car's back door to hide his face from me and I got out to stand where I could see them both.

'Okay, you motherfuckers,' I said between my teeth. 'How much?'

Big Hlati started to grin like a hyena with a thigh-sized funny-bone between its massive teeth, making soft little giggles much too girlish for such a large Frankenstein monster.

'Now look, Dhlamini, I had nothing to do with this, *bra*! I didn't tell him a thing! I swear it on my life!' Honest swore, putting his hands up, palms outward in my direction.

He looked so distressed I almost believed him.

'How much you got on you, Dhlamini brother?' Big Hlati asked.

I knew I was wrapped up like a mummy stapled in superglue, so I took out my cash-stash where Big Hlati the Bloodsucking Blackmailer could see it and counted out the remaining bucks. Those three thousand *amarands* disappeared so fast that I never even saw where Honest's *gattes* brother put them. Next, the Laughing Policeman reopened the back door of my car and pulled the shot-up tyre out again with one overlarge paw. He settled it between his knees and languidly brushed his hands one against the other in a brisk cleansing movement, that mean hyena grin back on his face.

'I'll just keep *our* tyre where it won't go missing or

anything stupid like that,' he giggled, slapping me so hard on the back I nearly had an oxygen-deficiency seizure. 'You have to realise, Dhlamini brother, this tyre could be conclusive evidence in a serious murder charge. I'll consider your contribution a down payment on your licence to freedom. I'll be seeing you around, right?'

He took off up the street, strolling blithely along and trundling the ruined tyre beside him. Thank the *shades* of the ancestors that I didn't carry a gun. The only answer *then* I'd have given his arrogant question would have made me a lifer behind bars, if not a free tryout for the hangman's rope.

I left Honest still sweating in his own home-made juices on the unfriendly curb and headed back to find The General. I was thinking in anticipation of all the deeply felt pleasure it would give me to get Big Bang Bongani to pay back every cent of those three thousand *amarands* when I caught up with the crazy gorilla again.

I was also being brutally honest with myself, realising that if The General couldn't help me, my new dazzlingly pyrotechnic career in these parts was at a dismal, fizzled-out end. Big Hlati Hlapane had me hooked like a moneyfish.

Accessory to murder.

Or at the least, manslaughter.

Attempting to destroy evidence.

Aiding in the concealment of a crime.

And I don't know what else, *mfowethu*.

Every time that giggling hyena-spawn of a diseased bestial whore needed pocket money all he had to do was give me a buzz and tell me to get it . . . or else get ready for a righteous fucking over.

I only had two choices.

To shut up both Hlati and Honest Hlapane the hard, eternal way.

Or get The General to put in a gigantic, earth-moving 'twist'.

I certainly wasn't going to sit still while that evil blackmailing motherfucker put the python bone-crusher squeeze on me. By the way, we actually never used that word 'motherfucker' in those days, but the deadly poisonous insulting expletive we had was so much worse that 'motherfucker' will have to do as a mild alternative.

Killing a cop never brought anything but trouble, *mfowethu*, so The General seemed my only valid loophole. I knew I was asking a lot. If this had been his personal *indaba* I could have asked for anything, even ultimate retribution, and it would have been served up quickstyle. But my predicament was something else, something that belonged *too good* to me alone, and as long I had stuck my neck out, it was solely up to me – and nobody else – to take care of it. Those were the unspoken rules.

And that's the way it turned out.

The General was bountiful with abundant ideas about how I could handle it, but assistance stopped right there.

The handling would have to be done by yours truly.

'Look at it this way, Dhlamini,' The General said in a solicitous manner. 'Vilakazi is *your* brother. *You* have to stick by *your* brother. That is our tradition. It is our forefathers' inheritance. Blood should always be thicker than water. I do not blame you in the least for having your priorities aligned as you see fit. I could call a certain someone to get the slate wiped clean. But Vilalazi is *not that certain someone's brother*. I only have so many favours I may ask, Dhlamini. I can see by the set of your jaw that you understand exactly what I'm getting at. One too many requested favours and the well dries up. And then I have no more favours. My people starve and nothing constructive gets done.'

He patted me fatherly on the shoulder and, whether he felt bad about it or not, my gut feeling was that he was sincere. Naturally, *tsotsi* paranoia always makes you question: '*Am I the sucker who's being fed the loser's lollipop?*' Nevertheless, I'll stick with my judge on The General. I knew and he knew that the only way I could get out from under Hlati Hlapane's bloodsucking shroud was to provide him with his own obliterating mortuary sheet, bury him with a mouthful of gravel and pound it in with a blunt, flat-faced, ten-pound sledgehammer.

We both knew I wasn't cut out for that line of non-reversible retribution, even though I could have it done from a safe distance, and I could feel The General approved of the way I discarded the very possibility of those bloodthirsty, barbaric actions. He was one grand-master puppeteer alright, who believed killing never solved anything satisfactorily. Yet that was not strictly true. The General had blood on his hands, blood that would never wash away, not in this life anyway. Yet, I reasoned with myself, it always absolutely had to be done when the sole purpose was to make things better for everybody.

Oom Kaffirboetie theorised that too much thinking bred too many brain cells, and overpopulation always led to anarchy. My chaotic brain told me maybe he was right and I was thinking too much.

Then The General interrupted my heretic mental meandering. He voiced the one thing I'd hoped for by throwing the ball right where it belonged, back into my court.

'What exactly are you going to do, Dhlamini?'

I told him I had to move out, far away.

I could see The General was pretty relieved when I unloaded my decision on him. Moving out, he agreed, was the only thing I could do. If I hung around I was only going to be an embarrassment of note to everybody.

For the first time I became aware that The General was looking out for me.

Something about my reluctance to get involved in madness and mayhem made him judge I wasn't just another *tsotsi laaitjie* working blindly subservient for him. As far as I knew, he never married, yet he was crazy about kids. Maybe that had something to do with it. All I knew was that he stood up for me many, many times, almost as if I was his own flesh and blood.

It took four hours and a telesales number of phone calls, but when I left The General it was to spend three weeks secretly getting lined up for a no-fanfare train journey down to Pietermaritzburg.

I was to set up a big drunk-man's drop with a 'warehouse', service garage and all, and with solid protection which The General, being a ruling Zulu clan chieftain by birth, could wrangle down in Natal better than anybody. I was to be the clearing station for all the imported stuff coming in by sea. The liquid merchandise that passed through, without the usual heavy import tax, directly to wholesale fabric-distribution companies owned by Bengal Tiger, who had understanding cousins working in Durban Port Customs. I was also to begin an *umPheki* operation with all its affiliated sidelines. And I was ordered to establish a retail and wholesale sales route for all the phoney-flavoured *skokiaan* alcohol The General's plants would soon be transporting southwards.

There were hundreds of busy productive factories all around that Pietermaritzburg area, employing hundreds of thousands of lonely, thirsty black men separated from their wives and families by the necessity of finding wage-earning unskilled-labour work wherever it was available. Pietermaritzburg alone (apart from nearby Durban) had timber and sugar concerns, producers of tannin extracted from wattle bark supplied by Natal Highland farms ideally suited to grow these trees because of the area's moisture-laden morning and evening mists, plus large-scale dairying and the rolling of aluminium, amongst many other smaller industries.

I expected to have to use a little muscle and make pay-offs in every direction of the greedy compass, but rather than facing imagined antagonism, I was received by all the local *indunas* with any clout as a messiah, an arriving saviour.

One of the major factors contributing to this unexpectedly warm welcome was that of shared hooligan street-level communication with every spiv and gangster I needed on my side. In those days we spoke an extraordinary *patois* that found purchase on black South African tongues when tribal labour first began moving into urban and semi-urban areas. The shared *tsotsi* jargon that made my new life easy for me and had me instantly accepted as a 'brother' had come to life as the result of language difficulties amongst new arrivals sharing common ground: black folk mixed willy-nilly with black folk. Confronted with a barrier of eleven different tribal languages, we found, or rather invented, a provisional means of verbal exchange.

A shared surface knowledge of Afrikaans, Zulu, English and Sotho plus all the other dialects served to fill the gap speakers encountered in vernacular dialogue. What was interesting was the fact that *tsotsi*-speak, or *tsotsi-taal*, was the *same* identical mumbo-jumbo in spite of vast differences between distant areas, from sprawling township to sprawling township. Furtiveness also helped build *tsotsi-taal*. The White Man didn't have a clue what we were on about, even if he was a linguistic master of every black language from Cape Town to Cairo. *Tsotsi-taal* brought about immediate camaraderie.

I was in like Flynn, *mfowethu*.

I'll give you a few brief written examples, a few lines. Read them and you'll understand.

Bra Shakes, ek sal gwila ommie tiemies te diet. (Brother Shakes, I'm going back to my spot to have a bite to eat.)

Shjee fuse, man. Sweet. Jislaaik, hey la, judge Bra Darkie Gattes. (Give me a cigarette first, man. Thanks. Hey, just check-out Brother Black Policeman there.)

Bra Gattes'se moegoe. Hy judge hy's monish. Kanti ek nortch hy'se guluva. (Brother Policeman's an idiot. He thinks he's a main man. Meanwhile I know he's just trash who can't get any other kind of work.)

Dja, hy'se eggstra alenlik moegoe. Judge hom hlombe. (Yes, he's a dedicated idiot. Just look at that girlfriend of his, for example.)

Sies, man! Sjy'se skarapafet! (Ugly, man! She's a street whore!)

Mette king-size ezzies. Hola. Kalakat king-size, Bra. (With a huge arse. Unbelievable. Monstrously huge, Brother.)

Enna fokken hans kanda. (And a fucking head like a horse.)

Hey, Bra Shakes, sjy mnca nette rawurawu mette magageba. Bra Gattes'se rawurawu. Of hoe sê ek? (Hey, Brother Shakes, she digs only gangsters with money. Brother Policeman's just a legal thug. Don't you agree?)

Dja. Warr joeleit gattes'se skarapafet? (Yes. Which area does the police-pig's street whore work?)

Sjy kennie om te joeleit, Bra Shakes. Net sjy line mette guluvas. (She doesn't work, Brother Shakes. She only hangs out with big-time criminals who don't need to work.)

Bra Darkie Gattes'se ware fokken moegoe mette

amaskarapafet. (Brother Black Policeman's a real dumb fucking sucker when it comes to prostitutes.)

Roeriet, forrie amaskarapafet soekie kuzak enne atshitshi. (Too true, those street whores only want money and drugs from anybody who can give it to them.)

En sulle fokken minkel nie die panis. Nette mbamba ennie beste koek. (And they don't fucking drink watered-down booze either. Only the best will do for them.)

En sulle willie die njombela. Sulle wil nette ndandas, Bra. (And they don't want peanuts. Just the cream of the crop for them, Brother.)

Dja, dja. Sulle wil nette Jewish enne Batas. Fokken skarapafet. (Yes, yes. They want only the most expensive clothes and shoes. Fucking street whores.)

Marr skarapafet ace ken om te rwa juicy, Bra. (But the sluts do know how to rob what they want, Brother.)

Sonna fokken gedindel, dja, dja. (Without getting fucking beaten up, yeah, yeah.)

Enne gepasa mette gonnie. (And without getting stabbed as well.)

Jislaaik! Enne gemang by die gattes! (Strewth! And too sly to get bust by the cops!)

Dja, dja, dja. Dis wat ekke ken die darkie gattes'se fokken poes-moegoes. (Yes, yes, yes. That's why I know all nigger cops are stupid cunts.)

Dja, fokken roeriet! (Yes, you fucking got that right!)

Hulle'se gal pil darkies, Bra Shakes! (They are such poison-bad dumb niggers, Brother Shakes!)

Fokken roeriet! Kom ons line, Bra. (Fucking right! Come, let's split, Brother.)

Dja, judge die fokken jampas. Betta ons nak vorrie gattes ons mang virrie stinkas. (Yeah, check out the fucking time. Let's get moving before the cops catch us without our reference books.)

Reference books?

Yebo.

Those days we all had to carry what we blacks called a *dompas.* A fascist herd-control identification document which had to be regularly stamped by the police, failing which you were automatically a non-person. If you were nabbed without an up-to-date one in any white area, you paid a cash 'fine' that you *knew* went no further than lining your arrester's personal pockets; or else you went to jail, where your services were required as government slave labour.

Those days.

Those were the days, my friend.

Meanwhile our homebrews of varying potency sold to the wonderfully patronised *shebeens* like hot-cakes. Some customers were particular about imported stuff. They insisted on the real thing. So I'd give it to them.

The way it worked was we watered it down by an average of twenty per cent. Back then there were no virginal-hymen, snap-off bottletops (that even today you can 'adjust' with crynolate superglue), but overlapping seals joining glass and stopper that swore to the untampered purity of the contents.

These we'd sweat off and then cut the prohibitively costly stuff one-to-five with distilled water and perfect colouring. And at 'imported' prices, that little artistic exercise equalled a magic profit in anybody's accounting ledger.

There wasn't a bottle seal made that you couldn't sweat off and replace without a trace if you had the right equipment. Try it yourself purely for fun on any household product available. Just put the neck in some hot water for a while and the composition seal will get soft and stretch. With a little care you can ease it off. With us, via back-door white liquor-stores paid cash-on-the-nose-no-questions-asked, it was government tax seals, just as easy as pulling the cork and putting the whole seal right back so that it would dry itself in a matter of half an hour or so. You could spit contagious bacteria in that doctored booze and no one would ever know the difference.

I got thirty-five per cent of all retail, but had to absorb the cost of procurement and delivery. I was pocketing around two thousand *amarands* for every *bakkie*-load I sent out. Whatever I could make on my other 'arrangements' was pure cherry on the top.

I planned to get *amafutha*, as tenfold fat as possible in the shortest possible time, *mfowethu*.

Ball And Chain

Besides beginning to take note of the lucrative openings fast-food franchises were starting to unlock, The General had read up on some of the early Italian-American *Cosa Nostra* methods and was about to introduce one of their first inaugural policies right here in the Land of Braaivleis, Sunny Skies, Chevrolet and *Brandewyn*. He was going to produce grocery-store items that sold commonly enough to Mr and Mrs Everybody, but which every black storekeeper *had* to buy from *him*, or else feel the outraged wrath that came from not supporting those who were your own. 'Outraged wrath', of course, meant anything from broken legs to having your shop *and* your home burnt to the ground. Apparently Italian olive oil was one of the Sicilian immigrants' first stepping stones to monopolising their *Mafia* business interests in the USA.

Ours was to be washing powder, a basic product purchased on a weekly basis.

Every township had its breadline *spaza* shops, small concerns which could never compete with the big, white-owned supermarkets, but which carried all the subsistence items suitable for dry shelving and available mainly in affordable, compact packages. And there were *thousands* of them, virtually one for every few blocks of congested brown-skinned humanity. *Exactly* copying the technicolour cardboard packaging of brands that spent hundreds of thousands on advertising didn't bother us at all, *mfowethu*.

At The General's behest, I met with a black lawyer to sort out all the necessary paperwork for this next sally into the world of approved commercial transactions. This lawyer had the strangest name, '*Bra-Bra*' Motshange, meaning 'Brother-Brother' Motshange. To top that unusual moniker, his offices were in the Indian business area *and* he had a pretty white receptionist working for him at the front. Mind-blowing, *mfowethu*, unbelievable.

Only she wasn't really white. She was Cape Coloured, but with her long blond wig, pale-base facial make-up, bright red lipstick, pastel summer dresses, blue varnish on her finger and toenails, her presence gave Bra-Bra an advantage of one-upmanship that was unbeatable during *apartheid*'s ironclad rule.

After passing muster with Bra-Bra's intimidating receptionist, I was about to head for his frosted-glass door, when I stopped like I'd been standstill-smashed by a fighting *knobkerrie*.

Until then I'd been too essentially concentrating on my own dilemmas to notice the girl sitting on a corner couch with her dimpled knees drawn demurely together, a porcelain-inlaid coffee table strewn with magazines in front of her.

What . . . she . . . did . . . to . . . me . . . had never happened before.

It's never happened anything like that to me since with anyone else but her.

For a second I couldn't even draw breath.

She had the first, shiny, Afro hair extensions I'd ever seen, all interwoven with bits of burnished metal, and big soft brown eyes. I don't know if you'd find her beautiful or not, but whatever she had, it was for me, *mfowethu*.

I went over and sat down beside her.

'*Sisi*,' I said, 'Sister, please don't tell me you've got legal troubles?'

She laughed at my audacity and it was the loveliest sound I'd ever heard. Just then the severely closed, frosted-glass door opened and a fat round butterball of a guy in a pinstriped suit popped out with a mouth packed full of overlarge dentures custom-made for smiling. He grabbed my hand and gave me the brotherhood shake for so long I thought he was never going to let go.

'Mister Bhekuzulu?' he asked, nodding away in the affirmative. 'Mister Bhekuzulu, this is my daughter, Zsa-Zsa.'

'Bra-Bra and Zsa-Zsa?' I gave back. 'Amazing.'

'Double phonetics run in the family, Mister Bhekuzulu,' he said. 'We like our names.'

'So do I,' I said. 'It sounds even better on her than on the Hollywood film star.'

'I see you two have already met?'

'Barely.'

Bra-Bra turned to his gorgeous progeny.

'Mister Bhekuzulu is from Johannesburg. He is going into business down here. The, ah, transport and grocery sales supply business.'

He dropped my hand and reached for his daughter's, almost pulling her off the couch.

'Mister Bhekuzulu and I have a lot to talk about,' he said, leading her in a sort of benevolent frogmarch to the door. 'His appointment takes priority, sweetness, so we'll have to part company for now, I know you'll under – '

'Listen,' I interrupted, aiming my words at Zsa-Zsa. 'Tell your father he'll be gaining big *lobolo* as well as a good son . . . ,' but my bold speech tailed off, because neither of them was paying me any attention.

Zsa-Zsa Motshange turned towards me, little spots of dark anger obviously meant for her *baba* flushing her smooth young cheeks.

'What did you say?'

'I'll tell you about it at Ma Motjadi's place over a grilled steak dinner,' I improvised, naming the top food and live-music *shebeen* in those parts.

'But I'm eating at home tonight.'

Eish, mfowethu!

'Don't bet on it, Miss Motshange. I wouldn't if I were you.'

Bra-Bra managed to peck her stiffly on the cheek in dismissive farewell and to ease her out into the corridor, clicking the entrance door firmly closed behind her.

'Maybe she had something important to ask you?'

'Daughters only want one thing from fathers, Mister Bhekuzulu. Seventeen-year-old daughters especially, and that's a fact recorded by an above-average legal brain.'

'Dhlamini. Call me Dhlamini. What she want?'

'Same as me, you and everybody else, Dhlamini, my friend. The root of all evil. Filthy lucre. *Amarands.*'

'She got what she wanted?'

'Half. *Hawu!* How many shoes does one girl need? And call me Bra-Bra.'

'Looks like we both know the nature of the beast, Bra-Bra.'

'My family knows nothing at all about this sort of business,' he said slowly, his mega-smile still firmly in place around the overabundant pearly dentures. 'That's the way I wish to keep it.'

'Okay with me, Bra-Bra. But I have to tell you here and now, your daughter's the girl I'm going to marry.' I was as surprised as he was when I heard myself say it.

His permanent smile vanished. Suddenly he looked shrewd and tough, even with all his baby-soft fat. He gave me a long, searching look, his eyes steady and unwavering.

'That might not be the worst thing in the world, Dhlamini, my friend. Can you afford her?'

I had twenty thousand in my back sky. I pulled it out and let him see the vulgar bundle.

'This do for a *lobolo* down payment? Bride prices being what they are today?'

The mega-smile came back like a witchdoctor's enchantment.

'There is a strong possibility of success in your favour,' Bra-Bra winked back at me.

'Great stuff, Bra-Bra. Now we've got that out of the way, are you going to invite me to your home for dinner tonight?'

I had rosemary-marinated pork chops and a superlative French rosé wine from the St Emilion district with the Motshange family that night.

Zsa-Zsa was not a modern girl in spite of the beautifully modern way she dressed.

Her mother, her grandmother and her great-grandmother were ultra-traditional Zulu dowagers, and she was brought up like that too. Most of her young life she'd been to a conservative, mission-influenced, God-fearing school, but she knew her own mind *sans* religion. Once she'd made it up, she'd do what *she* thought was right whether it suited her family's ideas and ecclesiastical upbringing or not.

Zsa-Zsa had it all figured out about how she was going

to live. This was relentlessly drummed into me during our formalised courtship.

She wanted babies and a piano. The grander the grand piano, the better.

She wanted a husband who loved her with a dog's devotion, and she also wanted that same husband to forevermore desire only one wife. Remember, this was Zulu territory and one wife was male marital anathema.

I never thought much about what actually being *married* to Zsa-Zsa would be like.

I just knew I wanted *her*, had to have *her*, and anything *she* wanted was good enough for me. I separated out my intelligence from the eager sperm-sacs of my testicles and, believe it or not, was faithful to her for the long months she made me wait before marrying me.

Our wedding was an event.

Township darkies knew how to marry, even there in Pietermaritzburg.

Vilakazi was my Best Man.

But that didn't stop him from being deprived of two top-gum incisors in a backyard scuffle well into the early hours after the final ceremony itself.

This was after Zsa-Zsa's best friend, Suzie Makheba, parted company with the flower of her innocence wrapped up in an abandoned hymen, which the girl's Reverend Dad who married Zsa-Zsa and me hoped she would retain until at least she turned eighteen.

Hawu, dadawethu! as my feisty old ancestors would have said.

It cost me a packet.

I was taken for a financial ride, *mfowethu*.

Being the *umkhwenyana*, the son-in-law, I had to pay for *everything*, unlike white weddings, where such matters are the bride's father's responsibility.

First it was the *lobolo* money, and I shiver involuntarily remembering just how much I gave Bra-Bra Motshange.

Then more for what is traditionally known as *inkomo kanina*, or 'the bride's mother's slaughter beasts'.

More again for the rings, and again more for my blushing beauty's designer wedding gown and my own and Vilakazi's black tuxedos, jewelled cummerbunds, frilly shirts and genuine pearl-studded bow-ties.

But first there was the preliminary 'party' to be endured.

Bra-Bra slaughtered a goat in honour of the *shades* of the ancestors, traditional prayers were said, sonorous hymns sung and afterwards, plenty of silent boozing took place.

By six o'clock, with the sun going down, the Motshanges' lounge was packed just as tight with black human life as any early-morning township train. It was even noisier, it has to be said, and that's saying something, *mfowethu*. The place was so full of the aromas of strong booze, tobacco and *insangu* fumes, that for me to breathe, Zsa-Zsa had to give me life support with the kiss of life.

The party went on right through the night.

Brutal, *mfowethu*, brutal.

The wedding was due to start on Saturday, one hour this side of noon.

At thirty-five past ten, my bridegroom's entourage automobiled to the church.

The bride's means of transport was a sight for sore eyes, eyes still radically sore through and through from the previous night's fun and games and jollification.

It was an open pink convertible that seemed larger than a Putco bus, but with sliced suspension lowering the long body to below waist-level. It was dolled up with fluttering ribbons; pink, white, orange, green, purple, blue, turquoise, yellow, cream, violet, saffron, black, vermilion, rose and red balloons floated out behind, trailing like helium-inflated polonies.

There was a fanfare of ear-shattering hooting as our limos flipped three times for flash-style around the already crowded block, packed with spectators and guests alike.

We were at the altar as the church clock read eleven-thirty-seven. Not bad, considering the spatial circumstances, *mfowethu*.

Suzie Makheba's Reverend Dad preached for far too welcoming eternity's forever long, and me, I wasn't the only one who felt that way. You could feel the pew-bound numb *ezzies* crying out for succour.

When the muscular old patriarch stopped his infernal gassing and the service was over amongst plenty of grateful and fervently uttered 'Amens' and 'Hallelujahs', we blew like the August winds back to Bra-Bra's place with all the hooters again going full blast every inch of the way.

What an occasion!

As we raucously approached the house, a group of aggressive Motshange female relatives swaggered down to meet us, some carrying nasty-looking staves and others straw brooms.

Suddenly, with a simultaneous leap skyward, they all parachuted swiftly back to earth *en masse*, singing loud, perfectly pitched harmonies and stamping out a dust-raising dance challenge. Those with brooms ceremoniously swept the way before us, while the others attacked unseen enemies; we slowed down to a crawl, engines barely turning over. They laid out *amacansi*, mats for us to walk on, as we came to a parked halt and got out of our iron carriages.

The reception was a lengthy affair.

It began slowly, with every involved old fart making an interminably long speech.

Zsa-Zsa and I had to be 'interviewed' one by one by

these grey-haired and dried-out ancient cow-bladders; but they *did* hand over compensatory gifts. Gifts both big and small, as well as unwanted advice – advice both long and longer.

More speeches, plenty more, senior family fathers reciting the valorous deeds of their hallowed clan's forebears as if every one of them had been a mighty conqueror only a little less successful than King Shaka.

It was long after dark when things really started happening.

There was the magic of the electric guitars.

The magic of the booze.

The magic of the sexy babes and their sinuous dancing.

I say these things because it was well after midnight when I caught sight of Zsa-Zsa's great-grandmother dancing as no octogenarian has a right to dance, not with all those voraciously used years behind her, *mfowethu*.

Not with the eighteen-year-old boy her sights were set on.

Suzie Makheba's Reverend Dad was the one who beat up Vilakazi.

Vilakazi was the one who deflowered his daughter.

Caught *in flagrante delicto*.

I was so tired and hungover, and my senses so shattered, that Zsa-Zsa and I only consummated our long-awaited union the following day, bolstered by half a dozen aspirins and a bottle of champagne watered down with orange juice.

And that was how I got married.

Marital Bliss?

By that time I was the busiest *tsotsi* in the province, and the *amarands* were pouring in hand over fist.

I had my organisation put together and running like oil on top of a downhill river in flood. Except that my personal road to riches was all *uphill*, as in mounting monetary heights. Vilakazi got a dental plate with false teeth that looked better than the ones he lost via the wrathful Reverend Dad, as well as four more driver-salesmen working full-time for him and indirectly for me. We were selling booze *and* washing powder like it was going out of fashion, *mfowethu*.

One of the first things I did was to get Bra-Bra to straighten me out with the local law and get the pay-offs going on a regular basis. Then I got him to make the rounds of any local competition he was in contact with and put a friendly proposition to them on my behalf, a proposition they would please spread outwards for all and sundry. I was willing either to buy or allow them to carry on, but the one thing I didn't want was rough stuff – and I avoided strong-arm pressure like the plague. As direct competition nobody scared me – there was plenty around for everybody.

You see, *mfowethu*, amongst Zulus feuds never end anyway. It's all tied up with ancestor worship – their vendettas go on and on for all eternity and I needed that like I needed a hole in the head. Besides, having to keep half a dozen killer-gunmen bodyguards sitting around on their *ezzies* eating away at your payroll can break you. Also they are guaranteed to give much *phindaphinda* multiplied trouble – they get restless when you haven't got any action for them and then out of boredom start picking fights with law-abiding citizens, knifing some guy over a girl, robbing cafés for kicks, that sort of thing. And if you *do* have manoeuvres for them, it's equally bad for business. Nothing gets public indignation up and the hot breath of the law down your neck like a series of gangland slayings that leave a trail of mutilated corpses behind in a nightmare of carnage.

I told Bra-Bra to let everybody know in no uncertain terms where I came from and who my heavy friends were. I told him to broadcast the word that I wanted to sleep restful on silk, not have raw insomnia keeping me bleary-eyed from an aggravating sandpaper mattress. That if they chose to work for me with their own connections, I'd *guarantee* to make them more money than they already were making.

Then I went right ahead with my plans and waited to see what would happen.

I ran into just one nasty spot of trouble.

The General sent down three slayers while I was deliberately absent from the area and inside half a week it was all over.

There were no bodies.

Just permanently absent local *tsotsis*.

The offenders' corpses were dropped into an acid vat housed in the spacious back of a minibus taxi, rendered down to liquid slime and dumped.

End of *indaba*.

I never ran into any more trouble the whole time I was in the Kingdom of Zulu. I didn't hurt nobody and nobody hurt me.

I had only one headache, a migraine in fact, because The General was sending me too much of the cleaning stuff. I had to find more warehouses and more *tsotsi* salesmen. Bengal Tiger was a big help with that problem, but of course he wanted his cut. The General complained a little, nothing really bad, but there it was just the same. He also let me know that he was thinking of branching out into laxative pills, and that made my heart palpitate a few extra beats in dread.

Finally, though, I had to have The General send me down a guy named John 'Abacus' Sexwale, a half-black, half-Chinese son of a sporting woman, to take some of the load off my shoulders. Abacus was fantastic with figures and passable at keeping things running. That left me time to organise more connected outlets all up and down the coast to offload the burgeoning quantities of washing powder products.

I was so busy that it was hard to see much of Zsa-Zsa, but she said that didn't matter.

Her old man was right.

She didn't know what line we were in.

I knew that if she ever found out, I'd be in the cooking pot with her holding down the lid with both hands, so you could say our marriage veered towards dishonesty.

Okay, *mfowethu*, it *was* dishonest.

Usually when I find somebody who tells me that *honesty is the best policy*, I judge that right there is a peculiar someone I would watch very carefully if I were engaged in mutually profitable business with him. Because usually it means that what *he* means is that honesty is the best policy for *you*, not for *him*. If *he* can count on *your* being honest all the time without fail, he will know just what you're going to do, how you're going to react and just *how* he can take *you*. The only *geeza* I can't judge true is the one who really *is honest*. He doesn't care whether *you* are or not as long as he knows *he* is, right down the line. This kind of *geeza* can be taken over and over again and he never learns from experience; he's always there ready to be a sucker for anybody who comes stalking along, looking for easy prey.

Honesty is the best policy?

In whose dreams, *mfowethu*?

The thing that gets to me is that this aforementioned species of *geeza* seems to find honesty a masochistic magnet: he seems to be drawn to *enjoy* it. I've only known two human aberrations that were completely honest like that.

One was a nun of the Franciscan Mendicant Order working amongst the rural and calamitously disadvantaged poor in an isolated part of mountainous Basutoland.

The other was my wife, Zsa-Zsa.

Beat that if you can – fate always hawking a gallon of tubercular mucus in my direction.

I didn't know then what I know now about Zsa-Zsa.

I judged that, once we were married, I could talk her out of her prejudices if she ever found out about me. I knew we loved each other and that that should be enough. I was *almost* right. If certain things hadn't happened the way they did, very fast and very blindingly hard, I might have got away unscathed with the whole kit and nefarious kaboodle. Now I guess I sound like every second emasculated, cringing human-male cur on the planet, don't I, *mfowethu*? Nobody likes a sorry-for-himself, moaning *mampara*, so I'll shut my trap.

It was funny, but Vilakazi had my situation evaluated far better than I did. He and Zsa-Zsa got to be really good friends. A few days before the wedding, Vilakazi did his best to talk me out of taking that one small step forward as an enemy of good bachelorhood, that giant step forward for the evil gods of matrimony.

What Vilakazi said after a lot of verbal fornicating around anywhere but the point boiled down to about this: that Zsa-Zsa *was* sure to find out about our clandestine operations. And when she did, we were going to lose something between us that would never return. Would our marriage stand up to the void of that loss, etc., etc.?

The spilling-over gut reaction that overwhelmed me was *how dare* my philandering *bhuti*, whose brain was always wrapped around his erect *umthondo* anyway, assume *he* could advise *me* on marital philosophy?

But Vilakazi had the verbal runs – he added more excreta, like that any discovery was going to dissect her mental stability into bleeding slivers of distrust for sure and that I had no right to do that to her if I really loved her.

Me, as I said, I got acidly annoyed, even angry, because I thought it was none of my brother's business. At the same time I was nearly losing my marbles trying to do so much, and I resented like hell being under fire with any kind of criticism. In my book Vilakazi was just being a nosey parker pain in the parking-lot of my defecation tube.

I made no bones about telling Vilakazi just that and a whole lot of other unnecessary macho *bulongwe*. You know what I mean, *mfowethu* – if it hadn't been for me looking out for him all his lousy, ungrateful life, he'd be rotting away in some forced-labour *apartheid* jail right now giving blowjobs and much, much more to twisted pervert white warders.

Vilakazi ended up calling me a know-it-all *gal pil*

fokken darkie son of a bitch, caught himself in the self-reference and then accused *me* of insulting our mother. He then got drunk three days in a row – that for sure was how the avenging angel of purloined virginity in the manifested form of a muscular Reverend Dad Makheba managed to whip Vilakazi, because normally my brother can punch his weight against all comers his own size and reasonably ominous weight.

Now was now, however, and I had just taken delivery of three brand-new Mercedes-Benz big babies. They were the sweetest wheels you ever saw, all shiny black and capable of hitting a hundred and twenty-five miles an hour without a ripple. From behind the front seats I had my specialist mechanics cut right through into the rear big boot compartment to make enough space to carry fifty cases of contraband, maybe more at a pinch. The German metallic confections' ostentatious air of wealth and prestige placed them way above any casual roadblock inspection. Special undercarriage springs were fitted to take the abnormal load, which set me back megabucks, as you can well imagine, *mfowethu*. I was shitting mental blood trying to work them into the operation to get back some of the boodle they had cost, when an addle-brained Bra-Bra Motshange had to get motherless and mindless drunk on me.

Zsa-Zsa and I were living in the Indian area of Pietermaritzburg in a sumptuous double-storey house with seven-foot-high walls, all owned by Bengal Tiger, mainly because blacks weren't allowed to own their own property in *apartheid* South Africa. I think Indians had a different property possessor's classification, maybe because they've always been smart bastards in any legal-document game. The rent was high but I could afford it, and for security reasons the ethnic isolation suited me just fine.

We had been there for almost ten months and Zsa-Zsa was just a few days away from having our baby, when she found out about my chosen occupation as a *tsotsi*.

She discovered the whole sordid maze of hidden truth from none other than her own father. The portly legal eagle had turned *malgat* conscience-stricken and became raving-lunatic melancholy and introspectively maudlin. He spent a whole night weeping, laying his guilt all over his nearest and dearest. Then he tried to off himself. But the gun jammed, and by the time he'd cleared the chamber he'd changed his mind.

I got back from a *spaza*-searching enforcer's trip down the north coast at about five o'clock in the morning.

Zsa-Zsa was sitting in our kitchen, which was big enough to open a *Taj Mahal* style curry chow-palace in. She was dressed in one of those shapeless diamond-stitched padded gowns just silently staring vacantly at nothing. I couldn't get her to speak. She looked ten years older than even her great-grandmother. I got her to bed and gave her a handful of sleeping pills before calling her mother to provide me with some clues as to the reason for her daughter's autistic condition.

No progress there.

Zsa-Zsa didn't say a word to me for four days.

By that time I was going around in square circles, *mfowethu*.

Vilakazi had been more or less avoiding me socially since we got spliced, although he would come over to the house between trips to see Zsa-Zsa when he knew I wasn't going to be there. My operation was at a point where every minute counted, and I had to be around the hub all day and night to keep things going right.

The cash was really starting to roll in. It had taken a year to get things into top gear, but now this combination of illegal effort was doing better than twenty thousand clear a week. The General's washing-powder was still a migraine, but even that was obediently coming into line. The only setback was that it took forty-eight hours a day minimum to keep the ball rolling – and there was only one *geeza* who knew how to keep it moving. If one piece of the action started to come apart, then all the rest would show signs of crack-up stress. On top of it all, old man Bra-Bra seemed to be going steadily off his rocker: he was threatening his own brand of loudly publicised suicide again. Zsa-Zsa's *mame* was on the telephone ten frantic times a day.

Finally I couldn't stand it anymore, *mfowethu*.

I went upstairs to where Zsa-Zsa was sprawled listlessly on the big double bed that I hadn't slept in for what seemed a century and I looked at her there deliberately not looking at me.

Suddenly I felt the unfamiliar wetness of tears rolling down my cheeks. A hot flush of embarrassment made me bury my face in the blankets. After a while Zsa-Zsa started to stroke my head, and I knew it was alright. I reminded myself that night to make a sacrifice to the *shades* of the ancestors and maybe even say a prayer or two to God in one of His churches; no harm in backing both your bets, is there?

Lying beside her, I tried to tell her how it was for me. I must have rabbited on until the whole night was talked away. I opened up and let it pour out, all the things I had done, how I felt about my 'profession'.

To me, making *ugologo*, or beer, without the permission of the sad motherfuckers who make up all the laws that control us like obedient sheep is not what you would call a real crime, then or now – especially then, with *apartheid*'s *gal pil* architects claiming alcohol turned *all black folk* into deranged berserkers *because our skulls, with our constrictive caps of dense, wiry, steel-wool hair, were too tight for the swelling with which imbibed liquor would disastrously inflate our brains.* Sweet *Nkulunkulu*, what did they think we were all drinking before the White Man arrived? Everybody and his brother was either making it or drinking it or both, *mfowethu*, but those parsimonious pricks said such things were against *their* laws. All my life I've been supplying items people really want, items the ubiquitous law in its barefaced manner says they shouldn't have. The people are going to get what they want anyway, even if I die today. History backs me one hundred per cent, *mfowethu*. So why not get whatever it is they want from me?

The mentally homicidal thought-police repeat their manacling litany about poor kids who stay legitimate and struggle their way step by grateful step up the ladder of success and end up chairman of the board. I've never met one of these prodigies and I've never met anybody else who's met one. I've known a lot of big shots, but without exception all the important, super-successful mainstream people I've ever met have had something undercover going for them that *allowed* them to get where they were. I make an exception here only for those individuals with unique talent who made it through prepared-to-starve commitment in the field of artistic endeavour. Either the big frogs in big ponds had silver spoons in their mouths when they were born, or somebody did something for them that let them float up to the top. None of the opulent upper-hierarchy lemmings of my acquaintance did it all alone, all by themselves.

In many ways you had a better chance of making it on your own on my side of the fence. For a darkie *laaitjie* like me there was no chance whatever of making it in the pure-as-the-driven-snow way. Ignorant lamebrains say it's easy money on the Wrong Side Of The Law. Well, me, I can tell you, *mfowethu*, that nobody ever worked harder for it than I did. I sweated like a many-headed hydra-dog to get mine. No *geeza* in straightforward business ever sweated or slaved any harder. And if my *tsotsi* profits were higher than most, my risks were equally so. I judge it works out about even-steven in the end anyway.

In the morning Zsa-Zsa didn't say much, but she had thawed a trifle: she was more like she was before, if you get what I mean. Me, I judged I had it made. She went over to see her *mame* and I took off in the direction I belonged.

I found Abacus Sexwale tearing at his Afro-Asian hair.

There were a thousand things to do and get done. There weren't enough drivers. We didn't have any loaders. There were seven *spaza* shops that hadn't paid what they owed for washing powder *and* under-the-counter booze. Vilakazi was overdue getting back with one of my big new black Mercedes-Benzes from a special trip up to Jo'burg with a load of rabidly popular *insangu* they called Durban Poisons – I withstood the maelstrom for ten hours before I gave up and went home.

Zsa-Zsa had spectacular food going. She was really talented with the pots and pans and could cook like a dream chef – and besides, she had two genius kitchen servants working for her. I could smell the goodness of thick, mouth-watering aromas when I went in the door. She didn't talk a lot and I couldn't once make her smile, but she put her hand tenderly on my shoulder like she had always done before when she leaned over the table. She went to bed early while I was still checking through

Abacus Sexwale's books.

The telephone jangled around eleven o'clock and my guts were in such a state of trepidation that it wasn't until that moment that I realised my brother Vilakazi still hadn't checked in to confirm his safe return. I knew something was wrong before I picked up the receiver.

Vilakazi's happy rumble of a voice was tense and thin with distance. It was a weak connection, but I could still hear him clearly.

'Dhlamini, *bra*, they took the fucking Merc away from me! They say if you want it back you better come get it yourself! The General says for you to keep your nose the hell away from Jo'burg!'

'Now *gahle*, *bra*, slow down, Vilakazi,' I said. 'What shit is this? Who took the Merc away from you?'

'Fuckssakes, *bra*, you stay away from here! It's the Boy's *amaskebberesh*! Boy Faraday! The General says that *moegoe* is stone-crazy, total *befok*, *bra*! Booze, beer, protection, drugs, whores, he wants the whole fucking country for himself! This Boy Faraday is a lunatic butcher, *bra*! His gangsters are knocking off anything that moves! The General says for me to go into hiding and he'll be in touch later! This shit scares me, Dhlamini, *bra*! I'm footing it out of here fast!'

'*Vilakazi!*' I suddenly realised I was shouting and straightaway I lowered my voice so that Zsa-Zsa upstairs wouldn't hear. 'Vilakazi, you listen *too good* for me now, *bra*. You go back to The General's and you wait for me there. I'm coming up to see for myself what's going on. And don't worry, *bra*, nobody's going to blow you or me away, trust me. What for? I don't bother nobody. I cooperate with everybody, you know that, *bra*. I make plenty-plenty *amarands* for the small *geezas* and the big *geezas*. Who the fuck would want to kill me?'

'Dhlamini . . . Dhlamini . . . you just don't fucking know . . . '

'You do what I tell you!' I found myself yelling again, the veins in my throat swelling up in imitation of melon creeper vines. I found myself squeezing the heavy black telephone receiver as if it was my own throat in order to lower the sheer volume of my vitriolic voice. 'Big boys don't cry – tough guys don't burst into tears like a fucking *mfaan*. Nobody put a bullet in you, did they? You're not fucking dead, are you? You go back to The General's and you wait for me there. I'll be up sometime tomorrow.'

I slammed the phone down.

I stood there shaking like an epileptic for a moment, weak with anger, wondering what I was going to do.

Then I heard a soft *click!* as Zsa-Zsa put down the upstairs telephone extension.

She'd been eavesdropping on me.

She didn't try to hide it, just hung up, and then I heard her footsteps moving across the wooden bedroom floor, footsteps that were theatrically heavy and slow.

I knew what was coming and I began to see red. I had taken about all I could stand, *mfowethu*. Who the fuck was she to tell me that what I did for a living was morally wrong? I felt a rage coming up so strong I was scared it would throttle me.

Zsa-Zsa didn't say anything until she was at the bottom of the staircase and we were facing each other.

'You better call Vilakazi back,' she said with a voice like whiplash. 'Tell him to come home.'

Red mists began to flourish behind my eyeballs. She didn't say *come back to your brother*, oh no, the big-head, fucking inflated-belly, egotistical cow. She'd said *come home*. It wasn't *Vilakazi's* fucking home and it wasn't *her* fucking home. It was *my* home and *I* was paying for it

91

with *my* blood, sweat and tears. *My* home. Me, Dhlamini Bhekuzulu, *nobody else.*

'Don't you worry about Vilakazi. Vilakazi can look after himself.'

She studied me for a quizzical moment, then spoke as if asking me to explain something she didn't understand.

'You're going to make your own brother stay up there where crazy *tsotsis* are murdering each other and maybe him too? When he tells you that he's frightened *for his life?*'

'For fuckssakes, woman – '

'Don't use that language. Not in my house.'

There it was again: *my* fucking house!

'You talk like a child, Zsa-Zsa. Nobody's going to make Vilakazi *eat the earth*. He's okay. He's just blubbering like he always does when the going gets rough.'

'What do you know about crying?' She chewed the words out and her eyes grew big and hot. 'Because you shed tears once in your life last night? You've never cried! You never will cry! What do you know about Vilakazi's "blubbering", as you call it? Or mine? Or this?' she said furiously as she put her hands on either side of her monstrously protuberant belly, fingers outspread, holding herself.

She knew she couldn't talk to me that way.

So she was entirely to blame for what happened next, *mfowethu.*

Everything was *hers*, was it?

Her home. *Her* child. Nothing left for me, was that her fucking story?

'What the fuck you got to cry about?' I blazed away at her, our faces only inches apart, angry little flecks of unaimed spittle missiles finding her cheeks. 'When you met me you were a spoilt little cunt of a stupid spoon-fed kid with nothing more than a whining mouth repeating, *please daddy, please daddy, please daddy!* You didn't have a pink dollar you could call your own! Now you got a house! You got two cars, servants and more clothes than you ever had in your whole fucking life! Half a million in the bank and you got a reason to fucking cry, bitch? And *my* kid that you haven't given me yet, you think he's got anything to cry about? He's got a *baba* who's a fucking big shot! My kid will have everything, hear me? Everything! My kid'll have the best!'

She moved back a step, her lips pulled down in clearly undisguised loathing, and started to turn away. Disgust radiated from her like heat from an infrared lamp.

I grabbed her arm hard and spun her around viciously. 'Maybe that's why you're so fucking worried about Vilakazi? Maybe my kid's Vilakazi's kid? Is that it, you bloodsucking traitorous bitch?'

She didn't say anything and her face was pale enough for her to pass for a half-caste *mlungu*.

Then, without warning, she spat slimy phlegm full in my face.

The red mists blossoming behind my eyeballs turned into a heaving carmine sea.

I punched her hard on her forehead and she dropped like a pregnant sack of potatoes. Before I could stop myself, I'd booted her twice between her legs and then I left the house without looking back at her lying bleeding on the floor. If she'd harmed our baby with her stupidity, I'd kill her, fucking kill her, kill her, kill her, kill her . . .

I didn't even slam the front door closed.

I still had time to catch the midnight train to Jo'burg.

Rabid Rabies

The General told me that Vilakazi was lying low and waiting for me at our mother's unpretentious shanty. He took me down to the basement of the Glass House and sat me facing him across the front of his huge, ornate desk.

'Look, *wena*, you know I didn't want you here. Not with a diseased dog like this Boy Faraday around. A hydrophobic, rabies-infested psychopath who bites anyone who comes near him. It is very foolish of you. A few thousand lost on a fancy car. That is not worth your life, Dhlamini.'

'How does *uthuvi* like him get away with it?' I fumed and ranted. 'Why not stop him, *umnumzana*? How does one *tsotsi* go crazy and all our hard work and planning goes up in smoke? How about Potato Crisp Nxumalo? Is he just going to let this kill-crazy *skebengu* take over and rule our lives?'

The General reached across and placed his hand on my arm as it trembled with anger.

'Wait, *laaitjie*, wait,' he said. 'There's a lot you don't know.'

The General was *very* serious.

Right away I began to calm down.

His calling me *laaitjie* was the tip-off. He'd never called me that before in his life.

'Let me tell you the way things are. Then you will do what you have to do, one way or the other. In the first place, Dhlamini, our organisation no longer has the police under control. Not like it was. Boy Faraday's short-sighted path of widespread destruction has seen to that loss. As of now, *everything* is on hold. Potato Crisp is compromised. He's heading for jail because of three witnesses under police protection. They have sold him out. We can't get to them. It looks like he is out of the picture. This Boy Faraday is a butchering hyena that would eat the bones of its own babies in its ravenous, consuming insanity. He is *not* going to "take over", because he has several warrants of arrest out for him as we speak. A witnessed bank robbery with two policemen shot dead is the most recent. He is murdering like a mad dog because of his uncontrollable rage. But his fire will be doused, nothing is surer. In the meantime he is terribly dangerous to be around and all illegal activity carries a virtually automatic death sentence. The resulting chaos is, how can I put it, a whirlpool of confusion, sucking everybody down. People lose their heads. People get hurt. People are dying like flies. That is what is happening, right here, right now.'

He looked at me very steadily, his raptor's eyes sad and serious.

'What does it matter if this man-eating animal Boy Faraday takes one of your new Mercedes-Benzes – when you no longer have a business?'

'*Hawu!*' I yelled, outraged. 'What're you saying, I haven't got a business? I've got more than a hundred thousand *amarands* tied up in stock and equipment alone. That's not a business?'

'Pay attention to me, Dhlamini. Listen to what I tell you, *laaitjie*. Inside of what will be, at most, a few extremely risky weeks, you must burn your bridges behind you. You are through. Out. Finished. *Phelile.*'

He stood up, walked around the desk and placed his face close to mine.

'You *have* to understand that, Dhlamini. You must start cashing in on all your assets quickstyle. Me, I'm going to take a nice long holiday. Maybe even a year. Maybe more. Let this all blow over. Because it is not going to be healthy to be around here.'

He studied my eyes and he could tell what was going on inside of me. He reached out again and patted my shoulder and smiled a little.

'You have no self-destructive bad habits, Dhlamini. You've done alright for a young man. Why don't you take a rest? There'll be other opportunities later when things cool down. Gambling beyond South African borders looks promising for the future. Fast food is becoming the country's biggest addiction. There are a load of new drugs young people want at any price. We have merely to follow overseas trends. There will be many other ways to earn pink dollars.'

I kept looking at him and I couldn't say a word.

Maybe it was Zsa-Zsa.

The General knew zero about that.

Maybe it was that I saw everything I'd been counting on and working for going to nothing, like an opaque early-morning haze dissipating in the heat of the rising sun.

Maybe I just couldn't take what he was telling me on top of everything else.

Anyway, I got up and all I could do was sort of wave at him.

I don't remember walking out of the Glass House at all, and I don't remember taking a taxi to catch up with Vilakazi again.

Out Of The Frying Pan

'What are you going to do?' Vilakazi asked anxiously.

I looked at him, at his worried face, at the deep lines running from his broad, flaring nostrils down past the corners of his mouth, and I wondered why he was such a sad *skebengu*.

'I'm going to get our Merc back, and then I'm going to tell that fucking Boy Faraday his fortune.'

'*Hawu!* Dhlamini, *bra* . . . ' Vilakazi looked like he was about to burst into tears. I wondered why I'd said that to him? Just to rev his engines, get him in overdrive? Then I realised it was because I was still in a state about Zsa-Zsa. And pissed off at Vilakazi for being right about our marriage. And pissed off at everything else in the world. I knew I wasn't going to get tough with Boy Faraday. I was going to play it smart. If The General was going to pull out and with Potato Crisp exiting the scene, then there was no reason I couldn't guide Boy Faraday and work alongside him.

We footed it to where I knew we'd find Boy Faraday, Vilakazi a step behind me, trying to keep up. When we got to the door of a little-known *shebeen*, Vilakazi pulled at my arm.

'Why not forget it, Dhlamini, *bra*? We're sweet now. We got plenty to get by.'

'Vilakazi, please stop fouling your pants like a flatulent old *madala*,' I said. 'You know where they've stashed our Merc. Go there and wait for me. I'll be with you in less than an hour. What I've got to say won't take long. And give me that *isibhamu* you're carrying.'

Vilakazi put his hand inside his black Vella leather jacket and hesitated, his face taut and worried.

'I don't have any plans to kill anybody,' I shrugged. 'But I need to protect myself. Come on. Hand over.'

He finally passed me his automatic handgun. I slipped it into my waistband. It was the first time I'd ever carried a firearm and this one was highly illegal – but then so were Boy Faraday and his amigos' guns. Mine felt immoderately comforting.

'See you later, alligator,' I said, remembering the words of a popular rock 'n roll song that used to play on soulless white Springbok Radio. Still Vilakazi hesitated. 'Go on, get out of here,' I said. He finally started up the dimly lit street. I waited until he passed the next corner.

Then I knocked on the door, gave the lookout ten bucks and walked inside.

Boy Faraday's choice of *shebeen* was an abominably foul-smelling joint with strangely contrasting, pristinely whitewashed walls covered with framed sepia-toned photographs of township pugilist legends. The place was not much bigger than my rented lounge and dining room belonging to Bengal Tiger in Pietermaritzburg.

There were four men in zoot suits all wearing snappy headgear of angled-brim fedoras sitting at a far table playing cards.

I knew Boy Faraday from when I'd seen him around: average height and a skinny build, but with a badly pockmarked, expressionless rodent face highlighted by flat insect eyes. I also knew two of the *tsotsis* with him. One was Dollar Two-Times, his number-one muscle, as wide as he was tall, and the other was Shoeshine Simunye, the *geeza* who set up the up-to-now infallible escape routes from any payroll heist or bank robbery.

The third spiv I had never seen before.

He sat facing Boy Faraday, his body fossilised and both hands on the table. I judged that he was in a state of lockjaw terror, obviously scared to death, *mfowethu.*

There was a proper solid bar in that *shebeen*, with a full-length smoky mirror behind it, not the usual mismatched spartan collection of Formica-topped tables and cheap plastic chairs that the shabby exterior proclaimed you would find within.

Nobody looked up when I walked in, not even the huge woman with a shaven head and shoulder-length earrings polishing glasses and tin beer mugs. Reflected behind her were two baseball bats studded with six-inch nails hanging within easy reach.

I walked over to the foursome and said as pleasantly as I know how, 'Mister Boy Faraday?'

Boy Faraday motioned me to rest my haunches. I could smell his expensive cologne a mile away.

I sat down next to him, but not too close.

If this *geeza* was a son-of-a-rabied-hyena-bitch hyena dog, I didn't plan to get bitten if I could help it. Here was the strange thing: I should have been incarcerated in abject fear, but I wasn't: I just didn't give a damn. I was as cool as a frozen cucumber, *mfowethu.*

'I'm Dhlamini Bhekuzulu, Mister Faraday,' I said. 'First of all I'd like to get my Mercedes-Benz back and then I'd like to talk to you about business.'

'Go ahead, dead man, talk,' he said. 'Mouth as much

as you like, it's your own *fokken* funeral service.' His voice was high: it came out like a whistling wind, like the rustling sound of dry river reeds in a fierce breeze, like the hoarse croaking of frogs also striving to be heard.

Dollar Two-Times and Shoeshine gave out sycophantic guffaws as if Boy Faraday was the funniest comedian in the world. The fourth, silent *geeza* looked on the point of weeping storms of liquid from his eyes as well as his trousers.

I stayed outwardly calm and collected.

'I've been working with The General,' I said confidentially. 'But the main man tells me he's pulling out. I judge maybe I could make the same kind of deal with you. I thought . . . maybe . . . we . . . '

Boy Faraday scowled. His pockmarked face darkened from brown to blue-black. I heard my voice lose itself and vibed I'd said the wrong thing, *mfowethu*. I felt clammy sweat break out on my chest, under my arms and at the back of my neck, but I still wasn't scared, just wound up and stiffly tense.

'Pay attention, dead man,' Boy Faraday said hollowly. 'I don't make any *fokken* deals, got that? Either you work for me like all my *rawurawus*, or you don't work, got that? I don't like *fokken* deals, no *fokken* cuts, no *fokken* percentages, *fokkol*. I'm in business for me. What, dead man, you think you some *fokken* White Man can come in here all *larney* and tune me the *fokken* rules?'

I stood up slowly and the scrape of the chair's legs on the cement floor made me jump.

Nobody said anything. The sudden poisonous silence was thick as stodgy *mieliepap*.

I had my eyes fastened on Boy Faraday's the way a boxer reads the flicker signal of his opponent's next move and I couldn't stop staring. If bullets were going to fly, I wanted to be the first to pull a trigger and I prayed Vilakazi had a full magazine in his *isibhamu*. You see, I'd finally retard-judged that The General was right. I never saw anything like Boy Faraday before – '*thing*' is the right appellation in his case, *mfowethu*. This mad-dog *thing* was mindless slaughter waiting to happen. Not much was needed to set him off, an imagined insult, false jealousy, maybe even his piles giving him fresh aggravation; *he should have been certified straightjacket cuckoo-crazy.*

Anybody who worked with him would by definition have to be certified cuckoo-crazy too.

Boy Faraday broke the silence.

'Look at this sad *fokken skebberesh* here,' he said pointedly.

I looked.

I couldn't have done anything else if I'd wanted to.

The fourth *geeza* at the table, the one I didn't know, had his eyes glued on Boy Faraday like a mouse hypnotised by a cobra. I could see now he was trembling all over and covered with a sheen of sweat which masked his face horribly like layers of transparent cling film. I wondered what kind of savage ritual I'd walked into.

'This *fokken skebberesh* wanted to make a deal,' Boy Faraday smiled, his mouth turning into the ugly slash of a gaping wound. 'But not only with me, got that? He made a deal with somebody else too, dead man. You want to know what's going to happen to him, dead man?'

His calling me 'dead man' was sawing at my nerves like a blunt breadknife.

Meanwhile Boy Faraday was grinning slowly, showing his teeth, slavering cruelly at some inner vision of eagerly awaited bloodfest. Dollar Two-Times was smiling broadly too, but Shoeshine was looking absent as if he wasn't hearing anything at all that was going on.

'How about that, *fokken skebberesh*? You want to know what's going to happen to you?'

The fourth man didn't reply. The trembling of his hands, fingers covered with chunky gold rings, was actually shaking the table and the liquor in the glasses sloshed about as if in shivering accompaniment. Then he let off an incredibly long, wet, terrified, noisy, vile fart that seemed in search of eternity.

Boy Faraday ignored this and turned to me again.

'I'll tell you, dead man, what I'm going to do to Fingers here. I'm going to cut off his *umthondo* and make him eat it as a starter. Then I'm going to feed him his *fokken* fingers with the fancy gold rings on, one by one, for the first course, got that? You still want your *skorroskorro fokken* Mercedes-Benz back, dead man?'

I didn't say anything.

Boy Faraday sat there looking at me with those flat insect eyes and my guts fell out onto the floor.

There wasn't any room inside me for anything else but overwhelming fear.

My hands had gone numb.

I couldn't have pulled Vilakazi's *isibhamu* if you gave me an hour to do it.

I was about to turn and start for the door when a big ugly automatic just suddenly appeared out of nowhere in Boy Faraday's hand *and he shot away Fingers' left ear along with a good chunk of facial flesh, the devastating explosion deafening me.*

The fourth man now identified as 'Fingers' *screamed* and *screamed* and *screamed*, clutching at the waterfall of blood that was gushing from the side of his mutilated head.

Then, as he involuntarily scrabbled his legs and pushed his chair away from the table, Boy Faraday plugged him in the groin. His genitals exploded from the heavy-calibre bullet in a blinding splash of red like viscous blobs of flying paint and he fell over backwards onto the cement floor, jerking furiously with an epileptic's electric, thrashing energy while his life's juice scattered wetly around him.

Boy Faraday casually blew smoke from the top of his gun barrel just like they did in the American cowboy films you saw at the bioscope, made the weapon disappear again as if by magic and sat there calmly feasting his inhuman insect eyes on the writhings of the wretched still-alive human being on the floor, now transformed into ragged burst and bleeding meat.

'I said, you still want your *skorroskorro fokken* Mercedes-Benz back, dead man?'

That was the longest ten yards I ever walked.

My legs wanted to run, but my mind wanted to hang onto my pedestrian sanity.

No ways was I hanging around to see how long it would take Fingers to die.

A passing minibus taxi took me to the faceless storage site where Vilakazi said Boy Faraday's gang had taken my Mercedes-Benz. All during the ride I kept experiencing the most peculiar conflicting emotions. I started out just being thankful that I wasn't full of holes, because I knew Boy Faraday was so unbalanced crazy that he should have been permanently locked away somewhere for the good of all mankind. Then I began to feel ashamed because I'd been yellow-belly chicken-scared shitless right down into the marrow of my wobbling bones. After that I began to get incrementally outraged again, furious that a strychnine slime-dog like Boy Faraday should be running around on the loose without a muzzle and leash.

The *amacrazy* red-haze anger was what I ended up with. I sighted Vilakazi on the corner near the unmarked 'garage' and stopped the minibus.

Vilakazi took one look at me and shut up.

I walked into the dilapidated undercover parking space with Vilakazi dogging my heels; my Merc was sitting in the first row of three-abreast cars. There was a hefty blubber-plus-muscle *geeza* in grease-stained overalls, with one of those new, exaggerated, blown-out Afro-hairstyles like a black beach-ball around his head, standing by a rack of mechanics' tools. He gave me the seriously penetrating evil-eye, making his attitude glaringly obvious. I took out Vilakazi's *isibhamu* and pointed it first at him and then at the Mercedes-Benz.

'Get my wheels out by the exit, *moegoe*, and make sure it's full of juice, or you're full of *fokken* lead, *got me?*' I said, parodying Boy Faraday for all I was worth.

It worked, *mfowethu*, but there was an insidious rancid piece of me that was begging for this oversize grease-monkey to make a wrong move so I could blast him. It was the first time in my life I ever felt that way. Homicidal. Purely homicidal. Vilakazi's automatic seemed to have a life of its own beseeching me to use it, and I came very close to murder. But the *moegoe* didn't give me any backchat and I eased my finger off the trigger.

Vilakazi and I tapped our toes while he started the car and emptied half a dozen tin jerrycans of petrol into the tank using an orange plastic spout and a length of hosepipe.

I was glancing around all the while actually hoping some of Boy Faraday's *skebengus* would show up. As I said, I'd never felt that way before, and I didn't ever want to feel that way again, but the march of time changes many resolutions, *mfowethu*.

Vilakazi looked in the perfectly disguised hidden compartment.

'Still packed with our load of Durban Poisons, *bra*,'

he said gleefully. '*Amamoegoes* didn't even *nortch* our consignment.'

'Get in the car. Let's get out of here.'

Vilakazi drove and half an hour later we were around the Baragwanath road heading first for a Lebanese merchant in the south of Jo'burg who'd pay us cash for the *insangu*; then, for safety's sake, we were going to turn around and follow the much longer Orange Free State route down to Natal. Vilakazi opened his trap to say something, but I viciously ordered him to be silent before he began to babble away with a hailstorm of clattering words. I loved him, but I had a lot to think about before listening to my brother's one-dimensional vocal outpourings.

I sat with my side window open.

The cold, moisture-sucking air of the dry Transvaal winter was a harsh but welcome tearing at my face.

Vilakazi was taking it easy on the narrow road.

I began to cool down to a point where I could think straight. It boiled down to this: either The General was wrong, in which case I'd have to make new friends: or he was right, and I had to judge some way to unload all my stock and equipment before anybody caught on to what was happening.

After my brain had buzzed in several square circles, it began to dawn on me that The General *was* right. I had been so busy trying to keep things moving that the filters on my thoughts had become as thickly congested as an elephant's mud-soaked hide. A lot of little things came back to me, little things that I had overheard or half-seen, *and they all added up*. I had to move fast if I wasn't going to get caught with my pants down around my ankles.

'I think somebody is on our exhaust fumes, *bra*,' Vilakazi said urgently, interrupting my chain of thoughts. 'Somebody following, maybe?'

I didn't really get what he said at first, and when I did it didn't seem important.

'Forget them, fuck them, let them pass. We're in no hurry.'

Vilakazi slowed down and pulled way over. I could feel the tyres bite into the dirt gravel on the shoulder of the narrow road. He was leaning forward and craning up towards the rear-view mirror, his face constricted with worry.

'*Hawu, bra!* You don't think Boy Faraday could have sent anyone after us?'

I turned in my luxurious leather seat and looked back.

The car behind was dangerously close, already starting to pull out to go around us – yet swerving near enough to give a close, cut-throat-razor shave. I didn't have time to open my mouth when I saw the blue-outlined fairy flash of dancing flames coming from the front window.

I heard Vilakazi grunt, a short, sharp exhalation of punched-out breath.

I don't remember hearing the sound of the AK-47 at all, just the screech of the tyres as we skidded out of control.

I don't know how many times we turned over and over and over, stressed metal singing rivet-popping songs like a forced aria to destruction. My body felt as if it was being broken and ripped apart, a garden spider having its legs intently pulled off one by one by some malicious child.

We jumped the road and went smashing pell-mell into the *veld* scattered with solid bluegum trees.

At some point on that terrible *bang! bang! bang!* banging-tangle of a trip I left the pulverised car; either the heavy door got ripped off like cardboard or I went sailing out the window.

My mouth was full of dirt and salty blood when I came to a slithering stop, and I was clawing at my eyes that seemed pincushioned with porcupine quills.

The big Mercedes-Benz went up in orange flames with a thumping *whoosh!* of detonation.

A fortune in compacted Durban Poisons *insangu* made the fire monstrous and filled the night air with thick, pungent smoke.

My vision cleared, but sharp grit still clogged my eyes like abrasive sandpaper.

I COULD SEE MY BROTHER VILAKAZI TRAPPED IN THE FRONT SEAT BURNING LIKE A HUMAN TORCH!

VILAKAZI!

VILAKAZI!

VILAKAZI!

He looked like he was just sitting there, twitching, with his hands still on the steering wheel!

But he was bright, incandescent red all over, an ignited phosphor statue, burning, burning, his eye sockets empty black holes!

MY BROTHER!

MY BROTHER!

MY BROTHER!

I let my face drop into the pebbles and dirt and lay there, anaesthetised, not feeling any hurt, only the heat of the roaring flames from that funeral-pyre Mercedes-Benz on my steadily blistering shoulders and singeing hair.

I don't know how long it was before I passed out, nor did I know that all that wet stuff on my cheeks was a flood of tears as well as copious blood.

Zsa-Zsa said I'd never cried, never would cry.

She was wrong.

That time it was for real, *mfowethu*.

How Much Is
All Of Nothing?

The next thing I remember is waking up in the Baragwanath State Hospital for Natives almost a week later.

So they told me.

There I met the first white *geeza* with whom I'd ever come into straightforward contact. It was via that *mlungu* doctor-brother doing his internship amongst us dark-skinned pariahs that I came to appreciate that a lot of white folk are just like us. It was he who first called me 'Shatterproof', and the nickname stuck like glue.

But not at first.

First there was conscious pain.

Such pain it was beyond the realm of conscious belief. A waking, enveloping nightmare that even heavy-duty intravenous painkillers did little or nothing to alleviate. They barely had the capacity to dull the vivid, excruciatingly intense, chainsaw *buzzing* of constant cutting agony that has no comparison you can think of, *mfowethu*.

Bad? Let me tell you about *bad*.

Every breath drawn or exhaled sent multiplying fragmented needles throughout my body and bombarding inwards, pain imploding towards the centre of *everything* that existed; I was the world and the world was me suspended in a preservative aspic of inescapable, thick, transparent torture.

To cough involuntarily was a waking nightmare. The easy, throat-clearing spasm that comes so naturally to all of us was a redoubling, a trebling of hyper-compressed suffering that sent shockwaves of an *unbelievable more more more more more more* omnidirectional ricochets ripping my sanity apart. It never *quite* made me pass out, leaving me hovering there, begging for the sickening blackness to swallow me whole, not caring if I ever woke up again.

My face and shoulders were a mess of suppurating blisters. The windscreen must have exploded sometime after the Merc left the road, because I eventually needed one hundred and thirty-six minuscule stitches to close all those tiny glass lacerations in my flesh.

That inconvenience forbidding me any facial expression was aggravating, *mfowethu*, but was nothing compared to the damage to my left thigh, which was splintered into bonemeal from just above my kneecap right up to my hip-bone. It rested swollen in front of me like a monstrously bloated beached whale, covered only in a protective binding of plaster of Paris so that restricted movement would pacify the internal bleeding. Below the same kneecap, three inches of bone had been pulverised into disjointed fragments. Further down, just short of my left ankle, the nutcracker of violently twisting car metal had again doubly split the leg bone.

Abuse toxins were swimming through my system like multiplying tadpoles with *piranha* teeth.

My big toe was mashed potato.

In the face of everything else, nobody noticed its poor mangling. Today it sits at the end of my foot like a crippled brown miniature jellyfish deprived of all identifying traits but a horrendously malformed toenail.

My left elbow was shattered. The doctors didn't pick that up either until it had reset on its own – repairing my internal bleeding was occupying all their skills and concentration. If you look closely, *mfowethu*, you can see I have a not-too-noticeable crooked left arm today.

Now came the real shit.

I had to *have* a shit.

The two very young trainee nurses on ward day-duty brought me the bedpan with enough alacrity, shovelled it under my *ezzies* and drew a screen around me, and I didn't see them again for another two hours. By that time I felt like sulphuric acid had been issued to me as an enema and I was almost weeping with embarrassment at being so contemptibly helpless. To speak, or worse, to raise my voice, was to summon blinding sheets of remorseless suffering, inflamed wretchedness. I was so weak, I couldn't even reach the buzzer over my head that sent out an electronic rattle for *urgent* attention.

Finally the two nurses birthed in twin sadism returned to my bedside.

One threw me a feeder packet of non-absorbent shit-paper squares and said, 'Wipe your own arse, *bhuti*. What you think this is, hotel room service?'

Then they left.

Eish, mfowethu!

I tried, but all I got was uncooperative, strengthless fingers covered in my own runny, blood-filled excrement.

Those bitches let me lie there until the acid in my excreta had burnt raw slabs into the skin of my inner buttocks.

After a period of time that felt as if it had been surrealistically warped and stretched by Salvador Dali, one nurse came back, cleaned me thoroughly with super-swift professional roughness, slammed shut the privacy screen and said, 'The evening shift comes on at seven. Maybe they'll be more sympathetic to someone who won't even attempt to help himself.'

There were bottles hanging upside down above my head from which pliable plastic tubes snaked down like vines into needles shovelled scooper-style into my veins, feeding me replacement blood and sustenance.

Apparently I had lost a dangerous amount of blood, enough to be life threatening, and much of what was left was going rotten *inside* my pulped leg, which still resembled an inflated blimp.

The night nurse, who was quiet, efficient and emotionless, told me that it would take three or four days for the swelling to reduce sufficiently for the doctors to be able to make a prognosis and decide what steps to take next.

I remember asking – croaking is more like it – 'Might I lose my leg?'

I was told that if medicine had not taken the massive advances it had in the last few decades that would definitely have been the optionless case. Then I was told it was more than likely that I would wear an ugly metal contraption, like a caliper on a polio victim, for the rest of my life.

While I was still digesting this bleak prospect, I was made to swallow a handful of pills and injected hypodermically with an infusion of morphine.

The morphine submerged the worst of my pain but didn't drown out the terrible, endless, penetrating yells of fiendish agony coming from down the passageway.

'What's that?' I asked the nurse.

'A poor man who had no choice but to have both his legs amputated' was the reply.

'Can't you give him more painkiller?'

'Doses are strictly limited to the prescribed amount,

which he has already received.'

'Why?'

'Because this hospital administration does not wish to create drug addicts.'

'Please, nurse, that poor man is in hell. Can't you break the rules just this once and ease his suffering?'

'I do my job and obey the rules. You go to sleep now.'

'How can I sleep with that poor bastard bursting his lungs and my eardrums at the same time?'

There was no reply.

She had turned her back on me and left the ward.

The screams, cutting as acoustic barbed-wire, gradually tapered off to a horribly choked, endless gargle towards the early hours of the morning.

Then there was a heavy silence so complete it seemed the very air was a vacuum of non-being.

When the day-shift staff came on duty, I learned the amputee had died from shock and loss of blood.

Why couldn't the poor, tormented bastard have spent his last remaining hours on earth in a haze of peaceful numbness?

Bureaucracy, *mfowethu*, is a very short-sighted, stingy and insensitive animal.

My swelling went down sufficiently for me to be trundled off to the operating theatre after a week had passed. Somebody gave me a shot of pentathol or pethadone, I can't remember which, during the hissing, rubber-wheeled journey there, and that stuff made me feel human for the first time since the nightmare of Vilakazi's death and broken bones had begun.

When the sick fog of gut-wrenching anaesthetic faded,

I hurt more than I did when I first awoke in Baragwanath. I will not try to describe it. Sufficient to say that it was demonic – Hieronymus Bosch turned loose on the flesh canvas of my body with a pickaxe instead of a paintbrush.

That was when I met my *mlungu* doctor-brother.

He explained that although the swelling had shrunk admirably, my shattered bones had begun to mend by themselves *at all the wrong angles*, and so it had been necessary to break every knitting bone-shard *all over again* in order to proceed.

Eish, mfowethu!

The good news was that something called a *Kunschner nail* had been invented in Germany. This small medical miracle meant that it was possible I would *eventually* be able to recuperate without having a permanent caliper clutter-structure – that I *might* even be able to walk normally sometime in the future.

It worked like this:

First a hole was drilled right through the thick solid walls of your hip, right at the fulcrum of the rounded top pivot of the thigh-bone. Then the *Kunschner nail*, a long, rigid, five-sided piece of metal, was methodically tapped through the aperture the sawbones had made there and forced into the marrow of the remains of the upper thigh-bone until everything fitted tight. Next, the thigh was sliced open from the skin, through fat and muscle, down to the bone fragments buried in the flesh. These were removed and the *Kunschner nail* measured to an approximation *of the length* of missing bone, and then *forced again* into the ball of the leftover thigh-bone above the knee.

The last phase of the operation was to open up the upper hip-bone, that jutting-out part just below the waist on which your trouser belt rests, chip away sections of this with a surgeon's chisel, pack these chips against each other

113

so that they joined the remaining pieces of thigh-bone from end to end, sew you back up – and in a matter of six to nine months, *your thigh-bone would regrow itself.*

Then the *Kunschner nail* would be removed by tugging it back out through the side of your opened-up hip and *hey presto!* An entire thigh as good as new, self-replenished marrow and all.

When I awoke from this latest ordeal, my *mlungu* doctor-brother was standing hovering over the bedside.

'There, see,' he said, pointing at the fresh plaster of Paris mould around a portion of my pelvis and the whole left thigh. 'The operation was one hundred per cent successful. You're just one of those lucky shatterproof fellows.'

The two daytime bitch-nurses were in attendance.

'Shatterproof?' the one giggled snidely to the other. 'There's still a lot more broken leg to take care of below the knee, isn't that right, doctor?'

'Two, three weeks to make sure there's no infection or complications from today's work, and repairing the rest of him will be a pushover, nurse.' He gave me his full attention again, deliberately turning his back on them. 'How're you feeling, Shatterproof? For a man who should be dead, you look pretty good to me.'

All I could do was nod and smile weakly.

My *mlungu* doctor-brother seemed satisfied with that. He scribbled something on my clipboard, placed it back at the end of my bed, winked at me and departed.

There *were* complications with the rest of my leg. Painful, repetitive, tedious ones. But I don't want to go into all that, *mfowethu.*

I ended up with one leg two inches shorter than the

other, but you compensate for this by the elastic fluidity of your hips and my limp is barely noticeable, much the same as my crooked arm. I can run as well as anybody and I still play social tennis. Keeps the abused limbs in fine fettle and an old man's blood circulating like ancient but efficient plumbing.

My *mlungu* doctor-brother took a shine to me during these protracted tribulations.

He taught me to play backgammon and scrabble, and as a direct result my English improved way beyond my education in that marvellously universal language by Oom Kaffirboetie.

There are two more things about my months-long stay in Baragwanath State Hospital for Natives I'd like to mention before going further with the story I know is the only one that really piques your academic curiosity, *mfowethu*.

The first has to do with constipation.

You see, after a big operation like the one performed on my thigh, the body withdraws into a form of shrinking shock.

For some reason your bowels go into protective custody as regards your waste matter.

One week passed and I was heading for a fortnight without having had a 'movement', as some people politely term it. The nurses were *pouring* laxatives into me, enough if recycled to start my own dispensary as a test run on behalf of The General for his new 'opening-medicine' scheme.

Nothing exited, in spite of my belly becoming more and more drumhead tight with ingested food plus a veritable pill army of sugar-coated motion manipulators.

Nothing.

Then, who should walk past the door of my ward,

glance in, recognise me and come ambling forward, knuckles nearly scraping the ground like King Kong in a zoot suit, but Big Bang Bongani.

'DHLAMINI, *BRA!*' he roared loud enough to make the walls vibrate, followed by his usual, subtle display of intuitive intelligence. '*HEYTADA!* WHAT YOU DOING HERE, MAN?'

The two bitch-nurses both had their hormones slipped into overdrive by Big Bang's overlarge male presence. The prehistoric Neanderthal caveman has that instant effect upon certain primal-type women: they are defenceless against the subconscious instructions of their own pathetically predictable DNA-matrixed genes.

'What's your friend's name, Shatterproof?' the plumper, more aggressive one asked me, oestrogen pouring from her eyeballs over Big Bang like an invisible net of tenuous spider-web pheromones.

Big Bang was so used to this sort of sexual adulation that he ignored her, but in response guffawed clouds of what smelt like *walkie-talkie* takeaweay halitosis in my direction. A *walkie-talkie* is an African-favoured snack of cooked chicken heads and legs with an unmistakable aroma.

'Shatterproof? That your name now, *bra?*'

Just then, and it *had* to be during visiting hours, the hospital wards packed to capacity with family, well-wishers and solicitous friends, my bowels announced that the onslaught of multiple laxative forces had finally arrived and that their spearhead troops were not to be denied the first flush of victory.

When the bitch-nurses heard the strangled urgency in my voice and saw the look on my face, a big stainless-steel bedpan was pushed quickstyle under my haunches by one, while the other whipped the privacy screen around me.

Big Bang, never one for finesse, pulled up a chair that belonged to somebody else. The somebody else objected to this high-handed reversal of first come first served. Big Bang simply glared the somebody else into submission and sat himself down, all the while nattering away about a girl he was seeing being in the maternity ward. She had just given birth to twins. Was he the father? He didn't know and didn't care, but she was one sweet girl and she knew how to cook the food he liked, which was usually defined by quantity as much as quality, and when it came to artistry in the bedroom, why, *bra*, she could have been a circus performer, the girl was double-jointed, the positions she could assume were fascinating, unbelievable, *bra*, do you know she can actually –

And my first missile, golf-ball-sized and feeling as solid and hard as a rock of ironstone, ejected at atmosphere-igniting speed from my backside and struck the echoing hollow bedpan with a noise that sounded as loud as the muscular mlungu geeza *in a loincloth striking a beaten-brass gong with a thundergod's massively crude hammer to announce the upcoming Rank Organisation feature film at the bioscope.*

*BO-*O-O-O-*NNG!*

Big Bang bellowed with infectious laughter.

'*Hawu!*' he announced to the spellbound ward in general. '*Bra* Shatterproof got his own dangerous cannon inside there, folks! Wait for the next blast! *Bra* Shatterproof going to hijack this whole hospital for ransom!'

I'll never forget it.

With every amazingly prolific anal projectile that followed, Big Bang kept up a running commentary until he had every one of the crowd there – except for a vocally silent and shamefacedly embarrassed me – a participating audience cheering and chortling as explosion followed explosion until finally my ordeal was at an end.

By then, visiting hour was over, the wards were empty, and I found that I was the recipient of admiring glances not only from my fellow patients, but from the two bitch-nurses as well.

Life can be sublimely strange, *mfowethu*.

Big Bang came regularly after that.

He brought me things that he liked to eat, so he could share them with me in a benefactor's magnanimous way and consume the bulk of whatever delicacies he chose without pangs of guilty conscience coming back to nip painfully at the heels of his quite fabulous indulgence. Bittersweet Black Magic dark chocolates, as well as silver-wrapped, liquor-centre, bursting-in-the-mouth delights, plus strawberries in cream and ice-cream in pound-weight tubs – you name it, *mfowethu*.

Apart from becoming saddled with 'Shatterproof' forever and a day, Big Bang's presence gave me something unique to fill the gap of Vilakazi's absence. I came to realise, over the long months of the constant battle with debilitating pain and the *repeat repeat repeat* bone-suturing operations, that Big Bang possessed a quality I had been unaware of up to that time. You see, in my making an island of unapproachable safety around myself, surrounded by a shark-filled moat with me the centre castle, I had become so self-absorbed that I couldn't see the woods for the trees.

Big Bang had loyalty.

Madcap psycho-batterer that he was, once he had given his allegiance, he stuck by that commitment – do-or-die glue as far as he was concerned, end of *indaba*.

He told me things about Vilakazi that made me weep. I shed no tears while Big Bang was there, of course. Only when he was gone. The dark, lonely hours, *mfowethu*, when all around you are asleep or unconscious, and you can let the salty, stinging liquid roll like caterpillar tanks with earth-ripping tread down your cheeks. I wept from the realisation that Vilakazi's concern had been, always, obdurately, *to look after me*, when I had always assumed it was the other way around.

That reminded me of Zsa-Zsa's bleak comment that I'd never cried, never would cry.

All I can say in answer to that accusation is, *Have you cried my tears yet?*

After I'd been in Baragwanath two, maybe three months, they put in the bed next to me a professor-type, classical music teacher *geeza* who'd confidently driven at one hundred miles an hour's ferocious speed down a deserted country road into the back of a donkey-drawn cart without warning rear-reflectors. He didn't even know he'd smashed into the virtually invisible wood contraption with bolted-on iron wheels. He was lights-out on contact. Apart from the usual metal-versus-flesh surface damage, his hips had been thrust forward at enormous trajectory into an unforgiving compaction of alloy floorboards, engine-block and steering-column, and the central bone structure of his bipedal balance was destroyed.

His only cure was to rest, immobile, in a pelvic plaster-cast for a minimum of nine months while his fragmented hips reset and knitted as best they could.

Traction hung him at an angle ceilingwards from the waist to prevent damaging or corruptive movement. He had a sensitive, ashen-grey, brown face and ashen-grey black-man's hair straightened and swept back from his forehead in careless academic style.

They had just stopped his three-day standard allocation of morphine.

Six weeks later, he was in exactly the same place, suspended by the same tensioned structure of dangling flesh and pulley wires.

The part of his body that rested on the bed beneath was scraped raw and bedsore-blistered from the constant, barely moving, centralised pressure. I never saw anybody so worn down by incredible doses of endless, compressed pain. Even his sensitive amber eyes seemed to have turned a cesspool's grey.

All the nurses would give him to alleviate his monstrous indignity and debilitating agony was three aspirin tablets in the morning and three at night. He used to save them, until he had twelve, fifteen or even twenty hidden in hand, and then he'd gobble them all and have a blessed night's sleep. Maybe one night's sleep was granted him through his own endeavour every four, maybe every five nights, and that's inhuman torture in anybody's book.

So I asked Big Bang to access me some potent pills. High morphine content would be a good guideline in choosing merchandise.

Big Bang duly arrived back with three thin cards of hermetically sealed pills, known as '*pinks*', which were big with homosexual rent-boy junkies and succulent-flesh young whores who had no choice as to who they slept with if they wanted the steamer's money. *Pinks* cooked up on a teaspoon and injected turned ugly monsters into cuddly teddy bears – foul-smelling, evil owners of erect scabby penises into perfumed paramours. You know what I mean, *mfowethu*. *Pinks* were pure morphine delights that could transform reality the same way an atom bomb blast could level an entire city like Hiroshima to a ghost-filled wasteland of rubble and fading memories.

Naturally, the music professor *geeza* couldn't spike himself with my contribution to absenting his agony, but popping a *pink* orally was no problem, and I could feel his gratitude seep out invisibly towards me after lights out, and his soft snores of calm, undisturbed sleep were sweet music to my ears.

After a few days the change in overall well-being of my music professor was astonishing, awesome even. Ruddy, warm brown health came back to his sunken cheeks. He smiled occasionally and even began talking to me about the great composers he loved so well – Brahms, Bach, Beethoven, and that just abridged the start of his auspicious musical alphabet.

I had Big Bang bring me in one of those reel-to-reel tape decks that could play four, five hours of uninterrupted music at a time, plus headphones on long extension cables with audio jacks. My music professor and I could listen to anything as loud as we liked without disturbing another soul.

And that was how I learned to love other music besides *mbaqanga* and jazz, *mfowethu*.

Then a terrible thing happened.

The music professor's knitting hips developed some sort of horrible internal infection.

They took down his traction assembly, laid him flat on his back on his hospital bed and sawed his pelvic plaster-cast in horizontal-midway-half with one of those strange wheel-saws that cut the cage of the hard cast with fierce vibrations, but not the soft, tender, vulnerable human flesh beneath.

Then they opened it up.

The rough movement this required sent my music professor into paroxysms of involuntary shrieking, screams that were nevertheless poor representatives of the drenching pain he must have been subjected to as his poor mid-section was lifted, turned side to side, and perfunctorily examined with cold, clinical eyes. His thrashing was so bad two male nurses had to be called to hold him down.

Surely they could have given him a mega-sedative, even a blanketing anaesthetic, for the incredible suffering *they knew* the helpless sad-case would have to endure?

They wheeled him out and a day later he was back again.

Something had changed in him, beyond the physical rebreaking and resetting of his hip-bone's shattered sections and the surgical slicing that must have been performed deep inside there. Something had replaced his will to live.

For seven days and seven nights, in spite of the double dose of two *pinks* fed him every morning and evening, my music professor mewled like a wide-awake cat castrated with blunt scissors.

On the morning of the eighth day he was found to have died in his sleep.

I should have known what he would do, but I didn't; there you have it.

You see, my music professor had grown so used to hoarding ammunition in his war against pain, he had been assiduously *saving* all those *pinks* I'd given him.

He must have had a stash of fourteen to twenty-plus high-concentration morphine bombs with which to earn himself a night's pain-free relief. The problem was they weren't your usual-potency painkillers. Those *pinks* had killed him as surely as if I'd blown out his brains by pressing a forty-five revolver close to his temple before pulling the trigger.

They gave him the sleep he so desperately required alright.

Permanent sleep.

In penance, I have donated a pint of my own blood ever since whenever I am able, *mfowethu*.

Eventually – long months later as I said – I was discharged from Baragwanath State Hospital for Natives.

Big Bang took me in – insisted on it, in fact.

I was still on crutches, my lower left leg beneath the knee still encased in plaster, with three metal plates bolted onto the bones down there to keep them in place. Only another four weeks, more or less, and then the cast could finally be removed. Meanwhile all the muscles in my left leg had atrophied through non-use and I felt like a cripple hobbling on a leg cut meatless down to the bone.

Big Bang was keen to know how I'd avoided any confrontation with the law.

It was quite simple really.

I'd had no identification documents on me. The Mercedes-Benz was registered in Vilakazi's name. My story was that I had been hitchhiking and a stranger in a German luxury saloon had given me a Good Samaritan lift. We were attacked without warning by unknown assailants. I had no memory of who I was or where I came from other than the cataclysmic flare-up of that disastrous night. Nobody thought to check Juvenile Criminal Records for my fingerprints and that was that. Just another abandoned and homeless *kaffir* who fortunately had been adopted by a new friend willing to care for him and take him off charity's already overburdened hands. End of *indaba*, no complications, *mfowethu*.

But not the end of my story.

I had plans to make and carry out.

When my lower plaster cast came off, I found I was

hopeless at walking without the aid of crutches.

There was a soccer field out back behind Big Bang's *khaya*.

One day, not long afterwards, as I sat exhausted on the ground after having made a weakling's half-circuit of the perimeter, Big Bang came up behind me unexpectedly. It was early afternoon. He should have been out working. Okay, not strictly working, but earning a living, if you get my drift.

'Run, *bra* Shatterproof,' he said with a peculiar leer on his gorilla's face.

'Don't make *fokken* jokes!' I snapped back. 'You lost your fucking mind?'

Then Big Bang Bongani kicked me hard in my side.

'Run, *bra* Shatterproof,' he repeated, his frightful leer just as enigmatic as before.

'I can't,' I whined. 'You can see I can't.'

Big Bang Bongani kicked me again.

'Run, *bra* Shatterproof.'

I got the message.

I was up on my feet and doing my best at perambulating forward at maximum speed to avoid painful contact with the accurate point of Big Bang's size fourteen shoe.

'Faster, *bra* Shatterproof' came from behind me, and a leather-encased, steel-tipped toecap jolted my backside unkindly from behind.

Six weeks later, Big Bang and I were trotting three reasonably swift miles every morning as the sun arose to announce the day.

I have that oversized, brainless brown brontosaurus to thank for my regained running prowess, my regained physical health.

So I brought Big Bang under my wing, took him into my special care and made sure that he wanted for nothing, so he too would share without miserliness in whatever came my way.

There wasn't much point on dwelling on Vilakazi's rotten demise, in thinking about the unfairness of it all. I had to shut my murdered brother out of my mind as much as I could, because if I allowed myself to remember him burning away, trapped inside the Mercedes-Benz Boy Faraday had hijacked from me, I would begin to scream worse than my poor pain-wracked music professor at his loudest.

I couldn't get in touch with Zsa-Zsa, because there was no ways I could tell her I was still alive and Vilakazi was dead, you understand, *mfowethu*? I knew our child must have been born and was well past the halfway mark to his or her first birthday.

Big Bang drove me down to Pietermaritzburg in his monstrous red Ford Galaxie with the white sidewall tyres.

We parked outside the central railway station and I footed it to the first payphone booth I saw.

I was shaking so hard, it was difficult to get the coins into the change slots. It was a freezing cold midwinter night, but I was sweating like a roasting pig having its fat turned to crackling. The phone rang and rang at the house I had rented from Bengal Tiger before it dawned on me that an answer was not on the cards. Finally I got through to Bra-Bra's house and Zsa-Zsa's mother answered my call.

We exchanged stiff greetings, our words like pillars of deafness.

'How is my wife, Mrs Motshange?'

She abruptly hung up on me.

I had to get more coins from Big Bang before I could

125

call her back.

She knew it was me back for repeat telephonic begging.

'Dhlamini, your wife has taken your young son and she has gone away, far away. I am not going to tell you where. She refuses to have anything more to do with you. We heard about Vilakazi's slaying. She warned you to take notice. That was the final straw that broke the camel's back. Forget about Zsa-Zsa, Dhlamini. You are out of her life.'

Then she slammed down the phone a second time.

At least I knew I had a son, although I hadn't a clue what his name was.

The first thing I did after Big Bang and I found a place to stay was to go to my bank. I knew I was going to need plenty *amarands* to trace Zsa-Zsa.

I was shown curtly not to the manager, who usually showered me with effusive welcome, but to some supercilious, big-nose *mlungu* dogsbody wearing narrow bifocal spectacles, in an office cubicle barely big enough to accommodate the two of us without an outsider suspecting that seriously anti-heterosexual advances were being made clandestinely.

There was a little over five thousand in my personal account.

The way-in-excess of half a million which I'd deposited in Zsa-Zsa's name – for obvious reasons – was gone, along with Zsa-Zsa. Everything I'd worked my fingers to the bone for was gone, *mfowethu*, down the toilet like it had never been there in the first place, a mirage that existed only in my own mind.

I didn't even bother with the account that needed both Abacus Sexwale's signature and mine to access. There was never more in it than enough to cover running expenses anyhow.

126

I was going to go over to Zsa-Zsa's mother and *demand with my fists* to know where she was, but somehow the void in my personal fortunes made it seem suddenly unimportant. All I could think of was *how could she have done this to me?* Her treachery was the last thing I'd anticipated, even though human nature had taught me to think otherwise.

I was left empty, without anger – I just could not believe it.

I morosely told Big Bang to go back to our lodgings and wait there for me. Then I walked the long, steady, deep-breathing walk the many miles to where my business used to be. Gradually the sickness and tiredness cleared from my mind and I began to think straight and earnestly judge all the things I had to do, to get started on.

First and foremost, I had to get too much *amarands*.

It kept bouncing around in my *tsotsi* brainbox to liquidate whatever I possibly – and I'm talking a *big* nebulous 'possibly', *mfowethu* – had remaining in assets. Finally it came to me what I should do.

With any kind of luck, I just *might* be able to salvage something out of the throttling mess that surrounded me.

My business premises were still there: nothing had changed physically during my absence.

Abacus Sexwale with his bizarre oriental eyes and a couple of hefty warrior *amadoda* were at the 'warehouse'.

You would have thought I was a transparent *tokoloshe* the way they treated me – a malevolent spook back from the dead no less.

Abacus deferentially led me to my own makeshift office, where I asked him directly what kind of shape we were in.

Abacus didn't ask any questions about what had happened to me or where I had been, but came straight to the point with what I wanted to know.

He told me what was on hand in the warehouse.

I gave instructions to cancel any incoming merchandise, for starters.

Things began perking up in my vision, but I should have known I was wearing rose-coloured spectacles. We had two *bakkies* out on the road and they were due back in the next hour or two. The premises were almost bare, no more than three dozen crates of *amaliquor* in sight, no sign of my other two magnificent Mercedes-Benzes. Within twenty-four hours I'd have everything I owned under this roof – that was the nucleus of my plan.

All I had to do was pick up a telephone to get to Bra-Bra Motshange. I needed him for what I had in mind. He was amazingly accommodating, wrote down the 'facts' and 'figures' I gave him and assured me there would be no problem.

Neither of us mentioned Zsa-Zsa.

I waited until the last moment before asking Abacus Sexwale how much was in our sturdy wall-safe.

He made no move towards that cash repository, just turned his empty palms out and shrugged.

'Everything's been going out, Dhlamini,' he said, as close to inscrutable as you can get. 'While you were gone, I've had months and months of wages and pay-offs to meet. When you vanished, the scavengers came out to feast, too much *nyaga-nyaga*, hyenas and jackals everywhere I turned. Pay-offs at honeypots and bribe-money doubled, trebled, *bra*, I had to pay, I had no choice. We owed big back-*amarands* to a lot of suppliers – check the books if you want. We've hardly been able to keep our heads above water, and that's the truth, *bra*.'

That was a lot of words all in a row for Abacus. He didn't blink while he spoke, but stared with his epicanthic-lidded black-button eyes straight into my own without wavering. I knew and Abacus knew I knew that there should be tens of thousands of *amarands* in that wall-safe. His story of losing it all to the bloodsucking leeches was all *bulongwe*, pure *bulongwe*.

Abacus sat there facing me, cool and relaxed as can be, his hands now out of sight beneath the desktop. He was patently waiting for me to say something, anything.

I wondered if he had a gun secreted down there?

Then I wondered what his reaction would be if I called his bluff and threatened to turn Big Bang Bongani loose on him?

Well, *mfowethu*, I never did find out, for the simple reason that that kind of blind, strong-arm stuff never pays dividends, believe me. At that negative stage of life's heartless imposition of sad fate upon my reduced circumstances, I had *nothing* going for me. Abacus Sexwale had it *all* – the very opposite of me, in fact.

It was more than likely he had covered his back well by splitting a percentage of the profit with his *amadoda*, in which case none of them would shed any tears if I were to change from nuisance to corpse.

At that stage I was certain he *did* have an *isibhamu* concealed under *my* desk, and doubtless the business end was pointing at me with a ready Afro-Asian finger curled around the trigger.

Abacus also for sure knew about Zsa-Zsa taking my not unimpressive bank balance, because he would never have been so barefaced a liar if he thought I had heavy funds to back me up – he would have known healthy *amarands* could have bought me his unhealthy cadaver anytime I chose.

I let the situation stay quiet and peaceful a while longer just so his nerves would settle. I could have saved myself the wasted time, *mfowethu*. Abacus wasn't even breathing fast, and his face was as blank and untroubled as a baby's smooth and featureless backside.

'*Lungile*, Abacus,' I said in a voice of acceptance. 'Right you are. I judge that if that's the case, then all the *amadoda* have been paid up to date?' He relaxed and nodded his head in silent agreement. 'Okay then,' I continued. 'I want this place cleared by day's end, no arguments, the lease is still in my name. Go start your own business with my blessing. Any questions asked, you don't have any answers, you sweet with that, Abacus? Good. This operation is finished. I will wrap up any loose ends. Anything you want to add to that?'

'*Yebo*,' he said. 'My personal papers in the safe.'

'Get them. You got the combination. But take your time. I'm leaving now and I'll only be back later. You'll be gone, of course. Hand over the keys.'

He did.

I walked out the door and that was the last time I ever saw him.

A Failed Phoenix

The house I had rented from megabucks crimelord Bengal Tiger, paying him for more than a year's occupation in advance was in darkness when I got there.

I could see both of Zsa-Zsa's cars in the garage, the filmstar open sports two-seater and the nifty little ultra-fashionable, ladies-preferred model with the smoky shaded glass.

I had to tape up an outside house window and silently break it to get inside. I nearly ruptured myself climbing over the high, tendon-wrenching sill. I felt nauseous when I padded into the dim, thickly carpeted lounge.

My telephone was still connected.

I called Big Bang, remembering the last time I'd held that phone in my hand; I almost expected to hear my dead brother Vilakazi's voice when Big Bang answered. It took a full minute for me to explain what I wanted. I had to concentrate to make it minutely clear and kindergarten simple. I couldn't take any chances on Big Bang misunderstanding me.

What I had in mind was for him to get hold of two girls who'd do anything for money, then pick me up and we'd all go to a *shebeen* miles out of town. I wanted our presence established with plenty of noise and plenty of shared booze as witnesses.

After midnight, we'd pay for back rooms to ensure carnal privacy.

Nobody would question that – it happened every night.

We would repeat this little exercise twice a week for the next month, at the same *shebeen* and with the same girls.

After the month had passed, Big Bang and I would be gone out the back windows. We were going to have business that would take us maybe an hour at the most to complete. I needed an unshakable alibi just for that one hour, for as many people as possible to swear that I'd never left the chosen *shebeen*'s premises.

After hanging up the phone, lacklustre energy told me to doss down and get some sleep into my weary bones until Big Bang showed up.

I went upstairs and had a leisurely shower.

I found some clean 'Jewish' tailor-made clothes in my side of the bedroom's chest of drawers, and once I'd put them on, my tiredness inexplicably vanished.

I began to wander around the large house, turning on the lights without apprehension, because *it was still my house, wasn't it*? *Yebo*, I'd paid the rent and I was *entitled* to be here.

Everything about the house was identical to my remembrance. Nothing had changed except for the stark emptiness throughout. It was like finding a fridge plugged in and working but totally devoid of any foodstuff on the inside.

There was a woman's fashion magazine on the floor beside one of the comfortable leather armchairs, Zsa-Zsa's white-tipped, lipstick-outlined cigarette butts squashed into several ashtrays. Dust was thick on the designer coffee tables. There was a bottle of Chivas Regal in the dining-room sideboard. I helped myself to a long drink. A packet of Lucky Strike, my brand, was on the bedside table upstairs.

SUDDENLY I FELT THE REALITY OF INSANITY DESCENDING ON ME LIKE A SWARM OF HORNETS STABBING ME WITH LETHAL MADNESS . . .

. . . *I ran to the bathroom!*

. . . *there was Zsa-Zsa's hairbrush, her towels, her shampoo, her toothpaste!*

. . . *I ran back into our bedroom and flung open the door of her her built-in cupboard!*

. . . *all her clothes were there, shoes, dresses, hats, scarves, everything!*

. . . *I sank down on my knees and poured out a prayer of thanks that she hadn't left me!*

. . . After a full ten minutes, it was sanity's turn to make a reappearance; the truth sank in.

SHE WAS GONE.

SHE DESPISED ME SO VIRULENTLY SHE WOULDN'T TAKE A THING WITH HER THAT WAS TAINTED BY MY HAVING BEEN VAGUELY CONNECTED TO IT.

NOT EVEN HER HAIRBRUSH!

I sank heavily, let myself slump down and felt my back jolt her dressing table behind me.

A bottle of prohibitively expensive perfume was sent sliding and smashed on the floor next to me, sending clouds of penetrating fragrance up through my nostrils as sickeningly as if it was cloying chloroform.

My head was pounding so fiercely that my vision seemed distorted.

Then it all hit me like a sadist's gigantic sledgehammer:
Vilakazi was gone.
Zsa-Zsa was gone.
My son I'd never seen was gone.
I couldn't judge why it had to be that way, or how I could have done things differently.

I was as puzzled as a child who has had his birthday presents taken away from him an hour after having opened those gifts.

I was sitting there, wrapped up in my own mental conundrum as the evening was tediously wearing on, *mfowethu*, when Big Bang came through the kitchen and up the stairs. I'd unlatched the back door, so I knew it was the mammoth-man following my orders.

Big Bang immediately judged there was something seriously askew.

He steadied me down the steep staircase, helped me like an old man into his Ford Galaxie.

I remember him telling the two ravishingly sexy, beautifully dressed girls he'd brought with him what we needed from them.

I remember the *shebeen* and the drinks and the back rooms with the girls giggling their enthusiasm, but then I passed out. I was so drunk and disorientated that I couldn't have got a stiff neck with a pavement for a pillow, never mind a worthwhile erection.

This went on for a whole month, as I explained it would earlier, *mfowethu*. The only change in routine was that I did manage to achieve a repeated stiffening of my *umthondo*. The whole thing was surreal, like being on the early euphoric downswing of fading Doctor Feelgood drugs and heading for the nirvana of dreamland.

The time came, the *right* time.

Big Bang and me, we left the *shebeen* without a sound

and parked his automobile not too close but not too far away from my very own establishment, the mental-sweat begrimed warehouse. The cold air struck us like a sobering knife and our alcohol-filled heads became as clear as the ringing tones of a gothic cathedral's brass bell.

'Hear me too good, Big Bang, *bra*. There's a pile of Zsa-Zsa's clothing she don't need no more in the corner and thirty-six cases of flammable booze lying next to them. We soak the clothes *too much* and everything else that looks like it'll burn. Then we make a bonfire, *inkalakatha* bonfire, you with me?'

'*Hawu! Bra* Shatterproof, you gone *amacrazy* on me? What you want to do that for?'

'*Ayikhona, wena!* Never mind explanations. My lawyer has set up big insurance on goods we don't have. *Too much* hundred hundred thousand *amarands* worth of nothing, you follow? That's what my insurers will pay us for fire damage. Let's get to work.'

I took a tyre lever from the boot of Big Bang's car and we went around to the back of my warehouse and forced an entry through the padlocked door. We didn't concern ourselves with the noise we made. At this time of night there were no open businesses in this industrial district of Pietermaritzburg and the surrounding blocks of buildings were as quiet as the grave.

We uncorked bottle after bottle of high-octane home-made liquor and poured the sinus-assaulting stuff all over the place until we had the whole building, including the wooden rafters overhead, soaked like a thirsty sponge. The strong fumes made our eyes tear up and I began to feel positively drunk purely on the repeated inhalations.

We both grabbed a last full bottle in each hand and headed back out to the connecting cobblestoned alleyway. We spilled the booze out in a wet trail behind us until we were beneath a clear, star-filled sky.

Then I went back inside my warehouse to make doubly sure we'd left no incriminating evidence behind us.

I found I'd neglected the tyre lever. I picked it up and returned to the alleyway. Big Bang and I backed away in reverse towards the street proper and I took a last, very fast look around.

There was not a soul in sight, but I could hear the faint, distant sounds of a portable battery-powered radio – once heard the tinny speaker amplification would always be recognised. There was a wide beam of light in the street behind us, a swathe of unwanted illumination.

'Okay, Big Bang, *bra*, light the whole box of matches and while it's still sizzling throw it onto our booze trail. *Sheshayo wena, go for it!*'

Big Bang reached into his pockets.

A sheepish smile came over his Easter Island face. He began to slap himself all over, hard searching slaps, seeking the answer of a matchbox's rattle and finding nothing.

I got out my own matchbox and lined up its tiny drawer in preparation for the contained fireworks.

But I could not fucking well do it, I swear on my life, mfowethu!

Maybe I'd known about my own chicken-shit inadequacy. Maybe that's why I'd brought Goliath-brains Big Bang along. Vilakazi leapt vividly back into my memory, a searing heat-picture, him burning like a phosphor torch. *But my fingers wouldn't obey me.*

I almost threw the box of matches into Big Bang's gorilla hands.

'Wait until I've reached the street back there. Then do your thing, *bra.*'

As I was leaving the narrow alleyway, I walked solidly, chest to chest, into an overcoat and peaked-cap garbed nightwatchman armed with a pair of stout *knobkerries*. It was his portable radio I had heard tinkling away earlier.

I could almost feel the vibrations of Big Bang's elephant's footsteps pounding down the alleyway behind me.

The nightwatchman and I stood there frozen immobile, our eyes transfixed upon each other in mutual shock.

Big Bang rubber-tyre screeched to a halt just short of colossal collision, angled his enormous shoulders, and headed towards the innocent nightwatchman like a hunting lion intent on the kill.

I managed to pull him back before any damage was done.

Then, quickstyle, I slipped the nightwatchman three hundred dollars, probably more than his monthly wages.

'You never saw either of us tonight, *umnumzana*. Please. I'll be back here to give you double, maybe more. I'll make it right with you. Trust me.'

The nightwatchman blew out a cloud of frost-whitened breath while his rheumy eyes searched me like lasers. Those eyes were as old as those of the *strandloopers* whose gaze had first acknowledged Jan van Riebeeck in sixteen hundred and fifty-two. Then he turned around and vanished in the pervasive gloom.

I looked back down the alleyway to see the lilac-outlined points of devouring orange flame start to lick the outer walls of my warehouse. Then Big Bang and me were heading full-tilt for his car.

We were five blocks away when we saw the fire shoot spiralling upward like a terrorist's bomb going off in a black-and-white Hollywood film made lurid Technicolor by the flames.

On our way back to our alibi *shebeen*, we heard the fire-engine sirens blasting away in the industrial part of town far behind us.

We were quietly parking the red Ford Galaxie when Big Bang said, 'Maybe the *madala* nightwatchman got fried?'

I was still holding the tyre lever. Big Bang deserved to be banged over the head with it to compensate for his gross insensitivity. But I couldn't have used the thing for a crude makeshift crutch even had my recent injury returned to dominate me. I was sick on the inside, not with remorse, but with an unnameable something so penetrating that I felt like choking myself on the ugly iron length, gagging myself like a suicidal sword-swallower.

The local *amapolisi* located me while I was still at the *shebeen*, as was only to be expected.

Everything worked exactly as I had planned it.

My alibi was as shatterproof as my new nickname.

After a brief interrogation, I was released.

I went back to my rented house and called Bra-Bra Motshange. I told him to contact the insurance company on my behalf with the good news and to set up a noon meeting the next day at his offices to file the claim which he had suitably padded with non-existent merchandise in the correct legal manner.

I had allowed myself too much celebratory booze in the early hours at the *shebeen* before the *amapolisi* came. I spent my waiting time nursing a *babalaza* you could reach out and embrace. It was a restless ordeal for me sleeping alone in Bengal Tiger's big double-storey house.

Next day I was at Bra-Bra's offices ten minutes early. We nodded politely to each other and sat down to wait, sharing an uncomfortable silence. Bra-Bra's cut was twenty-five per cent, so he was as eager to get this over with and settled as I was.

Spot on time, Bra-Bra's ersatz white receptionist knocked on the frosted door and ushered in a tall, hawk-nosed, tough-looking *mlungu geeza* in a dark undertaker's suit. His haircut was ultra-short, prison-style. You could see his scalp shining through.

'Mr Motshange? Mr Bhekuzulu? My name is Simon Pennyfeather-Jones, as you most probably already know.'

We shook hands.

Simon Pennyfeather-Jones sat opposite us, but did not so much as glance at the paperwork which Bra-Bra had so meticulously prepared.

'You understand why I am here, gentlemen?'

Bra-Bra and I both nodded sombre agreement.

'Perhaps you do not, gentlemen,' he said, allowing himself the trace of a thin-lipped smile. 'It is entirely possible that the purpose of my visit has been misconstrued by yourselves. I sincerely trust that *neither* of you assume my company will take your exorbitant claim seriously?'

Bra-Bra and I didn't *neither* of us know what to answer him.

I removed my hands from the desktop and folded them casually in my lap so Simon Pennyfeather-Jones wouldn't see them shaking.

'Mr Bhekuzulu,' he said, fastening his hard eyes like limpets on my own. 'My company is aware of the nature of your business. I can assure you that we have known about it almost since its inception. Please, gentlemen, do not bother to contest what I say. Quite frankly, we were prepared to let sleeping dogs lie as long as you paid your monthly premiums on time. But your claim is way beyond anything we are prepared to justifiably meet.'

Bra-Bra started to bluster, but Simon Pennyfeather-Jones lifted his hand and guillotined anything my legal eagle father-in-law was apoplectically going to come up with.

'My company feels morally certain that the fire which destroyed your insured property and its alleged contents was brought about in an illegal manner. We are most emphatic that you refrain from submitting your claim. There, that sums it all up admirably.'

'Cut out the *bulongwe*,' I finally managed. 'What proof do you have?'

'*Bew-long-gway*, Mr Bhekuzulu?'

'Bullshit, Mr Pennyfeather-Jones. I repeat, what proof do you have?'

'Footprints, Mr Bhekuzulu. Liquor softened the dirt edges of the cobblestone alleyway leading to the insured premises. When the fire subsided, two different sets of perfectly baked footprints were found, one an abnormal size fourteen, I might add. Forensic mouldings of them were made by our company investigators. Of course, one of them might not be yours, Mr Bhekuzulu, but the other smaller set may just possibly be a perfect match. We can bring an enormous amount of pressure to bear right now, this very minute, should you so choose.'

'So you accepted my money, but from the word go you never intended to pay out?'

'Mr Bhekuzulu, insurance concerns are amongst the biggest and most powerful businesses in the world today. How can you expect us to be honest with you if you do not show us that same quality in return?'

'So you're cheating me in the name of honesty? Why don't you turn me over to the cops?'

'We have standards, Mr Bhekuzulu. Besides, what good would such an action achieve? Live and let live is the creed we live by. You might be back sometime in the future for another, more legitimate insurance policy. One never knows, does one? Here. This is a release form absolving us of any responsibility. Please sign it, and then I shall leave you gentlemen to get on with your busy day.'

I signed with no further protest escaping my cauterised lips, *mfowethu*.

That night Big Bang and I headed for The General's rural family home on the Natal border.

Everything I owned was on the back seat of the car.

I was going to beg The General for a job, any job.

I judged I was still good enough to herdboy his many cattle.

Over The Hills
And Far Away . . .

The General acted like he was glad to see me.

He acknowledged Big Bang in the same way people respond to the rough canine inquisitiveness of your bluntly sniffing four-legged domestic pets heading for the choicest parts – a nuisance, but there nonetheless, and to be barely tolerated out of unwaveringly staunch friendship with the inconsiderate owner.

The General put us up in two clean and airy thatched *rondavels*, not far from the unpretentious main house which he maintained outside of *apartheid*'s authority.

We had dinner with him, prepared by his personal live-in five-star chef. It was wonderful food and the first decent meal I could remember having since leaving Pietermaritzburg to go after Vilakazi and my hijacked Mercedes.

Big Bang left us alone, excusing himself after the last course was wolfed down.

It was the first chance I'd had in a long while to talk to anybody of independent intelligence and it all came pouring out of me like unplugged dirty dishwater gurgling down the kitchen drain.

'Dhlamini, I have never heard a young man feel so sorry

for himself,' The General said when I paused for breath. 'What do you want from me? You want me to weep with you in sympathy?'

His casual indifference infuriated me so much that I found myself gasping for air like an angry asthmatic. I started to get up from my chair, thought better of it and sat down again. The General began to grin at me, his raptor's eyes smiling. I had to grin back eventually, because The General was, as always, one hundred per cent on the money.

He was absolutely right.

The General leaned back, fully at ease, stoked up his pipe with Holland House cherry tobacco and lit it with enjoyment. He puffed out smoke that was aromatic, fragrant even.

'Now that you have released all that negative self-pity of yours, Dhlamini, we can talk. As I have reiterated, the old days are breaking up, vanishing. With them, the old ways. Nobody is precisely sure what will happen, but this I do know. The ban on alcohol for we blacks will soon be lifted. This will destroy our illicit *amaliquor* business. I have plans afoot to take care of that side of things. Jo'burg is a hive of entrepreneurial activity, but with the ongoing fiasco of Boy Faraday holding up banks in broad daylight, that is a place to stay away from. For a while yet, Dhlamini, for a while yet. Meanwhile, tell me what you know of Nelson Mandela?'

I had heard of Nelson Mandela of course. The *Black Pimpernel* as we called him in those days, *mfowethu*. But politics, even the good fight against the evils of *apartheid*, was not my long zoot suit – my fight was for survival, *my* survival.

The General filled me in on *The Struggle*, on the infamous Treason Trial, on Nelson Mandela's life-or-death battle at the Rivonia Trial and his subsequent political sentence of life-imprisonment to be served on Robben Island, a bleak little sandspit a few miles off Cape Town's inhospitable rocky shores.

What had this to do with us?

The African National Congress, The General explained, far from being crushed by these adverse circumstances, was secretly growing stronger every day. For any organisation to effectively fight the wealth and guns of the ruling white supremacist Nationalist Government, it needed to have funds, inexhaustible funds. That was where we were going to come in. The ANC had 'friends' and 'businesses' overseas; money earned or raised there was funnelled back to South Africa in a hundred different ways in spite of the country's tightly reined banking rules.

The General had been invited by Chief Albert Luthuli to join The Struggle and to invest heavily in what they called 'A Gentleman's Gaming Club' in London. A *legal* gambling operation to which were attached fine money-spinning restaurants, top class, top prices. The General wanted me to go over there and learn the business from top to bottom. His reasoning was that eventually South Africa would follow suit and legalise gambling; in the meantime, there was a healthy profit to be made, in spite of the ANC taking the lion's share.

Would I be interested?

I had only one question.

'Ask it, Dhlamini, my boy,' The General said.

'I owe Big Bang Bongani. If I can take him with, I'm your man.'

'There should be no difficulty in getting him employment as a bouncer,' The General answered. 'You might say he was tailor-made for the occupation.'

I had time to kill while The General organised our passports – no mean feat in those days of white paranoia about terrorists and communists and *die swart gevaar* and subversives *et al*.

I wandered around the coastal tourist mecca of Durban on the Natal coast to while away the waiting.

Durban is a place I'd just as soon never see again, *mfowethu*.

There must be more dumb *mampara* suckers per square mile in Durban than in any other place in the world.

These holidaymaker *geezas* just love to be taken for a ride. They keep coming back year after year to be played like fish – a human version of the sardine run, when every year nature makes the ocean give forth her seething bounty and a miles-long swathe of fish swimming in their millions just a few metres offshore are caught with rods, nets, spears and even bare hands.

Everybody who *lives* in Durban, black, white or Indian, from *picannins* to playboys, has just one business in mind during the holiday season – to rip off every stranger in town. They shave these poor bastards bare a thousand times a day in a million different ways. You'd think you would hear the yells of abused and overcharged outrage from Potchefstroom to Pretoria, but you never seem to. These *mampara* holidaymakers get taken for breakfast, lunch and dinner. Old or young, doesn't matter – and if they are bloods on the lookout for some real action, then they are the rightful prey of true professionals. And those professionals don't let up or let go until their victim is shorn as clean as a sheep after shearing time.

A packet of cigarettes costs *too much* if you buy it from a vendor, and a long-past-her-sell-by-date cheap whore who should be paying *you* for sex wants hundreds of *amarands* for her debatable charms. These *mampara* suckers get rid of their cash as if it was infected and they hated like poison hanging on to it.

But that's enough about Durban.

To cut a long story short, that was how I ended up in London with Big Bang Bongani.

We both had jobs at a club called 'Browns' – which I thought was good right-side karma for starters, seeing as Big Bang and me were skin-cousins to the joint.

The General was a major unlisted shareholder, which goes without saying.

Personal introductions were made through an ANC exile living in London to people who could do me a lot of good, and I had eleven thousand South African in the bank. Four thousand were mine and seven more I owed to the generosity of The General. Those days you could buy a pound sterling for a buck seventy, a buck eighty, believe it, *mfowethu*.

In his farewell speech to me, The General quoted Nelson Mandela: 'This is what he said, Dhlamini. You would do well to remember it, my boy. "*I was made, by the law, a criminal, not because of what I had done, but because of what I stood for. Because of what I thought. Because of my conscience. Can it be any wonder to anybody that such conditions make a man an outlaw of society?*" Keep smart, Dhlamini. I'll see you when you get back.'

I can't say I took The General's advice.

I did a lot of headstrong things in the next few years and very few of them could be called 'smart' – but at least I started out smart, *mfowethu*.

It was around the mid-1960s when Big Bang and I caught 'the Tube', the underground railway, to our new jobs at Browns. My first impression of the English, travelling in those sardine-compacted carriages, was that they were fearfully ignorant of the beneficial properties of soap and water and that they stank.

Management was at first surprised to see us at Browns,

but any confusion was soon cleared up when they realised we didn't carry spears and eat our fellow human beings and we were on the employment payroll at a hundred pounds a week. Management remained offhand, to say the least, but they finally positioned us both as superfluous bouncers of a kind at the club's restaurant and we were told to keep the blue blazes out of the way of the hyperactively busy waiters.

It became routine for us to report for duty at five o'clock in the grey, sunless, already fading afternoon.

We'd stay through the evening's packed-out roster of much bejewelled and fastidiously dressed diners, amongst whom members of the aristocratic elite were regularly to be seen. It kept me out of mischief, but that muzzled watchdog duty was not nearly enough of a boring exertion to tire me out. It was all a laugh, but not that funny, *mfowethu*, because I hadn't been there a month before I lured myself into something that could have got me turned into just another Soho corpse.

Before I tell you about that, I must mention that Big Bang was having the time of his life.

While he was growing up, he had had his ear-lobes stretched in the traditional Zulu manner, but he'd neglected this ethnic fashion as he got older. With all the admiring glances he was getting from the creamy-skinned ladies who came to Browns, he hit upon an idea to make himself even more noticeable beyond his already eye-demanding abnormal size. He went to a local jeweller and had made for himself silver and gold circular wedges that filled the loose elastic hoops of his drilled-out ear-lobes, and had these studded with flashy light-reflecting yet affordable zircons, diamonds' poor cousins. They *looked* like diamonds, the genuine article. Each of my friend the gorilla's stretched ears appeared worth a million pounds sterling minimum.

Just turning his head in the subtle lighting of the opulent eatery – where we did very little except show ourselves – was like being spotlighted on centre stage; he gave the chandeliers serious competition. Those ears of his flashed, cajoled and tempted with refractive bursts of dazzling come hither, and within a very short time Big Bang was gaining himself an enviable reputation as a 'cocksman', which was the polite appellation they gave over there to an extremely potent horizontal artist of note.

Back to me, *mfowethu*.

One of the super-criminal godfather patrons of this club – there were two of them in fact, but one put in an appearance far more often than the other – was Ronnie Kray. He already had much of the infamous publicity that surrounds an underworld king, and he and his twin brother, Reggie, were said to have sadistically murdered more than a score of competitors to get where they were. But the 'Old Bill' (which they called the Law over there, or sometimes 'The Filth') had never been able to pin anything on either of them.

Three or four times a week we'd see Ronnie Kray filling his face at Browns in the pulsatingly plush restaurant. Once he even asked me to sit at his table and dine with him. Our differing accents made for a solid lack of sophisticated communication, but his questions were all limited to the savage habits of carnivorous wild animals, and the answers I gave him about lions, leopards, crocodiles and hyenas were such spur-of-the-moment lies, such tall tales, that they could have been the nucleus of a new wildlife mythology. I mean, he *believed* a whopper I invented about getting hippos to form a temporary floating bridge so that we could cross a flood-swollen river on their stout backs with lurching lorries to deliver a profitable cargo of contraband.

It was through Ronnie that I met the singer introduced

to me as Bubbles Nightingale, her stage name, who hypnotised me with her cleavage, huge blue eyes, masses of curly red hair and her breathless hanging on to my every *bulongwe* word.

I have no excuses.

I knew all about Ronnie Kray, stranger though I was to this startlingly new London scene.

I knew that if you wanted to operate *anything* in their territory, you got permission from Ronnie and Reggie Kray, or you didn't operate, end of *indaba*.

I knew the twins packed more weight than a piledriving, *amabulldozer* Springbok rugby scrum and that playing in their backyard was a certain way for your nearest and dearest to collect on your life insurance policy.

But I couldn't keep my eyes off this curved white accumulation of female hormones, who was obviously *the property* of Ronnie Kray. She had me in sexual bondage from the moment she encouragingly touched my hand with hers during the telling of my African fables – I was jolted with enough electricity to light up every shack in Soweto, I kid you not.

I've known a lot of women, both before and since, and the only one that made me feel beholden to her was my wife, Zsa-Zsa. Yet I have to acknowledge that many of the women I've known were a lot of earth-shaking fun – the spice of life, *mfowethu*, the spice of life. In point of fact, I used to spend much necessary leisure time at Miss Harriet Fortesque's Fabulous Feminine Escorts, which was about the most glamorous upper-class whorehouse I ever saw. You could take the gorgeous young women she had there to the Queen's garden party and nobody, including the over-amorous Prince Philip, would be any the wiser about their for-hire origins.

But Bubbles Nightingale did something for me and it

wasn't only because she was forbidden fruit, as well as pale-skinned jailbait back in *apartheid* South Africa. First off, she was small, really tiny, with these great big blue eyes as I said – as different from sturdy but sweet as chocolates Zsa-Zsa as it was possible to be.

Bubbles used to perform at a number of well-known nightspots, there was a seven single about to be released, and she had her own flatlet in fashionable Knightsbridge.

I got all this from Howard Postlethwaite, the headwaiter at Browns. I also got a brotherly handshake and a farewell pat on the back.

'Cheers, me old mucker,' Howard said. 'Its bin a reel fahkin treat makin yore short acquaintance orlroight.'

Since Howard Postlethwaite was about the only genuine *geeza* who'd bothered to give me the time of day since I started working there, I let him know that I was aware of the risks in which I was indulging. He agreed to slip Bubbles a note on my behalf.

Well, *mfowethu*, I wound up at her flatlet two nights later, and I didn't leave it for consecutive days, except to foot-it quickstyle to the nearest neighbourhood grocery store to obtain essential provisions.

What was it like sleeping with a *white* woman, my number one paleskin without remuneration, but not my last?

Her nudity was shocking to me at first.

Her nipples seemed surrounded by pain they were so bright against her pallor, her pubic hair a dangerous red burning bush that threatened to incinerate any invader.

But *Nkulunkulu* made us all from the same essential mould and I coupled with her as Adam coupled with Eve, blissfully, joyfully and without guilt. She had a massive overhead mirror on her bedroom ceiling and the visual entwining of our two body colours gave her great pleasure.

She was as inventive as they come and tireless – more was always on the menu and the menu changed from day to day.

We ended up being fast friends.

In fact, through the years she was one of the few women I ever had as a good friend.

But those first weeks we couldn't get enough of each other.

We couldn't look at each other without ripping off our clothing.

Her flatlet had central heating, so we could stay comfortably naked for as long as we wanted.

We had to have each other carnally *so much* we were drugged sick with it.

She made me dizzy with lust. I couldn't walk up a flight of stairs without getting vertigo. We didn't talk much, but she loved music and I introduced her to *mbaqanga* and township jazz, which was influential in her later career. Besides, there wasn't much time for talk. We hardly had time to eat or sleep. We were both addicted to one thing, and we both felt that if we didn't have each other *right then and there*, we would die.

It was as if we were fated to die anyway, tomorrow or the next day, and we had to know *everything* about each other's bodies before that happened.

I don't know what sort of a future we might have embarked upon together, but one day I caught her nosing up a line of white powder and it shocked me, *me*, the big bad *tsotsi* from the big bad township slums. It was the first time I'd come face to face with hard gutter-drugs being used by someone I knew and cared for, and it repelled me as well as scaring me ice-cold sober. I ripped the powder away from her, and when she told me to mind my own fucking business, I got unforgivably violent. I lifted my hand to her. I never felt more like hyena vomit in my life, *mfowethu*.

We started to talk then, afterwards, for the first time and after a while I began *listening*, not just going through the motions, and it turned out amicably. She told me her powder was cocaine mixed with crushed methamphetamine crystals and she took it occasionally *just like everybody else she knew in the music business* when she was tired and she wanted to party. She could take it or leave it, *but I'd better be aware that it was the designer drug everybody who was anybody was taking, and it carried enormous status, because you needed to be flush to afford it.*

That gave me pause for thought. Still, I didn't want to fool with it. In my backwoods South African mind, powder equalled heroin, and I'd read about too many junkie *mamparas* who might just as well be dead from having to continually feed their short lifelong habits.

Bubbles skinned up a joint. She called it 'blow' and we smoked what I considered to be very low-grade *insangu* and lolled around for the rest of the day. I couldn't believe it. In London it was 'cool' to smoke *dagga* almost anywhere and at any social occasion, and users who called their tastes sophisticated paid up to *forty pounds sterling* for a minuscule plastic bank-bag of the stuff. I saw riches glowing on the horizon. For forty pounds of the Queen's currency, I could buy an acre's worth of the world's best dynamite *insangu* down in the hot, humid coastal regions of Natal.

Meanwhile, that crazy, mad, devouring feeling Bubbles and I had for each other felt like it was fading.

We still wanted each other, don't get me wrong, *mfowethu*, but it was different now.

We carried on talking like never before and got a host of things out of our systems. Bubbles was about the only woman I was ever able to talk to like that. We had a lot in common emotionally besides our rampant libidos, and we still do.

She told me she wasn't really Ronnie Kray's piece of skirt, although he paid for her little nest, and I thought silently to myself, *Man, tell me another one, Bubbles.* Ronnie Kray was welcome to use her flat and her at the same time. She said he never showed up more than once a week anyway and he always telephoned first, adding that she thought his primal urge was really for boys, something of a not-uncommon preference acquired by spending a misspent youth as a guest courtesy of Her Majesty's Prisons. According to her, the Kray twins had plenty other nubile young skirt available whenever they wanted them. But that didn't mean it was kosher for me to work the same side of the street – know what I mean, *mfowethu*?

If I got caught, I would probably have my amputated legs handed to me feet first – a favourite, chainsaw form of Kray retribution, if the stories were to be believed.

Bubbles said she was due for a holiday that we should share and had told Ronnie Kray that she was going to visit her mother in Birmingham. If I was Ronnie Kray that was one story I wouldn't buy if my own sister tried to peddle it to me, and for the first time I gave serious thought to what might happen to me if somebody should walk in on us. But somehow it didn't seem to carry that much importance right then.

I don't really know how we got away with it, but get away with our *rawurawu* robber's sex we did. For the next year we'd see each other two or three times a week and we never got caught.

By that time I knew Mister Kingpin Ronnie Kray a little better because I did errands for him now and again. Maybe my dangerous dallying escaped The Firm's notice (the Krays called their outfit 'The Firm') because Bubbles was more of an exotic envy-creating female corsage to be displayed on Ronnie's lapel, and not a full-time penis possession. Sometimes he wouldn't call upon her services for a month or more, although she'd have dinner with him at least once a week.

Be that as it may, *mfowethu*, Bubbles and yours truly were to be seen together at most of the high spots at one time or another – the races at Ascot, Brighton Pier, Butlin's Beach Clubs, even once the fabled Monte Carlo Casino. We had one *inkalakatha* good time and it cost me most of my eleven thousand before I was through, even though Bubbles was never shy about digging into her own purse to get us around.

The more I saw of this ravishing and musically talented English girl, the better I liked her.

For a while I even fantasised that the two of us might get married, but that would mean never being able to bring her home to South Africa. We had our *indabas* about that, but it never came to anything for a lot of other reasons – the main one being I was still married to Zsa-Zsa.

I thought a lot about Zsa-Zsa when I was on my own. Sometimes I would hate her. Sometimes I would wake up in the middle of the night missing her so much that I wanted to trash my bedclothes and run stark screaming naked out into the pea-soup London fog. Whatever I felt about her, I knew that she was stuck fast somewhere deep inside me.

I don't know how long things might have gone on like that with Bubbles. I was just drifting, having a good time, catching up on all the theatre and shows with her and Big Bang, and every time I thought about engineering something for myself, I couldn't seem to get serious. Maybe I'd expended too much energy in the *amaliquor* business back home and was having a delayed psychological reaction of some kind. At any rate, I couldn't work up a head of steam to get the locomotive of my ambition going.

It took Howard Postlethwaite to jar me out of my waster's lethargy.

I was having a pint of lager and a game of darts in a pub near Browns when Howard came up to me with a worried look on his usually imperturbable, craggily bland face.

'Wotcher, me old sahn,' he said in his *h*-dropping Cockney accent. 'Oi've got some tasty fahkin news for yer, oi 'ave.'

'Have a pint, Howie, mate?'

'Don't moind if oi do, Shatterproof. You'd better prepare ter scarper, me old sahn.'

'Says who?'

'A big fahkin geezer wot oi'll point out ter ya ternoight.'

'I should be worried?'

'Yew'd be a roight dumb fahkin nigger cahnt not ter, me old sahn.'

'Truly?'

'Trooly, mate, as oi live an' breave. Finish yer game. Oi'll give yer the gen when yer done.'

Later that night, Howard pointed out a heavy-set individual who looked like he'd been formed by pouring him into a cement mould. He was sitting alone, the aura of jail everywhere about him, eating at one of those hidden, uncomfortably cramped tables reserved for discouraging a return visit.

I knew this *skebengu*-muscle was waiting for Ronnie Kray because I'd seen him around for months. Wherever he was, it was a certain bet that Ronnie Kray was going to turn up shortly. The grapevine said he was fairly big in The Firm and one of his priorities was to make sure there were no surprises in store for his boss when least expected.

His name was Riggsie Leitch, and as far as I ever saw

he never did more than case out wherever Ronnie was due to appear. He was strictly a strong-arm butcher's machine to look at, but looks can be deceptive. Nevertheless, I couldn't judge why I was on his mind. I'd never said more than three words to the psychopathic slag-heap, and as I remember it those were '*Two's company, blindman*' when he'd made a move to join Bubbles and me while we were having a duo-by-definition drink.

'Lissen up, me old sahn,' Howard had said. 'It's none orf moi fahkin business, oi'm just the messengerboy cahnt, innit? But 'ere's wot that Jurassic bulldog geezer said abaht yew an' that gel. You got ter back orf an' 'e means loik yestirday. Or else 'e'll run orf at the mouf abaht yew screwin the skirt orf of Ronnie Kray's Bubbles babe ter the fahkin guv'nor 'imself. Besides which 'orrible event, Shatterproof, me old sahn, Riggsie Lcitch is an hugly son-orf-an-'ound-from-'ell an' e'd orf yer soon's as spit on yer. Am oi fahkin gettin threw tew yer, me old sahn?'

That was a fairly long speech for Howard. It lacked his usual abundant supply of humorous hot air, *but I could register on the annihilation-scale that he meant every innuendo.*

'Oi fink at rock-bottom reptile level, me old sahn,' Howard added sagely, 'the only reason Riggsie ain't done nuffink abaht it orlreddy is that 'e don't want ter get the gel inter any kind orf bovver. Spoil 'is fahkin pickings, loik.'

I could see what Howard was driving at, *mfowethu*.

Riggsie the Hopeful Rogerer had his monochrome lizard's eye on Bubbles, and would probably go to her with his cold-blooded, scale-covered penis in hand mouthing an identical rephrased horizontal proposition. It would be an offer she couldn't refuse unless she was prepared for Ronnie Kray's retribution when Riggsie ratted on her. If she didn't play along, who knew how vicious and vindictive

Ronnie Kray would get? A favourite punishment of Limey hoodlums for women who'd wronged them was to fling vitriol in the face of the offender, transforming her into a permanently scar-layered horror-house gargoyle. Ronnie Kray could laugh the whole thing off, or he could chop her into postage stamp-size meat squares for an ego-soothing goulash, but how would he be disposed towards me? A *geeza* who is laying out high-rental dough for a skirt's domestic comforts can get downright homicidally tense when he catches another *geeza* using the oven for which he has paid.

'Orlroight then, Shatterproof, me old sahn,' Howard said. 'Yer a good mate an' oi don't want ter 'ave me mince pies see yer get 'urt. Tell yer wot, oi've bin offered a graft as restaurant manager in a new club wot'll make Browns seem loik a fahkin shit'ole. Oi kin even get meself a share if oi 'ad the fahkin dosh. Why don't yer take orf an' meet me there? Oi'll get yer connected loik?'

'How much, Howie?'

''Ow much wot, me old sahn?'

'How much to get in?'

''Undred fousand fahkin smackers.'

'What percentage?'

'Twenny-foive. Fahk orf, me old sahn, geddout orf it. Next yew'll be tellin me you've cracked the fahkin pools, innit?'

'I'll get the hundred thousand, Howie. But this is how it works, *bra*.'

I told Howard Postlethwaite about why I was in London. Who I was working undercover for. About how The General would want at least fifty per cent of *our* earnings sent back to South Africa. About how whatever *our* percentage was, it would be a thousand times better than being a lowly wage-earner. What did he think?

157

Howard was over the moon.

'Yew fahkin jungle-bunny cahnts got a few ace tricks up yer coon-carnival sleeves then, aintcher, me old sahn?'

So that was how it went.

I even had the gumption to call Ronnie Kray and tell him I would be leaving Browns and hoped he would patronise the new establishment where I'd be running things.

I didn't call Bubbles because I judged by this time she'd know which way the wind was blowing anyway. If she couldn't take care of the situation herself, there was nothing I could do about it.

I told master fornicator Big Bang to keep an eye out for her.

When I got around to thinking about it, after The General's courier had dropped off a hundred thousand pounds sterling in used US dollars, I was pretty glad to leave Browns, *mfowethu*.

Earning A Living

It had got to the point where I *had* to make some real money for myself.

I had finally got it through my now bleached platinum-blond woolly head that I was never going to make any big-time *amarands* here in this miserable freezing city of rain and sleet and snow. It was just not my kind of country, know what I mean, *mfowethu?*

The only big chance a poor penniless *geeza* like me had was the football pools, or better, the races, or even the gambling clubs I was a small part of – but nobody at any of those money-devouring joints was going to let you stay a winner if they could help it. Casinos were a closed corporation – their doors opened to let the dosh come in and closed the second it threatened to depart.

Not that there wasn't acres of the folding stuff around.

While I was at Browns, Lord No-Name, the international commodities baron, lost one hundred and seventy thousand quid in one evening and didn't bat a jaundiced eye. That was a big one, but there were just as outrageous shenanigans going on all the time. I saw Sir Bigwig Forget-Who drop fifty thousand in half an hour, then try to cover himself by going double-or-quits. *Sucker.* Of course, he got to owe double and had twenty-four hours to come up with the cash, or have his predilection for pre-pubescent boys exposed to the castigating, castrating public.

But not for me this high-rolling path to inferno. I never had the wad necessary at any rate to get into the no-limits action.

Besides, as I said, *mfowethu*, gambling is for suckers, dupes, the incredibly hopeful in a hopeless environment. Most professional games are rigged, but even if they're not, the house has the built-in leverage. You may make a little but the house makes a lot. The only way they are going to let you walk away with a big win is if they're certain you have a lot more where that came from – your personal bank account. *And* that you'll come back to try and pull it off again. That way, even when you score big-time, it's only a temporary loan that you'll pay interest back on in spades. That lovely lucre will sooner or later always fly away home to roost.

There's also only one way to play horses at the racetrack, and that's to have your own son riding one of the temperamental beasts eventually heading for a winning post at the glue factory. And then only if your son has enough solid evidence against the rest of the jockeys in the race to send them to HM Prisons for a minimum life-sentence each. Just to make sure, you ought to have every *other* horse in the stakes so loaded with equine valium and veterinary mandrax that the fastest nag can hardly uncross its hooves. That way your son has an outside chance of winning, provided his steed doesn't drop dead in the final stretch. I've been witness to that too, *mfowethu*. Besides all the aforementioned, there's nothing to stop your son from placing his bet on some other fancied runner and falling off his own nag as it gallops around the first turn. Say he wins – you've still got some shop steward sure to make noise about an unethical foul – in other words, you're better off putting your Dunhill lighter to your money. At least the blaze will keep you warm. The only decent living to be made from horse racing is made by the horse, who, being speechless, never gets a chance to claim, never mind spend, any of the winnings.

Not that I haven't tried putting my wishfully multiplied money down on these things, bets that covered the spectrum of instant riches.

I've seen plenty of my 'dosh', as the Londoners say, go down the drain at the gaming tables, and I wish I had a pink dollar for every time I've placed a small fortune on some knacker's tenpenny-a-pound upcoming meat-and-bones when the whinnying wanker came stumbling in after dark.

It took me due process of elongated time to realise that the only way I could make myself comfortable was to work for it – to get something going just for yours truly, nobody else. Luck is for the free winged denizens of the no-charge air, *mfowethu*; real luck is what you make with your *ikhanda* and your own two hands.

The only other way to make a lot of dosh is to steal it.

Nkulunkulu knows there's plenty-plenty too much of it around and it's not that hard to come by if you don't mind taking your chances on being absent from society for as long as the judge hands down to you when you're nabbed. I *mind* taking my chances. About the most important thing to me at that time was Dhlamini 'Shatterproof' Bhekuzulu. I couldn't see then and I don't see now any gain in taking a chance on some stupid wealthy squealing victim, or a nasty detective with an aggravating ball-and-chain giving him such constant grief that loosing off explosive lead projectiles into your belly soothes him, or on spending years in some dank grey hole eating your heart out for the good things while your youth passes you by.

There had to be an easier way of making it than that, *mfowethu*.

So, like it or not, minnow shareholder that I was, my only option was a job, the job that financing Howard Postlethwaite could grant me.

There were plenty of times when I didn't like it, hated it with a lunatic's fervour in fact.

But that's life, and I learned a new business, a profession that's come in very handy over the passing years.

Howard Postlethwaite was a good teacher, I'll say that for him. He was a peculiar *geeza* in that the only thing he really cared about was running a high-class ultimate snob restaurant. Don't let his gutter accent fool you: Howie knew what he was doing from pie chips and gravy to gourmet truffles and *coq au vin superior*. He had worked his way up as a dishwasher, busboy, kitchen help, assistant chef, head chef, waiter, and headwaiter and was now at long last general autonomous manager. He never did any other kind of work and he never wanted to either. As *geezas* go, he was honest. Not that Howard wouldn't grab a quick over-the-top profit if he could, but he wouldn't chance his arm doing it blindfolded. Whatever fancy eatery he was involved with took precedence over all else.

I judge I can call Howard a 'mate' like the English do, though you never know because him and me, we don't think things through the same way at all. But we've been together many seasons and I've never had to get physical with him and he's never had to get physical with me, not once. Between us friendship has always prevailed. That's about par for the first, second and third course concerning

Howard Postlethwaite and yours truly.

In these exclusive clubs like Browns that attract the wealthy big spenders, it was exclusively the nameless 'Big Fish' that got things started. Money, bribes, securing upmarket premises and unbending rigid fixed legalities, the works. Then they had to have somebody run the place for them. First off, an essential linchpin in the convoluted machine is a human computer-brainbox pro. He oversees the gambling. This VIP is somebody they have to trust. Or at least they have to coerce him with fear so badly that he'll think twice about helping himself to a pack of fags without paying for it first. Sometimes this *geeza* is on a salary. Sometimes, if he is the *crème de la crème*, he's on a percentage of the take. There is only one way to keep him reasonably honest – the more the Big Fish make, the more he makes. Simple mathematics. Even so, he can beat you fifty ways to fuck your lover *if he wants to take the chance*. Depending on the size of the casino, he's in charge of maybe twenty or thirty hustling employees – stick men, dice ferrets, dealers, shills, cashiers, protection heavies and checkers. These are the gambling staff. They don't lower themselves to converse with the operating staff except when they're owed money or need to know the time of day.

Most of the successful gaming clubs in those days had to have a *numero uno* restaurant on the side – because even a slot-machine junkie sometimes liked to fill his face with good nosh. The days of franchising suitably accommodating food outlets had not yet arrived, *mfowethu*.

There also had to be entertainment, at the very least a small hot-sounds combo or a fairly well known singer, top acts on tap at least once a month.

I met prominent show-business *geezas* like Matt Munro, the 'English Frank Sinatra', and Max Bygraves, later *Sir* Max Bygraves. Even a handsome up-and-coming young Welsh songster called Tom Jones, his first seven-single 'What's New Pussycat?' well on the way to Britain's Top of the Pops.

This entertainment is strictly a come on – the food and drinks and pulsating heady music just a glamorous something to get the big spenders inside so they can get rid of their dosh at the gaming tables. But since it *is* a come on, it has to be done suavely. Just right, *mfowethu*. Food high-priced but not *too* high-priced. The very best of cuisine temptation there is. Plus superior service and the drinks affordably inexpensive, because inebriation breeds fiscal foolhardiness. Atmosphere understated and impeccable. Take your pick.

And this is where the operating staff, including me in my new persona, come into job prominence.

There are any number of sound *geezas* like Howard Postlethwaite. The only difference is that some are excellent and others not so excellent, merely of above-average competence. These specialists command top pay and they deserve every penny. They've got to know everything there is to know about running a huge restaurant – marketing, staff, purchasing, kitchen, bar. Plus myriad other dodges and sharpster angles nobody ever thinks about, including how to get a drunk-out-of-her-mind, titled society belle with a cocaine nosebleed all down the front of her pearl-studded evening gown out of the ladies' shithouse, while she's slur-shouting 'RAPE! RAPE! RAPE!' loud enough to shatter the crystal chandeliers.

Howard Postlethwaite was better than superlatively excellent. He was up there with the Olympian Gods of Flawless Bacchanalian Repast.

He taught me everything he could. I picked up a few useful odds and ends for myself on the side.

He put me through the heavy-metal wrangle at first. It

was weeks before he would even deign to let me pick up a starched linen serviette, much less seat a paying party with suitable decorum. Finally though, I was upped to assistant manager.

The new gaming club was a terrible, blood-vessel-bursting headache to begin with.

Howard fired, rehired and again fired all the staff, *three* times, *mfowethu*, before he was happy with the desperate-to-please human putty he felt he could mould to his own stratospheric standards. Waiters were the prime targets for his ego-thrashing of our employees in general – waiters in those days had to pay for their own uniforms and food, but a good table hustler could average well over a monkey a month in grateful tips from flattered patrons. That's five hundred solid sterling we're talking here, serious dosh in those days, *mfowethu*. A bad week would glean him a pony or more, twenty-five quid no less, guaranteed on any given night. That was in addition to what he could thieve, and there is no *geeza* in the world who has more dodges to steal from you or the customer than your average smarmy professional waiter.

I don't want to bore you, *mfowethu*, but The General's hundred grand bought Howard and me only a percentage of the restaurant's profits, not those of the gaming tables. Fifteen went back to South Africa and we split ten.

Sounds tight? It was.

There was still good money to be made.

Healthy money.

But there were a couple of catches to collecting it.

To repeat, the restaurant was just the come-on in the big-picture entrapment-scheme of things. That meant the food and service had to be top-notch. *And* cost less than a parity establishment on the same echelon.

I helped Howard Postlethwaite there with my *tsotsi*'s

inbuilt inventive ability.

I made it known that any meal from Monday to Thursday entitled you to free Irish coffees. I'd treble load the first *gratis* ones with cheap-cheap whisky laced with hundred-proof pharmacological alcohol. Then I'd drench the steaming-hot liquid confection in rich cream and molasses-thick brown sugar, and then again shamelessly layer their tipsy '*What the 'ell, let's 'ave anuvver boys, we've already 'ad one free ain't we?*' Pommie attitude with six or seven more single-tot Irish coffees on the customers' bill at eight pounds a pop. Our ten per cent share began returning to us a hundredfold.

The menu also had to include something affordable for the out-of-towner out on a big night in the Big Smoke – the *geeza* all set to impress his beloved, dour wife or impress the flimsiness of filmy panties right off a would-be young mistress. We didn't want to scare him away. His money was as good as anybody else's even if it came in lesser incremental amounts; it all added up.

This meant that you had to have eyes in the back of your head to keep the profit rolling in. It meant you had to cut every corner and plug up every hole. Believe me, *mfowethu*, this is an enterprise that has more holes in it than that yank tank's tyre Big Bang Bongani so filled with buckshot that I had to *make myself* flee Jo'burg in the face of black-faced blackmail. Everything had to run like a perpetual-motion machine. Any breakdowns and you'd be the one forking out hard-earned money, right back into your own losing game.

The gaming club had the gambling rooms upstairs.

Ours was the silverware polish and dazzling glitter below.

There were nineteen regulars on the gambling staff and part of our deal was to feed these freeloaders at only two pounds a head before the regular dinner hour. That catch meant that meant that Howard and I started off with nineteen daily no-profit items, even if we fed them heavily disguised dishes left over from the day before yesterday.

Then, at dinner, we could seat two hundred and fifty paying patrons like affluent sardines granted elbowroom in accordance with the fire laws. Or close to three hundred if you jammed them into the sardine can a little tighter and took the risk of the fire department inspector dropping by for a free sample of your *Rack of Spring Lamb marinated in Garden Garlic and smothered in Hellenic Red Wine.*

Allow me to inform you, *mfowethu*, what else the manager of a culinary zoo like that had to grow ulcers about.

First take the kitchen employees, those we used to call 'potboilers' or 'tapeworms'.

There was the head chef at the top of the pots and pans heap. This so-called Munch-Artist can make or break you from the second you open your doors to customers. If he's on your side, you're halfway home. One almost infallible way to ensure this is to cut the overweight *piranha* in on the 'dropsy' – the kickbacks from your suppliers. If you don't, he's going to bleat louder than a goat on LSD amplified through Pink Floyd's PA system at a hippie rock festival. For instance, the temperamental wanker will say the meat is of an 'unusable' quality. Then the grot-headed ghastly ghoul of a gastronome will take a couple of *sides* of good baby beef, exorbitantly expensive in the UK, *and deliberately spoil it, vandalise it unfit for human consumption, just to prove his point.* That is a lot of tender beef. The complacent profit-slaying joker has just serial murdered your next few days' take right then and there. Or if this fuckbag head chef is pissed off at you? Because you perhaps rationed his morning supply of *your* engine-starting whisky? He will pass the word to serve nine king prawns instead of five in a fearless outlay of show-off seafood *hors d'oeuvre*. Or, say, serve a slice of roast lamb that would choke the wide gullet of an adult male lion, instead of one that would rightly only choke a ten-year-old Biafran anorexic. It's basically the same thing as him putting his hand in your till and helping himself. Only you can't prosecute the rectal-tube-occlusion for the aggravation.

If the scurrilous swine is *really and truly* angry with you, the fun can get drastically out of hand. He'll just let fragile things drop. Ceramic dishes the same as those '*made by appointment to HRH Queen Elizabeth*', silver-filigreed butterbowls, crystal glasses, you name it. Even thirty gallons of soup – you could hear the crash and the swearing of those menials with boiled ankles all the way over in Buckingham Palace. After four or five hours of this you either take an automatic cheese-grater to the sick psychopath's balls, or you find out what's got those same testicles in a terrible twist. Then you free them for him so that he can be a happy fat chappy in his delicate *prima donna* work again. Afterwards, to show his gratitude, maybe all he'll do to you is accidentally drop all the solid silverware in the garbage disposal unit. Just to make it definitively clear who's big boss.

The bulk of restaurant proprietors who are not chefs themselves simply give up. They organise him a percentage on the side. He'd rather have that than having his salary doubled. That's the way a head chef's mind works.

He has other ways to make himself money at your expense. Because making it *at your expense* is what motivates him. He's known as the 'Fat Man', not because he is necessarily corpulent, but because he is the individual who saves all the fat. This animal goo is divided up into three separate categories – *one*, clear frying fat – *two*, frying fat mixed with trimmings – *three*, fat scraps comprising bones and offal, the last but one step away from outright useless garbage. This is all judged and weighed by a specialist *geeza* in such queasy commodities who comes calling once a week. He actually *buys* this stuff, which commercial exchange lines exclusively the head chef's pockets, naturally. The entrepreneurial 'Fat Man' also makes plenty more from the garbage proper. This is separated into stale table leftovers, rotten trimmings, and 'hard' garbage – cans, bottles, broken glass. The oink-oink pig-farmer-fellow comes and collects the whole disgusting mess in order to feed his porkers the choice edibles. This way *all* the garbage is conveniently hauled away at no charge to the restaurant.

The head chef doesn't do all of this himself. Anything that causes sweat is done by the dishwashers, the porters and the 'swiller', who cleans off the dishes before they get washed. A head chef doesn't even wipe his own arsehole unless he absolutely has to.

Under the Kitchen Kingpinis the *sous chef*, his personal assistant. Then a *garde manger* who only does the broiling. Then there's a *sauce cook* and a sort of mutant *garde manger* who works only on creating salads-to-die-for, visual explosions of high-class rabbit food. And a *pantry man* who does desserts and cold dishes. And a virtuoso *general cook* for any little speedy extra that needs doing right away. On top of all this there is the *meat maestro* – because none of these other aforementioned tosser twats dare risk nicking their fingers with a butcher's knife. And if you think any head chef with a helium-inflated ego can get along without any of his darling parasitic little helpers, just try asking him, *mfowethu*. He'll be out the back door *too fast* with you owing him two months' severance pay, pausing only to urinate in the *avocado consommé* and defecate in the *chocolate mousse.*

In the dining room of an elite restaurant like ours, you also have a head wine-steward.

This alcohol-serving *geeza* can really help tote up the profit. I've seen wine-stewards who are nothing less than sleight-of-hand magicians. If you, the customer, are sitting there with a gorgeous girl who's shifting your libido into overdrive, and you *don't* buy a svelte imported wine with each course, a necromancer wine-steward can and will make you look and feel like the lowest cheapskate pariah leper-cousin in the universe. A wine-steward can deftly make you order the most expensive bottle on the winelist. *And* have elegant compliments waiting to ensure you think you're actually *enjoying* it to boot. They have prepared flattery ready to bazooka fire at you so effectively that women glow under the verbal bombardment and men puff out their chests like steroid-overdosed barnyard roosters. They are worth their weight in gold.

Then there's the *maître d'hôtel.*

It's up to him to supervise half-a-dozen captains, a dozen or more waiters, and an always sufficient number of busboys or stackers. If you think this is a piece of rat-fanny cake, you don't know what rodent vermin waiters can be, *mfowethu.*

Each waiter has his own 'station', or set of tables he is exclusively responsible for – depending on the number of seats needed for any particular dining-party. Each waiter is duty-bound or *supposed* to take care of his own set-up – linens, silver, the immaculate presentation. In addition, it is his job to keep up with the side work – cleaning and filling the condiment containers, and placing bread and rolls, scalloped butter, shard-iced drinking water and all the rest of it on the tables.

When the rush gets chaotic, waiters hate each other with an enmity that makes that between Jews and Arabs look puffball-tame by comparison. One of the serving brigade wouldn't lift his pinky to loosen the throttling, twisted collar of another dying by asphyxiation; he'd even stuff a moisture-soaked starched napkin down his gasping mate's air-starved throat if he got the surreptitious chance. But when *you* want to impress with your five-star-advertised service and joined tables that necessarily cross 'station' territory, your waiters have mystically bonded like Siamese twins. They bunch brotherhood-style, becoming virtually inseparable in some unavailable, shadowed corner, closer than incestuous siblings. When harassed by onerous duty to pitch in and share said joined tables, they become deafer than doorposts and meaner than junkyard dogs.

Waiters can destroy you more efficiently than killer landmines placed at strategic points in the restaurant aisles. They'll try it on at first, just to see which way the cookie crumbles and how much they can get away with. They maliciously confuse orders, lose bills, spill gravy, stick their fingers in the butter and do so many other disgusting things that sane imagination quails at the deformed limits of their creativity.

The only way to overcome this is to take the biggest, most aggressive one out into the backyard and beat the living shit out of him. This can be a problem, especially when he just happens to be a *karate* expert with a tenth dan he's earned in his leisure hours. But I had an ace up my sleeve – Big Bang Bongani. One look at an aroused Big Bang and his fireworks of light-exploding ear decorations, and I swear Godzilla would have turned tail and fled in fear-soaked ignominy. I used Big Bang only once. The story, almost an urban legend, of an Incredible Black Hulk got around fast and saved me an immense amount of hassle.

There was no labour union then. Different from today, *mfowethu*. Now if you call an English waiter anything but his real name, you get more official legal watchdogs in your nosh house than you've got customers.

In the restaurant game, you have to constantly bear one thing in mind. Never ever lose sight of it, *mfowethu*. Each and every one of your employees has just one single-minded aim in life. To *rwa* you of anything and do it every-which-way he or she can. And there's more ways to do it than a Zululand *ishongololo* millipede has legs.

Making this lunatic asylum appear to have a respectable facade was my job.

Starting with the kitchen, first and foremost I had to keep the 'Fat Man' happy. Then I had to microscopically watch everyone who worked for him. Because those sweet little helpers could destock a kitchen faster than a voracious army of mutant-enlarged African soldier ants.

The refrigerating rooms were locked. Howard and I were the only ones with keys. But please allow me to elucidate.

One time, near Christmas, fifty turkeys went missing.

Don't ask me how anybody can get *fifty* adult turkey carcasses out of locked freezer cabinets, but I oversaw them being stacked in there and thereafter my frozen turkeys had vanished, gone completely awol.

I could not judge where the culprit or culprits had stashed them; no staff had gone home, no delivery trucks had called. It was driving me crazy.

Then I saw an alley cat out back ripping away at what looked like the splitting image of a turkey drumstick sticking halfway out of the snow-covered ground.

The wide-o motherfucking wankers had *buried* my turkeys right there in my own backyard!

Let's take another look at that aberrant species misnamed waiters.

They bring their orders to the kitchen.

The kitchen fills their orders.

The waiter picks up his meals and leaves to serve them.

Nothing sounds simpler, does it, *mfowethu*?

One waiter I caught and fired had his inside pockets lined with pliable plasticised asbestos, and had gloves made of the same stuff for a specific purpose. Every time he'd pass the smoking grill, he'd zap a juicy-hot baby chicken or a sizzling fillet steak quick as a wink. Into the asbestos kitty it'd go. He had an after-midnight trolley stall selling fast food and manned by his brother outside the late-nite dance clubs. They were coining it at my expense. I was so impressed with him, I set him and his brother up legitimate-style and my cut was fifty per cent. Big Bang guaranteed no welshing.

The next thing you have to watch with waiters is when they total the bill. I had my waiters bring their bills back to me to verify the total amount. I'd stamp the bill and the waiter would go and collect the tab. Between then and when your waiter shows up with the customer's money, many strange and bizarre occurrences may implement themselves.

Here is a favourite.

An ambitious waiter can have a duplicate set of bills made up for him by any Tom, Dick or Harry printer in the city. Then he substitutes one of his for one of yours – ups the total within reason and pockets the difference. Or he has his own identical rubber stamp made – reworks the bill after he's left me and adjusts it again before he brings it back. Who's to be any the wiser, *mfowethu*? Today's double-check computerised till systems are even easier to beat, but that's another story, not this one.

This one deals now with *another* wide-o waiter move from those days, which was to have a simultaneous big tally from one table and a small one from another ready for presentation at the same time. The big one goes to both parties. It can work well, provided the smaller bill's diners are smashed out of their skulls. If the waiter pulling this scam is caught out, he'll mouth something like '*My apologies, sir, my apologies, madam, so sorry, it seems I've made a terrible mistake, please forgive me.*' It is the most peculiar thing; the majority of customers think all waiters are automatically servile morons. Ninety-nine times out of a hundred they'll spuriously laugh it off. But take it from the horse's mouth – those waiters are slicker than a Teddy Boy's greased hairstyle. I never knew one who didn't have a head for figures on par with that of a qualified chartered accountant.

Then there are the bartenders. There were three of them in a place like Howard's and mine.

How can anyone control these *geezas* and their super-fast action? They have *so many ways* to skim your cream. The best you can do is tell them you have an inside informant's snitching eye watching out for any flaws and hope for the best. A barman can take ten pounds for a round and ring up three. He can sell his own stuff right along with yours and you'll never be any the wiser. They are wizard witch doctors with invisible spells they use when short-changing. They can bleed drunks dry of a week's wages. They can steal drinks. They are able to rob you blind while listening to your troubles and sympathising better than an empathic priest, looking you straight in the eye all the while.

You take inventory as often as possible because you have to.

The open stock behind the bar is always the big problem. There's no ways you can use a dipstick to measure alcohol because so many bottles are so many different shapes. I got so proficient that I could tell within a half-inch how much was in a bottle and how much dished out was accountable to the ledger. If you demonstrate this skill to a bartender, you'll earn his respect. But that's about as far as it goes.

It is also an unqualified axiom that bartenders are always somehow able to punch their weight. It goes hand in hand with the territory. Bartenders are *always* too efficient with their fists and too capable of handling themselves to take them out back and introduce some wisdom. Waiters are saplings, barmen are oak trees. That's just the way it is.

There is only one lever you have going for you as boss over this cross-section of humanity who choose to work unusual hours.

Hatred.

And a street-smart boss builds his fires and stokes that hatred. He not only keeps it going, he *grows* it. The waiters hate the kitchen staff. The kitchen staff hate the waiters. The captains hate the waiters. The *maître d'hôtel* hates the captains, etcetera, etcetera, *ad infinitum*.

The bartenders slip each other a free drink and have a good guffaw.

The biggest hater of all is the wine-steward. He hates absolutely every co-worker in the place. Because he judges every one of them is taking what's owed to him.

It helps management immeasurably that this is the cannibal nature of the beast. If restaurant staff ever got together like good proletarian communists are supposed to, all you'd have left over after the siege would be the toilets, and you'd have to beg a discarded newspaper to finish up your ablutions.

I had to keep the place supplied with everything – from soap, wax, mops, deodorants, rags, buckets, tools; through aprons, towels, napkins, tablecloths; silverware, cutlery, pots, pans, glassware, china, trays, serving tables; as well as the infinite variety of food and liquor – not to mention the codeine-content painkillers for those who still wished to dally in spite of having to contend with the day's second hangover.

For every item you need, though, there is a supplier's salesman trying to sell you his particular brand of merchandise. When you have so many hopefuls all trying to sell you something, you have an excellent avenue open for manipulation. Food and liquor top the bartering range because that is the most lucrative area with the largest turnover.

In food there are categories of major suppliers. Butchers and seafood companies for meats, fish, special sausages and hams, crabs, lobster, prawns, shrimp and venison. Dairies to be found around outer London for cheese, butter, eggs, ice-cream and special desserts. Bakeries for various epicurean breads. Wholesale grocers for garden-compatible canned goods made realistic with added dye, plus condiments, herbs, spices and bulk items. And farms supplying true-blue fresh vegetables and fruit. You depended mostly on whatever seasonal fresh produce was available.

All of these suppliers would kick back five per cent cash on your total purchases for the month – this regular windfall of 'invisible' dosh helped by not having to draw taxable and therefore recorded wages from the business.

As far as our in-with-the-in-crowd restaurant was financially concerned, clever buying made all the difference. Like any other capitalist democratic organisation, the object was to buy cheap and sell frightfully dear, to *justifiably* hike your better-than-average retail price as high as the bruise-free market would bear. Economics, *mfowethu*, basic economics.

But there was so burgeoning much you *had* to know, and you *had* to learn it all yourself the hard way. For instance, take a side of beef. That's where your variety of steaks and ingenious stews comes from. When you buy it, it weighs maybe fifty pounds deadweight. But when you section it, it comes down to thirty pounds or less – depending on how good your *meat maestro* is. You have to know *exactly* how many servings you can obtain from this. Then you have to gamble on how many diners are going to order these scrumptious items on any given day. If you estimate wrong, you have to dream up what new dishes will go the furthest and still keep your paying diners from hurling the offensive contents of their plates to the floor.

To keep your doors open, you had to be on your toes every ballerina-style performing minute of the day.

All in all things were going pretty good. I was picking up healthy pocket-money on the side, as I explained earlier, what with one thing and another. You might judge I was in the pound seats.

Am I boring you with all this graphic but mundane business-business, *mfowethu*?

Let me reward your listener's patience for hearing out these repetitive details that are, to me, important in grasping influences that were irresistibly attractive to my *tsotsi*'s nature, my Dr Jekyll and Mr Hyde flawed psyche.

There was change brewing in the air.

The adrenalin-releasing kind of change that makes the hackles on a sensible *geeza*'s neck rise and a voice in the back of his head start whispering to watch out and beware.

A youngish Colombian named Poco Batista Salvador started to frequent the restaurant.

Poco did some gambling upstairs as well, but mostly he was on the lookout for skirt. Somehow he never seemed able to make what appeared to be the beginnings of a semi-permanent relationship with the opposite sex last more than the brief lifetime of a candle in the wind. This was odd, because he was a tall, good-looking *geeza* with fine facial bone structure and a head of jet-black curls, a filmstar's easy charisma and a poet's limpid pools of romantically seductive, deep brown eyes.

Poco didn't seem to have any particular connections, but he loved it when I introduced him to Tom Jones and Tom shook him by his hand and called him by his first name. After that, Poco thought the sun shone out of my posterior. He never stopped talking about it, and it became embarrassing the way he would dog my heels whenever I had a spare moment.

At this particular conjuncture of events I was seeing Bubbles again.

Ronnie Kray seemed to have become bored with her, and it became routine for Poco to hang out with us.

Poco was always flush with dosh. He finally told me, in such a hushed confidential manner that you would have thought it some heinous crime, that he was the only son of an extremely wealthy *aristo* family from Colombia that owned lucrative mines and vast lands. He insisted on paying the bills almost everywhere we went – theatre – short stopovers to Amsterdam, Venice or the Louvre in Paris – country inns – you name it. I never objected too strenuously when he reached for his wallet.

You could see he had fallen in love with Bubbles, but was happy to take a back seat as long as he could be near her. It was transparently clear that he thought she was a flame-haired leprechaun goddess come to earth amongst us mere bog-bound mortals.

All of Poco's always-elegant clothing was stitched with a monogrammed family crest, so it seemed he was telling the truth about being a playboy kept ridiculously spoilt with limitless funds from his indulgent, loving parents.

Then, after a few months of this comfortable threesome, when we were at the motor races at Silverstone where Stirling Moss led the international Formula One field from start to finish, a name passed Poco's lips as casually as if he were recalling fond memories of some boyhood friend. It turned out this person, whose name made pyrotechnics kaleidoscope in my head, was a distant relative of his and at one time had been dead keen on amateur sports-car racing himself, but had never made the grade to the major circuits.

The casually dropped name was that of a shadowy *geeza* known in the underworld as the Main Man, the Cocaine Czar, the *Numero Uno*, the source who handled the export of virtually *all* nose candy coming from Bogotá to England.

I beamed in on Bubbles and she beamed bright signals back at me like a communicative lighthouse. Both our noses twitched like twin divining-rods and immediately sourced the smell of underground money.

Bubbles was always looking for a supplier of her favourite drug who wouldn't charge her an arm and a leg, and I knew something she didn't know: the Kray twins were moving big-time into the millions to be made in the 'snowbound' market, one of the thousands of names by which cocaine was already getting to be known.

I swear this is the truth, *mfowethu*, that my first thoughts were purely aimed at picking up a little folding by getting the Kray twins a connection they could use. That's the way I should have allowed it to happen, because if there is one *tsotsi geeza* who knows you shouldn't go poking your nose

179

in somebody else's business where it doesn't belong, that *tsotsi geeza* is me.

I excused myself to go get another round of drinks and left Poco for Bubbles to apply her feminine wiles without distraction.

I stayed at the bar counter, bought some Jamaicans a pint, and smoked three cigarettes before heading back. I judged Bubbles could get herself included in Poco's will as sole beneficiary, given sufficient time.

She had milked enough information from him to be a source of supply to the Greater London Dairy Co-operative. Our boy Poco was in the Colombian Cocaine Czar's good books for occasionally carrying hefty diplomatic-marked pouches through customs for the drug emperor to the embassy, where another 'uncle' was one of many ambassadorial assistants.

Poco knew what he was carrying, but to him it was all a frivolous game. He fancied himself a romantic swashbuckling desperado figure, something like a masked modern-day Zorro without the sword.

By giving Poco my ears and by prompting him now and again, the floodgates opened and he was boasting openly about how he could get anything he wanted from the *Numero Uno* and for a price that was hard to believe.

According to Poco, a kilo of pure-as-it-comes cocaine would cost me two thousand quid. That started my cerebellum humming. I could easy get many, many times that amount from the gluttonous Firm right here in the Big Smoke. It didn't seem to me that getting the stuff from Bogotá to London would pose that big a problem. It would take some convoluted brainwork, sure, *mfowethu*, but I was confidently convinced I could get it done.

Right then and there I knew I was going to give it my best shot. That kind of profit was just too handsome for my *tsotsi*'s avaricious instincts to resist. I had ideas growing in my head so fast that remembering them all would take dedicated concentration.

Pure cocaine is a white powder with no smell the human schnozzle can detect. The taste of cocaine is bitingly bitter. If you rub it into your gums it thoroughly numbs them, but still will reach your pleasure centres as surely, albeit slower, than through the vacuum cleaner of your greedy nose straight down into your absorbent lungs.

Street-level cocaine contains only about thirteen per cent of the stuff; trust me, that's a police laboratory-tested analysis. This is such a small amount in the average sales made in grams you could lay it on your pinky's fingernail. So the way it's done is to cut the cocaine with Borax baby powder, which looks exactly like cocaine and has no smell or taste. When you mix the two you get a 'ching' mixture bulky enough to handle, and easily suited to putting it into cellophane squares, or a 'paper twist'.

You can cut high-grade cocaine five times easy with Borax. As long as there's thirteen to twenty per cent cocaine in there, it will give the customer his bang and you won't get any complaints of being ripped off.

Starting with my kilo of pure cocaine, I judged I'd be cautious and cut it only three ways with Borax. That way I'd have three kilos, which starts to add up to some serious dosh. If the customer is satisfied, who's to complain, *mfowethu*?

I was in overtaxed overdrive because I could *visualise* that beautiful big bundle of beauteous banknotes. All of a sardine I was fed up to the teeth with what I was doing, with the way I was living.

What I needed was a gigantic stake so I could get the hell out of England and back to South Africa, land of the sunshine gods, where I belonged. Aiming low, as you may have gathered, has never been my long zoot suit.

Then the news arrived which I judged was an auspicious sign indeed that the new venture I was considering carried Lady Luck's stamp of approval.

Boy Faraday, king of payroll robbers, monarch of filling-station cash marauders, slaughterer not only of men both black and white who dared block his way, but also of unsuspecting strangers who happened to glance at him sideways and catch his malevolent mad-dog eye. He had reigned *carte blanche* supreme during his period of hydrophobic and tyrannical lust – but at long last he had been shot dead in the Mofolo Marshes by his most bitter enemy, Captain Frik le Grange of the Brixton Murder and Robbery Squad. Township dwellers from Springs to Randfontein and beyond must have felt suddenly freed and mightily relieved. He was so feared and such a callous life-sucking vampire that the UK *Daily Mirror* carried photographs and a lurid byline-story about the monstrous cancer of his career.

Back to me, *mfowethu*.

I put every fact-finding question I could think of to Poco to be certain that he could follow through on his promises. Three nights later I was sold on the fact that there was no ways he was bullshitting me. Too many pertinent details were repeated under my gentle cross-examination and verified in that part of my brain that clicked a consensus of one plus one equals two confirmation.

When I said I could *maybe* get him front-table seats at a club on the outskirts of London where the Rolling Stones, at this tadpole stage of their bullfrog career, were giving a 'private' concert, Poco *volunteered* to catch the plane to Bogotá and set the deal up – *no* problemo, *no charge, leave it to me, Shatterproof*, sport.

If all was well, as he repeatedly assured me it would be,

he would telephone my restaurant's public payphone and confirm that he had secured the goods.

I was completely sold on my boy Poco, but I judged now was the time to go looking for a go-between to introduce my interest to the top *geezas* at The Firm, without being named a player in the game. I needed a *geeza* who was no contest with me in the brains department, but one who was not entirely a *mampara* and also had a fine nose for the magic multiplication of money.

I decided to drum up a little interest in Riggsie Leitch, the same psychopath Riggsie Leitch who had shown so much priapistic interest in Bubbles Nightingale, who now, incidentally, had changed her stage name.

Bubbles told me she had given Riggsie the big come-on approach, and then had hired a diseased whore to take her place after a lot of foreplay-boozing. The whore was planted, waiting, in the bathroom of Bubbles' Knightsbridge flatlet, the switch with all the lights off went smoothly, and Reggie the sucker fell for it. He ended up with a virulent dose of leaking penis and avoided Bubbles like the plague thereafter.

I knew where to find him.

He was playing cards in a back-room school always held at the Old Picadilly Hotel, upstairs, on the fifth floor. Problem was, if you sat at Riggsie's table you couldn't go home until Riggsie had won all his money back and yours as well, so he was finding it harder and harder to find playmates at the card table.

He was at the mini-bar eyeing all the occupants like a shark eyes a shoal of salmon. I asked him to come for a drive with me and we made circles around the slush-filled streets while I repeated my sales pitch until it seemed the essence had sunk in.

When Riggsie nodded his head without making any untoward comment, I knew I was halfway home.

This was the imperfect and dangerously volatile balance of a seesaw agreement because a hardboiled criminal like Riggsie *mon amour* is mercurially swift to become irritable, and his behemoth breed of tyrannosaurus-rodent becomes *murderously irritated* if he judges you know too much about his business. He'll also burst your mouth in a second if he feels you are taking the piss or being condescending. In many ways he has to be paranoid-suspicious because he is responsible to some very bad people who are very unkind concerning mistakes.

I think what sold Riggsie was my price, my price to him. I could almost hear his homicidal predator's brain click as he worked out how much he was going to pocket with nobody being any the wiser, no fingers being pointed his way.

''Ow much dooyer fink yew can get then, Shatterproof?'

I began to spill the beans about my Borax-assisted three kilos, but something made me pause.

'How much can you pay for upfront?'

'Oi fink aroun' foive kilos max, we ain't talkin' a bag orf roice 'ere, mate.'

I hoped he couldn't hear *my* brain click with unbounded joy.

'Three kilos of good stuff do for starters, Riggsie?'

'Sounds orlroight ter me, mate. Sound loik.'

I drove him back to his no-takers card game.

I judged our little deal would stay sweet and secret because talking about it would mean sharing, and Riggsie wasn't about to do that, no ways, *mfowethu*.

I didn't prolong my farewells, because I had things to do.

The first got done at a chemist and the second at the local grocer's.

I bought plenty sachet packs of talcum-lined 'Big Boy' condoms and a clear plastic pouring funnel. At the same place I bought a flowery container of superflow Tampax sanitary towels, plus a 'period belt' women used to hold their fanny-mattresses in place, safety pins and rubber bands.

My next call supplied me with Borax and one of those old-fashioned manually operated flour-sifting sieves.

When I got back to my digs I began trial-and-error experimentation with my new equipment.

I found that three condoms, one inside the other, could stretch to safely contain an incredible amount of compacted Borax, while rubber bands kept the powder solid and stable.

I had myself a cocaine-polony conveyor belt, and my home-industry *drugwürsts* flattened into accommodating contours most pleasingly when you applied shape-altering pressure. It was as easy as falling off a log to take a Tampax napkin apart and pack it groaning at the absorbent edges with trial-run cocaine substitute.

Feeling like a transvestite, I stripped, donned the menstruation-mechanics belt, my packed double Tampax almost making me bow-legged, and fastened the whole contraption securely with safety pins.

My pussy swag-bag sat tight and safe – nothing short of an earthquake would dislodge it.

I got dressed, gathered up my goodies, telephoned Bubbles and told her I was coming over.

I was whistling and jiving in my head to a lively old township *mbanqanga* tune, feeling lighter than air, my conscious mind filled with lovely pictures of how I'd soon be leaving London, aptly named the lung-smothering Big Smoke, for good . . . ten trips should do it . . . and then I'd be heading back to South Africa as King of the Kool-Kat Castle.

With that kind of rocket-fuel *moolah* to boost my take-off, there was nothing I couldn't do, permanent stratosphere here I come, *mfowethu*.

There were countless enterprises I could get into back home.

Why had I stayed in gloomy London so long?

My bones hated the marrow invasion of this damp and cold, antiquated, bourgeoisie-ruled hole from the moment I had stepped off the plane at Heathrow to make an undistinguished arrival, and it was *still* a damp and antiquated hole now that I was leaving it. No colour, no vibrancy, no spontaneity; everything as calculated as Arthur Wellesley, first Duke of Wellington's '*Publish and be damned*', while he had most probably owned all the printing presses and literature distributors from Napoleon's flunkeys downwards.

Bubbles was worried by my rabid euphoria.

My babbling made her nervous.

I sat her down and poured us both stiff drinks, insisting she accept a loaded refill. I explained it all one more careful time, concisely and at a verbal snail's pace, just so there could be no mistaking the finer points of my own brilliance.

'Not for me, brother,' she said, shaking her masses of red curls. 'South American jails are not for the likes of this songbird. Thanks, but no thanks, sweetheart. Besides, you're messing with the Krays. There are easier ways to commit suicide, dear thing.'

'How is *anybody* going to bust us? Come on, Bubbles, love, my contact's got lockjaw. We'll all make dosh, plenty of dosh. Now who's going to object to that?'

'What's my take, sweetheart?'

'One tenth.'

'Half.'

'Come on, Bubbles. I'm paying, doing all the legwork, the organising, the ideas, all of it.'

'Half, dear thing, or you can find yourself another pigeon.'

'Bubbles, hear me, all you have to do is sit tight on your artificially swollen and uncomfortable fanny for the comfortable flight there and back. It'll be a pushover through customs. Who'd dare embarrass a menstruating woman sitting in first-class passageway? It'll be a breeze, you know it will.'

'You want *me* to wear *that thing* through customs, I'm worth half, sweetheart.'

'It'd look bloody funny strapped on me, wouldn't you say?' I said, and that got her laughing.

Once I'd agreed to her half-share, there was no more argument about going together to Bogotá.

I really needed Bubbles as a partner – I needed her for more than just being my mule to carry my score, but this is not the time to go into the particular details of those extrapolations, *mfowethu*.

I arranged with Howard to give myself a short break from our restaurant and went to my bank to draw the necessary money – with travelling expenses, almost every penny I had managed to save, I might add.

I shopped around for some additional items I fancied

I'd need in faraway Bogotá if this dodge was going to fall into its allotted place.

Then I packed my newly purchased rich tourist's crocodile-skin suitcase with all my gimmicks and hung around the payphone waiting for Poco's come-ahead call.

When it came, my hand held the receiver with a Parkinson's grip, the thing rattling in my ear like an inanimate epileptic against my gold-link wrist-chain.

Poco's voice sounded as far away as the moon, but I had no trouble hearing what he said to me.

'Listen, sport, the curios are going to cost a little more than I first thought.'

'How much more, Poco?'

'Maybe a thousand, give or take a couple hundred either way.'

'I'm still in the market. Secure the consignment.'

'Will do, sport. When you arriving?'

'Tomorrow's connecting flight.'

'I'll check on the timetables. See you at the airport, sport. Give my love to Bubbles.'

I fumed briefly, like a last flickering burst of metered gas announcing that coins were needed in the council gobble-box to get the flame reconnected.

What was a paltry thousand when you're heading where the sun shines all day and you can wrap your overcoat up in mothballs and forget about it?

Three hours later, Bubbles and I were on the first leg of our journey to Bogotá.

South American
Shenanigans

The approach to Bogotá, the capital of Colombia, is very mountainous, and it seemed those crags were sucking us down to our doom as the aircraft skilfully circled, came in for a light landing and taxied directly up to the airport terminal.

A few minutes short of two interminable hours later, minus fifteen pounds sterling in what I'll euphemistically describe as 'tips, and after verging-on-violence differences of opinion with a customs official, plus a porter who did his best to separate me from my luggage, as well as suffering a surly taxi driver who smelt as bad as he looked, Bubbles and I were sitting frazzled in a nauseating shade of flamingo pink-daubed *suite superior* inside a morgue-grey hotel, waiting for Poco, who had not been there to welcome us at the airport as he had promised he would be.

I still had the adrenalin shakes and Bubbles gave me a purely restorative sister-style platonic back massage to soothe me.

Hours passed and Poco still hadn't put in an appearance.

I walked down the shadowed and steep, angular, echoing stairs to the reception desk because the fragile birdcage-elevator looked like a suspended accident searching for a trusting victim.

Waiting for me was a sealed envelope with my name dramatically splashed across it in bold, thick-nib fountain-pen ink.

How subtle can you be, *mfowethu*?

Its contents informed me that a 'meeting' was to be held at a specified cafe-bar on the morrow, no time given, no street guide and no signature. *Please not to use a taxi, sport, much safer and less conspicuous if you take a slow stroll to get there.*

I had to beg the *concierge* for a street-map, but no go, there weren't any.

A suitable exchange emptying my pocket and filling his resulted in a fair proficiency – a well-signposted hand-drawn effort.

When I got there it was as dark as a nun's undergarments at midnight.

Nothing much was happening for the South American legal *shebeen*'s proprietor during the interminable hour and a half I waited for Poco to pitch up.

I think the proprietor's vast turnover during that time totalled three beers, but he exchanged greetings and flurried *sotto voce* short exchanges with at least two dozen swarthy individuals whose only purpose in life seemed to be to wander in, exchange a few incomprehensible words and wander out again.

Nobody gave me a second glance, conspicuous as I was – black with a white halo of an impossibly coloured hairdo.

Poco came in at long last, with a greasy, pop-eyed, roller-gait *geeza* in tow wearing a baggy yet somehow voluminously puffed out thermal-protective jacket better suited to hiking the high reaches of the Andes than to trolling the humid lower-altitude streets of sweltering Bogotá.

Poco said nothing, brushed past me without acknowledgement and headed directly for the Stygian atmosphere of the table furthest away from the entrance, right at the very back of the rathole establishment.

I could judge from the sweat-layered vibes that my heroic smuggler friend was close to farting up a nervous windstorm.

He would not look me in the eye, and if anything is guaranteed to make me equally nervous, it is this avoidance of visual *bonhomie*.

'Listen, sport,' he said urgently. 'There's something we need to discuss.'

'No discussion. You got the curios or not, Poco?'

'*Please!* Don't use my name!'

'You fucking crazy, Poco? Who the fuck's to hear us, mate?'

'This is *my* country! You don't understand how things work here!'

'Same as anyplace else. We doing a deal, or what?'

'I have the stuff for you, sport. My *amigo*, Vesper here, he has it all ready for you.'

'So let's get on with it. Then you can show Bubbles and me the sights, right?'

'It is going to cost more, sport, like I told you.'

'How much more?'

'The thousand I mentioned plus five.'

'Fuck. Fuck. Okay, I'll cover that. Let's get on with it.'

Greasy-haired frog-eyes, the owner of the dirty padded puffed-out jacket next to Poco, reaches down and produces *for fuckssake a fucking brown fucking paper bag* from under the mind-wrecking stale beer and vomit aroma of the table. Out of this, like a magician producing a white rabbit from a top hat, he boldly displays a kilo cellophane sack of very white powder. He pats the transparent plastic

191

package with affection and says, 'Yeah, yeah. Far out. Groovy. Yeah, yeah.'

Before I had time to touch the merchandise, he slipped the sack back inside the recycling-board-approved brown paper groceries container and *my merchandise* was once again hidden under the frightful pong of our unsavoury table.

'Yeah, yeah,' Vesper said again, a litany of *muchos-muchos* approval conveying that I'd seen all I needed to see. 'Far out. Groovy. Cool. Yeah, yeah.'

'It has been very dangerous, sport,' Poco added. 'You must understand the risks that I person – '

'Poco, you're the best,' I answered fast, cutting him off. 'Nobody else could have done it, I know.'

I silently wished I'd brought Big Bang along – they'd have given me the nose candy free just to get rid of him.

'So there is no problem with the extra five hundred, sport?'

'What problem?'

Wait until we got back to London – I'd make the spaniel-browneyes motherfucker pay in spades.

Poco looked like he didn't believe me. I reached over and gave his silk-draped shoulder a brotherly squeeze.

'Bubbles said I could trust you to come through. That Poco friend's a real trouper, she said, and that's the truth, *amigo*.'

'Bubbles said that?'

'*Dadawethu!* Would I lie to you? Ask her yourself. Bubbles gives praise where praise is due.'

Twenty minutes later I had reduced the price to the original one thousand quid increase.

'Let's have a butcher's at the goods,' I said. 'Bubbles warned me about buying blind.'

'You don't trust me, sport?'

'Come on, Poco, I *know* you, you're a straight ace. But *you* know how women are.'

'What do we do, sport? Vesper hates complications. Let's just get on with it.'

'Do they have toilets here?'

'Why, you want to piss, sport?'

'I want to try some powder. Same as Bubbles told me to. You want to tell her she's wrong?'

'You carrying the money, sport?'

'Taped to my ankles.' But it wasn't. It was wrapped around my waist where I had a fine eight-inch switchblade knife Riggsie had given me in parting, with the words *Don't corst nuffink ter be too careful, mate.*

This was the hard part.

The hole in the ground squat-style shitpit of a toilet was just big enough to accommodate the three of us at a wedged-in squeeze. The uprising gas of unflushed excrement was atrocious, beyond horrible. There was the additional luxury of a dirty permanently stained handbasin with a cracked mirror above it. My fly-specked reflection was not one to inspire confidence.

'Why don't we open it up, Poco?' I said. 'I want to sample top, middle and bottom.'

Vesper began backing away, his pop-eyes swollen like jaundiced yellow ping-pong balls. He turned his back on us briefly, but Poco had a hand on his jacket sleeve and stopped and turned him around again in one movement. Poco then took the bag away from him. The space was so confined any getaway flight was blocked by our bodies. Poco blistered his mate Vesper with a string of fireball foreign words and then handed me the bag.

The contents looked like the real McCoy, but trusting just my eyes, I could have purchased anything from powdered sugar to my own illusionist's Borax.

I tasted some from a wetted forefinger dipped into the cocaine and my gums and tongue turned to ice. For the first time I began to believe the gods were smiling on me again.

I took a hand mirror from my pocket and removed a scooped sample from midway down the bag. Next I slid a folded cut-throat razor from my pocket, took a fat pinch from the centre and chopped it into two small lines. I snorted them both with a rolled-up five-pound note the way Bubbles had demonstrated I should do with repetitive coaching – and the back of my brain exploded.

I thrust my head back, closed my eyes and let the locomotive rush of *pura-pura* cocaine charge down my rattling rails.

No need to dig down to the bottom – this stuff was so unadulterated pure you could cut it eight times and still have the customers lining up for more.

I handed the bag back to Poco.

'Let's go for it,' I said, my senses churning like the gigantic wheels of industry filmed in blurring fast-forward motion. Cocaine sang uninhibited wild songs in my ears and raced roaring around my bloodstream like hurtling greyhounds accelerating around a closed-circuit racetrack, *mfowethu*.

I felt good, ten feet tall.

The three of us went back to the table.

Nobody said much.

Poco bought three beers.

The sweat started rolling down the back of my neck and my shirt felt like it was made of glue. Without a word, I handed Poco the dosh. I took the brown paper bag from Vesper, who seemed to be sweating as much as I was for no apparent reason, and headed for the street. Poco followed me to the door, stopped there, flashed me a white ear-to-ear Zorro-triumphant grin, and waved farewell.

'Don't forget, sport,' he called out to my back. 'While you're here, we don't know each other.'

What had happened to my Poco-guided sightseeing tour? No time for that but, *mfowethu.*

'See you back in the Big Smoke,' I answered over my shoulder, the brown paper bag suddenly seeming to be illuminated by repeatedly flashing neon lighting calling every lawman in Bogotá to come over and request a routine spot-check inspection.

Then an incredible aroma hit my cocaine-savaged nostrils – the wafting warmth of baking bread floating on the air and pervading my senses with pleasure. Not hunger, I was way too whirlpool-wired for that, but my recognition circuits remembered the call of simple staple food delight that infiltrated my olfactory inlets.

Then I saw the bakery.

There was a queue of people lining up, spilling out of the entrance.

A sage *tsotsi*'s instinct for survival made me join them immediately.

What better place for a man with a large brown paper bag to be seen other than at a bakery? Half a dozen rolls and some local pastries on top of my kilo of cocaine – just the very thing to proclaim my empathic tourist's innocence.

More people formed up behind me as the queue snaked forward into the busy warmth of the shop itself. The place was very orderly and the customers patient. Two dark-haired girls in baker's hats at the glass counters were serving as fast as they could from the stacked metal trays of golden goodness fresh from the ovens.

A cocky *geeza* wearing huge mask-like spectacles and an absorbed look of total self-concern, browsing the displayed confections on one side of the shop, decides he wants to visit the other side. Instead of walking around the queue, or even perhaps pausing to say 'Excuse me' before plundering through the tight orderly rank, he *shoves* his conceited way with his shoulders between two frail middle-aged women like a barracuda cutting through minnows.

That angered me.

I can't tell you how much or why, just that it made my blood boil.

When he did it *again*, going back to his original speculation of glass counters displaying cakes decorated with icing to look like fragile palaces, I switched my bag from my right arm to my left and let fly with an excellent right jab that caught him flush on the nose. There was a most pleasing *pop!* sound as my knuckles connected and dislodged gristle and bright red blood sprayed out over his mouth and down his white-on-white embroidered shirt.

He just stood there, dumbfounded, hands hanging at his sides, eyes wide with accusation and staring twin beams of solid outrage at me.

'You can't *hit* me!' he suddenly screamed, making no other move, either to come at me or to back away.

'I just did,' I said. 'So what?'

'I will have you *arrested!*'

I suddenly realised he was talking English, *good* English. My brain buzzed and see-sawed with cocaine power – I'd just given a fellow tourist a slapping. But once again – *so what?*

The *so what?* was that *he* could call the law down on *me*.

Me, the high as a kite remodelled *mampara* I'd so bafflingly become and *that* meant – *what?* The – cocaine cat – would – be . . . *what?*

Let out of the fucking brown paper fucking bag!

'You were out of order, mate,' I said, still with no control over my righteous indignation. 'Manners cost nothing. But a lack of them does.'

Just then one of the women he'd jostled hit him with her handbag, a looping overhead blow, startling in its accuracy and finding his bloodied bullseye of a nose.

He staggered back, both hands to his face.

The crowd were murmuring appreciation and encouragement.

More women kicked his ankles and swung heavy-clasp, hefty leather handbags. He turned and fled out of the bakery.

I felt like a hero, even more so when they called me to the front of the queue, gave me what I pointed to and indicated that it was all *gratis*, on the house.

I found myself holding two brown paper bags, not one, *mfowethu*, and back out on the narrow street again.

At that time of day, apart from the bakery, the street wasn't overcrowded – it was almost empty in fact.

I walked along as casually as I was able, fast, but without making it obvious, my every nerve ending begging me to break into a run. I wanted the anonymity of a taxi. As I came around another sharp corner, I was grabbed by the elbow. A mouth jetting fumes of abrasive chillies sizzled something like a peppercorn barrage of incomprehensible words into my ear.

Mfowethu, I nearly voided my bowels – this was it! I'd been nabbed!

But it was only a street vendor, pushy bastard, hawking black-and-white monochrome postcards of unbelievably gross pornography, women with men, women with women, women doing it in both lower orifices with dogs and donkeys and Coca-Cola bottles.

I tried to push him away with my elbows, my hands full with my packages, but he wasn't taking no for an answer.

This was not the attention I needed.

Zero attention was what I needed.

I managed to fish out a crumpled note, dropped it on the ground and turned to make my getaway. In seconds he was behind me, pushing something into my jacket pocket and muttering his thanks, and then I was on my own again.

A taxi cruised by and I hailed it.

Inside it stank of burnt marijuana.

I felt for what was lining my jacket pocket.

The pornographic postcards.

There must have been at least ten of them.

While we were yet stationary, the engine rumble-idling, I gave the taxi driver the name of my hotel, wound down the passenger window and threw the lot fluttering into the gutter where they belonged.

Next thing, two armed Bogotá *amapolisi* wearing knife-edge creased uniforms are right there, appearing from nowhere – one standing in front of the taxi, traffic controller-style with his white-gloved hand held authoritatively up in the air, the other cop knocking on my passenger-side door imperiously inviting me to step outside.

Quick as a flash, I grabbed one of my breadrolls and stuffed it into my face before obeying him, my stomach dropping down to my knees as I stood up.

The South American popinjay policeman carefully picked up my discarded porn postcards, dusted them off, searched the image on each one and then cast his mirror-shaded dark glasses on me.

'You are aware thot thees feelthy theengs ees against the law?'

'They're not mine,' I said, my brown paper bags behind my back on the taxi's rear seat burning holes between my shoulder blades.

'Then why deed you 'ave them een your possession?'

'This is a misunderstanding,' I blustered. 'They were pushed into my pocket.'

'Thot ees what all feelthy perverts say.' He held them out to me.

'You can have them,' I said. 'They're all yours.'

'My partner ees weetness to the ownersheep being yours. You most come weeth os to be formally charged.'

It was a wide-awake nightmare, *mfowethu*.

There was no ways I could go with these two Bogotá bogeymen to some torture-chamber police station with my bags of cocaine and baker's delights; no ways I could leave them on the back seat either.

I reached for my wallet and pulled out a note.

Held it out to him with the note hidden by the leather folder itself.

'Surely these ees no an attempt to bribe me?'

I added another note with no attempt at disguising what I was doing.

'Your fine for possession of feelthy theengs illegally purchased weel be moch more thon soch a gesture.'

I trebled the offering.

He considered this for a long moment, then disdainfully made my large cash disappear.

It was painfully obvious that *he* was doing *me* a huge favour.

'Better thees way,' he said nonchalantly. 'No *problemo* weeth so moch paperwork, eh?' Then he turned his back on me and he and his partner headed off in search of fresh tourist prey.

I leaped back into the taxi, telling the driver to put pedal to the metal, thinking about how long I'd have wasted in jail if I'd been bust by bad luck. He must have been delivering me by the longest route he could dream up to increase his fare, because as we turned past yet another

199

featureless grey city block, I saw the two immaculately uniformed *amapolisi* chatting amicably with the street hustler who had pulled the move on me in the first place – *and then actually hand him back his filthy postcards.*

I swore long and loudly.

The taxi driver guffawed equally long and loudly.

'What you laughing at, mate?'

'The policemen, thos ones there, thees ees a game they like to play on toureests.'

'You call that a game?'

'People here are poor in ways you can never *comprendo*. You toureests, you 'ave moch money. Ees not so bod, eh?'

'They set me up.'

'Ah, *si*, thot they deed. Bot now you are a wiser man, eh?'

'Why didn't you tell me, say something?'

'Ees no my beeseeness.'

I fumed all the roundabout way back to Bubbles and the hotel. I could cheerfully have leaned forward, put my hands around his neck and strangled my taxi driver from behind by his philanthropic throat. But there was sturdy wire-mesh barrier separating us.

Time was getting short, but at the hotel Bubbles and I did what we had to do. Together we trussed up her nether parts like roast-bound chicken, then headed for the airport without further delay, any vague ideas of taking in the sights definitely gone forever with the capricious wind.

After all that fear-sweat and smuggle preparation, we strolled through Heathrow customs without a suitcase being opened, without even being asked if we had anything to declare. I could have been carrying the cocaine in candyfloss cone-wrappers openly in my hands. Nobody gave us a second glance. Bubbles was magnificent – you would have thought she was royalty returning to her adoring subjects.

When we got free of the hustle and bustle, who should I see but Poco Batista Salvador, lurking conspicuously well dressed amongst the airport crowd.

What was he doing there?

Whatever it was, I didn't want him privy to what I was going to do next, so I bundled Bubbles into a taxi, made sure he saw me, then commandeered and rode the next taxi I could find.

Bubbles was headed for her Knightsbridge flatlet.

I was headed for my restaurant, where my car was parked. Poco's taxi was behind me all the way.

Having disembarked at the restaurant and overpaying the taxi driver for added speed, I headed straight through to the kitchen without seeing Howard Postlethwaite and out the back door. My car was right there in the alleyway where I'd left it. It started first time and I was on my way, without Poco on my tail, to Bubbles' place.

On the way I stopped to get boxes of Borax from a convenient outlet.

Bubbles was in the bath when I let myself in.

She sang out to me that the goods were on the lounge coffee table, a big square affair with a solid glass top. Perfect. I opened up all the condom containers with a razor blade and poured the cocaine into a big mixing bowl. Then I poured out five boxes of unsullied Borax, a little more than two kilos in total.

I started by filling a man-sized beer mug a quarter to a third full of cocaine and topping it up with Borax. I mixed it as well as I could with a wooden kebab skewer. Then I sieved each mugful through my flour sifter, juggling it as much as possible so that the mixture would be passably intermingled. This I repeated three or four times just to be sure of an even spread.

Bubbles came naked out the bathroom while I was still labouring and poured us a drink while she watched in her birthday suit. She helped me pour our score into three large plastic bags, which we weighed and reweighed on the kitchen scales until we had three transparent packages of just over one kilo each.

The last thing I did was sprinkle pure cocaine specifically kept apart for that purpose into the top of each bag, and then I taped each one up into a solid compact square. Adding the pure cocaine was like 'salting' a gold mine. Any test taken from the top would show a high resolution, an undeniable concentration of the real thing.

I put all three packages into a fashionable shoulder-sling gymbag and I was ready to make my move.

Next stop Riggsie Leitch, *mfowethu*.

On the telephone Riggsie sounded like he was waiting to hear from yours truly.

We arranged to meet at his digs, a smallish penthouse-type hotel suite, not the best hotel, not the worst, but it had enviable-to-a-*tsotsi* access that could only be gained by leaving the lift behind and trudging up a narrow stairwell to double-barricaded steel entrance gates.

Bubbles had gone to her cubbyhole kitchen to mix us a last drink for luck when her doorbell rang.

Through the spyhole I saw it was Poco.

What was his game?

I opened the door at supersonic speed and dragged him inside before he could blink.

'What's going on, Poco?' I snarled, Riggsie Leitch's switchblade at his throat. 'You planning on a short life?'

'Just want to make sure your deal was sweet, sport,' he said, nodding his head fearfully at my dominance and looking terribly scared, the Poco I knew.

I let him go, snapped the blade closed and pocketed the

knife, then marched over to my gymbag.

Next thing I knew, a lethally ugly gun appeared in Poco's hand. He grinned his *Latino* filmstar's grin and said, 'I have to thank you for taking all the risks, sport, but playtime's at an end. Hand over the merchandise.'

He never saw a naked Bubbles come up behind him and whack him sideways in the head with one of those incredibly heavy, solid marble squares used for dicing meat or vegetables. Bubbles had swung it square-point just above his temple. Poco's head sort of split open and he collapsed like a rag doll, blood pumping out onto the carpet. Bubbles dropped the marble square on his face, smashing teeth, turning his lower lip to pulped liver, and spat down at his limp form like an enraged red-headed wildcat.

'I knew he was a wrongo, Shatterproof, I just *knew* it, sweetheart.'

I didn't answer.

I was down on my knees, feeling for the double-crosser's pulse.

There was none.

Bubbles had killed him.

He was stone-cold dead.

'Jesus Christ, Bubbles, we've got a corpse here.'

'He'll wake up just now. Better tie him up.'

'No need. Hear me, Bubbles, the motherfucker is *dead*.'

'You sure, sweetheart?'

'Oh yes, I'm sure.'

'Well then,' Bubbles said almost calmly, with detached feminine arachnid logic, 'we'd better make plans to get rid of the body, hadn't we, sweetheart?'

'I can't believe it,' I muttered.

'Me neither, dear thing. I didn't think I'd hit him *that* hard.'

'No, Bubbles.'

'What do you mean, no? The wrongo's dead isn't he?'

'I mean I can't believe that was his game all along,' I said patiently, getting to my feet. 'He was using *us* as *his* mules. Think he'd have done us in, Bubbles?'

'There's two years' good luxurious living by anybody's standards in your bag,' Bubbles said pensively. 'Two years to find another couple of twats like us, sweetheart, if there's nobody left alive to tell the tale.'

'Any ideas on making Poco disappear?'

'Yes. Get a hacksaw, a wood saw, a ten-pound hammer, lots of binliners and wide plastic packaging tape. Bring it all back with you after you've seen Riggsie, sweetheart. Too risky to take Poco out all in one piece, wouldn't you say?'

I couldn't argue with that.

I was up to my neck in death-penalty *Murder One* with her.

I downed half a bottle of scotch in one long pull, pulled myself together and headed for Riggsie Leitch. An earthquake was giving off seismic rumblings inside me, *mfowethu*.

In Riggsie's penthouse, things went far more rapidly than I expected.

When I spilled out the three kilo weight packages of cocaine, all he did was make a tiny opening, put a little into a glass vial, mix it thoroughly with water until it was dissolved and then taste it like a wine connoisseur.

Then he sealed the bag he'd opened with Scotch tape.

'That it, Riggsie, mate?'

'Wot yew fink, Shatterproof? Numbs me bleedin' tongue, no bovver orn moi side, innit? If yore merchandise ain't wot yew sais it is, oi'll know where ter find yer, mate. Yew ain't a worried geezer then, innit?'

He had a point.

But the way I had it judged, *if* Riggsie ever had a need to come looking for me, he was going to have to do an immense amount of travelling to make contact. He passed me over a rectangular black leather briefcase, first snapping open the catches.

'Orl there, mate. No need ter count it. Wot oi says oi'll do, oi does. Wotcher fink, oi'm a fahkin crook?' This was followed by chest-heaving cement-mixer laughter.

There it was.

Stacks and stacks of beautiful pounds sterling, the Queen's own currency, a multitude of multiplied money. I took it all out, wad by wrapped wad, and forced it into my gymbag. It was an awful lot of money, *mfowethu*.

'Orlroight, mate,' Riggsie rumbled. 'Don' spend orl orf that fahkin dosh orn fanny an' the tables. Save some fer yer old age. Yew'll need it then, innit?'

I was out Riggsie's double-barricaded doors and made my way down the steps to the lift, and it was as easy as that.

When I got back to Bubbles' flat, Poco was still lying exactly as I'd left him, only the blood from his head was congealing and *rigor mortis* was setting in. His stiffening limbs looked horrible, grotesque, like some nightmare window-dresser's posed store dummy carelessly discarded but still wearing a creased Pierre Cardin suit with a flashy silk scarf. Bubbles was smoking a thin, brown, wooden-tipped *cigarillo*, two lines of cocaine from the personal stash I'd given her as yet unsnorted on the glass-topped coffee table.

I upended the gymbag next to Poco's corpse, careful not to let the money touch him. All that beautiful green spending stuff dumped just like that on the carpeted floor.

Bubbles and I just looked at it and looked at it and looked at it.

Finally we packed it all into one of her suitcases, covered it with some of her lingerie and underwear, and pushed it under her bed. It was as safe there as anywhere else.

I'd remembered the saws and the crusher hammer and the rubbish binliners and the wide stick-to-anything plastic tape.

We undressed Poco together, carried his naked body to the bathroom, dumped him in the bath, got naked ourselves and began dismembering him bit by bit.

It was easier than I'd imagined it would be.

After the first hour, it ceased to be a human being we were slicing and dicing and became T-bones and chops and spare-ribs, just another butcher's task at the charnel house.

Dawn arrived by the time we'd finished and now all that remained of Poco was several slushy watertight parcels of soft bone-splintered meat.

We scrubbed the lounge carpet and scoured the bathroom.

By mid-morning all was spic and span, Poco wasn't yet beginning to pong.

For the next week we repeated the routine, and Poco went piece by piece from Bubbles' chest-freezer into the building's basement furnace when the caretaker wasn't there. Everything continued just as it had before, no hiccups whatsoever.

At the restaurant Howard plied me with some questions, but I gave him all the replies he wanted to hear and that satisfied his curiosity.

What he didn't know wouldn't hurt him, *mfowethu*.

One night only a few weeks later, Howard found me in the kitchen and told me Ronnie Kray was amongst our diners and that he wanted to see me. I went over to his table and sat down by invitation, completely unsure as to what was going to happen, what was wanted of me.

I looked directly into Ronnie Kray's face.

Then I realised something was wrong.

Ronnie Kray was sitting *next to Ronnie Kray*, there on the unfocused periphery of my vision, limited as it was by the stares of their disturbing double-vision. *But that could not be so.*

Oh Christ, then it hit me hard, *mfowethu.*

I was being called to book by both Kray twins.

What serious kind of shit had I got myself into? The twins' expressions did not suggest they were going to shower me with praise.

'Orlroight then, Shatterproof?' Ronnie said after a prolonged silence. *Or was that Reggie?*

'Great, Ronnie, great. Any problems I can sort out for you?'

'Yeah, that's kind orf why oi'm 'ere, Shatterproof. Wot kin yew tell me?'

I started to say something, my brain searching for a thousand answers, all of them rejected before I could mouth a single one.

Ronnie Kray held up his hand. It was covered in diamond rings.

'Fer a bright boy yew've bin actin' fahkin stupid, me old sahn. Dooyer know that? Steppin' roight in where yew 'ad no fahkin business ter be steppin' in loik some dumb fahkin jungle-bunny cahnt.'

This time I *had* to talk, and I judged I'd better do it quickstyle.

No chance, *mfowethu*.

'I didn't judge I was stepping on your toes, Mr Kray, I swear, I – ' and that was as far as I got.

Ronnie Kray repeated by Reggie Kray looked at me the way you turn the sole of your shoe upwards to examine it after you've trodden in a particularly offensive dog-turd.

'Its not moi fahkin toes yore steppin' orn, ya fahkin Einstein golliwog. Wot do oi care yew make yersell a pigeon's piss fahkin nest egg, roight? But yer fahkin wif the system, Shatterproof, yew unnerstan' that? Now, me old sahn, tell me 'ow many toimes didjer cut the fahkin stuff?'

My face was blank. My repertoire of response was blank. Therefore my mind was blank. With my platinum-blond hair I must have looked like a darkie goldfish spilled out of its bowl and frantically gulping useless air.

'Nevvah moind,' Ronnie or Reggie Kray said. 'It makes no fahkin difference, unnerstan'? Now oi'm gonner tell ya just 'ow you got fahked like a wide-open blind cahnt, blond niggerboy. An' oi'm gonner tell yew precisely wot yer gonna fahkin do abaht it, orlroight?'

By this time I was a series of nodding affirmations, not a squirt of individual essence in my foreigner South African soul.

'In the firs' fahkin place,' Ronnie, I'm sure it was Ronnie, continued, 'yew pick up the fahkin consignment in Bogotá. So far, so good, me old sahn? But yew don' fahkin know oo yore dealin' wif or pickin' it up from, right? Yew gotter be outer yer fahkin moind, Sambo Shatterproof, 'cause that fahkin stuff orn offer ter tourists is cut by some wide cahnt maybe two three toimes orlreddy. Yew fink them Souf Hamerican cahnts're gonna give yew the pure harticle if it suits the fahkin cahnts ter rip yew orf?

Oi'll say it again, yew mus' be outer yore fahkin moind. So yew geddit back 'ere, bright fahkin cahnt that yew are, an' 'ow many toimes dooyer cut the fahkin consignment? Free toimes is moi bet, roight? Oi fought so, now stay 'onest wif me, orlroight? Ven yew give it ter Riggsie. Riggsie's a good mucker, but 'e's bin brought up the 'ard way, so 'e orlso sees hopportunity knockin', innit? Riggsie cuts it anuvver two toimes, nuffink 'eavy from 'is point orf view. By the toim the nose candy gets back ter moi distributors, it'd maybe give me old granmuvvah a bit orf an 'igh, yew wif me? Oi can't 'ave that, or oi'll go fahkin bankrupt, innit?'

'Mr Kray, Mr Kray,' I almost begged. 'I *know* that stuff was ninety-plus pure!'

'Wot yew knows an' wot oi knows, is two differen' fahkin fings, orlroight?'

'Right, Mr Kray.'

'Only fing yer did roight by me is getting' rid orf a nuisance wideboy fahkin cahnt, way oi 'ear it.'

'I beg your pardon, Mr Kray? What'd I do?'

'Yew orfed a cahnt oi've 'ad me mince pies orn fer ages, Shatterproof.'

'No, you've got it wrong, Mr Kra – '

'Shuddup, arse'ole. Me source is himpeccable. Now lissen ter me, yer deaf as a fahkin doorpost nitwit cahnt, them Bogotá bog'ouses pulled a fahkin wide switch orn yer. Yew came 'ome minus sevenny per cent orf wot yew thort yew'd bought. No fahkin arguments, darkie desperado, that was yore fahkin lot, me old sahn. Me an' moi bruvver 'ere, we 'ad ter lay orf that pigswill-powder quarter proice down Birming'am an' uvver fahkin teenage dance clubs, innit? No easy fahkin task, oi can tell yer. 'Ow do oi know wot 'appened ter yer if that ain't the troof? They done the double switcheroo orn yer, me old sahn.'

'Impossible!' I blurted. 'My female test-kit had some

back on English shores. Says she's never had better! The best, the *best*, Mr Kray!'

'So yew did orf that Souf Hamerican vampire cahnt. Knew moi source was himpeccable.'

Then it hit me.

How many life-stealing games were being played by how many criminal money-ghouls?

''Ow it works is loik this, me old sahn. Yew gave me a fahkin fahk. Oi've forgiven ya 'cause ya did me a big favour wif that Dracula-bandito, may 'is soul rot in 'ell. Bygones is bygones, innit? Oi tole me connexshuns they'd get their dosh back an' they're gonna geddit back. From yew, innit? Oi want them wankahs ter stay 'appy.'

His pause was like the roof of heaven had fallen, shattering the earth I walked upon.

'Yew, Shatterproof, yore gonna give me back orl orf that dosh, geddit? Orl orf that dosh yew got from Riggsie. Riggsie don' know yew fahked 'im up the arse'ole. Not *yet*, me old sahn. So, ter save yer fahkin black 'ide, yew gonner give me back orl orf that dosh, geddit? Dooyer? Knew yew'd see sense wif the business brains an' orl loik yew an' 'Owie Postlethwaite the cripple got, innit?'

'Howie's not crippled, Mr Kra – '

'Now yore catchin' orn, me old sahn. If oi don' get every fahkin penny yew got stashed wif yore 'ungry fanny, oi can't promise the star orf me good 'umour'll remain hascendant, loik them fortune-tellin' wankahs gives out. Orl oi kin do, is hassure yew, if me dosh don' come back, every fahkin penny orf it moight oi remind yer, oi'm goin' ter personally oversee 'Owie's legs absenteeism below 'is fahkin knees, geddit?'

Something twinged away in the back of my mind about Boy Faraday.

Same hyena bone-ingestor.

Different name, different country, but down-home, *same hydrophobic mad-dog difference.*

Ronnie Kray nudged his twin brother.

Reggie, in a very high-pitched silken voice, said:

'Oi *personally* will furver see yew nevvah need dosh again, yew got that, fugbrain?'

I didn't acknowledge him with eye contact.

To be honest, I didn't dare.

Not then. Not now.

Not ever. Perhaps that says it better, *mfowethu.*

No ways was I standing up to what is best described as a human embodiment of a vindictive natural disaster.

Bubbles wasn't there when I let myself into her fashionable-address flatlet.

I retrieved the suitcase from under her bed, carried it into the lounge, opened it, bundled the flimsy underthings to one side and sat down to take one last long greedy look at the wealth I was saying goodbye to.

For the life of me, I could not judge what had happened, what had gone wrong or where it had gone wrong.

I replayed every scene in my mind frame by frame – London – Bogotá – London. Perhaps when we had been in those atrocious back toilets in that dingy bar in Bogotá, when I'd closed my eyes with cocaine ecstacy, had Vesper somehow switched the pure powder for a watered-down version similar to the original? *But that didn't make sense.* Bubbles had snorted plenty thereafter, and according to her, it was the best, purest, high-potency rush she'd ever had. Besides that fact, if it *was* bullshit *bulongwe* crap cocaine, why had Poco come after it like a ravenous man-eating bloodhound on the trail of what *he must have known was the real thing?* Could it be *Riggsie who had done the dirty on me?*

Whatever the truth was, what I had to face was that I was the one who was being royally fucked over from whichever angle you viewed my unenviable *tsotsi* peasant's arse-in-the-air situation.

There was not a thing I could do about it, *mfowethu.*

Any independent move at this stage would guarantee a manhunt, and a black *tsotsi geeza* with platinum-blond hair like me didn't have a lot of camouflage going for him in England's savannah-less jungle.

To be honest, I judged the Krays would *lose* money to make sure I got what they would see as my just desserts if I scarpered with the dosh.

Even back in South Africa?

Yes.

If I ballsed up The General's link through Howard Postlethwaite and all that regular-funding funnelling through contract-channels back to the ANC's anti-*apartheid* coffers, I was a dead man.

Hawu, mfowethu!

What the Krays might do to me paled beside what the ANC heavies *would* do to me when they caught me. No place to hide from those dedicated warriors. *When* they caught me was as sure as sunrise. I sighed the biggest sigh of my life and accepted my fate.

I was a loser.

I had tried to play out of my league.

It was as simple as that.

Right or wrong didn't come into it.

I left the megabucks suitcase with Howard at our restaurant.

Now, almost directly after having forfeited all that cash, a peculiar awareness seeped into me, one that I knew wasn't paranoia. No matter that the Krays had promised *'Bygones is bygones, innit?'* – I was still an uppity, thieving jungle-bunny *tsotsi* who had dared flaunt disrespect in their savage faces. My days of working side by side with Howard Postlethwaite in the public eye were over. Sooner or later, Ronnie or Reggie would decide an 'example' had to be made of me, and all either twin had to do was lift an eyebrow and I'd be food for the fishes at the bottom of the broad, faceless River Thames.

Within twenty-four hours, I had dyed my hair back to black, had dreadlock Rastafarian extensions expertly fitted to my skullcap of tight curls, bought myself billowing, loose, hip-hop casual garments, sold my luxury car for cash, and invested in a Lambretta scooter with a huge super-dark bolted-on windscreen and custom side-saddlebags – as well as a full-face mirror-fronted crash helmet. My disguise was so effective I didn't even recognise myself in reflective images from glass-fronted shop windows, as I made like a two-wheeled mod fashion-plate.

I was going to miss Bubbles.

I was going to miss my tailor-made suits.

Survival was survival.

I moved in once again with Big Bang Bongani.

What choice did I have, *mfowethu*?

Pregnant Possibilities

For nearly two months, I stayed mainly indoors at Big Bang's digs.

I practised my culinary skills, read a lot and watched a lot of TV, while my mind never stopped churning, turning over every stone in a search to find that elusive little flash of brilliance that would guide me to finding my own riches, to get me a suitable stake to begin making my dreams a reality.

Big Bang was out working at Browns most of the time, but whenever he was home, he always brought a woman back with him.

We'd exchange vague pleasantries, then off the two of them would go to his bedroom and I'd have to turn up the hi-fi or the TV to baffle the shrieks and moans of female sexual pleasure while Big Bang vigorously exercised his *umthondo*.

A lot of his women used to smoke *ganja* or 'blow', as most of them called *insangu*, which raised the level of their penetrated appreciation for Big Bang's tireless stud-bull coupling to an unprecedented high.

How that oversize *geeza* could *phatha-phatha*, *mfowethu*!

214

He was a tireless tumescent male miracle!

A non-stop pumping black piston!

One of his regulars was Samantha, a white university student with skin the colour of alabaster, violet eyes and long, depthless-sheen, dark brown hair which fell almost to her waist. She was drop-dead gorgeous in anybody's estimation and on top of that she looked as innocently virginal as those religious pictures of the mother of Jesus. You know what I mean, butter wouldn't melt in her mouth.

During one of her privileged visitor's nights, or should I say basically extremely early mornings, she asked me if I had any blow to spare?

'Don't really use it much, Samantha,' I said, shrugging.

'Why don't you and Big Bang get some of that great Durban Poisons gear over here? I'd be your first customer and all my girlfriends'd be lining up next in the queue.'

'It's an idea, maybe. But big risk for small profit, not my game.'

'We're all paying thirty pounds a one-ounce bank bag. Forty easy for the really good stuff.'

'I'm not into street dealing, Samantha. Did that when I was a kid, no percentage in it.'

'Hey, *bra*, maybe she got a point,' Big Bang interjected, animation finding his face like an aimed spotlight.

'*Ayikhona*, Big Bang, *bra*. You want to go out there battling for territory?'

'No problem,' Big Bang laughed, an elephant sneering at the prospect of a muscle-bound mouse. 'Serious though, *bra*, I got Jamaican connections. Those brothers'll take anything we can bring in wholesale anytime. The more we give 'em, the more they can lay off. Sweet, but they want buy it by the sackload when their own source go time to time dry.'

'You got a *serious* connection?'

'Me an' the Rastas, *bra*, we tight like I told you.'

'Cash up front by weight?'

'The way it works, *bra*. No *mlungu* gangsters invading their turf. Them Jamaicans is tough *tsotsis*, don't take no shit from nobody. Tell whitey go fuck himself.'

'*Hawu!* Big Bang, *bra*, I think I been a blind man *mampara*. Been staring us in the face, man.'

'Anybody can get it in safe, that be you, Dhlamini, *bra*.'

'A phone call get your sister to score for us?'

'Sharp, Dhlamini. Sweet Cherry her own Jo'burg township *shebeen* queen now, *bra*. Don't even have to go Durban-side. She get it brought up for us. Sweet like a lemon.'

'Let me think, Big Bang. Go on, you two, leave me alone and have a good time. I need headspace. I got a little leftover coke, Samantha. That do you?'

'Fucking hell. You mean it? You got ching?'

'Sure I got ching. Not a lot, some just stuck to my fingers a while back.'

'Jeez, thanks, Dhlamini. Any favours I can do you, just ask, huh?'

I gave Samantha half a gram. You would have thought it was a pound of gold. Big Bang was like me – after a youthful ingesting of anything from *skokiaan* to *malpitte*, he didn't use much of anything besides guzzling beer, which he absorbed like a behemoth sponge.

The penny had dropped, *mfowethu*.

Big money was in the offing.

Not as big as cocaine maybe, but with industry and a steady work ethic, it would add up to *bankable* thousands and thousands after living and operating expenses. Forty pounds sterling per tiny plastic bank bag? At five quid to me for the same weight, a sackful of South African dream weed would be worth monstrous money easy, and nothing compressed into manageable shape like *insangu* if you knew how to go about it.

But weeks passed and *the idea* just wouldn't come to me.

Hundreds of plans came to me of course, but every time I put them under my inner microscope's scrutiny, I found flaws, nasty cracks in the masonry of what my mind built. And flaws got you sent to jail.

I took a long stroll through Hyde Park.

I wandered amongst the swimming ducks and swans, watched kids playing, listened to madmen gesticulating and yelling their lungs out, poised atop soapboxes like vultures laying barbed-wire eggs. Mothers with prams all seemed to bunch protectively together – some of them were pregnant with bellies so swollen it looked like they were sometime soon going to give birth to an adult . . .

. . . huge bellies . . .

. . . huge storage space . . .

. . . the sacrosanct womb of untouchable motherhood, fragile new life . . .

. . . never to be tampered with under any circumstances . . . the holiest of awe-inspiring temples . . .

I had found my *tsotsi* smuggler's masterpiece.

Simple as that.

A false stomach bloated not with life, but with compacted *insangu* pressed into the right shape and sealed with glue-edged cling film so sharp-nosed customs canines couldn't smell a thing – and lastly an overcover of inch-thick rubber foam, just to give that feel of taut human flesh should any explorative fingers presume to dare make a cursory outer inspection.

Oh yes, *mfowethu*!

Oh *yebo* yes!

The game was on!

Big Bang was impressed. So he should have been. Even I was impressed with myself.

One small problem.

Neither of us could pretend to be pregnant.

We needed a female accomplice.

Samantha said *yes* straightaway without hesitation. Added it was a bit of a fucking lark, wasn't it, and she'd always wanted to see 'Affricarrh' anyway.

I won't bore you with the details of slipping into South Africa and out again.

My single niggling worry was that some observant customs snoop might notice Samantha going in with her beauty queen's sylph-like figure and exiting nearly seven, eight months pregnant after only ten days.

Post-morteming that first successful trip, I made Samantha a false belly to go *in* with that matched *exactly* her cumbersome shape when fragilely leaving.

Once the Jamaicans had received and paid for our first load, there was a standing order for as much as we could bring in and supply them with. '*Bes' dope Jah make inna whol' worl', mon,*' was the unanimous stamp of approval upon what we back home took for granted.

There were only so many times we could use Samantha. Sooner or later somebody would start wondering how one female could stay poised-to-give-birth pregnant for so long.

So we made Samantha our 'recruitment agency'. Nobody but her got to see our faces or know who Big Bang and I were, a perfect set-up. Each courier was paid five hundred pounds a trip, a lot of money in those days, and used a maximum of twice.

There was no shortage of willing employees, confidence was at an all-time high and it was going to go on forever . . . forever . . . forever . . .

This marvellous state of affairs continued for a lovely period of lovely years, a lovely steady accumulation of lovely incremental dosh.

Then we had our first bust.

The girl's fault.

She got pissed out of her mind, fell all the way back down the boarding ramp and ended up unconscious on Jan Smuts Airport's tarmac, legs sprawled apart and her camouflage maternity dress hiked up under her breasts. Her 'stomach' had slipped to the side from her fall and the bone-jarring impact, but even so, she was a trouper and nearly pulled it off.

As she came to, she had the presence of mind to cover herself immediately and start wailing, '*My baby! My baby! Please God nothing's happened to my baby!*' She was helped to her feet, assisted back up the ramp by solicitous stewardesses and seated.

But the British Airways bosses or management at Jan Smuts didn't want any comebacks which could lay a sue-for-damages claim at their doorstep, so they sent in their own doctor to examine her before the plane took off.

Curtains, *mfowethu*.

Just plain old bad luck.

The South African Police wanted nothing to do with her. She was deported to the UK after making a statement incriminating imaginary drug-dealers. Big Bang and me were right out of the picture.

But the English rozzers weren't nearly so affable.

They wanted blood and guts and they worked her, scared her shitless, until they got what they wanted. She grassed a description of Samantha, where she hung out, where they could find her.

Still, they had nothing on Samantha, and she proved too wise for them. Interrogation and threats got them precisely nowhere – they had to release her. Big Bang and I were subsequently warned by Samantha of the situation, and we stayed cool, calm and collected, model 'goodfellas', one employed, one unemployed.

Only problem was the *amapolisi* got hold of Samantha's savings account number and next the revenue police were after her to explain how and where she'd come across the vast sum of money (for a subsidised university student) deposited regularly in cash in her name, *by none other than herself*, over the last few short years?

Samantha said she'd won it over in Monte Carlo, but they had their methods of checking the veracity of such a claim. Before long, her account was frozen and Samantha had a charge of defrauding the state lined up against her.

I judged it was only a matter of time before Big Bang and me were up in the dock with her.

We had accumulated good dosh, not as much as we'd have liked, but enough to make a careful fresh start.

The Pregnancy Scam was over – it could never be used again, more's the pity. We must have caused untold pregnant women an embarrassing body search in the years ahead, but that wasn't any of our concern.

It was time to go back home with our ill-gotten gains.

Time to go back to South Africa.

And that's what we two *tsotsis* did.

Home Sweet Home

The first thing that happened to me back in Jo'burg was to get arrested.

A stupid thing.

Sweet Cherry was housing her brother and me. I agreed to fetch a consignment of illegal liquor for her, got drunk, got stopped at a roadblock and got thrown in jail.

There wasn't anything to do in that dirty place but think. I judge I did plenty of that, a surfeit of useless thinking.

What had happened to me?

Where was I going?

Would I ever get anywhere?

A time comes in a *geeza*'s life when he always has choice. A chance to get ahead or get left behind. Yes or No. Backwards or Forwards. The difficulty lies only in making the right move.

Then there I was, in a stifling courtroom, up before the *moegoe magistraat* and feeling about as low as you can get, *mfowethu*.

I can still hear that sanctimonious Afrikaans voice saying, '*Ses duisend rand of ses maande in die tronk, meneer Bhekuzulu. Die keuse is joune.*'

Choice. Choice. Choice.

This time an easy one – *Six thousand rand or six months in jail, Mister Bhekuzulu. The choice is yours.* I let my spare change answer for me.

The white *amapolisi* took my fingerprints with unnecessary harshness, pushed me around like a no-account darkie *skebberesh*, and made me sign for the return of my miserable possessions taken from me after they snapped the handcuffs on and threw me in the back of a police van.

Outside in the blisteringly hot sun, my jacket smelling foul even to me and my shirt sticking sweatily to my back, I heard the sound of a familiar voice coming from the radio turned up loud in a nearby Greek café.

Unbelievable.

It was Bubbles Nightingale's singing style, an infectious pop song way up on the hit parade, but with a very un-English and very unusual *mbaqanga* backing, obviously pirated from the vinyl long-playing records I'd lent her years ago.

Good for you, Bubbles, I thought, immediately cheering up.

Cast your mind back, but no, I guess you can't, can you, *mfowethu*? You're not old enough, I should have known. Still, many people will recall that phenomenally popular song that made its mark around the world. Think hard enough and maybe it'll come to you. Only don't look for Bubbles Nightingale as the female vocalist's name, know what I mean?

The liquor laws forbidding we blacks access to strong alcohol had been relaxed, another source of good *tsotsi* revenue shot to hell. I stopped at a bottle store, entered the Non-Whites section and bought a litre of Oudemeester brandy and two litres of Coca-Cola. I found a Non-Whites boarding house and paid for a cubbyhole of a room.

I opened my brandy, sat down on the sagging steel cot

that passed for a bed, and gazed out the tiny but spotlessly clean little window at absolutely nothing.

How had I missed out?

What should I have done differently?

I laid out my whole life, year by year, and still couldn't judge what had been happening to me.

It was dark by the time the brandy bottle was empty.

I opened the tiny window.

A rustling evening breeze came rushing through and it felt marvellously cool and fresh on my skin.

I knew suddenly what I had to do to get my life on an even keel again. It came to me as a blinding revelation that manifested itself even through the haze of alcohol I'd steeped myself in.

I had to get back to Zsa-Zsa and my son.

That was all I had that seemed to make any kind of sense.

And not forgetting –

She had well over half a million.

Half a million plus of *my amarands.*

Sitting in *her* bank.

I crept into that pavement-hard steel cot.

Then I had the best night's sleep I could remember having had for a very long time.

Next on my agenda was to ask Big Bang to find Zsa-Zsa for me.

Big Bang was a hard *geeza* to say *I don't know* to, trust me.

What the mammoth-man lacked in the sleuth department, he'd make up for in the positive-results sector.

Of that I was certain.

While Big Bang was away on his errand, I spent most of the time imagining what I would tell Zsa-Zsa, how I would get her back again and what I would feel for our toddler son.

Choice, Choice, Choice

I dreamed of a multitude of scenarios.

But I knew only one would get through to Zsa-Zsa.

That I was going legitimate for good.

For the first time in my existence, I really applied myself to conjuring up how I could earn a living in the straight and narrow Honest Joe world. What was a *skebengu tsotsi geeza* like me to do?

Amazing – when I thought about it – there were a surprising number of things I could actually turn my hand to.

I could run a *gourmet cuisine* restaurant or one of those standard fare 'Pub & Grub' taverns with my acquired expertise – but where would I get the opportunity to do that in White South Africa? Where my customers would be segregated? Where offering the best meant less than nothing because of *apartheid*?

Equally, I could efficiently run a liquor store, but that occupation was precluded by law, *mfowethu*.

I knew how to dispatch and run a fleet of trucks, but those managerial positions were exclusively reserved for '*die Wit Baas*'.

I could probably sell almost anything as a sales rep,

but any approach made to white-owned business concerns would place me in the *kaffir-who-thinks-he's-too-white* category, so that was another dead end.

Perhaps some sort of overseer's job with the big breweries or local alcohol manufacturers? No ways – the only job they'd give me would be driving a delivery truck for peanuts.

People made good *amarands* doing the things I could do equally well, but in this country it was like some select Get-Your-Name-Down-At-Birth Country Club, Members Only, No Darkies Allowed.

The trick was to have a white skin, not the kind of skin I had.

Then I thought why not open a little *bon vivant* restaurant just outside South African borders, a place like Mbabane in Swaziland? No colour bar and only a short ride away from Jo'burg. Not too big and not too small. Just *haut monde* posh enough to attract serious diners and with an ambience I'd learned to create over in London. If I could get my hands on some of those remaining *amarands* of mine that Zsa-Zsa had, combined with what I'd brought back from London, I could pull it off, I knew I could. With a busy restaurant as my home-base and camouflage cover, there was nothing I couldn't do, no new heights I couldn't strive for and attain.

And then the truth sank in.

I knew in my bones it wasn't any good, would never be any good.

Yebo, I could likely get the *amarands* from Zsa-Zsa. I could probably even fantasise some gossamer illusion into making her believe I was a nine-to-five goodguy. But I couldn't bullshit Dhlamini Shatterproof Bhekuzulu. He was the *tsotsi geeza* who knew how the cards were stacked. All the while I'd been working my mind on running a classy eatery, the back of my devious brainbox was busy judging overtime how I could use the restaurant as a front for at least five other ways to make easy illegal bucks.

That's just the way I was.

Nothing was going to make me any different.

It took a lot of complacent hypocrisy to manipulate my inner iniquity. But once I had it lodged in my mind that *that* difference ingrained in me wasn't such a terribly, *terribly* bad thing, *mfowethu*, I decided yet again that I had a right to what was left of those freedom-buying *amarands* now controlled by Zsa-Zsa. I was the one who had sweated and risked his life for it. So what if Zsa-Zsa couldn't accept me *and* my way of life? I would handle that hurdle when the time came.

I knew whatever story I gave her about the last few years of my absence would have to skirt extremely warily around murder and women, and especially drugs – despite the glaring fact that it was supremely naive to expect drugs to be exempt from the laws of modern consumer capitalism – especially when, as a product, they best helped define it.

I would have to prepare an impeccable tall tale to fool Zsa-Zsa, to make it stick. It was, for me, like dreaming up the false pregnant belly packed with *insangu* all over again. The idea hadn't come to me yet, but I was sure, positive in fact, that it would.

It always did.

No use worrying about it, *mfowethu*.

Big Bang returned in a remarkably short time.

Only a few days had passed.

Zsa-Zsa was living *right here*, up in Jo'burg; she had a house in a new upper-echelon development in Meadowlands.

The address was on a slip of paper Big Bang handed me.

'So now I'm going to lose you, *bra*?' he said, all downcast and totally unlike him.

'Big Bang, when Vilakazi died, you became my *bhuti*. You family now, big man. I never turn my back on you, my brother – they got to make me a corpse first.'

'Yeah?'

'Yeah, *yebo*, yes, yes, yes. Don't you forget now, *bra*?'

'I never leave you, Dhlamini, *bra*.'

'You never going to have to, *bhuti*. So relax. You going to come with me while I get myself some good Jewish?'

'Long's I can criticise your bad taste in shit suits, *bra*.'

That was more like *my* Big Bang Bongani.

First stop was Hillbrow – home of the best sartorial shops – with the best service – didn't matter there whether you were black or white – your money carried no stigma.

Come afternoon, I was fixed up with two new off-the-peg imported tailor-adjusted *mnca* suits, plus shoes, socks, ties, shirts – the works.

Big Bang drove me over to Zsa-Zsa's and I just sat there in his monster automobile for a long while – elastic, sticky, nauseating time – while I tried to raise the gumption to open the car door, walk over and knock on her front door. I was as jumpy as a paws-blistering cat on a red-hot tin roof. My hands were sweating so badly that I had to keep wiping them harshly again and again on my new silk handkerchiefs, utterly ruining two of them beyond the realms of redemption. At the rate I was going, I judged my boy'd be grown up by the time I moved my backside's fossilised *ezzies*. I forced myself to get out of the car, a massive exertion of willpower.

Some kids, local *abantwana*, were playing down the road; couples strolled along arm in arm. The same township aromas, the same familiar and nostalgic sounds from my childhood. There was a new chauffeur-driven and ostentatiously gleaming Cadillac parked nearby, but I paid neither it nor the immobile driver a fraction of attention.

All of a sudden, a rushing need descended like a tropical cloudburst, drenching me from head to toe with urgency – I *had* to see her.

Then there I was, knocking on her front door, watching myself as if divorced from my own body.

I could hear voices inside.

The demanding, earth-pawing, snorting bull in me wanted to charge forward and smash my way through.

But then the door opened.

A man stood there in gracefully flowing Zionist robes. Taller than average, he was corpulent and heavy-jowled, but still the essence of ecclesiastical dignity.

The first thing that entered my mind like a bullet of high-explosive adrenalin was that *something was wrong with Zsa-Zsa or our child.*

I almost knocked down one of the most powerful men in the country with my brusque impatience to get inside. That man was Edward Lekhanyane, famed leader of the equally famed separatist Zion Christian Church, formed back in the late fifties and continuing to grow juggernaut-fashion, attracting *millions* of doting adherents. Edward Lekhanyane was their Black Messiah, a miraculous Prophet for the people of Zion, the personification on this earth of the spiritual link between themselves and their God. He had psychic powers unrivalled by ordinary men – the gift of healing by way of his Holy Stick of Office, healing with his Blessed Hands, healing with Water made

Holy and healing with Spoken Prayer.

But now, I was in a fair-sized lounge, with afternoon sunlight streaming in through the windows.

Zsa-Zsa was standing in the middle of the golden rays. You could see tiny dust motes floating around her like magical dancing sprites all performing an elaborate adoration.

'Reverend Bishop Edward, *Baba* Lekhanyane, this is my husband, Dhlamini Bhekuzulu,' my wife said, introducing us simply and without preamble.

I shook hands formally with the Black Messiah and then we were all solemnly squatted down like it was the most natural and ordinary thing in the world to do.

Zsa-Zsa had slimmed down a lot. No, more than a lot – she could have held her own now against all those beautiful sexy English girls I'd known. As usual she was wonderfully dressed, nothing fancy, but she was elegant and poised in an uncommon outfit made from common African cotton-print.

I was eating her with my eyes, but also telling her and him what a killing I'd made in the eatery business back in London.

They sat there taking it all in.

Reverend Bishop Lekhanyane murmured encouragement now and again whenever I paused for breath, but Zsa-Zsa said nothing, just quietly looked at me with unblinking big eyes. I told them how I had hungered for home, rabbited on about how I'd sold my shares for an excellent profit and had come back to South Africa to see Zsa-Zsa and my – my – my – *right there I became tongue-tied*.

I didn't even know my own son's name.

Zsa-Zsa smiled mysteriously, knowingly.

'Vilakazi will be back very soon, Dhlamini,' she said softly. 'He's out playing. The older twins next door are looking after him. Yes, I named him after your deceased brother. To bring honour to him in place of murder, and to us and to our son.'

Vilakazi!

My son named after my brother!

Vilakazi!

Vilakazi!

Vilakazi!

I vaguely recall standing, shaking Reverend Bishop Lekhanyane's hand again when he excused himself and left, and then I was on my haunches once more facing Zsa-Zsa across the tea-service-covered casual table that separated us. She had had light silver blond streaks professionally bleached into her relaxed hair which made her look more sophisticated, but also somehow gentler and softer. Her eyes were so big and deep and dark that I couldn't look away. Those eyes told me Zsa-Zsa was aware of all there was to know about me. In returning that gaze of equanimity, I knew right there and then that Zsa-Zsa and my son were all I wanted in the world. But my heart did the dying death-lurch and thumped zombie-style way out of extant time, *mfowethu*, because I knew I wasn't going to get her.

Eish! Dadawethu! What was the use? The odds on my suitor's likelihood of success were a foregone conclusion of failure.

A sentient snowball condemned to the furious fires of hell had a better chance than me.

I got up and she stood facing me.

'I know you've seen through my *bulongwe* concoctions,' I said. 'My life in London wasn't quite as grand as I made it out to be. I made some money, bankable money, but you don't want to know how. Before I *shiya* forever out your front door, I want you to know that if you judge we could make it back together again, I'll make it up to you. *Dadawethu!* I swear it!'

Zsa-Zsa moved slowly towards me.

I wanted to wrap my arms around her but something delayed me.

She abruptly put her hands up to her face and I could hear her sudden chest-heaving sobs, *improper* sobs which she quickly brought under control.

'How can I believe you, Dhlamini?' she said, knuckling embarrassed tears away.

Just then the front door unlatched.

Two giggling seven-year-olds in pigtails urged a small boy inside.

I was looking down at a miniature replica of myself.

My knees went weak and my legs turned to overcooked spaghetti. I collapsed back down in an armchair with a jarring thud.

Zsa-Zsa gently took Vilakazi's small hand and led the wide-eyed boy over to me.

'Vilakazi, this is your father.'

He touched my knee with his free hand. Then he pulled away from Zsa-Zsa. Next thing he was in my lap. I hugged him tightly but carefully, experiencing feelings I've not had before or since. I could see Zsa-Zsa's searching eyes over Vilakazi's shoulder . . . watching us, watching us, watching us.

I knew from the look on her face that I was home.

Honeymooned And Hobbled

For the next few ecstatic months, I judge there was never a more blissful *geeza* than me, *mfowethu*.

Zsa-Zsa, Vilakazi and yours truly had a lot of lost time to make up for, a lot of things to do together. All three of us.

We started out sightseeing.

I borrowed Big Bang's same blood-red Ford Galaxie with the flagrantly white sidewall tyres – he'd never got rid of it – and we toured the country: the Kango Caves in Oudtshoorn, Table Mountain via the perilously swaying cableway car, the Kruger National Park, the big aquarium in Port Elizabeth, the Knysna Forest, the Drakensberg Mountains, Shaka's Rock – you name it.

I learned something new about my family each and every day.

The greatest knowledge was that I realised for the first time in my life, *I had something that truly belonged to me*. But for ages the insidious suspicion haunted me that I was only on probation – that it couldn't last because I was cursed to never measure up.

Then one balmy evening Zsa-Zsa came to me where I was lying on the floor wearing only a pair of shorts and reading, believe it or not, a book titled *Famous French*

Cooking Techniques. She handed me one of those oversize chequebooks that the banks dole out to preferred bigger businesses. I raised my eyebrows.

'The bank requires both your signature and mine so that you can make payments with our money.'

Up until then we had been sharing expenses, not worrying about who paid for what. I was having such a ferociously good time I had for sure contracted some virulent form of pure tunnel-vision pleasure-disease.

I was, in effect, being served notice that it was time to get up off my *ezzies* and put the grey matter to work again. An iron-hard hint hidden in a velvet glove.

I opened the embossed chequebook cover.

The account balance was *close to a hundred thousand more than I'd parted with*.

'How?' was all I managed to croak in astonishment.

'I joined the Zion Christian Church, Dhlamini. *Baba* Lekhanyane advised me where to invest as long as I returned a contributing percentage of any earnings to Moria, City of Zion, to aid their aims.'

'*Hawu!* You've lived on the money and you've *increased* it?'

'*Yebo*, Dhlamini. And I've sworn to continue the same biblical division with any profit we may make in time to come.'

'Let's wait until the good time we're having right now starts turning stale. No need to rush things,' I said, looking at the massive chequebook and fighting off the animal instinct that I should tear the tempting thing into confetti shreds. Zsa-Zsa leaned over, weighing her breasts deliciously against me, kissed my cheek and went off to take a shower.

When Zsa-Zsa came out of the bathroom, I feigned sleep.

It had been a long day; I was within my rights.

But I lay there unmoving a long time in the dark, thinking some essence of me was gone forever, there was no turning back. I was happy, make no mistake, *mfowethu*, but somehow I wasn't quite as happy as I remembered being only a little while before. The image of a black crow with one wing fiercely clipped to prevent it flying away, which I'd seen at Hampstead Heath's zoo, came suddenly to mind. The feather-amputated wing looked terribly sore, terribly absent.

Then I joined Zsa-Zsa and went to sleep.

Zsa-Zsa was as much of a child at heart as my son Vilakazi.

Both of them could be senile serious until something ridiculously spontaneous happened to break the dirge-like mood, and then they would light up like exploding fireworks and giggle and hoot uncontrollably until tears ran down their faces. That would reach deep down into my gut every time it happened. I never had so much innocent merriment in my life as watching the two of them ignite themselves with fun.

I told them a bit about England, just casual rambling reminiscence, letting my mouth warble all by itself.

Zsa-Zsa said she'd like to go there, but the dour expression this instantly wrought upon my face must have told her that wouldn't be a good idea. She changed the subject on the turn, but her laughter was absent for too long after that.

We were in Durban, a place I said I had no time for, I know, *mfowethu*.

But there was the sea, we blacks had our own segregated

beach and the Indian Ocean was warm and friendly.

After dinner we would tour the beachfront in a rickshaw hired from that place near Addington Hospital, the rich salty smell of low tide blown towards us by a steady breeze seducing our senses.

When we came into range, the highly decorated, muscular drivers would come forward like front-row men from Zululand's proudest regiment. There were always many to choose from. Vilakazi would squeal with joy once inside a fierce warrior's cart, the cow-horn headdress leaping skyward up-and-down as the embodiment of pagan strength raced us south again with great bounds in the direction of The Bluff.

Then it would be time for Vilakazi to go to bed.

All of us had a good time getting our little boy to sleep. In many ways, that was the best part of the day. He would say the strangest things out of the blue, things you'd never expect of a child, and all three of us would laugh, push the quirky essence of whatever he'd come up with hilariously further and further until we couldn't laugh any more.

Then Zsa-Zsa and me, we'd lounge around under a big overhead fan, taking it easy, maybe drinking a few cold beers until sexual excitement built up to that stage where we knew what was coming, but prolonged the heightened moment as long as we could. And then, *mfowethu*, then we'd go at each other in a raging storm of *phatha-phatha* passion. Sometimes it would last long and drawn out into the early hours, and other times it would be so vital and violent we'd feel as if we'd torn each other apart.

One day, not too long later, we were having lunch in a rudimentary and basic 'African' restaurant. I got talking to the owner. He told me he was having a hard time making ends meet. I gave him a few tips on how to improve business that he clicked onto fast, and then tore up our bill to show his heartfelt thanks. Zsa-Zsa could judge I knew what I was talking about.

That night was different.

Zsa-Zsa talked non-stop about nothing else but the restaurant business. I judged it *was what I wanted*, but I was queasily apprehensive of total commitment. What it boiled down to was that I was scared and she wasn't – that's the truth. By the time we went to sleep in each other's arms, it was settled.

I was going to open a restaurant in Swaziland.

We headed for Mbabane just as soon as we could get our affairs in order.

It was the worst move I ever made.

But how was a *tsotsi geeza* like me to know that?

Opening a restaurant has some of the same snagging problems you encounter when putting up an infant *umPheki*. The most solidly important aspect is your location. You can't expect your customers to come too far to get to you. Therefore you have to go where they are. Give me a restaurant right next to the most successful place around – I'll get rich on the overflow.

It took me weeks to find what I was looking for.

But I found it.

A large hovel of an old rambling Indian tailoring shop with living quarters above, just one street behind the main road and within easy walking distance of the town's two biggest hotels. There were another five restaurants nearby, all within one contained mile of each other. Nothing wrong with that, *mfowethu*.

I gave the astonished suit-making head of the household ten thousand to move his tailoring premises by month-end.

That was only the *first* pay-off.

After that I went to Zsa-Zsa and my bank's on-tap lawyers to get a lease signed and to clear zoning laws and ensure commercial enterprise rulings were correctly catered to, just to be on the safe side.

I knew to the letter what I wanted to do with the place.

I drew up a rough set of pencilled amateur plans, including an outside rough-and-ready bar that was part of yet separated from the restaurant. Those Swazi *geezas* sure liked to booze and the last thing I needed was beer swillers in my restaurant eating nothing but 'soup-sandwiches', as some of my old London mates termed the preference for a diet consisting solely of alcoholic liquid.

I took these drawings to a reputable mixed-breed contractor called Mendez. He was a half-Portuguese half-African builder come hurriedly over from nearby trouble-brewing Lourenço Marques, capital of Portuguese East Africa. I wanted his estimate for a ballpark quote on finished construction.

What I got from *Senhor* Mendez was a polite laugh and free advice to go visit the offices of the 'Minister of Buildings', along with precisely drafted professional plans for official approval.

At the end of that visit, I was again thousands of bucks poorer, but I had written permission to get estimates and was officially 'under consideration' to be allowed to build. This did not mean I could actually bring in bricklayers, electricians or carpenters, not just yet. That would come later.

My set of professional plans was stunning. The draughtsman had achieved exactly that soft effect with lighting that made it difficult to read the small-print line-up of the nags listed in a racing guide, but easy to see a woman who was subtly shadow-airbrushed into good looks on her own at a far table.

I wanted to panel the place with warm-effect wood halfway up the walls and install indirect illumination above the panelling. I wanted non-reflective grass-weave type material on the upper half of the walls to give an ethnic feel. It looked great in my mind's eye.

When I brought Zsa-Zsa to see the place, I thought she would burst into tears.

I was so full of inner visions of what it would eventually look like, that it hadn't sunk in what a dreadful picture the dump presented to an untrained eye. It stank of stale, rancid sweat. On a first inspection the rotten odours of old oil and layers of curry-grime on the walls were close to overpowering. The place hadn't been scoured clean since the Indian families, plural, had moved out.

When I showed Zsa-Zsa the plans and imaginative impressions of what it would look like, she softened but wasn't entirely convinced. She couldn't visually match what she saw, present tense, with what she *would* see, future tense. I don't think she accepted the evidence even when the restaurant was at long last completed. To my wife, some sort of witch doctor's magic had taken place; a sorcerer had arrived and waved his *insanusi*'s magic wand. Sweat and perseverance had nothing to do with it.

When the day's toiling frustrations were over and evening settled in, we'd sit around and I'd tell her how things were progressing. She'd just laugh in reply with an almost hysterical high note overriding her usual warm gurgle. But she signed whatever I wanted her to without question, not once asking what the money was for. She even offered to sign blank *pages* of cheques so I could deal with costs whenever they arose without our partnership palaver, but I was steering well clear of that one.

You want to know why, *mfowethu*?

Because if a 'right cock-up', as the Limeys say, occurs from your solely solo move, you're in a mountain of shit shovelled unsparingly on you by your spouse so deep, you need gills to breathe your way back to the surface of survival.

But *our decision* was another kettle of fried fish altogether, right?

It wasn't until I began to have the old inner structures of my newly acquired business premises torn down that the hyenas and jackals really started biting big chunks out of me and our bank balance. Every one of the building fraternity – plumbers, plasterers, carpenters, electricians, painters and all the rest of their ilk – was into blackmailing me with schedules that went from uncertain to improbable. I had to grease their putrid palms with monotonous regularity to make sure the ball kept on rolling. There was no doubt in my mind that all would grind to a standstill if I didn't.

It bothered me, but I accepted it. There was no choice. I judged maybe I was in the wrong business though – extortion seemed a fine way to double your tradesman's wages.

But then I lost control of my endurance limits.

I began to get angry.

I'd been around long enough to wise up to the fact that palms have to be greased in any business if you desire things to run smoothly. If a *geeza*'s got something *you've* got to have at all costs, he's got a certain right to pad his bill a little. But there's a limit to what the camel's back will bear before shattering. These motherfuckers were just too *inkalakatha* greedy – and there was sweet fuck all I could do about it. Here I was doing my best to be Mister Nice Guy, and every time I blinked another scavenger had his voraciously vile hand in my personal accumulation of pennies.

It seemed it would never stop, an unfolding ordeal of hellish proportions making Dante's *Inferno* seem puny by comparison.

That devil's spawn bastard from the municipality, the electrical inspector, kept finding countless discrepancies in the wiring according to 'regulations', and for a time I played innocent just to see how far he'd push his luck. That bullshit-master would've had the place rewired until my hair went snow white if I hadn't passed him his thousands in a plain manila envelope. Thereafter he was honey and cream. Even gave me unasked-for advice about how to disconnect the electrical meter in an undetectable way and thus cut my monthly electricity bill by half.

The worse-bastard of a building inspector never had to bother to make the sham of a cursory inspection. I met him by appointment at the bulldozed wreckage of the entrance with his safely sealed wad and it wasn't long before I received written and rubber-stamped approval in the post.

I allowed myself to have acquisitive fun by zapping around to every auction within a few hours' driving distance, taking Vilakazi with me and filling his face with ice-cream and hotdogs with tomato sauce and oily chips, to hell with my car's upholstery. I found an awesome five-star hotel's mahogany and brass bar for a pauper's song, plus matching handcrafted barstools that Prince Philip would not have been ashamed to place his royal philandering arse upon. I found antique serving sideboards with lead-framed crystal windows, the ultimate in snobbish presentation.

There were beautiful *banquettes* along three accessible sides, coverings made of to-die-for tooled leather, which rounded off the corners of what was becoming my opulent dining palace. I used forest-green starched linen tablecloths with sparkling white on white napkins held by serviette rings made of polished green malachite.

The seating capacity was around sixty to seventy patrons, not too crowded, not too small.

My china service was blindingly white, almost translucent, with a matching rich-green filigreed border, and it set me back massive *amarands, mfowethu.*

The silverware was genuine, magnificent stuff – I was lucky to find it in the necessary quantity.

Glassware repeated the same carefully chosen quality.

Light-reflecting crystal-glass chandeliers were an extravagant indulgence, but I judged I'd be the only proprietor *geeza* in the whole of Swaziland who could show that kind of class. '*Glass*' and '*class*' reminded me of Howard Postlethwaite's Cockney slang, a good omen surely, even leaving out the '*arse*' he was sure to tack on as the third inevitable rhyme.

When it came to equipping the kitchen, the heart and soul of any worthwhile eatery, I was not looking for any price-incentive deals. I laid out well over a hundred thousand to get precisely what I knew was needed. No questions, no arguments, *mfowethu.* There was no better gourmet-preparation stainless-steel cooking equipment guaranteeing succulence available anywhere on the southern African subcontinent. I had culinary orgasms just standing there and casting my eyes over the chef's treasure.

The next tentative forward step was the health board's investigative inspector, searching for diseased microbes, contagious bread boards, meat that still mooed – you tell me what else was on that pernicious person's particular inventory – guessing at it is beyond me. I judged as a consolation to myself that this was my last major pay-off – *please God it was my last major pay-off!* I was *gatvol*, as our Afrikaans *boeties* in a mood of shared impotent rage would have phrased it.

The health inspector turned out to be a fat – amazingly fat – relative, so he said, of King Sobhuza, Swaziland's ruling monarch. His sweat-shiny obese corpulence didn't surprise me – if he shaved the fat off everybody else on his investigative list the way he sundered me from my padding of monetary comfort. He ended up with a king's ransom and I ended up with my permit and permanently homicidal tendencies towards all grossly fat black men who never stop smiling while they suck away your lifeblood.

Yet I breathed the relieved sigh of a man reprieved from the gallows. Now I could apply myself to getting down to basics. All I needed was staff willing to do things my way and then I would be ready for that last essential hurdle. The one that had to be surmounted – my liquor licence.

Following that I would be on the gravy train, my coaches carrying food *fantastique* and enticing aromas pouring out from the locomotive engine's smokestack.

I began the interviews necessary to find a top-class chef.

I was exhausted by the time I found the right one.

He was a middle-aged Malawian called Beston who had worked for years as head honcho at the Italian and German embassies there and had recipes under his belt that would make any connoisseur salivate and weep for joy at the same time. He brought along with him two 'cousins' who were his self-trained assistant cooks and I judged they were a steal at the salary we agreed upon.

I found five waiters who had that necessary poise and also a willingness to please that made customers request a table where said waiter would serve them again and again *and again*. I sat them all down together after their employment had been confirmed and read them my rules. First off, all tips were to be pooled and shared equally. I half expected them to walk out on me *en masse*, because all waiters think they are the best in the universe at squeezing the biggest tips from their worshipful customers. Pooling tips made waiter *numero uno*, being every single one of them, *mampara*-judge that he was carrying all his serving *bras* on his back. The response to this was silence, a *respectful* silence. Great stuff. Then I told them the rest of my requirements. Then I hit them with my *pièce de résistance* – each *geeza* was going to get a percentage of the profits, paid biannually. This had the advantage of guaranteeing long periods of service. The harder the waiters worked and the more they pulled repeat business, the more money they would make, and the only way to benefit equally was by unflagging team effort.

I could positively *hear* the adding machines in their heads spilling out narrow ticker-tape paper as they balanced the possibilities. In an amazingly short time they all volunteered to sign the contracts I had prepared. It was communism the way Karl Marx's communism was *supposed* to work. Working together, they all had above-average expectations of building up an untouched golden nest egg, without having to dig deep into their own pockets every month-end for a hefty pension fund contribution. If any single one of them got greedy and stole or slacked off, he was robbing his brothers as well as yours truly. I judged my boys would be bird-watching each other with indoor binoculars and hawk's eyes far, far better than I ever could, *mfowethu*.

Then I did something that had been at the back of my mind since the beginning.

I called Howard Postlethwaite in London.

Fifty-fifty shares money-wise in a full-partnership

business with me carrying all the upfront expenses,
straight down the line, including his airfare to Swaziland
and initial accommodation. Funds channelled to the ANC
indirectly through Howard's endeavour over in London
were handled by a small, obscure law-office there and
would continue in the established manner with or without
Howard's input.

'Yer mean it, me old sahn?'

'You never seen black dolls like we got here in
Sobhuza's kingdom, Howie. There's a casino, the works.'

'Fahkin 'ell. Not pulling me leg are yer, Shatterproof?'

'Come on, Howie, mate, you know me better than
that. Just think about it. You and me, the black and white
bosses, ebony and ivory, we can handle anyone from Idi
Amin to the Klu Klux Klan's Grand Dragon, no sweat. We
got all the presentation aces up our sleeves.'

'Fahkin 'ell.'

'You already said that.'

'Fahk orf, me old sahn. Don't come the golliwog cahnt
orn me, mate.'

'What's it going to be, Howie?'

'Get me a gallon orf that suntan lotion shite,
Shatterproof. Orn me fahkin way over, innit?'

I could not lose out. Howard Postlethwaite on my side
was like having a billion bucks' inheritance pending. He
was one Pommie *geeza* I knew I could trust implicitly.
When he arrived in Mbabane, I left the rest of the staff
recruiting to him so that he would have status equal to me
in our employees' eyes.

In spite of all the exacerbating skinned-alive irritations
and brain-popping migraines suffered on a regular basis, I
was still having a good time, enjoying myself thoroughly,
mfowethu. It was hard work, no diluting that, because
there were endless streams of *fix-it* or *fuck-it* tasks to

be dealt with every day, day in, day out, when you were starting a restaurant from scratch. And you had to plan each minute of your time so that everything got done in the correct order, the *horse before the car* kind of applied logic. One foul-up concatenated into dozens of tangled pitfalls, each one sufficient to give you peptic ulcers.

There was still leisure time over to have fun at home.

I'd march upstairs, tired and dirty, to where we were plushly renovating the old Indian tailors' overhead living quarters, and the first thing I'd do would be to hop into a bath with Vilakazi. It was an ancient, free-standing oblong tub with ball-and-claw support feet and the plumbing would rumble violently when you turned on the hot water. I don't know who screamed louder in mock fear whenever this took place, me or Vilakazi, and Zsa-Zsa's pleas for a little peace and quiet were raucously disobeyed.

On weekends, we'd go out to Mantenga Falls, a cascading series of torrentially plunging waterfalls, massive curtains of thick white water – deep clear pools at rocky intervals along the fiercely tumbling downward course – and surrounded on either side by lush ferns and dense green forest. A magical place. Those were irreplaceable times we shared together there, none better.

Reverend Bishop Lekhanyane, the supreme Black Messiah of the Zion Christian Church I'd met earlier, would call around to visit every now and irregular again in his newest chauffeur-driven Cadillac.

At first he used to make me irrationally nervous.

Something in me automatically mistrusted any charismatic figure deeply involved in religious matters as being a charlatan always on the lookout for personal gain. I judged they all had something to sell by way of making inroads into your hidden guilt or fear of the unknown. Whether you were in the market or not made no difference to their persuasive zealot's zeal, *mfowethu*.

But I would sit there passively while *Baba* Edward and Zsa-Zsa talked, all the while wondering what the powerful *Geeza*-of-God thought about me and what my wife had told him. I felt he had some mystic control over my family and therefore over me, so I'd deliberately blaspheme just to see if I could get under his religious crusader's skin. It was like pouring water on a duck's back for all any of my jibing stuck to him.

Then I discovered Edward Lekhanyane liked to play backgammon.

Ah yes, backgammon, that wonderful game combining skill and chance that my *mlungu* doctor-brother had shown me how to master back in those days I was pulped wreckage at Baragwanath State Hospital for Natives. The Black Messiah was pretty good himself and, given the chance, we'd play for hours at a time. Because it made Zsa-Zsa happy, I'd even let His Holiness win occasionally – but surely you know I'm filling your ears with my backgammon-grandmaster *bulongwe*, *mfowethu*?

Let me tell you, the Reverend Bishop was no slouch when it came to the intelligence agility department. With every game we were like two warring generals out to decimate each other with every means at our disposal.

But while immersed in the demands of the workplace though, that remembered *bonhomie* of shared verbal and mental wrestling perched on either side of an indifferent backgammon board *was different, became somehow warped*.

I had this unshakable feeling, like a curse almost, that Zsa-Zsa and the Reverend Bishop were one kind of species while I belonged to some lowly branch of lesser animals.

Still, the big shots and the not-so-big shots I met every day weren't so different from me, not as far as any introspection allowed me insight. They were all after *amarands*, the hand-in-hand fawning respect wealth brought you on a humbled kneeling platter, and they were all trying desperately to find the quickest way to accumulate it. *Yebo*, what a rat-infested rat race life was, because none of them at heart was ever after the most honest and scrupulous methods of achieving their goals, but *always* the quickest sure-fire method, heedless of who got hurt along the way. Maybe many of them would baulk at murder and breaking bones, but you sure as eggs are eggs couldn't tell it from dealing with them face to face. There *was* a difference between them and the gung-ho *tsotsi* criminals I knew and had known, and it boiled down to this, *mfowethu*: *the criminals were honest about their evils.*

Something was wrong with the tenets of society's philosophy in practice. Perhaps Zsa-Zsa felt the way she did about glorious incorruptibility purely because she didn't know how the world worked. The world was still a permanently atavistic arena – the powerful gorged on the weak and the weak preyed upon the helpless, a vicious and pernicious never-ending cycle.

Maybe Zsa-Zsa never had a chance to find out the way things were: maybe she'd been too sheltered by her doting suicidally inclined *baba*, Bra-Bra. What I knew for definite was that if a *geeza* was one hundred per cent honest just in this innocuous restaurant business alone, he had no business being there. But I had to keep up the appearance of noble straightforwardness if I wanted to hang on to Zsa-Zsa. That was for sure. Ever felt like yelling, *stop the world, I want to get off, mfowethu*?

The time came when I was ready for my liquor licence application formalities.

My meeting was with two clean-shaven pickaxe-visaged interrogators, one white, one black, but believe me, they looked like twins chiselled hard faced from sharp intractable granite.

We shook hands and sat down facing one another across a big desk as bleak and uncluttered as the wastes of the Kalahari.

There were numerous forms to fill out produced from severely black briefcases that matched their severely black suits, and that done, the three of us blandly faced one another again.

'Very well, Mr Bhekuzulu.' This from Pickaxe One. 'Next we will need written character testimonials.'

'Essential, Mr Bhekuzulu, at least four,' added Pickaxe Two.

'I assumed my bank had taken care of that detail, gentlemen,' I said, warning hairs pricking up uncomfortably at the back of my neck.

'Your bank is merely a financial reference, Mr Bhekuzulu,' Pickaxe One replied, frowning slightly as if I'd dropped an unnecessary and grossly vulgar expletive amongst a crowd of innocent seven-year-old school kids.

'We must have commercially uninvolved testimonials from responsible citizens,' said Pickaxe Two, also frowning ever so slightly, making me feel I was suffering from some kind of cross-eyed double vision.

'I thought that was what lawyers were for,' I answered, trying out a confident smile. 'Let mine handle that aspect. My testimonials are my finances. Nothing better than that rock-solid security, is there, gentlemen?'

'I do not think you fully understand,' Pickaxe One said. 'Apply yourself, please, to grasping what is required of you.'

'We must have affidavits from contactable persons who have known you for ten years or more,' Pickaxe Two added in a voice so acerbic it seemed his spittle was made of hydrochloric acid.

'Upstanding-community-minded-citizens-as-previously-stated-who-can-and- will-vouch-for-you,' Pickaxe One added, enunciating each word as if it was an entire sentence.

'We must be morally certain your liquor licence will not lead to abuse thereof,' said Pickaxe Two.

What neither Pickaxe One nor Pickaxe Two understood was that I could be jailed long term by 'character references' from the characters I knew. But naturally I couldn't explain that to them, even if it took as diplomatically long to put forward my vindication as it would take for hell to freeze over.

'Let's leave that on hold for now,' I said in my best placatory manner. 'May we move on to the next step in your agenda?'

'We know your assets,' Pickaxe One said. 'Your assets are acceptable.'

'What are your liabilities?' Pickaxe Two interjected immediately.

'No liabilities, gentlemen. I am debt free.'

'What is the source of your income, Mr Bhekuzulu?' Pickaxe One demanded.

'Also please inform us if due taxes are paid up to date and receipted in South Africa?' added Pickaxe Two before I could draw breath.

'Gentlemen, gentlemen, what has that to do with anything?'

'Although our government does not agree with your country of birth's policies, the legalities of the status quo must be observed,' Pickaxe One explained with the only barest veneer of politeness.

'We have economic ties that are delicately maintained. We may not tread carelessly on sensitive toes,' said Pickaxe Two.

'What difference does any reciprocal agreement between Swaziland and South Africa make if I have the necessary capital to facilitate my own business?' I asked sincerely, almost at a loss for cohesive thought. 'We're talking mutual benefits here.'

'Our state authorities insist upon this information, Mr Bhekuzulu,' said Pickaxe One while Pickaxe Two nodded sternly in affirmation.

'Every applicant must be thoroughly investigated,' said Pickaxe Two, still nodding.

'Thoroughly investigated,' Pickaxe One echoed, parroting Pickaxe Two.

'Whoa, steady, gentlemen,' I held up a hand. 'My wife's father left her the money.'

'There is a will, of course?' Pickaxe One asked.

'Some sort of legal document?' Pickaxe Two added his query.

'Naturally,' I answered blithely. Anything they needed in that category, Bra-Bra Motshange could conjure up, no problems. Still, I was feeling like an incontinent elephant was defecating tons of excrement upon my head. These crazy cretins were examining *me* like starving dogs coming across a used menstrual pad. Moneywise, I could buy and sell both of them as easy as breathing, but *how?*

It started to get to me.

I bunched my fists and censored my impulsive responses.

'That's covered,' I said evenly, but unable to force a smile. 'What do we move onto next?'

'You must advise us in writing of any arrests or

convictions,' Pickaxe One said, stern as a cement priest.

'A criminal record will automatically debar you from successful application,' Pickaxe Two pointed out with the same intractable detachment.

That was the waterfall that broke the crocodile's back, *mfowethu*.

I saw red.

I went bonkers, as the Limeys say, ballistic crazy at what my ego saw and interpreted as malicious victimisation. I could have killed them both with my bare hands. Instead, I upped on the spot and hit the street, tearing up my liquor licence application forms into little pieces and strewing them like a dedicated litterer carelessly behind me.

By the time I began to breathe normally, those paper scraps were all gone, scattered by a vagrant breeze, just like my restaurant – a scattered impossible dream. Opening a restaurant like mine without a liquor licence was like trying to manufacture Napoleon Brandy from pigswill and hydrochloric acid, strictly *cul-de-sac*.

ALL THAT MONEY SHAT DOWN THE FUCKING DRAIN! *DADAWETHU!* WHY ME ME ME? HOW *MOEGOE* STUPID WAS IT POSSIBLE FOR ONE *GAL PIL* DARKIE *MAMPARA* TO BE? JUST STROLL UP AND SIGN YOUR FUCKING NAME ON THE DOTTED FUCKING LINE! REGISTER YOUR ARSEHOLE SELF AS A CUNT CUNT CUNT!

Why did honest boys have to make it so fucking hard on good bad boys? I'd close my doors! Smash their complacent faces! Fuck them all! Look at these wankers walking the same fucking street! Disgusting dog-shit slobs all of them! All their miserable salaried lives they save save save, get sick, and then suddenly there's a great big fucking nothing in their bank accounts! Fucking suckers! You, me, them, all of us! But any one of these bastard shit-eating wanker cunts could get a liquor licence by using his cock-sucking ignorant thumbprint and with his fucking fucking fucking eyes closed! Cunts! Cunts! Cunts! I can never be one of you! Never! Never! Never!

When I got back to our upstairs apartment, I was still boiling, but also wondering how I was going to break the news to Zsa-Zsa without her demanding instant divorce in return.

Reverend Bishop Lekhanyane was sitting in my armchair.

His usual flowing robes were replaced by a Zionist paramilitary-type uniform, the five-pointed ZCC silver star backed with green and black ribbon seeming to glare malevolently at me from his bomber-jacket lapels. He was studying a scroll of some sort, deep in thought. Feeling the way I did, he was the absolute last person in the world I wanted to exchange social *bulongwe* with.

'I see you, Dhlamini,' he said, glancing up. 'I assume Zsa-Zsa's out with young Vilakazi. No locks yet, so I let myself in.'

'Don't let me delay your departure' blew out my mouth like a spray of none-too-polite venom. 'Feel free to come back another time.' I was staring out the window and seeing nothing but an opaque white haze.

I heard the scroll rustling as he rolled it up, the whispering sound informing me he was still solidly there. I was about to add more verbal pleasantness, but he beat me to the punch.

'I know you are deeply troubled, Dhlamini,' the Black Messiah said, his voice soothing, penetrating, captivating, cajoling, all of those things at the same time. 'Something is eating you from the inside, like a sickness with poisonous teeth. I cannot leave the temple of your family home without first offering whatever help is within my healing powers to grant you. Let it out, Dhlamini. Anything that comes into your mind. You do not have to speak it. Just *think* it, and I shall be able to focus on your essence.'

I glowered daggers at him.

My mind leapt into violent cacophony all on its own, no encouragement necessary, *mfowethu*. Terrible thoughts erupted within me –

YOU, YOU FUCKING SANCTIMONIOUS SO-CALLED DYNAMIC PROPHET, YOU WANT TO FUCKING HELP? YOU? A BIG FAT FUCKING CUNT IN YOUR WANKER'S PLAY-PLAY PRETTY UNIFORM? DO ME A FUCKING FAVOUR – SUCK ON YOUR OWN SYPHILITIC *UMTHONDO* AND FUCK OFF OUT OF MY SIGHT! MAYBE YOU'D LIKE TO VOLUNTEER AS A *CHARACTER-REFERENCE* FOR DHLAMINI BHEKUZULU, EH? GET GOD TO GIVE THE ARSEHOLE AUTHORITIES A FUCKING CELESTIAL BLOW JOB SO THE CUNTS'LL GRANT ME A LIQUOR LICENCE, EH? FROM YOUR SEMEN-FILLED GOB TO GOD'S EAR, EH? TELL THE SAME FUCKING CUNTS I GOT MY *AMARANDS* FROM SELLING YOUR FUCKED-UP SHEEP-FOLLOWER ZION CHRISTIAN CHURCH ZOMBIE-BRAINDEADS THEIR FUCKING STUPID SHITHEAD COLLECTION OF USELESS FUCKING RELIGIOUS ARTEFACTS? THAT'S MORE LIKE IT! YOU CAN WORK FUCKING MIRACLES FOR THE FAITHFUL, BUT YOU CAN'T FUCKING HELP ME, CUNT, CAN YOU? YOU'RE AS FUCKING MUCH HELP TO ME AS A COCK-SUCKING SEVEN-RAND NOTE! STICK THAT UP YOUR BLACK MESSIAH'S FESTERING SHITSPOUT AND GET HIGH ON YOUR OWN FUCKING FART FUMES!

Reverend Bishop Lekhanyane held up his hand for my attention, breaking the vile spell of invective that dominated me to my core.

'What is the problem with your liquor licence, Dhlamini?'

My mouth dropped open.

Up till now it had been clamped shut in rage. How could he know what my problem was so accurately, so precisely? But know it he did. His eyes shone with inner knowledge.

'You asked me, *Baba* Edward,' I answered, now deigning to grant him an elder's address that conveyed respect. 'I'll tell you. The trouble is there's no ways I can get a legal permit to sell alcohol in any form, which is the backbone of the business I've poured Zsa-Zsa's and my money into. No licence, no restaurant, *Baba* Edward. I couldn't feed stray animals on those restricted profits. I have a criminal record, *Baba* Edward. No matter that I'm honest now, my past condemns me. Please, *Baba* Edward, if you want to help, please leave me alone here until my wife and son come home.'

'You almost sound as if you have gained some sort of humility, Dhlamini,' he said. Then he sat there looking at me, and stayed utterly silent.

His silence did it to me.

All the injustices and all the anger inside me came up like acid-searing vomit scorching the lining of my mute throat. There were runnels of sweat pouring down my chest, but inside I felt like winter's frost had withered my soul.

'Sit down, Dhlamini,' was all Reverend Bishop Lekhanyane intoned, and my body obeyed independent of my will.

He got up from my armchair and stood towering over me. All at once he seemed enormously big.

'I have listened to your innermost thoughts of corrosive

despair and destructive damnation for the last ten minutes,'
he said slowly and with a vocal grandeur that miniaturised
you. 'Detrimental recklessness that makes a snake find evil
in my stomach. *Nkulunkulu* never meant man to crawl
like that snake without legs, to seek the lowest level of
survival. We are given two legs to stand upon. *Nkulunkulu*
in His Merciful Generosity gave us the means to think for
ourselves, to accept what we are. Despite my strength, it
made me physically ill that you chose to cast your anger
over me like a foolish fisherman throwing his net in the
hope of finding fish without knowing their habits or, in
fact, if the waters contain fish at all. You are blessed with
a loving wife and a loving child who want you for what
you are, not what you *think* you are. You have no faith in
yourself, nor them, nor of the songlines which the *shades*
of the ancestors made for us all to follow. Are you listening
to me, Dhlamini?'

That very instant, a sudden vision filled my mind
– clear as crystal I saw an awesome overhead view of
Reverend Bishop Lekhanyane with arms and face raised
towards the heavens as he addressed a multitude of doting
adherents. There was an uncanny hush over this densely
peopled City of Zion that I saw so clearly, a hush loudly
echoing the Black Messiah's melodious voice. Then he
completed his sermon and the ZCC band, permanently
stationed there, led him away from his raised pulpit to
the strains of 'Swanee River', that old Dixieland strain
that called upon the souls of black slaves to take heart
and believe in a better hereafter. The multitude lining
the route of his exit from this place called Sacred Moria
acknowledged his friendly smiles and praised him with
tumultuous applause . . . he left the vast prayer-ground in
his chauffeur-driven Cadillac . . . over the dust-bedecked
roads to his headquarters . . .

. . . and I snapped out of it, came back to the here and now.

'I'm listening, *Baba* Edward.'

'It is time to look not outside of yourself, but within, Dhlamini.'

I was glaring at him once again in response to this when Zsa-Zsa walked in. She took Vilakazi to the kitchen, fed him some biscuits and milk and came back to us.

'*Baba* Edward? Is everything alright?'

'Dhlamini has run headfirst into obstacles preventing his obtaining a liquor licence to operate your restaurant. There is a solution, as there is always a solution to most setbacks.'

I thought he'd become unhinged. His demeanour was so unfazed, so calm and confident, that it belaboured belief. His eyes positively beamed elation at me.

'You must register fifty-one per cent of the restaurant in Zsa-Zsa's name,' he said. 'As controlling ownership dictates, the new application will be made in her name. I shall provide all good character testimonials. There shall be no further problems, I assure you.'

Zsa-Zsa's eyes went wide. She said nothing, but came over and sat beside me, her arm resting on my shoulder.

'That means I have no control!' I blurted. 'I'll just be a dogsbody, a menial manager, a nothing!'

'Dhlamini, that is not true. All earnings besides those agreed upon with your foreigner partner will still be yours and your wife's. Nothing has changed, except you are now in a position to go forward, not backward.'

'How do you know about my, sorry, *our* new partner?'

'Some things cannot be explained by words.'

'And that's it?'

Reverend Bishop Lekhanyane just smiled his most gentle smile.

'If we are to dwell in the sight of *Nkulunkulu*, each of us must rise above circumstances that would confound us every day. I am leaving you now. I came because I felt you had need of me. I leave you with something to give pause, something to think about in your own time, my children.'

Then the Black Messiah departed, leaving us alone.

'You believe him?' I said, turning to Zsa-Zsa whose eyes were moist and shining with joy.

'His words are my faith, Dhlamini,' she replied. 'Why can't they be yours?'

'*Yebo*,' I said. 'You're right. We've got ourselves a restaurant.'

Full Speed Ahead

It didn't take two months before I knew we were riding a winner thoroughbred racehorse of a restaurant.

Business surged ahead, solid funds came in during the week and weekends were packed to capacity. It looked like we were set to stay on top of things for a long time to come.

There was a major problem when the doors were first opened, but it didn't take that long to overcome.

As I've mentioned, *mfowethu*, those Swazi *geezas* loved to booze, and that was why I'd had a separate bar built to the side and at the back of the restaurant proper with its own street entrance. The only complication was that nobody took any notice of the rules. Flash guys with their flash dolls would bounce into the restaurant, grab a prime table, soak in the ambience *and* soak up a steady supply of beers – and nothing else. To add insult to this pauper-making injury, they'd become raucous, drunkenly self-conscious and overloud, making wild gestures emphasising some pointless point – and they'd chase the good spending customers away.

Big Bang was there in three days.

I had to have a tailor-made tuxedo put together for

him; no men's outfitters nor even the clothing factories that supplied them carried his breathtaking size in stock. To top this, I got him some of those built-up platform shoes in vogue at that time, so that Big Bang ended up looking seven feet tall. Immaculately attired, with those kaleidoscopic stretched-ear-lobe fillers of his, he made Hercules look like a shoddy midget. He was stationed permanently at the doorway.

Next, I had 'Reserved' signs made for *every* table in the place. If we liked you, the 'Reserved' sign was removed and you were seated. If we didn't like you, it was *Sorry sir, but every single place we have is booked – reservations are our policy.*

There were brash bloods in their best suits who pushed past you and sat down defiantly with their giggling girls. Big Bang would come over and politely ask them to leave. If this got no positive response, he would simply lean down and gather up two or three of them bodily in his massive arms. Next, they were deposited without violence back outside on the street. This was so embarrassing for the would-be gatecrashers that they seldom made a second attempt. A second attempt might invite harshness from Big Bang, and even featherweight harshness from Big Bang was a complete censuring of a third try for glory.

Howard Postlethwaite brought with him a super-smart sleight-of-hand Scots barman who could have sold drinks at a temperance revival. He might as well have been handling liquid lucre the way our big interior bar poured money in, cocktails being his speciality. We many times had patient diners stacked three deep at that bar waiting for a vacant table, and we turned those tables over several times *every* weekend evening.

After half a year, we were barely able to handle the steadily increasing traffic.

I knew we would have to have more space.

There was only one way to go.

Up where Zsa-Zsa and Vilakazi and me made our home, where that assiduously redecorated and soundproofed space was already happily occupied by our small family. We had no choice but to move out. Within weeks I had carpenters knocking through an elegant balustraded stairway of impressive width and professional redecorators renovating full speed ahead.

This addition to our restaurant's seating capacity took care of the overflow nicely, thank you.

Then we settled down to a steady trade that looked like it would last for all eternity. I worked the hardest I had ever worked. You had to stay on top of every fluctuation every minute, or else mice nibbling at your larder would turn into monster omnivorous rats digesting you and your outlay wholesale.

I cut Beston, our Malawian chef, in for a small percentage because he was cannily astute at 'marketing', as we called the acquisition of necessary provisions. He would go with Howard and me at five in the morning to be first at the various fresh-food suppliers we purchased from. We had to buy our own frozen-storage truck to bring in fish and other highly perishable items; the restaurant name emblazoned from rooftop to chassis-level on the truck's windowless sides was good advertising proclaiming that we dealt only in the best.

We closed the grill at eleven-thirty sharp, but never closed our doors to go home until well after midnight, even on weekdays. It got so that Howard and I would take turns to catnap on a canvas camping cot installed in the tiny office where we kept the safe and the double set of accounts books. Everybody was in the same boat, working tremendously hard – waiters, cooks and cleaners

– but somehow we managed to keep going, lessening the pressure by using regimented shifts. My incentive plan worked like a dream and internal theft turned out to be virtually non-existent.

Now a reverse situation came to plague me.

I was seeing so little of Zsa-Zsa and my cherished Vilakazi that they might have been living on a different planet. Our social get-togethers had been honed down to a Sunday lunch at the restaurant, not exactly a successful family sit-down because I was more on my feet than on my *ezzies*. Reverend Bishop Lekhanyane was irregularly there to keep her company.

The Black Messiah was in the soul-saving game, or so I thought, and because of my attitude I considered myself a daunting prospect. But he could never resist releasing a broadside of spiritual advice at me and in return I could never resist allowing his verbal *bon mot* barrage of devout yet high-explosive entreaties to pass unanswered.

Zsa-Zsa loved this somewhat sectarian interaction between the two of us, and thought oral salvation was coming my way. But these exchanges always left me feeling irritated and with that niggling barbed-hook sense that I'd come off second-best still stuck inside me.

In my defence all I can mumble, even to myself, is that you can't live today by a set of biblical laws made by manna-eating patriarch prophets thousands of years ago – today demands you make up *your own* set of laws as you go along to embrace whatever comes your way. Who's to know what tomorrow may bring, *mfowethu*?

Faced with any radical situation demanding fast reflexes for survival, I know any given response of mine would be utterly different to *Baba* Edward's and Zsa-Zsa's. Chalk and cheese. Black and white. But who judges these things in the great overall scheme, if there is such a thing, which

I doubt very much? Who's Right? Who's Wrong? Is there never a Grey Area?

After one Sunday lunchtime serving that was so sardine-packed I couldn't even find a table for my own wife and son, Zsa-Zsa gave up on me.

She stopped coming.

I solved this by hiring a relief-manager Howard Postlethwaite had come into contact with and for whom he vouched. That gave me five working evenings only instead of seven and every third weekend off after Saturday night's crucially busy trade – and my family life regained some normalcy. As much as I trusted Howard though, I hated bringing in that manager. Because the quickest way to go bankrupt is to delegate authority. He can steal you blind, and if he's cut in the other staff and suppliers on the deal, he's practically impossible to catch. Why? Because nobody talks who's in on a good thing.

Still, I'd made my decision.

My family came first.

It worked well for a while.

Quite a long while actually, *mfowethu*.

Long after my old mates Ronnie and Reggie Kray got arrested and convicted of murder in London for the premeditated daylight slaughter of 'Jack the Hat' McVitie plus another shady underworld mucker known as George Cornell, The General walked with his usual *panache* into our fine food and fine wines establishment.

The new decade was barely a year old.

I was delighted to see him, the happiest *geeza* on the block. I gave him my undivided personal attention and the best of everything, including vintage treasure from the grape, all on the house.

When he had eaten his fill – and he could eat enough for three men, small and thin though he was – I joined him in an after-dinner imported brandy liqueur and he lit up his pipe, insisting on an *espresso* to go with it. He leaned back, puffing away with enjoyment, and it gave me a huge thrill to have him in *my* restaurant and so obviously enjoying himself. His spade-bearded face creased in a grin reciprocating mine and we clinked our brandy snifters in a toast.

'To your continued success, Dhlamini, my boy.'

'Thank you, *umnumzana*, and to yours.'

We drank. The General set his glass down and those raptor's eyes lunged deep into my own.

'I have not eaten this well, quite frankly, since I cannot remember when. I am so pleased you have this place and that you are making a good living.'

'Again, thank you, *umnumzana*.'

'Which makes me come to the point of why I came here.'

'More than my superior cuisine?'

'Much more, Dhlamini.' The General's gaze suddenly got serious; his eyes increased their penetrating intensity. 'Of course I have enjoyed catching up with you again, my boy. But there is a lot more to it than that. I have a proposition I am sure will arouse more than a spark of interest in you. A set up that you are well qualified to operate to huge financial advantage. Huge, Dhlamini, my boy, huge.'

Right away my intestines began to knot themselves. I could almost guess what was coming.

'I'm content with what I have here, General, sir. My family and security give me more than I could have dreamed possible.'

'Ah, but I *know* you, Dhlamini. A man is as big as his dreams, and you dream of much more than this,' The General said, using his pipe-stem to indicate our surroundings. 'Forget about peanuts, Dhlamini – peanuts are for monkeys. I am going to talk to you for five minutes. During that time, my boy, you will do me the courtesy of not interrupting me. After that you may accept or reject my offer.'

I said nothing.

My instinct was to get to my feet, say good night and farewell and walk out of there straight back to my wife and son, but my instinct evaporated in the time it takes to blink your eyes.

I could no more have walked away than I could have committed fellatio upon myself.

I was mesmerised like a rabbit is mesmerised by a cobra.

'Dhlamini, remember when I talked to you way back in those old days at the Glass House? I judged the times of illegal alcohol were coming to an end. Meaning illegal for those of our race to purchase and to drink in public. I was convinced the oppressionistic Nationalist Government would be smart and take our profits away from us. I was wrong. How stupid could I ever be to think a government is smart? A government is many things but being smart is not numbered amongst its talents.' The General paused, letting his words sink in before continuing. 'Perhaps it is hard to believe, but right now we are able to make a hundred times more bankable money than we ever did in those halcyon guns and gangsters days. We can make more money than you realise exists.'

I had a sneaky feeling that someone was lurking behind my shoulder. My nerves were making me jumpy – and with good reason. That *being-watched* feeling is something you can trust; ignore it at your peril. There were customers still propping up the bar. Nobody could hear us unless we used a PA system to amplify our voices. Still, I had this recognisable feeling. It persisted undiminished in an uncomfortable manifestation and without lessening.

Then I understood what it was.

Tsotsi's paranoia, the thing that keeps him alive, keeps his senses tuned to the nuance of every threat.

'Now pay attention, Dhlamini,' The General said, his confiding voice banishing my septic apprehension as fast as Saint Peter refusing entrance at the Pearly Gates to a recalcitrant Hendrik Verwoerd. 'I have to fill you in on the whole picture so that you will see opportunity beckoning as clearly as I do.' He took a long, pleasurable puff on his pipe, then leaned forward so that his face was close to mine. 'When it became legal for we darkies to drink the white man's liquor, it meant the end of an era, my boy. There is no more easy profit in one-hundred- per cent illegal home-made booze. Not when legitimate retailers can buy and sell whatever they need without breaking the law and going to prison for their requisite indiscretions. Now something else has happened, a cropping-up of fortune's fancy with all odds to our providential advantage. The Nationalist Government is making a killing by massively taxing all imported liquor. That means *every* bottle of whisky, gin, vodka and even brandy – any strong liquor you care to name that comes *into* our homeland, South Africa. There are billions, yes, *billions*, being earned in taxes. But to give relief to some favoured importers, if any of these specific-type alcohols are brought into the country in huge liquid-filled vats via shipping containers and – *if the product is decanted, bottled and labelled on our shores, the tax falls away*. Only a small surcharge is levied. Right *there* is where we come in. Do you see now how opportunity knocks as loudly as a cathedral's clarion call to the faithful, Dhlamini?'

'Am I allowed to speak now?'

'By all means, my boy.'

'I'm all ears, *umnumzana*. Please explain.'

'Bengal Tiger is one of those who through a maze of connected but well-camouflaged separate corporations has several permits that allow him to *legally* bottle, label and distribute. Now things are different. Why bring the various preferred alcohols in from overseas *when we are able to manufacture the identical liquor ourselves at a fraction of the cost?* Ah, Dhlamini, my boy, I see the erstwhile penny is dropping. You have already figured it out. *We have government-approved bona fide paperwork to cover every gallon of excellent high-quality booze that you, who are our specialist, can duplicate and supply so that even a connoisseur will think twice about what he is imbibing before passing an opinion.'*

I had to give myself a minute to catch my breath.

The prospects were staggering.

'When we have billions behind us,' I whispered, 'there will be nothing we can't "twist" – nobody we can't buy off.'

'Exactly. That is all the talking you need to do, Dhlamini. You come with me, my boy. I have people who want to meet you.'

We went out together.

I could no more have stopped myself going with him than I could have stopped breathing, not to mention that cessation of oxygen inhalation was the last thing I wanted.

Canned Cheat

We went to see people the whole country was searching for, people with summary execution warrants hanging over their heads. Corrupt *tsotsi* murderers, of course, but amongst them those outlawed for their bold standpoints and commitment to The Struggle against *apartheid* – *and* willing to fund their ideals any way they could.

During the days of subsequent meetings to iron out our plans to defraud the *apartheid* government of millions and millions of *amarands*, I got to know many men who are now the backbone elite of our present democracy. They needed me to become a combination of general supply-manager and production bright-boy, a human glue-stick who could make the practical side of the whole operation weld solidly together. It was a daunting job, but believe me, *mfowethu*, it was one I was confident I could do with my eyes wide shut.

In character with my luck, there was an ugly pus-filled boil threatening to burst that surfaced in our first discussions, when a certain controlling Comrade X said, 'There are still independent *tsotsi* diehards manufacturing cheap *skokiaan* in some of the areas we will need. They must be permanently removed from their unauthorised businesses, an example made of them. They are an outdated loose-end threat that cannot be tolerated.'

I couldn't believe my ears.

'What you mean, "unauthorised"? What you talking "outdated", *bra*? Just a few harmless brothers making a living same way as we going to.'

'Your outlook on political economics is sadly lacking in effective strategy. And never, *ever*, refer to me again as your *bra*, understand?'

'Fine by me we lose the *bulongwe* pretence of brotherhood, but *your attitude* towards a few no-account wildcat backyard booze-makers means the difference between eating or starving for homeboy people we supposed to be on same side as. What? A few gallons *ugologo* going to hurt us? Ever heard of live and let live?'

'We need a populace whose fervour is unilaterally in favour of change.'

'I can't credit the way you judge this,' I protested on the instant. 'Fancy words mean nothing when you got no food on your table and your kids' empty bellies are making them cry with hunger.' I turned to others in the room, containing my anger. 'This is way outside the parameters of what I'm prepared to do for you. I want strictly *nothing* to do with murder or with physical coercion by crippling and maiming. *Nqodo!* You with me?'

'But you must agree the end justifies the means?'

'Perhaps. But me, I want nothing to do with it. Please consider the fact that any strong-arm acts of violence will ultimately call unwanted attention to our entire secret operation. We cannot afford that. Persuasion can also be convincingly understated and quiet. Why do things the hard way if there is an easier option?'

Comrade X looked at me with cold flat eyes, and I briefly wished I'd kept my big mouth upper-sphincter shut.

'Sometimes the only option for an activist committed to The Struggle is that of reprisal. Next time I want your opinion, I'll ask for it, understand?'

'Now, now, Comrade X, my boy-genius is right.' The General spoke clearly and you could see his words carried authority even here in this volatile place. 'Why borrow trouble? Dhlamini has a "persuader" who works for him. A man as close as his own brother, who needs only threaten to get results.'

I could see Comrade X nodding, not looking happy, but nodding all the same.

'You,' he said curtly to me, his expression unchanging. 'Be ready for another intensive meeting at the same time tomorrow. I have more people I wish you to explain rudimentary working details to. The General will tell you where.'

I had no taste for the way Comrade X talked down to me.

I was the acknowledged expert and I wanted to be treated as such.

'Okay by me,' I said as distantly as I could manage from under my uncomfortably hot collar. 'But first I have questions that preclude "working details" about how the operation should be set up. And if your answers are not an exact fit with the category *I* require, then, Comrade X, you might as well go and fuc – ' *and something stopped me right there.* Not The General's hand on my arm, but something in those cold flat eyes that told me Comrade X would feel little if any compunction about killing yours truly for 'justifiable' revenge. I suppose The Struggle needed ruthless men like this one, but that didn't mean I had to fall in love with him.

I held those dreadfully merciless eyes, but for any indication of what he was thinking I might as well have been looking into a satiated snake's for all the hungry response I got. I had made my point and even my vanity told me to let it go at that.

'This is some *tsotsi* you got, General,' was all Comrade X said in dismissal.

Minutes later I left.

Big Bang was driving me. He still had his gigantic Ford Galaxie, but had had it sprayed a sombre diplomatic-corps black. The white sidewall tyres remained unchanged.

'You upset, *bra*?'

'Me? Not me, Big Bang.'

'Don't give me *bulongwe*, *bra*. Give me the word, I remove your *gal pil* fleas, whoever they are.'

'Big Bang, *gahle*, *wena*. You'll get us both buried.'

'We'll have company, *bra*, lots of company.'

Yet I was excited in an indescribable kind of way.

I was jived-up big time as if the most exhilarating thing in the world had happened to me. All I can remember is the flooding sensation of: *this time you're going to be an emperor-tsotsi – this time you'll establish such power nobody anywhere can ever touch you and yours.*

When I got home, sleep was as distant as Saturn.

Little Vilakazi began sniffling and hiccup-sobbing in his sleep, and all of a sudden it infiltrated my defence mechanisms just how much I was risking.

If BOSS, the Bureau of State Security, ever caught up with me, I would be placed in the hands of white-supremacist sadists who'd make the Marquis de Sade's cousins, the Kray twins, look like benevolent spinster aunts.

My next thought (and it came to me with the veracity

of one of the Black Messiah's staggeringly straightforward sermons) was there wasn't a snowball's chance in hell of anybody being able to nail me to any sacrificial cross. Even Zsa-Zsa would never tumble to my new occupation. The way The General would have his expert hand at work in setting up what we darkie *rawurawus* needed, we could blatantly disguise ourselves as impossibly skin-transformed *mlungu* Nationalist Government state employees and still never come within a hair's breadth of being caught. The only *geezas* the law would chop off the hands of were *mampara gal pil* amateurs who were set up as fall guys anyway.

The only excuses I would have to make would be to cover my tracks as far as missing family-time went.

But I had that judged to a fine degree already, *mfowethu*.

I would let it be known that King Sobhuza himself had undercover appointed me Royal Swaziland's Examiner of Potential Commercial Income from Foreign Investment. I could already see the perfectly printed and mightily distinguished counterfeit calling card in my mind's eye, brightly emblazoned with an embossed Royal Coat of Arms, comfortably cached in my wallet.

Such a big lie was sure to be believed, wouldn't you agree, *mfowethu*? With my alibi confirmed for a relatively small fee paid to the bribed health inspector, who turned out to be a genuine bloodline-relative of the ruling monarch, my cover was foolproof. *Dadawethu!* I suddenly noticed I had emptied a full bottle of brandy while I was thinking these things through.

Time for bed.

Time for dreams.

Our following meetings with political *bras* and outright money-grubbing *bras*, including one or two radical and idealistic *mlungu* sympathisers, continued apace.

What I saw clearly, and what even the most intelligent whiteys and darkies seemed to miss entirely, was that this was *not* about equal rights and justice, not at all, *mfowethu*, but a transfer of power from one set of harsh administrators to another set of better camouflaged would-be administrators.

Tell me I'm wrong, *mfowethu*, before I continue?

Why so quiet?

My rambling reaching home?

The end result was we had a pyramid corporation all set up by The General's old friend Greg Morris, in legalese which covered almost any eventuality, including brain-brutal BOSS raid techniques. We even had it superbly organised so that a *white* security firm, armed with all those explosive death-dealers we blacks were forbidden by amputating law to possess, would guarantee our immediate safety. What a laugh, *mfowethu*.

The General got to be the overall boss without portfolio. That was his talent, his knack of *allowing* you to grant him full autonomy, his trusted control over all things relative to cash money, promised money, and even gossamer money, the diaphanous kind that needed mystical fairyland-elfish scrutiny to analyse and compute.

There were other bosses, but notwithstanding their do-or-die dedication to a 'New South Africa' they were well schooled in the gutter level of how even the highest noble aspirations worked. Not some United Nations soporific blanket of 'Human Rights' – but back to the old axiom of sacrificing lesser ambitions for the telescope-focus of the greater good. Shaka Zulu, peerless King of the Land of Heaven, had that implacably in mind with every 'atrocity' he generated.

There is always a vast difference between what people

will accept *now* and what they will give their word to accept in the nebulous future. My argument, relative to making my new assignment work at grassroots level, is proven by offering any creditor either your bank-guaranteed cheques, or half the owed amount in cash for an extension of credit. His polemic choice is always defined by the alacrity with which he reaches for the money.

The General, as I said, was the controlling doyen. That's the way it was lined up. He was an expert at performing plastic surgery on volumes of subcutaneous profit coming in and going out. He was the governing *geeza* who invested not in arms and foreign support, but in Bengal Tiger's visionary view that property anywhere *would eventually* equal vast wealth with no labouring sweat attached. Buildings that nobody but a moron would pay good rent for were obtained through fabricated companies and became ours, separate from all the other cream we were busy spoon-feeding ourselves.

The General was the sole *geeza* I gave my feedback reports to, and it couldn't have suited me better.

Comrade X furnished protection and on-the-spot capital and procured the validating paperwork for the *umPheki* locations where I needed them. He also supplied transport and drivers.

Key man for me was Zachariah Mbelu, a flourishing entrepreneur who had opened up his own shoestring chain of mini-markets in the townships. It was from him that I would get all my bulk sugar and other essential ingredients. Without someone like Zachariah Mbelu, there was no manufacture of bogus-imported bulk liquor.

Finally, there was a high-ranking white Afrikaans official, way, way up in the police hierarchy, who was vitally important to us, essential for our 'protection'.

Times had changed, you see, *mfowethu*.

No more paying off local *amapolisi* and taking blind chances thereafter. This time around we had to depend on past experience and my savvy to keep the size of our swindle a closely guarded secret. The plan was to have only a limited number of alcohol spewers gushing glug-glug at any one time, but others would additionally be set up and ready to operate if one of those busy working happened to malfunction, or had to be deserted through the bad luck of haphazard legal scrutiny. The 'twist' now had to be applied where it counted – in the courts – cases dismissed for lack of evidence, bumbling prosecutors, negligible fines and minimal jail sentences if otherwise unavoidable. Our powerful well-positioned 'contact' meant that even should an *umPheki* be terminated, the basic loss would be just that, the price of construction only. Much safer than licking the rectums of the local law, *mfowethu*, and this way the *sonta*, the 'twist', was underwritten.

Our 'contact' became a very rich white man indeed.

Building materials divorced from run-of-the-mill type articles for our liquor plants were sourced through The General's lisping Lebanese friend, the same one who had originally supplied us with as much alcohol-containing commercial cleaning liquid as we needed in the old days of separating the poisonous additives. From him we got everything we needed – tin, copper, electrical supplies, plumbing and construction items. Bulk purchases for unusual products could be made without prying questions being asked by anyone.

My prime task was exclusively to make awfully close to two-hundred-per cent proof pure alcohol, which made production reasonably simple for me. Adulterating, colouring and flavouring would come later and was the least of my worries. My job was limited to regularly turning out the quantities needed and not getting apprehended doing it. For the time being, all the other steps in the swindle – bottling, counterfeit labelling, grading the brands, distribution and so on – were somebody else's headache. The General had Greg Morris set up several corporations to take care of the money that would be pouring in and to stay sweet like a lemon with any Receiver of Revenue bloodhounds.

There was nobody better at doing precisely just that than The General.

Things were going to be accomplished relatively slowly and with great care. No overnight miracles were expected.

First I had to find *umPheki* locations that would service an entire country, and believe me, *mfowethu*, there were many bridges to be crossed before I could begin doing what I was best at. It may sound easy, but before I was ready to perambulate positively, I had to account for *every* item prior to any location being given the go-ahead.

Now you can grasp, without thinking too hard about it, that I was spending far too much time away from the restaurant, *mfowethu*, and naturally and understandably Howard Postlethwaite was souring on me.

I knew his upset ire was my just dues, so one night after we had closed our doors on the last customer, I told him as much as I dared, without providing incriminating names or details. I also intimated that I was selflessly doing it for The Struggle – a revolutionary hero who had no choice.

When I'd finished, Howard, not one born yesterday in any previous lifetime never mind this one, was remarkably complacent about the whole thing.

'Orlroight, Shatterproof, me old sahn, yew got ter do

wot yew got ter do, wot yew fink is roight. Ain't no fahkin use cryin' over spilt milk, innit? Oi'll see yer around then. Drop by when yew feel loik 'avin' a pint orn the 'ouse.'

'Thanks, Howie. You sure that's all you got to say?'

'Wot yew expect? No use in natterin' orn loik oi'm some fahkin guardian angel cahnt.'

'So there's no hard feelings?'

'Look 'ere, me old sahn, 'ow much yew got in the bank?'

'I got good dosh in the bank, Howie, you know that.'

'So wot's yore fahkin case, mate?'

'What're you trying to say?'

'Oi ain't *tryin'* ter say nuffink, me old sahn, oi *am* sayin' it. 'Ow much fahkin dosh dooyer fahkin need then?'

'As much as I can get my hands on, Howie.'

'Fahkin crazy. That's wot yew are, mate. A fahkin crazy greedy cahnt, can't see 'is fahkin nose in front orf 'is fahkin can orf mace.'

'You judge I'm crazy? That it, Howie?'

'Fahk orf, golliwog. Yew know wot oi mean. 'Oo wants ter be the richest wankah be'ind bars, yew wif me, me old sahn?'

'I'm with you, Howie. But let's just leave it at that.'

'Yore call, innit, me old sahn.'

And that was the end of our conversation.

What could I say, *mfowethu*?

Howard was one-hundred-per cent right the way he saw things.

But not from where I stood. How could I explain to Howard that what I was doing was about more than the money? It was an adrenalin surge of addictive excitement – a drug if you will – something that had me doing joyfully ecstatic cartwheels inside myself? How could I get it across to him that I was back in the one career I knew better than anything else? A trade I was so good at, I could be *the best* with my eyes closed and using only minimal applied concentration? Howard got his rocks off running a top-class eatery. I got mine from a gorgeous curved *umPheki*, and I was as proud of my talent as he was of his. How could I ever hope to get that across to Howard Postlethwaite, my *mlungu* Limey mate and partner?

We settled on my taking a lesser proportion of the incoming profits and agreeing to hire yet another assistant manager to fill in for me. It was a fair deal with no advantage on either side. I, or rather Zsa-Zsa, officially the fifty-one per cent owner, still had her shares and my position was open to me anytime I wanted to come back permanently.

'Please remember, Howie, in case it ever comes up, I'm working indirectly for King Sobhuza.'

'Yer mean if yer ball an' chain gets nosey, yah cahnt yew.'

'Exactly.'

'Fink she'll swaller it, me old sahn?'

'If you're going to lie, tell big lies, Howie.'

'Yer got a point there, me old sahn.'

We left it at that.

For the next accumulating months, I travelled extensively. I started in Jo'burg and worked my way southwards, giving Pretoria, the administrative capital of *baaskap* South Africa, the lack of attention it deserved.

I concentrated primarily on fledgling industrial sites with reasonable access, because that's where you had the best chance of getting away undetected with an operation requiring the constant in and out of delivery vehicles.

When I was done, I had far more rural locations than city ones, mainly due to the fact that each *umPheki* was relatively small, capable of producing perhaps fifty to a hundred gallons, and especially because the simpler black folk in the country would turn deaf and dumb for a few monthly *amarands*.

You'd be surprised, *mfowethu*, how difficult it was to find precisely what I was looking for. My *umPheki* sites had to conform to a rigid set of specifications. If a site lacked some of the necessary requirements, I had to dream up a way to create them with the least possible outlay.

No Honest Joe businessman trying to find himself a new location worked harder at sourcing his requirements than I did.

There were many headaches.

First off, there had to be a flow of everyday traffic around the spots I picked so that our transporters wouldn't be so noticeable going to and fro. Then it had to be a legitimate business area, basically of *any* sort, to give the unostentatious trucks, kombis and panel vans a reason for being there in the first place. You can't have a flotilla of delivery vehicles pulling up to a deserted warehouse in the middle of nowhere, can you? Right away some nosey parker's going to start asking questions. What I had to have was an existing building, however dilapidated, which could house an *umPheki*'s tallish and obvious cooking-column, necessitating a solid brick-and-mortar coverage – a shell if you will – of visually impenetrable containment.

The chosen site also had to have an excellent network of roads surrounding it, with at least two or three different approaches and departures. Because nothing gives you away faster than using the same route over and over again, no matter how congested the traffic is.

Next was a continuous water supply.

An *umPheki*, even a small one, uses an amazing amount of water, say seventy to eighty gallons minimum to produce a worthwhile day's output of alcohol.

Out in the country, you can sink your own borehole, or use a nearby stream if it's available, but in the city you are stuck with a watermeter. The municipality *sells* water to you, it's all recorded monthly, and if you're using far in excess of what your bogus business *should* be using, a nasty meter-reader comes calling and wants to know *Why?* When he arrives, you'd better have a spot-on answer prepared. That's why one of the finest places you can erect your *umPheki* is right alongside a bulk agency-affiliated dry-cleaning laundry concern, or a wholesale aerated soft-drink factory, anything that's got a legitimate excuse for using tons of water on a regular basis and all housed in the same umbrella complex

On the manufacturing side, an *umPheki* needs a ridiculous amount of sugar to make six or slightly more gallons of close to the required two-hundred-per cent proof base-alcohol. Into this witch's brew also goes fresh yeast, and a selected portion of what old Oom Kaffirboetie used to call '*Der Bazooka*' or '*Hitler's Piss*'. There are more disputes about what makes this ingredient the best than there are cumulative seconds in the day.

It takes three days average for your first mixture to ferment. You use urea, the main catalyst of your '*Der Bazooka*' or '*Hitler's Piss*', basically a crystalline solid found in the urine of mammals. This can reduce the fermentation time to forty-eight hours, but this particular method requires refined or granulated sugar. If you can get hold of syrup cheaply – syrup is potent but costly – your fermentation can be completed in just twenty-four hours. Urea is not hard to obtain, because it is synthetically mass-produced and used in making formaldehyde, tanning leather, varnishes, paints, explosives and fertilisers.

Oom Kaffirboetie would add several of his own 'specials' to the urea, and he came up with an incredible formula which he passed on to me that brought slow-and-steady fermentation down to a mere *sixteen hours*. This godsend from my touched-genius Teutonic teacher meant that I could manufacture our completed batches of alcohol far faster than any average or even legal professional outfit, and I'm prepared to put my money where my mouth is in that regard. See, old Oom Kaffirboetie had died on the job some time back while contravening the *Immorality Act*. What a way to go, eh, *mfowethu*? I must be the only *geeza* in South Africa who now knows that shrouded secret formula of his, and I'll give it to you just to prove my point and establish that I am indeed the law-breaking *tsotsi* transgressor I once was.

You use roughly fifty pounds of urea, one hundred and twenty pounds of disodium phosphate, fifty pounds of dried yeast and twenty pounds of calcium sulphate – the correct portion added of this combined mixture will give you the best fermentation *and* fermenting time available in anybody's analytical book.

Now once your *umPheki* is cooking, there are still plenty of things to worry about. The fermenting *smell* of your basic bulk ingredient is a major problem. It is as strong as an unclean and faulty-flusher public urinal with blocked drains on a diabolically hot summer's searing midday, and the rotten aromas are twice as pervasive. Once that particular pungency is identified upon entering your nostrils, it is never forgotten. So, close to an *umPheki*, the best neighbour you can have for desired obfuscation is a chemical plant, or any other manufacturer that makes a worse stink than you do. A factory district – a rural one being the best, as I've said – is tops because all the multiplied smells intermingle and the hotchpotch assault on the senses makes for great olfactory confusion.

When it comes to disposing of your used by-product, more problems arise. You can't just hurl it away, out of sight out of mind style. You'd get arrested quicker than you'd believe possible, *mfowethu*. Sounds ludicrously simple-solution manageable for an inventive brain? Let me tell you, the leftover piles up so fast you'd think you were hallucinating the staggering size of it. You can't just dump it into the local sewage. Sewage 'farms' are inspected all the time and even with all the other atrocious smells, your leftovers can be identified as easily as a naked porno star at the Pope's tea party for the best-dressed Vatican cleric. That's why the country, or near-country, makes the best site. You can haul it away in oversize plastic bags and simply bury it somewhere unpopulated.

The ecological damage?

We didn't know ecology from enema in those days, *mfowethu*.

UmPheki locations sited on the banks of a river were pretty near perfect. You can thrust a broad underground drainage pipe deep enough beneath the water's surface and far enough out so that force-pumping the stuff takes it miles downriver before it rises to the surface. That makes it difficult to pinpoint any source and dead fish tell no tales.

Being near a pig farm is also a good spot. A lot of pigfeed is basically fermented edible rubbish, and walking bacon will devour every scrap you can part with, and may even become alcoholically fond of being mildly inebriated.

Coincidental to establishing *umPheki* sites, I also searched for 'warehouses'. The finest cover for this is a transportation-trucking firm doing countrywide deliveries, with its own storage and maintenance facilities – something like the old set-up I originally ran for The General after that police raid and shoot-out when I'd barely escaped with my life and subsequently been given my first 'managerial' job for his organisation. It was essential to have *apparently* good legitimate reasons for pickup and delivery. These sites were only available to us through rental, *apartheid* property-ownership laws being what they were then.

Sometimes, to camouflage ourselves to the degree necessary, we'd finance a 'home-industries' bakery, a cheap whitewash paint factory or an old-fashioned laundry service next to our own *umPheki*. That's how thorough we were, *mfowethu*.

With all the hither and thither moving around I'd been pressurising myself into, the only time left spare for Zsa-Zsa and little Vilakazi was a portion of the weekends. I was never home for meals because distance and driving-time absolutely prohibited it.

Business was beginning to wreck my home life all over again.

But unlike being able to adjust my restaurant hours by bringing in qualified help, this time I was locked lonely into an unstoppable routine with the key thrown away.

Within a year the ball was really rolling and gathering both size and momentum.

Once the market was created and established for our products – and at our prices every brand was selling like hotcakes – you had to keep the customers regularly supplied.

So that was the whole side of my responsibility in the bag.

First, the locations.

Second, the *umPheki* housings or concealing structures.

Third, getting the distilling output to function like Swiss clockwork.

Fourth, and last, overseeing flavouring and packaging of the goods.

What happened thereafter was not my baby, but the smooth operation Bengal Tiger had put into motion for marketing and selling the bottled and labelled stuff would have taken your breath away — so perfect it came close to infallible.

This went on for years, but as I've said, *mfowethu*, when my life and *magageba* mega-profits are floating above all the worries and problems of existence like oil on water, I begin to fret. And sure enough, something kicks my feet out from under me.

It happened again.

At the time I had nothing but minor annoyances to contend with, but apart from these, we were running like an express train without brakes heading for money nirvana.

Then disaster struck like a terrorist explosion with no countdown given to first clear the endangered area.

It happened so fast, *mfowethu*, so blindingly fast that it eclipsed the breathtaking magnitude of any maestro magician's stage illusion. Picture this: *There*, on the raised stage, *right in front of you*, only ten or twenty rows away, is an elephant. *Yebo*, an *elephant* in all its mammoth majesty — and yet the magician does nothing more than clap his hands *and the elephant is gone!*

I felt like I was that unshakable elephant of permanent solid substance. A poor pachyderm that without warning could be callously vaporised by the metaphysical hand of dire necromancer's fate . . .

There was one of those interminable bimonthly meetings with Comrade X chairing the agenda.

I was not initially included, my input not needed until later. So I sat outside on a comfortable leather armchair in an adjacent room with the door closed, waiting my turn. I relaxed, because it was purely logistic routine and I had been twice reminded not to forget to be there.

I *knew* everyone inside. Their faces. Their names. Their rank and status.

There were raised voices – so strident and loudly passionate you could almost *feel* straining vocal chords stretched to volcanic rupturing point.

A heated argument was obviously taking place between the major players.

Then there were gunshots.

Followed by silence.

After a few shocked minutes, the door opened a fraction and Comrade X allowed his face to be seen by me.

'Get out of here. You were never here, understand?' was all he said, but his cold flat eyes were startlingly ablaze with inner fire.

Naturally, I obeyed with alacrity.

I didn't want to know what had happened.

Ignorance was strictly bliss to me.

Out of sight and out of mind, *mfowethu*.

A short time passed, maybe a week, and then I received an urgent message to call upon The General. I was so frightfully busy that I hadn't even had spare time to hear if anything untoward concerning that *isibhamu* incident was being bandied about through the grapevine. I stopped what I was doing and went straightaway in answer to his summons with an open mind and untroubled heart.

'Have a seat, Dhlamini, my boy,' The General said. 'Prepare yourself for a shock.'

'What, have profits trebled instead of doubling?' I grinned back at him. Then I saw that his raptor's eyes were deadly serious and his spade beard was jutting forward like the prow of a ship.

The General leaned back in the huge, padded swivel-chair that encased and dwarfed his small dapper frame and steepled his fingers, resting his chin upon the apex.

'What I have to say to you is important. I want you to concentrate. Every detail is vital.'

'I'm all ears, General, sir.'

'I want you to recall for me every second of your last visit to Comrade X.'

'Haven't been there for a month, General, sir.'

'I am not the *amapolisi*, Dhlamini. Please do me the courtesy of relinquishing any games.'

'My apologies. Yes, I was there, a week ago more or less.'

'You know the identities of the other men there while you were present?'

'Yes, yes I do. I saw them briefly and was told to wait my turn.'

'And then?'

'Shots were fired, General, sir.'

'How many, Dhlamini?'

'I counted five.'

'And how many men did you see leaving that meeting?'

'None. Comrade X showed his face to me and ordered me to disappear. I left quickstyle.'

'Two men died that night, important men. A third was presumed dead. But he lived long enough to alert the police to the identity of his slayer. Yet no more than that. Subsequent to this, BOSS raided Comrade X. They have the murder weapon. The bullets match the corpses, but they have no fingerprints to say who pulled the trigger.

The arrest of Comrade X has thrown this entire operation into jeopardy.'

'But why, General, sir?' I asked, feeling that icy cold *déjà vu* prickle of impending doom approaching like a blanketing black-cloud storm about to bombard me with cannonball-sized killer hailstones.

'How long do you think Comrade X will hold out against the expert interrogators of the Bureau of State Security?'

I nodded, following the direction he was taking me.

'Not long, General, sir.'

'They have truth serums, hallucinogens, and terribly sophisticated inhuman physical torture methods at their disposal. Comrade X *will* talk. And he *will* divulge every detail of what we are involved in, *if his interrogators bother to question him beyond the murders that presently concern them.* We may be lucky, Dhlamini, my boy, but then again, we may not. What is certain is that Comrade X will answer any question asked of him with the spartan truth. Whether he believes he has fooled them, or whether he believes he has not, the fluctuating state of what he perceives to be his own mind will be immaterial to their findings. It makes no difference. We are on temporary, perhaps even permanent, hold. As of now, this instant. Bengal Tiger is already covering his tracks, deleting, destroying and burning any evidence that can lead back to him.'

'Oh well,' I sighed the sigh of one resigned to defeat. 'Back to the restaurant business for me, General, sir.'

'Not quite, Dhlamini, my boy.'

'I don't follow?'

'You will. Matters have become terribly complicated. The complication ensnares you.'

'I'm just one small cog in a big gearbox. BOSS won't be

looking for me and even if they do, what can they prove? I'm a family man living in Swaziland, minding my own business. Nobody cares about me, General, sir.'

'Ah, but they do, Dhlamini, my boy.'

'Again, I don't follow you. What's that about, General, sir?'

'Comrade X is himself the source of your complication.'

'But he's been arrested. Nothing to do with me.'

'Wrong.'

'Wrong, General, sir?'

'Unfortunately so, Dhlamini, my boy. Comrade X is convinced that if any witnesses to the murders he committed fortunately expire or vanish, the murder charges against him cannot be proved.'

'I would *never* give state testimony!'

'You know that and I know that. But Comrade X does not. Besides which, he does not consider the slayings "*murder*" but "*political exorcising of enemies of The Struggle*". That is the category he has sufficient power to place you in, Dhlamini.'

'This is unbelievable.'

'Admittedly. Unbelievable or not, believe this. Two other men at that meeting behind closed doors are now mysteriously dead. One was hijacked and killed. The other was knifed dead during an eruption at his favourite *shebeen*. A coincidence which is blatantly not a coincidence. Comrade X has a highly lucrative contract out to make sure you join the ranks of the deceased. This is corroborated by my sources. The word is out that you are a traitor to The Struggle. Hatred for *apartheid* is such that from today you are a guaranteed corpse, Dhlamini. None of this is my doing. I simply relate the facts of the matter. You have very little time to make a decision, my boy.'

'What do you mean, General, sir?'

'Firstly, you have to get away. No, do not speak as yet. Far away will not save you if you are perceived as an enemy of The Struggle. They will get at you through your wife, your child, your friends, anybody, anywhere, anytime. You must prove beyond the shadow of a doubt that you are committed to The Struggle. A man willing to sacrifice all for a shared aim, a believer in the one ideology.'

'I'm not a political person, never have been. I'm a dead man, General, sir.'

'No, you are not, not yet. You are very much alive and I wish, for selfish reasons perhaps, that you have every chance of remaining so.'

'But what can I do?'

'You must join MK. Then you will be above reproach.'

'*MK*? Militant struggle? I have no moral commitment to violence! I hate guns!'

'Do or die, Dhlamini. It is the best I can do for you. It is *all* I can do for you.'

'A soldier for *Umkhonto we Sizwe*, the Spear of the Nation?'

'Yes, MK, as you know. You will be outside South African borders and part of a basic training camp within twenty-four hours. Safe for the time being, Dhlamini. But I must have your decision *now*, if I am to help you.'

Again, what choice did I have, *mfowethu*?

That was how I became part of a small, neophyte, underground army embracing sabotage, guerrilla warfare, terrorism and open revolution.

Our initial strategy was selective forays against

military installations, power plants, telephone lines and transportation links – targets that would not only hamper the military effectiveness of the Nazi Nationalist Government, but badly frighten all *apartheid* supporters, scare away foreign capital and weaken the intrinsic structure of the white-power-dominated economy.

That was the altruistic vision.

In reality it degenerated into the foulest dregs of outright depraved loss of respect for human life and human dignity and human ideals you can imagine.

It was a nightmare time, a savage time, a brutal bestial time, when to allow yourself feelings of right or wrong, or fair play, was to invite catastrophe to come calling with the Grim Reaper's scythe held firmly in both bloodied hands.

Here, *mfowethu*, read this. I am not proud of it, but that was how it was.

What is it?

A diary of sorts, a record more of my immediate thoughts than listing precisely what we MK did.

Excuse me now, will you? I'm going to take a short but welcome nap.

Call me when you're ready to continue, eh?

Please use the toilet there if my scribbles make you feel like vomiting.

Only joking.

See you later, *mfowethu*.

Thursday. Night.

South African recce soldiers in force herd the inhabitants of this remote village suspected of being MK sympathisers towards a central compound. We watch hidden from thick camouflage, but we are too few to risk open conflict. Men, women and children are still sleepily naked or in scraps of night-garments. They look and behave like drugged two-legged cattle. The soldiers interrogate the adults, one by one, harsh flashlights held up to their faces. A young woman is struck with a rifle butt. She collapses, teeth and lips smashed. She pushes herself up again with violent effort. A man rushes over to help her, possibly one of her brothers; it is difficult to tell in this torch-lit night. He is thrashed mercilessly to the ground, heavy boots thud into his side; you can hear his ribs crack. The young woman has deftly broken free from her interrogator with this distraction and she runs away with flying feet for the darkness. A hand-held searchlight is snapped on. She flees like a black gazelle trapped in the glaring white light, now darting between the trees that form the village's perimeter. Bullets spray after her from flame-spitting automatic weapons. Wood chunks burst in violation from heavy-calibre impact, tree trunks explode, and the young woman sways first left, then right, then her head bursts in a fountain of dark blood. She becomes an amorphous shadowed patch of shapelessness on the ground. Soldiers fetch her body and carry her back carelessly slung between them. Blood flows in thick streams from her dangling dead nostrils, making a wet trail that marks her cadaver's return to the compound. Three days ago she fed our starving men and also me. We made love. She was sweet and innocently compliant and wanted only to help. An elderly man next points northward. That is where we supposedly have gone; the South African soldiers will follow that direction. We MK men fade further back into the darkness to layer their upcoming route with trip-string grenades and a profusion of invisible landmines. That is all we can do for tonight.

Saturday. Late afternoon.

We receive a covert supply of AK-47s and fresh loads of much-needed ammunition. These are hidden inside bleached raw-cotton sacks of mielie meal delivered to an Indian bush-trader's faraway commercial outpost. AK-47s are robustly constructed weapons, ideal only for killing, killing, killing. We wrap them after cleaning them in cheap, brightly-patterned, lightweight rayon blankets, ready for distribution and future use. We halt a battered bus spewing foul diesel-fumes and carrying happily chattering schoolchildren along the single-track bush-surrounded dirt road. Once inside this forcibly commandeered excellent camouflage, we head for a preselected rendezvous to deliver the fresh arms to a more northern cadre of our MK brothers. Half of the children are boys and half are girls, none of them in the least bit frightened of us. One of our group, the one who prays morning and evening without fail and was once upon a time a schoolteacher, or so he said, begins an indoctrination harangue. The children love it. They repeat the phrases of political mumbo-jumbo with an enthusiasm that should be reserved for the ABC of school. The bus grumbles and groans, lurches and sways, but we are making good time, much better than footslogging it. Our expert tracker now gives instructions to the petrified driver, who sweats an acrid waterfall of wet fear but obeys without question. The bus leaves the road, almost capsizing into a hidden depression, miraculously rights itself and slows down to a jolting crawl, heading deeper into prolific bush, carefully negotiating the rough terrain it was never designed to traverse. We stop just before sunset. The children make our evening meal of thin maize-porridge and brackish water. One of the girls is fourteen, but her figure has ripened _ to look at her she is a grown woman in school uniform. The comrade-schoolteacher talks charmingly to the girl, layering her with good-natured frivolity, touching her hair, her bare knees. The bus driver opens his mouth, and then promptly shuts it again, as he catches the comrade-schoolteacher's rapid eye suddenly focusing on him. The girl follows the comrade-schoolteacher into the bush with very little urging, her eyes bright in ignorant anticipation at being so favoured, the chosen butterfly from amongst all her less vital caterpillar friends. Three men shiftily follow them. Not much later the girl screams horribly, long, drawn-out interminable wails, but eventually this turns into pitifully choking sobs and finally dribbles away into silence. The men return one by one to our fireless campsite, buttoning up their flies, looking sheepish and full of bravado at the same time. There is no sign of the girl. During my midnight shift on guard-duty, I notice there is no sign of the bus driver either, not as far as I can see anyway. Should I report it? I decide not to, let sleeping whipped-lapdogs lie. In the morning neither she nor the bus driver are to be found anywhere within the area it was specified they must on no account leave. They are gone. Two men, it is decided, are sufficient for the task of finding them, and they set off after the easy-to-follow spoor. I am ordered to accompany them. I obey. We reach them miles before they have any chance of reaching the road and are as distant from posing a threat of discovery as the North Pole is close to our position. South African patrols at this stage have about the same chance of spotting them as has a terminally myopic man with smashed spectacles. She sinks down hopelessly to her bare thorn-scratched haunches, and the bus driver bravely puts his arm around her shoulders and turns to face us _ not trained for long-distance endurance of any kind, he also is clearly exhausted way beyond his stamina's limits. One of my two companions steps forward when we are within face-to-face conversation distance and smashes him repeatedly about the head with his AK-47, even after he is prone and lifeless, until greyish-pink matter starts seeping out between the visibly sharded bone fragments of his skull. The girl points pitifully between her legs and makes the only sacrificial offering she imagines might save her from a similar fate. One MK soldier goes behind her while the other pulls out his penis pretending to accept her offering; she actually smiles before his companion opens up a pocket-knife with a stubby blade and saws raggedly at her throat until she is dead. He is covered in her blood at this merciful stage. He was one of those who had raped her last night. We stand over her mute corpse. I did nothing but watch. There is no going back now. The two men laugh and joke on the return journey, their false jollity permeated by the lunatic relief of near-hysteria. If I did not know it before, I know it now _ my soul will rot in hell. Nevertheless, we make our arranged meet with our waiting MK comrades not much later, and the AK-47s are distributed as essentially needed. The mission has been successful, that is all that counts.

Monday. Early morning.

We walk into a trap. An ambush near a trickling stream, a withered shadow of what was once a turbulent river because of the enervating and blistering drought that curses the land. We have had to come here in desperation to replenish our long-evaporated meagre water supplies. Bullets fly around us with the intense buzzing of a deadly swarm of wild bees. There is heart-stopping confusion as we fall into our trained pattern of scatter and retreat, form up again, scatter and retreat, all the while firing short bursts blindly at where we can only guess our attackers have secreted themselves. Our tracker's stomach is suddenly shot away; it literally vanishes in a spray of cloth fragments and cauterised meat. He is dying, but dominates his pain and shock with insane courage, gathers up what remains of his flapping entrails and, using an anthill for cover, hisses at us to flee while he holds our enemies at bay. We are far enough from the stream for immediate safety when we hear a last distinctive explosion, an isolated AK-47 shot, then no more for long seconds. The echoing sound of a fragmenting grenade that follows eventually reaches our ears as we run steadily southwards and we register from this suicide farewell that our tracker is dead. As he dominated his pain, so we dominate our raging thirst _ the nearest water is two impossibly far days distant. I pick up a pebble and suck on it until my mouth contains no more saliva and I am certain I am going to die. More than that, I know infallibly that death from dehydration is my destiny. But then it rains. Dry dust turns to weltering mud and we fall onto our backs with mouths open to receive heavenly liquid life from the heavy dark clouds overhead and we survive.

Thursday. Night.

Our routine has become even harder. We have been recalled for an escalation of intensive training. Stupid, as we are hard, lean, fit, and only half-starved _ a pillar of strength in comparison to most of the new recruits. Every day we drill with heavy cut-down saplings, we practise hand-to-hand combat. We work with AK-47s until we can strip them sightless and put them back together again in less than a quarter minute. We learn how to boost landmines with plastic explosive, powerful enough to shatter and destroy any all-terrain armoured vehicles and the occupants within. We hone the art of guerrilla ambush; cowardly cruelty is our praiseworthy doctrine. We live on the thin gruel of insipid maize meal and birds eggs and lizard flesh and protein-rich insects, meat happens only when it happens, AK-47s make poor hunting rifles. At midnight sometimes, like now, we are allowed to stagger away for blessed sleep. We are woken before the sun rises. Perhaps death from the instructions of Comrade X would have been preferable, a better fate than this living hell.

Sunday. Aftermath.

We have come to the encroaching borderline lands of white farmers. On the dirt roads we lay abusively heavy new-design landmines. These improved instruments of destruction have a mind-numbing capacity to effectively annihilate or horribly maim forever over ever-increased areas. We have carried these metal murderers on our backs for so long, we almost weep with relief to be able to unbuckle them and commit them at long last to callous and indifferent mayhem. We routinely attack the white farmhouses. In one week alone we destroy five generations-old buildings and three times that number of flourishing families, including all their servants and labourers. Darkness is our ally, because we know the South African recces will not come to the aid of those we are slaughtering for the lethal reason that we have mined all the approaches before our killing attack. Mines are virtually invisible in the dark even to a highly trained expert with all the latest infrared technology at his disposal. We have all night to finish our merciless job and escape before dawn. Our technique is flawlessly developed. At sunset's twilight we poison the faithful dogs and cut the thick barbed-wire surround. We fire rockets into the doorways and windows and rush through these breaches with AK-47s firing the second the dense impenetrable smoke clears, screams of terror goad us into frenzied insensate action. The horrors we leave behind are a deliberate provocation to white succour that can only arrive at first light. What atrocities they will find, creatively engineered or just haphazard reality, will drive them into a careless paroxysm of blind rage and thus drive them into dull death at our hands. Low on ammunition, we retreat, back into the sheltering bush, laying explosive mantraps as we withdraw. We come across a farmer rushing his wife to hospital, three daughters and two alert sons with searching eyes and bolt-action rifles in the back of the dust-billowing pickup truck travelling with him. We blast his big bakkie from the back with a heat-seeking rocket. One barely teenage daughter and the pregnant wife survive the metal-ripping detonation of the fiercely flaring impact, still alive, jerking spastic feminine defiance at us, but on their doomed way to the grave, they bleed hideously. The MK men queue up and take turns to have brutish sexual intercourse with the almost-cadavers, the two white females with shattered bodies. I refuse to participate. I am told I will be shot if I do not join the ghouls orgy. A pistol is placed to my temple. All the men are watching me with vampire-expectant eyes. To my shame, I unbutton my pants and perform what can only be described as nauseating necrophilia. I am alive and the girl and her pregnant swollen-bellied mother are both dead within the hour, stripped naked, abandoned on a sandy road next to five other white bodies and a ruined vehicle.

Tuesday. Bush hospital.
An ancient Dakota drops the enemy from its innards. The parachutes pop open only seconds before the South African recces hit the ground. They snap their harnesses and hurtle forward in a crouched run, firing as they come. Half of us are killed in minutes –

Put that horrible diary aside, *mfowethu*. Don't look surprised to see me back so soon. I couldn't sleep. What you've already copied and written down, I'm convinced, is more than enough. Please close those covers now and I'll continue while I'm yet full of memories. A lot of years passed in that manner, years I'd rather forget, so let's rather get on with the more relevant story of *tsotsi* business.

This is what took place when I just simply could take no more of life amongst living homicidal zombies.

I deserted.

The news filtered through to us that Comrade X had been given free flying-lessons from one of the upper storeys of John Vorster Square, and that was incentive enough for me.

I camouflaged my return so that the first time I called home was from Swaziland's airport, but there was no answer to the insistent ringing of the telephone. I judged that perhaps it would be more sensational to surprise my family in person, they having no clue whether I was alive or dead at this stage of the absent game I'd been forced to play. I took a taxi home. Once inside, I thought I was in the wrong dwelling until I realised I was seeing new furniture and new curtains and all the rest of it. But there, *mfowethu*, there were my favourite small photographs of Zsa-Zsa, little Vilakazi and yours truly, beaming out in a tight huddle from the picture frames. My best brandy was still in the same place in the familiar cabinet and I poured myself a drink and sat down to wait.

I worried.

By late afternoon I was more than a little drunk, when the front door opened and in they walked.

Zsa-Zsa looked pretty much the same. Gorgeous. A dusky delight. Fashions had changed but she hadn't.

But, oh my, *mfowethu*, how little Vilakazi had grown. He had on long pants, a relaxer in his hair, and he had shot up to be nearly as tall as his mother's shoulder.

They both stood there with frozen, searching stares, taking in my country-labourer's frayed jacket and patched trousers – perhaps not recognising me at first because I had lost so much weight. I was all threadbare lean muscle, skin and bone, not an ounce of fat, and still wearing my bush-beard. I held out my arms to Vilakazi, expecting him to rush forward for a hug and a wrestle. But not *this* grown Vilakazi. He stepped forward and stuck out his hand for me to shake, more formal than a bunch of conservative bankers meeting themselves face-to-face in a three-dimensional mirror. I could see Zsa-Zsa's reaction over Vilakazi's shoulder and she was crying, but next thing she was laughing through all those tears. Vilakazi stepped back and then she was in my arms. How good it felt to hold her! How good it felt to be home!

For the next few hours I answered a fusillade of questions, and my inventiveness had plenty of opportunities to scale the height of new imaginative peaks. Of course I was forced to avoid the desolately macabre real issues of the missing years by claiming there were many areas in that past which, for their own safety, I couldn't talk about.

But they weren't interested in all that; they were interested only in *me*.

I talked until my tongue ran out of fuel.

Then Zsa-Zsa told me to wash. She begged me to shave off my dreadfully unprepossessing chin-fur so she could see my face. Thereafter I was *ordered* to find some respectable clothing, get dressed, and make myself ready.

For what?

I needed fattening up, she said, and there was no time like the present to begin just that absolutely necessary feeding process. After complying, when I was clean-shaven again and smelling sweet, she said she had a surprise for me and into the car we three piled.

Zsa-Zsa parked right in front of the glittering facade of a main-road restaurant and left the keys carelessly in the ignition, herding me and Vilakazi at top speed through the swanky entranceway.

Howard Postlethwaite was standing there, an enormous goofy grin on his craggy Londoner's can of mace.

"Ullo, Shatterproof,' he said blandly. "Ow d'yer loik yer new rest'rant, me old sahn?'

Now that is what I call a surprise, *mfowethu*!

Howard and Zsa-Zsa had had the magnificent initiative to cook up and carry out this grandiose move years back and had turned it into even more of a success than our first Swaziland venture. Here it was all set up for a luckily surviving me to come home to. That benevolent angel of good fortune was back, perched solidly once again on my absurdly blessed shoulder.

Howard set up a table at the rear and spoiled us royally, trotting out a variety of dishes that would have pleased the narcissistic Roman epicures Caligula and Nero at their most lavishly fastidious.

Only problem was that my belly had shrunk, but still I ate until I could hardly lift my knife and fork to my surfeited mouth.

Howard finished off our feast by personally serving us filter coffee and liqueur brandy in elegant snifters.

Each flavour was treasure to my atrophied taste buds.

Zsa-Zsa kept watching me with star-shimmering intensity as if I'd vanish the instant she chanced to take her eyes off me for even a second.

Vilakazi was studiously polishing off his third ice-cream with hot chocolate sauce, his other hand holding mine under the table.

I just sat there absorbing it all, taking a good butcher's at them and every miraculous thing around me.

This was some diner's palace I owned all of a sardine, *mfowethu*. It was full to capacity with nary a dissatisfied face in sight. I couldn't help noticing that while I was there some of the tables had turned over twice, and there was still a packed crowd at the same beautifully sculpted bar taken from the first restaurant.

I watched Howard Postlethwaite at work controlling the ambience. Nobody smoother, *mfowethu*, nobody. He looked marvellously happy. His beautiful suit of sartorial perfection must have set him back London's finest tailor's prices, because that's doubtless where it came from, lousy exchange rate or no lousy exchange rate. The splendid suit vastly improved Howard's outer lack of natural attributes, his craggy English face with enormous bushy eyebrows set above a pear-shaped body. That suit made him positively, assuredly, emphatically elegant. Howard raised one of those dust-broom eyebrows while I was observing him and I followed its fringed aim to a waiter a good ten tables away with a messy, carrot-coloured soup stain bespattering his sleeve. So help me, the waiter might have been hit by an invisible laser blast the way he stopped in his tracks, spun about, vanished and reappeared in a fresh, sparklingly clean, white serving half-jacket in place of the soiled one.

The low hum of voices that are peculiar to a large area filled with happy human beings is a peculiarly recognisable and individual collective sound. It is a good sound. A contented sound. A sound that may be a complete *potpourri* cross-section of young and old – including guys together after a night on the town – secretive lovers exchanging subdued verbal passion – a whole bunch of girls out on a ladies-only female foray for loudly proclaimed independent togetherness – impossible to pin down every source, impossible to tell with any exactness. What you could tell, *mfowethu*, was that that special sound added up to accumulating money, the sound of success.

Then the forgotten penny dropped.

'Where's Big Bang?'

'Over at the old place,' Zsa-Zsa said, lips curled in a smile. 'You didn't think we'd forget Big Bang, did you?'

'What old place? Why isn't he playing tuxedo peacekeeper here?'

'Which question first?'

'Both.'

'The old restaurant. Downstairs it's pool tables, game machines, a serving bar knocked through from the old one you built at the back, and turned inwards with protective barricades so there's never any "barman versus customer" violence. Upstairs Big Bang serves time-honoured African food buffet-style – iron pots with succulent meat stews and vegetables and one price for as much as you can eat. A roaring success. Big Bang hasn't had to break any heads for months.'

'Big Bang *runs* it?'

'Like a traditional tribal chief over his own fiefdom. Any backchat or unpleasantness and Big Bang *bans* you, you become *persona non grata*. His customers always come back *begging* to be reinstated in his good books. Big Bang might have been created for the job. Plenty of women. Plenty of beer. Some occasional gratifying violence.'

'That's wonderful.'

'It is, isn't it? He loves Vilakazi too, spoils your boy rotten.'

'He got shares?'

'Of course he's got shares.'

'How much?'

'Fifty per cent. Treat a man right, he'll treat you right.'

I sat back and let this all sink in while we had more coffee.

As I said, *mfowethu*, I was stuffed to the gills with good

food, almost feeling nauseous with contentment. Vilakazi was slumped in his seat, his eyes beginning to droop, clearly ready to go home to bed without any protest.

I was aware I was in a cloudy daze myself, and I found my eyes wandering pleasantly all over the place like a compass seated in a gimbal's tilted housing during mildly rough weather. *Mildly rough weather?* What's that called again, *mfowethu?*

That's it, thank you.

An oxymoron.

Then the moron in me began to surface, because there was a large, well-polished copper coffee contraption at the end of the spectacular bar and it glinted a silent Circe's siren song under the subdued lighting. My eyes remained fixed on it while my mind roamed like an Australian on a backpacking tour through Europe, my body as blissful as if it was on a surfeit of pentathol, that lovely drug they calm you down with at hospitals before a severe surgical procedure. All of a sudden I knew what the alluring attraction of the coffee contraption was. The swollen belly of the jug looked like a *bonsai* liquor-making *umPheki* steaming away and doing its productive thing. I began to experience immediate withdrawal symptoms.

The next few weeks were spent just loafing around, filling myself with recovery vitamins the natural way, soaking up soothing leisure and healthy food, and getting close to Zsa-Zsa and not-so-little Vilakazi again. My boy had a brain like a Venus flytrap, and it was jammed full of ideas he'd caught and was busy digesting, many of them the most startling combinations of fact bolstered by fantasy that you could ever imagine having thrown at you. Any conversation would trigger off some reference point he could relate to, and while he'd make you burst into laughter with some of his preposterous conclusions, the performance of his inquisitive intelligence always came shining through. I could be amused in Vilakazi's company for hours on end without ever becoming the least bit bored. His face was so mobile; he never held the same expression for more than a fleeting moment at a time. And the energy of that boy – he just never stopped moving and he moved like he was bouncing on air.

It took a while to get back that father-son good mates trust again.

I was hesitant and afraid deep inside myself to open up. Those years in the bush had made me place an emotional shield around myself and I was fumblingly hesitant with my spontaneity. But that passed. We got to know each other all over again from scratch.

There were, however, some unbridgeable differences between father and son.

Vilakazi had become passionately interested in music while I was away. When he'd play his Motown records of Percy Sledge and Otis Redding and even whitey groups like the Beatles and the Rolling Stones, I started going down to the restaurant, just to give my ears relief from these audio insults to *mbaqanga* and township jazz.

I judged Howard Postlethwaite knew how things were going to line up for me, canny Limey that he was.

He didn't seem surprised or dismayed when I told him I was going to find out at some stage in the future if The General still had a place for me in his organisation. Besides, there were big, banked *amarands* owing to me, and I knew I'd never collect without first offering my services.

'Orlroight, Shatterproof, me old sahn,' was all Howard said. 'But oi could use a fahkin 'and around the business 'ere while yore waitin' an' if yer'd be disposed ter feel loik gettin' up orf yer fahkin lazy golliwog's arse.'

Even his insults made me feel good, *mfowethu*.

You see, he didn't *have* to ask me to participate in the restaurant's management again; Howard had it all under iron control. I could see for myself how the place was continually dovetailing the way it should, never a glitch in sight, and never a rough patch of destructive staff interaction-reaction.

But *modus operandi*, plural, had changed since I'd been away, trying my best to make myself learn to hate blindly, yet somehow never quite succeeding.

For instance, the waiters.

We used to work them to the bone. Now, if you didn't allow them reasonable shifts, the good ones would be away like the wind, the bad ones waiting until you were in a real jam before deserting to allow you to dig your own hole of helplessly abandoned horrors even deeper. If you swore at a waiter, all of his comrades would back him up until you apologised to all of them – singularly and as a profession. Their basic pay had risen drastically. In keeping abreast of the times – if you snooze, you lose – that's how it worked. Waiters were even insisting on medical aid and unemployment contributions from *your* pocket. The only way you could actually fire any obstreperous bastard was to catch him red-handed stealing, being blind drunk on the job with witnesses to corroborate your assessment of his sobriety or lack of it, or physically assaulting a customer.

The new restaurant was twice as busy as the old one, seating double the number of diners.

The first time Howard showed me the pay schedule, I nearly had myself a hernia. The head chef with four cooks under him was earning a qualified accountant's salary. And all the rest – wine-stewards, dishwashers, barmen, cleaners, the works – were all making the kind of money I'd have judged stratospheric ten years ago.

Food prices were up too, that goes without saying, but *our* food prices were nowhere near where they should have been in relation to our overheads. No wonder we were in the hurricane's eye of gastronomic popularity, *mfowethu*. On the turn I had new gold-embossed leather-bound menus printed with adjusted charges. Howard was sceptical, but not a single diner blinked at the shift in eating economics and business surged forward as robustly as always.

We were inundated with sales-mad suppliers.

The world seemed to have climbed aboard the food-business bandwagon. Five, six, seven, eight and more merchants representing anything from bar requisites to meat and condiments plagued us on a daily basis. My best use for them was to check and counter-check competitive prices, one against the other, and so become conversant with what we should be paying for what we needed.

Frozen vegetables were now rearing their frosty heads, coming rapidly to the flawless greens forefront and the convenience aspect made for a much lighter workload. We still had several fresh-food suppliers and from the moment the doors opened in the early morning until lunchtime, we were busy, busy, busy, and then after lunch, even busier one way or another. Dairies, bakeries, meat and wholesale grocery suppliers were all scrambling for our business.

Competitors each had a foot jammed in the door trying to sell you something he or she claimed was the *crème de la crème* of whatever harvested crop they had their hands on.

They all offered kickbacks. Here's an example, *mfowethu*:

'*The total comes off your income tax. You see that*

clearly, don't you, Mr Bhekuzulu, Mr Postlethwaite? So you lose nothing. But the percentage of personal monetary return I'm offering you is paid cash and therefore to do whatever you wish with whenever you wish, gentlemen. There, my cards are on the table. All I need is your signatures at the bottom of this order form and I'll expedite the delivery immediately. I didn't quite catch that, Mr Postlethwaite, would you please repea – Mr Bhekuzulu! That is not necessary! Yes, I know the way out, take your hand off me – I'm leaving, I'm leaving, but think about what I said, won't you, gentlemen? One can always change one's mind and – alright, alright, I'm on my way! No need to be abusive, only doing my job!'

A gold mine for managerial employees of owner-uninvolved restaurants, *mfowethu.* Some of them must have been making more money than their employers.

Another significant difference had crept in unnoticed.

Credit cards were replacing cash and, strangely enough, that took a lot of the fistful-of-notes enjoyment out of balancing the night's take. Plus you lost five per cent in cold-blooded discount to the synthetic credit card-issuing banks and that was why I, along with a lot of other incensed restaurateurs, never carried Diner's Club facilities. Can you believe, *mfowethu,* that those particular plastic vampires wanted *seven and a half per cent of your money* for the privilege of allowing *their* customers to eat at *your* establishment? That's the way it was, Big Business always shafting small business whenever it gets the opportunity.

It was no longer necessary to venture virtually pre-dawn to the market and work your larynx hoarse fighting for bargains. It all came right to you. The biggest fight remaining was to beat off salesmen who'd have you overbuying your way into bankruptcy as soon as look at you.

Months later, while I was well and truly embroiled in all of this roots-level trading, a call came for me.

It was The General. He'd contacted me before I'd got on my *tsotsi*'s bicycle and contacted him. I was flattered.

Howard must have read my face as soon as I'd replaced the receiver.

'Break a fahkin leg, me old sahn,' he said, before turning his back on me. 'Show them cahnts wot yer made orf.'

Back On The Boil

This time around there was none of the inherent frenzy there had been before.

Incredible, but there were a half-dozen precious *umPheki* cookboys sitting out there untouched at various excellent locations and all they needed were minor repairs to start them functioning full-head-of-steam-ahead once more. Years of idleness hadn't made them obsolete, which just proved my wise *tsotsi*'s choice of always using the best materials. I'd have them operational within a fortnight.

My only worry was, was there any competition? In this game competition doesn't like competition overmuch and your rivals show their antipathy by doing their best to remove you from any fond attachment to this mortal coil. Life back in the townships of Jo'burg had got both tougher and harder, and there were desperado *skebengu rawurawus* aplenty for hire who'd blow you away for as little as five hundred *amarands*, no questions asked, I kid you not, *mfowethu*.

Political unrest against *apartheid* was peaking again and the whole of South Africa was as volatile as an active volcano. The army patrolled the streets in strength. A black man never dared break into a run – that was reason sufficient to shoot you dead or arrest you with an immediate savage beating, so you played it cool and kept your head down and made it a practice never to stare too hard.

'Listen, Dhlamini, my boy,' The General lectured me like a kindly father. 'Please get it into your *ikhanda* not to concern yourself with anything but our operation. Once we manufacture what we need, *we are a legitimate concern*. Leave politics to politicians and let the gangsters annihilate one another – we have left that far behind. Bengal Tiger has the "twist" in everywhere you can conceive of, so let him and me take care of any little upsets or annoying bumps. Our markets are very well established – stronger than they were before and perfectly safe. Take it from me, my boy.'

Within a few short months, I was fully operational again.

The hierarchy of my immediate bosses was somewhat rearranged, but controlling politics and controlling profit went happily hand in hand together, all interests concentrated on working industriously for shared benefit.

There was no problem with supplies. The General had meantime bought into diverse linked companies which manufactured yeast and refined sugar and other basic essentials in the amounts we needed, so there were no hiccups anywhere along the way to being totally cost-effective.

Things were smoother, better organised.

My second time around I was able to studiously avoid many sneaky pitfall mistakes that had trapped me before. I could take my time; I didn't have to rush things. There was ample opportunity for a prior assessment that the swimming pool was filled with water before diving off the high diving board.

We were all going to be in business for a long, long while, and we were all going to become multimillionaires. Aims and aspects of supporting The Struggle at the same time were taken care of. Bookkeeping and inventory work that used to be my baby and that had plagued me so remorselessly were now, through The General, appointed somebody else's headache. My share of the split-many-ways profits was a straightforward percentage and believe me, *mfowethu*, each and every *umPheki* was distilling increments of liquid gold. My heaviest task was making up and submitting a bimonthly written report to The General, much like a sea captain keeping the daily ship's log.

Once I was decisively back in the driver's seat and firmly established, The General threw a private party at our new Swaziland restaurant.

Outside (barely) of South Africa, it was the perfect place for bigwig *tsotsis* and powerful political personalities, outlawed by the edict of equally powerful politically advantaged personalities weighing in on the permanently paranoid side of unfairly weighted scales, to let their hair down.

The restaurant doors were closed, just for that one time, to all outsiders and it was a singularly fantastic get together. If BOSS had known about it and overkill-bombed the place with their usual heavy-handed *no survivors no witnesses* techniques there would be no New Democratic South Africa as it exists today, believe me, *mfowethu*.

I was helping Howard Postlethwaite out that evening, but also downing a good couple of drinks while I was at it. Because I was such a busy bee, I didn't eat. When the party started finally breaking up, I was drunk as a skunk.

A few of us who were not on anybody's most-wanted list headed over to the Royal Swazi Holiday Inn and fooled around at the gaming tables.

Somebody slipped a note of much doubled-over hotel stationery into my hand.

I fumbled for ages with inebriated fingers, at long last unfolding it.

There was a Royal Swazi Holiday Inn suite number hand-printed there, as well as a time and the date indicating the following day.

I searched all around me with bleary eyes, and so help me, through the smoke and muzziness, *I saw Bubbles Nightingale.*

She was sitting at one of those *rest-your-legs-from-feeding-us-money* casino convenience tables amongst a small group who all had that stamp of the professional musician about them: long hair, dark glasses at night, outrageous clothes. She deliberately avoided my leeringly intent gaze. She looked exactly like that red-headed froth of boiling female hormones I remembered so well – me and Bubbles stark naked in a bathtub together cutting up Poco Batista Salvador's murdered corpse into steak on the bone and sectioned spare-ribs – covered in bright red, red so bright it did its best to outshine her neon pubic bush and equally neon head of Medusa-curls hair. It wasn't erotic then, but now, *mfowethu*, my testicles dropped with the weight of hundred-pound cannonballs and my cast-iron artillery barrel straightened up in accurate elevation towards the target.

Of course.

She'd had that first major hit and a second and a third not quite so big, but good enough to get into the international top forty. The world was beginning its Sanctions of Suitable Conscience against South Africa, and Bubbles (now with a different stage name) had made a public announcement that if she couldn't perform to a racially mixed audience, she was turning down a mega-lucrative offer to tour the country that birthed *apartheid*. The resultant publicity that was splashed worldwide didn't hurt her record sales at all, *mfowethu*. In fact it doubled them across the globe, because South Africa had become a focus for indignant armchair hate, outrage indulged in by a spectrum of mealy-mouthed warriors, from pretentious pop stars to *de rigueur poseurs*, from Paraguay to Portobello Road.

Now she was giving a one-off open-air concert in Swaziland and there were other big-name overseas musicians tagging along because it was all going to be made into another highly-publicised Woodstock-type film. All proceeds from this braveheart venture by the songster microphone-adventurers were pledged to fight *apartheid* – and the production would naturally become the music industry's most-spoken-about hallowed flavour-of-the-year vehicle for quadrupling said record sales yet again. *Eish, mfowethu!* And they'd have us all believing that wicked messenger's tale that they were knights in shining armour no less!

Be that as it may, droves of fans – black, white, Indian and Cape coloured – were crossing the border in veritable flotillas of anykind wheeled transport; tickets were already a sell-out. Swaziland would soon be swimming with music lovers more numerous than a homosexual's arse swims with millions of competitive but doomed-to-failure post-sex spermatozoa.

Bubbles crossed, uncrossed and crossed her legs again.

Even from where I was I could see she wasn't wearing panties.

I was turbulently testosterone-conscious of *her* every single waking moment endured thereafter and I couldn't wait for the time to arrive when we were going to be alone together.

My wife?

My family?

They didn't enter my head.

I was possessed.

I was bewitched, a slave chained to reawakened passion, an erect phoenix rising up from long-ago London's post-coital ashes. You would have had to amputate my legs to stop me footing it to the Royal Swazi Holiday Inn. Next you'd have to chop off my arms, *because I would have dragged myself inch by inch over whatever distance separated us.* An effective but distastefully abhorrent method would have been to guillotine my *umthondo*, but the French Fellatio Revolution was far, far away, non-existent, and no ways was my male member a member of the guilty by birth Bourbon-fostered Gallic aristocracy.

When I walked into Bubbles' hotel suite, I'd been throbbingly tumescent since waking up that morning. My head ached with a crushing *babalaza* and my middle leg ached with an engorgement so skin-burstingly tight I could hear my heart thump along its elongated centre, from base shaft to swollen helmet-head.

She'd known it was me arriving and she stood in the centre of the room with her silk dressing gown pooled around her feet, shimmering like glistening water. My throat was so constricted I could barely croak out a greeting – and then we collided. My mouth was everywhere while she ripped at my clothes as if they were the evil embodiment of everything she hated and despised.

Bubbles somehow straddle-walked me over to the blatantly open door and kicked it closed with a bare foot. I was down on that flame-lily fanny of hers, drawn to it like steel filings to a magnet, enjoying my stretched tongue's exploration, taking my time before sucking hard on her cheeky clitoris. Her fingernails were digging deep into my neck, but I couldn't have cared less if she drew blood.

Then she was raking my face and making those synchronised gasping sounds peculiar to sexual passion, pulling me to her so hard I found it almost impossible to breathe, suddenly realising her juices tasted incredibly like the sweet smell of a cooking *umPheki* finally giving forth its honeyed bounty should taste. She forced me back, moving around me, but I hung on tenaciously to that irresistible focus of womanhood – no ways was I giving up munching on that delicious mango. It came to me after a measureless age that her relentlessly fierce effort was a forced attempt to get at my *umthondo*, so I loosened my hypnotised wrestler's grip. Her electric-eel tongue immediately struck my stalk with high-voltage flicks of that wrap-around mouth snake. Then she enclosed it, *it felt like all of it*, in her hot mouth.

This went on and on until we both had to come up for air.

Our eyes slammed into each other like loosened arrows striking bullseyes, and time slowed down to where every movement was made in a melting bath of sensual gelatine. Our hands ran like hunting spiders all over each other's flesh. We were mirrors of each other's explorative enterprise – not slow, not fast – and I could feel every muscle, every sinewy tendon, every bubbling vein and artery below her oh so white unblemished skin, and in turn I felt she was paring my flesh down to the bone.

Then we entered a red-orange haze, a searing miasma of poisonous need that gave life instead of death and she locked those fragile-looking but steel-tempered thighs around me. She had hold of the end of my *umthondo* now, and she was rubbing it frantically, spastically, against the moisture of her outer vagina lips. And then – then it inched slowly up into her, a journey to the end of the world by the time it was all the way inside her.

We rode each other languorously, with infinite drama, until we both got there and the culminating concatenation of mutually shared explosions exhausted us so that we both felt we were on the point of expiring.

We dragged ourselves over to the bed, neither of us wanting me to come out of her, but of course it had to happen. There was cold champagne on the bedside table. As Bubbles poured with her back to me, I almost choked on the beauty of her cascading red hair above rippling vertebrae and that stunning mesmeric view of her twin calabash buttocks beneath. My fingers went between her cheeks from the back like searching blindworms, over her puckered little anus and then home into the soaking hotness of her vagina.

Mfowethu?

Is this bothering you?

Am I being too graphic?

My apologies if I have offended your fine young sensibilities, but those particular memories are so sharp, so clear. When you get to be an old *madala* like me, when you reach this age where remembered images are as precious as diamonds, then you'll understand, eh?

To cut a long story short, or to put a marathon measure of lascivious lust in a nutshell, we did it for the rest of the day and most of the night as well.

I got home in the early hours of the morning and I had no excuse prepared.

My scurrilous hangover was back in sadistic spades.

I tiptoed into bed and balanced myself as close to the edge on my side as I could manage. I *couldn't* touch Zsa-Zsa. In my fevered brain the very thought of being touched *by her* was anathema, horrible, like being touched by a rotting cadaver. I was too depleted to even take a wash, and I must have reeked of Bubbles' feminine musk from the tip of my toes to the top of my head. But I had had the presence of mind to splash myself with pungent petrol from the spare can in the boot of my car, so that I could claim my nose-numbing odours were due to a mechanical breakdown.

I lay there, weak as a kitten, drugged out on an overdose of sex, promising myself just a little nap and then I'd get up and spring-clean this adulterous fornicator's body. I'd get the sheets changed in the morning. Maybe on my next lie-down on that same bed I wouldn't feel so dirty.

I can't explain this Pavlov's dog reaction of mine to Bubbles. I suppose it was pure addiction as bad as any junkie's. I couldn't get enough and I couldn't stay away.

Even when the superstar music concert was over and the fans had long gone home, Bubbles opted to stay behind on a kind of semi-permanent vacation.

I think I began to hate her after the first few days – despise *both* of us is perhaps a better descriptive analysis of the situation. But that was surely a wretched victim's predictable antipathy to his body housing a debilitating disease and I knew it.

Bubbles had no shame: she knew precisely what she was doing and she felt not a hint of remorse. She'd call me anytime, anywhere, during the day. She had me running like an Olympic sprinting champion to be the first of my family to reach the jangling telephone if it went off with the sound of doomsday firecrackers in my home. I'd always obey her invitation. After we'd satiated ourselves with each other yet again, I'd wander the streets like a lost soul in a turbulent sea of frazzled nerves. Bubbles had to go back to England *sometime*, didn't she?

But meanwhile, whenever I was home, I couldn't speak to Zsa-Zsa, much less look her in the face. I was short-tempered with Vilakazi. He couldn't understand my abruptly bleak moods at all, and was there anybody who could blame him, *mfowethu*?

Then something happened that shook the cornerstones of my foundation, reverberations from an earthquake, a *tsunami* of an unexpected evil event.

I came back to my home early. We all had an awkward supper together. We had tickets to a film that Vilakazi wanted to see, an historical adventure that related indirectly to his schoolwork. During the screening, I found myself enjoying the story in a detached, cynical way – the forces of good triumphing at the last possible moment over the unbeatably advantaged forces of rapacious human demons.

Zsa-Zsa was in bed as soon as we'd chased Vilakazi to his. Ordinarily I would have joined her on the turn, but instead I found excuses to wander around finding lame little anythings to do that would delay the moment. I poured myself drink after drink, turned on the hi-fi, reread the same trailer-trash dog-eared magazine I'd been nauseated by on first scrutiny, and ended up staring out a window at nothing, liquor-bile rising up bitterly in my throat.

Zsa-Zsa called to me from the bedroom.

There was no ignoring her summons.

I stood halted in the doorway, staring at her.

Although the lights were off, illumination seeping through from the lounge outlined her.

'Come to bed,' she said in tones that told me I had no choice in the matter.

Then, *mfowethu*, in that inexplicable moment, the

handcuffs of Bubbles Nightingale's arrest on my sanity fell away from my wrists and my manacled mind. The power of my enveloping need for my spouse returned tenfold. She was what I wanted, what I needed, what I could not live without. We would find out why no further pregnancy had followed after Vilakazi's birth, fix whatever it was, and have loads more lovely children. Nobody else would ever come between us ever again. Strange – inexplicable as I've said – but suddenly that's the irreversible way it was – had become.

Naked, we held on to each other as if we were holding on to dear life itself. Zsa-Zsa wanted to make love, a subconscious need for physical affirmation that we were indeed man and wife.

And for the first time I could ever remember, my sexuality deserted me, my libido went into hiding and I was left as limp as a length of soggy over-boiled cannelloni.

Nothing helped.

Nothing got me going.

I'd been abandoned by the very carnal essence that had forced me to the brink of marital catastrophe. Eventually I rolled over in burning shame onto my back. I just lay there wondering if Bubbles was employing potent witchcraft to cause my impotence, to emasculate me, rendering me incapable of moving with layers of sweat lashing out of every pore and soaking the sheet beneath. Zsa-Zsa kept stroking me, soothing me, but that motherly loving simply made me feel worse, lower than earthworm excreta.

I knew what I was going to do, *had to do*.

I phoned Bubbles from the restaurant first thing the next morning and set up a meeting in a semi-public place where she would have as much chance of seducing me as a mouse has of raping an elephant. The *monkey was off my back* as fully rehabilitated junkies proclaim their new freedom. I felt wonderful, *mfowethu*.

I met Bubbles upstairs in the hot-buffet eating section of Big Bang's place, my old restaurant premises, filled with the rich aromas of flavoursome meat stews. I had told Big Bang what my meeting with Bubbles was going to be about, and if Big Bang commanded discretion, that was about as discreet as you could get.

Seated across the table from Bubbles, I waffled on and on to her, because I didn't know how to begin saying what I had to say. By the time we began eating, I still had made zero progress in the pull-out stakes. My rehearsed lines spun around in my head like an aimless proliferation of tongue-tied butterflies and they were still fluttering haphazardly there when Big Bang came up and towered over us, almost blotting out the light.

'Hey, *bra*, there's a *geeza* down by the first pool table downstairs. Says he needs to see you quickstyle.' Big Bang paused. 'He don't smell good, *bra*, but he's there. You want I should exit him?'

'No, no, Big Bang, *bra*, I'll go *nortch* what he wants. Thanks, my man.'

I didn't bother to ask if Big Bang had a clue as to what this *geeza* wanted. I was so overwhelmingly grateful to delay what had to be said to Bubbles, I knocked over my chair as I shot up like a jack-in-the-box.

It turned out I knew the *geeza* who was requesting my presence.

It was Vuka Shabalala, a vicious *guluva* from the old days who sold whatever was going in the pills and powder category and always used hungry *abantwana laaitjies* to front for him when it came to exchanging goods for

money. As far as I knew, he'd always been arrest-free.
I couldn't imagine what he wanted from me, because
although I knew he was connected, I steered clear of him
the way a pubescent virgin niece avoids being alone with a
venereal-disease-carrying profligate uncle she knows can't
wait to try his luck.

'Where can we jaw?' Vuka hissed, his eyes imitating
ping-pong balls at a Chinese table-tennis tournament.

'What's problem with right here, *bra*?' I returned,
not particularly concerned, my mind still cocooned by
Bubbles, you understand, *mfowethu*.

'Serious, *bra*,' he said, gripping my forearm so hard his
fingers felt like a hyena's bite.

'The toilets do?'

'Let's get there, *bra*.'

We sidled our way, unselfconsciously on my part and
separately by urgent request from Vuka, to the men's
pisshouse. There were two Swazi guys I knew from the
local soccer team there, so we washed our hands until they
left us alone.

Vuka pushed open the doors of every toilet cubicle to
make sure they were vacant, leaving nothing to chance. He
was visibly tense, drawn as tight as a stretched bowstring.
I still didn't know what he was after, but there was a
vacuum in the pit of my stomach that told me I wasn't
going to be crazy about it, whatever it was.

'*Bra*, I won't fuck you around with *bulongwe*. There's
drug-squad *amapolisi* over there drinking beer at the bar.
They going to nail me the minute I step outside into the
street. You a *rawurawu*-brother, you got to help another
rawurawu-brother, *bra*.'

'You listen to me *too good*, Vuka. You fuck off *now*. I
don't know you. You got my message?'

I thought he was going to physically attack me – he

looked that brain-disconnected, wild and unanchored to anything but the clamorous, clutching spectre of being collared by the law flooding his survival synapses.

Then he grinned a regained-confidence grin of unsubtle evil. His mouth was full of gaps interspersed with crooked gold teeth.

'Those *amaboere* get me, they get you too, *bra*. And Big Bang. I tell the *uthuvi* you and him and me, we partners. We all deal same-same goods. You can't deny fokkol. Why else'm I here, *bra*?'

'I have Big Bang kill you for this later, Vuka.'

'Later is later, *bra*. Now is now, sure-sure. So be cool, *wena*, let's get rid of *now!*'

'What you want, motherfucker?'

'There's a fancy big box'f sugar-style whole fruit the drinks waitress put *phakathi* her locker for me soon's I came in. She going to give it back me when I split, *bra*, can't change that, I tipped her heavy *imali*. Inside I got Burmese Brown, came in sweet like a lemon through these check-*fokkol* Swazi customs.'

'Fuck's sake, you got heroin *in here?*'

'I *told* you, *bra*. You think I'm fucking you around?'

'What you want me to do?'

'We got to play it smart, *bra*. We go back out, you first, me next. I can't leave normal-style, *bra*, that waitress she going to give me the *pasella* Chrismas box, then I be *too good* fucked, then the drug *gattes* got me.'

'So?'

'You start bad-mouth me, *bra*. Say where all those *amarands* I owe you? You hit me, we have big fight. Me, I lose, *bra*, I lose *too good*. You grab me like no-shit kung-fu *bulongwe* badguy and run me out the door, *too much* quickstyle, *bra*. Secret is quickstyle. Those *amapolisi* too surprised to make they move. Moment I hit tarmac where

319

you boot me, I'm gone, *bra*, I'm gone *too good*, they never catch me. Even they pick me up later, no problem, *bra*. No heroin, no problem.'

'Let's go.'

'Me, I'm not yet the finished, *bra*. Lot of people will know where the goods is left behind. No funny ideas, hey, *bra*?'

I was impatient to get started.

All it took was one furious yell in his direction and I punched him in the mouth, bursting his lips. He went down as the two drug-squad *amapolisi* turned on their bar stools in vacant surprise. I hauled him to his feet, impressive blood spraying everywhere, grabbed his collar and the seat of his pants and rushed him out the entrance – putting the boot in from behind for good measure as he'd suggested. He went down flat on his face as a tirade of swear words poured from me. But he was up like a shot and away like the wind, leaking more fluid from badly grazed hands and knees.

A woman behind me somewhere was screaming her head off.

The drug-squad *geezas* were on their feet and pounding flat-footed in hot pursuit.

One shot me a look of concentrated suspicion, but he was too busy on his captive-intent imperative mission to stop and make a thing of it.

I went straight to the drinks waitress, who knew me, of course, and told her to make haste and get the crystallised whole fruit out of her locker. When she brought it, I grabbed it from her quickstyle, the big box noticeably heavy but truly a lovely embossed thing that looked like it was made from real hammered silver, just the thing to justify the weight, *mfowethu*. Then I threatened the waitress with her job if she didn't induce permanent memory loss with regard to gift-packaged *glacé* fruit, and pounded up the connecting balustraded stairs to rejoin Bubbles as if nothing had happened.

She was nonchalantly enjoying her food, eating with undisguised relish.

'We got to leave, Bubbles. Not later. Sorry about this. *Right now.*'

Bubbles arched a sculpted eyebrow.

'Food first. You can eat me for dessert, dear thing.'

'*Now*, Bubbles,' I insisted, and the urgency in my voice must have got through to her, because she didn't even murmur further protest or ask questions.

In less time than it takes to tell, Big Bang had a taxi waiting.

I didn't want to use my car – and have it recognised – and then we were on our way to the Royal Swazi Holiday Inn.

I felt as if I'd completed an iron-man triathlon event and my hands were clammy with sweat that stuck like sticky glue.

'Mind telling me what that was all about, dear thing?' Bubbles asked.

I was speechless.

I stared open-mouthed at her.

She was as cool and unruffled as if she'd just left some beauty parlour after a female overhaul. Then, *mfowethu*, then it came to me through my adrenalin fog that there was no reason for her not to feel that way.

Eish!

And Bubbles was repeating her probing words, distracting my desperate concentration.

'I need silence. Please, Bubbles, I'm begging you. I've got to think long and hard.'

'Pass me that silver treasure-box of yum-yums,

sweetheart. I'll guzzle while you tax your grey matter.'

'No!'

'Don't be so touchy. Saving it for the wifey, dear thing?'

It had all happened so blurringly fast that my mind was still revolving in circles that spun in contrary orbits. I was kicking myself for getting involved, but I didn't see I had any other choice, *mfowethu*. Hindsight told me I should have walked away, let the drug squad pick up that vermin, Vuka, and play the village idiot if ever they got around to interrogating me. I was clean, no matter what they might've tried to pin on me. I could see that now that the fear pressure was off. What a mess, *mfowethu*, what a fornicating unnecessary mess.

Now I was burdened with a load of heroin that I had no idea how to get rid of.

What was more to the point, if I was nabbed with it in my possession, I'd be as guilty as if I'd bought and imported it myself. I'd have liked to flush it down the nearest lavatory, but I knew the odds were much in favour of Vuka and some psychotic gun-happy buddies sooner or later coming back for their merchandise. I'd better have it ready and waiting when that did happen.

With all the choices open to him, wouldn't you just know it was Murphy's *Mampara* Law that that vile viper Vuka would *have* to pick Big Bang's place, and that I'd just *have* to be there, a million-to-one shot with bad luck dealt the best hand. It was also a sure thing that when those drug-squad *amapolisi* got through with Vuka, as they were bound to do having had him in their sights for all this time, they would be heading my way and looking for Bubbles as well. There were dozens of people who'd seen us at Big Bang's place, and to top that, Bubbles was *famous*. She'd handed out three autographs before we'd even sat down.

I didn't know who Vuka's associates were.

If I did, I'd have given them their big, silver, fake-bottomed box of crystallised whole fruit via the fastest illegal courier available, believe me, *mfowethu*. In that trade you don't look for enemies.

Then again, suppose I got hold of the *wrong* drug barons?

Do you think they'd *tell me* it wasn't their consignment?

They'd take the heroin off my hands and chortle themselves silly when my body turned up in an act of vengeful revenge. I'd be presumed the bad baggage, no doubt about that whatsoever.

When we reached the Royal Swazi Holiday Inn, I told Bubbles exactly what had unfortunately taken place.

I had to, that was only fair.

That also solved my Bubbles problem.

She was gone on the next interconnecting flight out of there – precisely fifty-nine minutes from Swaziland *terra firma* to the eventual air-conditioned comfort of an executive-class luxury passage aboard a jet airliner winging its way through the wild blue yonder back to Heathrow Airport – and doubtless a chauffeur-driven limousine to transport her in the style to which she was accustomed to her sumptuous superstar suite in the heart of the Big Smoke.

By the time I finally got home, after accumulating long hours puzzling things out in Bubbles' deserted hotel rooms, I learned from Howard Postlethwaite that the narcotics nasties had *already* been to our clean-as-a-whistle swanky restaurant as well as revisiting Big Bang's place, and had gone through both establishments with a fine-tooth comb. Apparently they were very polite and well-mannered, didn't bother the customers at all – nobody knew what the blue blazes was going on.

That left only Bubbles and me to be found in the flesh. Bubbles had, in effect, self-destructed. She was gone forever.

Which, of course, left me carrying the jailable can, *mfowethu*. That lovely, heavy, silver box of *glacé* whole fruit.

I suggested to Howard that he close the restaurant and go home, but I didn't answer any of his rather pissed-off questions. I told him I'd see him the next day and left it at that.

Before the *gattes* cops came, as I was sure they would, I opened up that box of crystallised '*yum-yums*', as Bubbles had called the contents. I took three pieces out of it so that it would look like it had been nibbled at, stashed these wrapped in tinfoil in the fridge, and left that rich-looking box conspicuously and casually open on the dining table, an honest wage-earner's treat for his loved ones.

I poured myself a beer that I didn't touch and sat down to wait.

Then I rumpled my shirt with its turned-brown dry bloodstains, pulled it thoroughly relaxed man-at-home out of my trousers' waistband, reached for a magazine and left it opened on my lap. I smoked ten cigarettes, breaking them off near the filter, puffing a half-inch and stubbing them out to make the ashtray look obviously used, the leftovers in my pocket. I wanted the *amapolisi* to see an unconcerned *geeza* come back home to relax after a long day's hard work meeting clients, looking for advantageous publicity. If they harboured the slightest suspicion I was not what I appeared to be, they would tear my home apart.

It was getting late.

Zsa-Zsa and Vilakazi were both visiting slumberland – they'd been asleep for ages.

It wasn't long after I'd prepared myself that the

expected representatives of the law arrived. In spite of my self-hypnotic litany to act the frazzled businessman, I couldn't help myself – I was out of that chair like a charging leopard the instant I heard the first ominous knock at the front door. Thank all *tsotsi* gods I had the presence of mind to wait a few seconds before opening it. The two drug-squad heavies who'd been at Big Bang's stood there, not looking friendly.

I deliberately made an exaggerated point of studying my wristwatch.

'It's very late,' I said, blinking sleepily, as they flashed badges at me. 'Oh, you're police. How can I help you?'

No answer.

They pushed past me as if I'd invited them in – not overly aggressive, merely doing their job.

I went back tiredly to my chair and lit up another cigarette so they'd be sure to notice the used coffin nails in the overcrowded ashtray.

That they were both *very big* men bombarded into my awareness.

Big *white* men.

One sat uninvited to my side and the other stood where I had to look up at him. He came straight to the point like a ventriloquist's lip-synch puppet-bulldog, as if his silent partner was pulling the strings.

'What started the brawl where you was seen earlier and identified, *meneer* Bhekuzulu?'

'Are you South African?'

'Please answers the question, *meneer* Bhekuzulu.'

'Were you there when it happened?' I asked artlessly to add a hastily fabricated smokescreen around my defensive position of innocence.

Silence.

'Bastard queer tried to grab me in the toilets,' I let

spew from my mouth, as if barely contained outrage had suddenly consumed me. 'Soon as I'd buttoned up, I followed him out and gave him what he deserved.'

'You was talking to him by a pool table before that, *meneer* Bhekuzulu.'

'So what's unusual about that? He asked me the time, must've thought I'd given him the come-on. Followed me to the toilets as I said. Filthy pervert.'

'So why did you shouts he owed you money, *meneer*?'

'Thought he'd taken my wallet when he grabbed my genitals. Come on, gentlemen, you're men of the world. He could've been an expert pickpocket.'

'You is saying then you wasn't robbed, but you was sexually harassed, *meneer* Bhekuzulu?'

'You think I punch strangers because I don't like their faces?'

'I are asking the questions, *meneer* Bhekuzulu. Please remembers that.'

'What am I supposed to say? These things happen sometimes, don't they?'

'Has this happened to you before, *meneer* Bhekuzulu?'

'Not since I was fifteen or sixteen and got wise to the ways of urinal bumbandits. I didn't think I looked the type at my age. It surprised and shocked me, on my oath. I couldn't control my anger.'

'Doesn't you perhaps know the man you attacked, *meneer* Bhekuzulu?'

'Are you out of your mind? No offence intended – I mean that sincerely.'

'I takes your point. Now tells me, *meneer* Bhekuzulu, why did you and the *white lady* leave in such a hurry? Her food were half eaten and yours were untouched. What were the rush, *meneer* Bhekuzulu?'

'Enough to put anybody off their food, wouldn't you

say? Besides, the *white lady* is a famous entertainer; I wanted her to publicise my restaurant. My shirt was covered in his blood – still is, as you can see. Not a good way to beg for an endorsement recommendation of any kind, wouldn't you agree?'

They both stared at me in silence until the surrounding atmosphere became heavy as airborne lead.

'She also has to shun negative publicity like the plague,' I added, carelessly breaking the golden rule that he who speaks first loses the verbal tussle. 'The newspapers would have a field day if they found out she had anything to do with a common bar brawl. Why don't you tell me what you're after? Maybe there's a chance I can help you?'

A sarcastic snort was the reply. But my ears were deaf to this subtle innuendo, this nasal nonsense – my sensitive hide as thick as that of a rhinoceros.

'Don't concern yourself, *meneer* Bhekuzulu. *If* we needs you, we'll come back to you, rests assured.' He smiled at me in a purely predator's way. 'Helluva good punch you gave him there, *meneer* Bhekuzulu.'

The silent but manipulative half of the drug-squad monsters duo rose titanically to his feet. He looked square at the solid-silver illusion the box of *glacé* whole fruit presented. You could see where three pieces were missing. I'd crumpled the pleated wrappers within which the plump sugary confections were displayed and placed these with the cigarette butts in the overflowing ashtray.

For a foolish bold moment I thought of asking the two Goliath killjoys if they'd care to sample, but my nerve deserted me. He stood there looking anthropoid-wistfully at the fat pears and apples and figs and apricots for so long, I could hear my heartbeat amplifying with each adrenalin thud. I was now so paranoid that I didn't even dare lean forward to knock the length of growing ash off my burning cigarette. If I stretched my hand forward, I was sure it would give me away by shaking like a naked Bushman transported into the deep howling-blizzard wastes of the frozen Arctic.

'Okay, okay, *meneer* Bhekuzulu, we won't troubles you any more tonight,' the first one said, breaking the spell of his partner's sweet-tooth fixation. 'Thank you for your time.'

And then I was fawning over them with pleasant goodnights all the way to the front door.

I waited there while the two hulks shambled in their shapeless, crepe-soled brown Grasshopper shoes to their unmarked car, climbed awkwardly inside the space designed for human beings, started up, switched on the headlights and then drove away.

When the sound of the engine vanished, I went back inside.

The beer I had poured myself earlier was flat and stale, smelling like rancid yeast.

So I poured it down the kitchen sink and then sank several triple brandies in a row.

Next I retrieved the three pieces of sugar-soaked chubbily rotund fruit from the fridge, uncrumpled their pleated wrappers from the refuse-filled ashtray, dusted them off and placed them back in the eye-catching silver box.

What to do with *that* box?

Swaziland was hot, very hot, at that time of year, so I decided the fridge would be the best place to keep the heroin box, and inside it went, with some lettuces and cold ham placed casually, carelessly, conveniently on the top. Trying to hide it somewhere ultra-devious would somehow be drawing due attention to it. If I did have a second drug-squad visit and the *gattes* cops looked inside the fridge, there it was, *why look inside it?*

There was nothing more I could do that night, or rather very early morning, besides do battle with visions of a matchbox-sized grey prison cell. Weariness injected itself into me so virulently that I felt as though the very bones that supported me had become transformed to some feeble geriatric's skeletal structure of brittle calcium – with this debilitating sensation additionally intensified by lethal sleeping sickness thrown in for good measure. I threw off my sweaty, blood-stained clothing and lizard-crawled into bed next to Zsa-Zsa. It seemed I'd hardly closed my eyes and I was fast asleep.

I rose fairly early as was my habit.

The Reverend Bishop Edward Lekhanyane was holding a Zionist Christian Church meeting near Mantenga Falls for the faithful masses, and I'd promised I'd drive my wife and Vilakazi there. I moved carefully and quietly so as not to disturb the still-sleeping woman I loved and the child I adored and turned on the bathroom light to shave. The electric illumination sliced a patch across the bed where my wife lay undisturbed. She mumbled and rolled away from the brightness before I closed the door. For some unfathomable reason I had this dreadful doomsday feeling that I was closing her right out of my life, and the feeling was so immaculately brain-batteringly strong that it manifested a physical hallucination perfectly imitating the real thing in my mind.

I shaved carefully, repeating the razor strokes, making sure my face was free of any missed stubble, making my jaw as clean as my conscience should have been. My thoughts strafed me like those splinter-shrapnel bombs the

South African recces used to layer an area with where they thought we MKs were concealed . . .

. . .

. . .

How can you be such a gal pil fokken *darkie* mampara, Dhlamini? *When you have heaven in your grasp, a dynasty to father? A wonderful, bright, talented boy, and already all the* amarands *you can use with unburdened scruples if you grow to be a white-haired ancient* madala. *Now you've got yourself so fucked up that if you make one wrong move, one wrong step, you're for the high jump to break any previous jail-record you've yet attained. That is, you* fokken mampara, *if you don't get yourself killed first by Vuka Shabalala and his cretinous sanguine cronies. Any other* geeza *would put that heroin in the post addressed to the nearest* amapolisi *station, or burn it on a garden bonfire; not you have a garden, but any port in a storm will do. But not you, sucker. Carry on with your voracious appetite for easy dollars and you're dead meat. Tell me you don' know that, sucker? You're heading for an early grave, so come right. Get your shit together,* bra *Shatterproof.*

. . .

. . .

Then the old *tsotsi* in me came back juggernaut-style like an avaricious homunculus feeding off my brain.

That greedy little motherfucker wondered how much that Burmese Brown was worth if I could lay it off and was prepared to take my chances? Oh, so help me, the megabucks not my own started rolling in front of my eyes like I'd pulled jackpot on a one-armed bandit. Talk about being enslaved to Bubbles, *this* was the ultimate enslavement. I was rolling over several possible strategies in my mind to make sure some of the mentally projected money would adhere in passing to my magically adhesive fingers, when I glanced back at my unflattering image in the shaving mirror above the handbasin. It came to me then, that given the right incentive, I'd probably manufacture a wedding cake of superlative quality laced with strychnine for a Sicilian *Cosa Nostra* betrothal. The Dr Jekyll and Mr Hyde syndrome was rampantly flourishing in my obscene persona. On that homicidal confectioner's warped note, I finished shaving and went to make myself some coffee.

Early-morning sunlight did the sleep-antagonistic task it was meant to do.

My wife and child were stretching and yawning, both arriving by rote in the kitchen. Outside under an almost cloudless sky it had begun to shower – rainfall and sunlight, a monkey's wedding. The glass windows were smeared with running water. Vilakazi had a piece of leftover chocolate cake and a plastic bottle of homogenised chocolate skim milk in his hand.

'You eat that everyday for breakfast, Vilakazi, you going to get beaten up by every girl in the neighbourhood, and with one hand tied behind her back. When it comes to girlfriends, you going to be last in line. You going to be the amorous young *geeza* who gets the one with the braces on her teeth can bite your nose off, never mind any other ideas you got in mind.'

'Dhlamini! What're you feeding the boy's mind with? Pay no attention to your father, Vilakazi. I think he's had too much to drink.'

'Have you, *baba*?' Vilakazi said, all concerned for my well-being.

'Booze gives you muscles,' I gave back with an impervious grin. 'But not until you reach eighteen and pass all your exams with honours.'

'Aw, c'mon, stop bullshitting me, *baba*.'

'Vilakazi! Such language!' Zsa-Zsa tried to hide her

amusement. The doors I'd seen closing so irrevocably on our loving seemed to open a fraction again. 'Using swear words means you have to eat *all* your fruit, yoghurt and cereal before you think about leaving this kitchen.'

'Can I have a fried egg afterwards, *mame*?'

'Two, if you finish.'

'Hear that, *baba*? You want half?'

Love for my son nearly drowned me.

How much like his mother he looked. How luckily he'd been gifted in the looks department. No scars, no drawn-downwards tough exaggerated mouth and nose creases of inherited cruelly bulging features like mine. My son was a young god to me – my love for him was pristine and unadulterated.

Vilakazi smiled shyly and ate his cereal with yoghurt and a sliced banana. Zsa-Zsa broke eggs into a sizzling butter-filled frying pan and popped sliced bread in the toaster.

'Thanks, Zsa-Zsa,' I said. 'Me and my son got to build up our strength.'

We ate our fill. Then it was time for them to get ready for the Black Messiah's revelations.

My wife gave me a wet slurpy kiss and went about dressing in her ZCC robes for the big occasion.

I was as unflaggingly conscious of that expensive *glacé*-fruit giftbox as if it was a burning silver laser boring a tunnel of seared flesh directly into the back of my incinerated crisp-curl-covered head. I hated to leave it behind.

It wouldn't surprise me if those sniffing drug-squad dinosaurs instinctively followed their noses and their barely hidden suspicions, and had a good undisturbed look between the panties and the plastic binliners in our apartment while we were gone. My paranoia convinced me they'd even slit open menstrual pads, the same smuggle

Bubbles and I had used all those years ago. Thank the pussy-products producers for the arrival of internal tampons on the feminine-hygiene scene – one less mess to worry about.

Sure enough, there was an unmarked car following us. It gave me a kick to think how the Black Messiah would react to being accused of drug dealing. What with hundreds of thousands of dedicated acolytes ready to physically exonerate his innocence by peacefully breaking heads, that would be a memory worth treasuring if the impossible ever took place.

I dropped off Zsa-Zsa and Vilakazi on the outskirts of the swelling crowd, all facing the sides of a sloping hill where the Reverend Bishop would no doubt be highly visible for his Swaziland sermon. There were massive loudspeakers hung from gumpoles temporarily erected at spaced intervals so his every word could be heard in booming clarity.

A female friend of Zsa-Zsa's spotted her and came over to say hello. She told me not to worry about coming back to fetch my wife and son: she had brought her car and would do the return-home duties. *Go catch up on your business or read the* Sunday Times, *Dhlamini. We know we can't persuade a pagan like you to stay and attempt saving his immortal soul.*

That left me free to drive to the restaurant office, where I made telephone calls to anybody and everybody I had even vague *tsotsi* connections with.

I drew a decapitated blank as regards who the heroin cartel was – *if* there was one and Vuka wasn't a solo operator, which was unlikely – but I did discover that he had been apprehended in spite of his scurrilous *skebengu* evasion skills and was being held by the police. The beating I'd given him would be powder-puff stuff compared to what he would sure-sure be going through now, *mfowethu*. The

General was away and whoever answered the phone was clueless as to when he would be returning and available. No mobile phones in those backward days, of course.

That left me still holding the Burmese Brown Baby, and I had no more idea than before how I was going to get rid of that junkie's gold.

Judge die djampas! I said to myself, reverting to ingrown *tsotsi-taal,* because when I glanced at the time it was heading for late afternoon. Zsa-Zsa and Vilakazi would've been back home hours ago. *Kom line, bra Shatterproof.* Time to split and spend some leisure time with the two of them.

There was a cluster of people around my apartment's frontage when I turned the corner and home came in sight. An ambulance started up and pulled away, siren wailing, just as I pulled alongside.

What was going on?

I leapt out of my car, barged through the collection of motley bystanders drawn together by macabre curiosity, and hurtled through the front door.

From the lounge I could see through to the kitchen.

It hammered at me like the shocking impact of a ten-ton invisible bludgeon *that the fridge door was wide open, and the extravagantly ornate silver box of crystallised fruit was sitting open on the breakfast-nook table.*

Reverend Bishop Lekhanyane was standing there looking down at it, his flowing robes transforming him into a celestial being keeping steadfast guard over the Ark of the Covenant.

'Where's my wife? Where's Vilakazi?'

'Your wife has gone with Vilakazi in the ambulance.

Your son is very ill. He has been vomiting blood and appears to have gone into a coma.'

'*What?*'

The Black Messiah pointed at the box of sugared preserves. One was missing. I snatched the nearest fruit and ripped it in half. Brown-white powder in a miniature golf-ball of spherical plastic cling film was inside. It burst at my rough handling and heroin powder floated down spilling like dust to the tiled floor at my feet.

Mfowethu, hear me now, I swear I thought the addictive narcotic *was hidden in a false bottom beneath all that camouflage of tasty delights.*

'Vilakazi *ate* one of those things?' I asked, but it was more a statement of fact than a question. My head was vortexing, my vision going white-spots crazy with threatening insanity as the Reverend Bishop nodded, giving affirmation to what I already knew.

'There are two exceptionally large white men who look like policemen at the door,' he continued. 'I suggest you get rid of that box while I delay them.'

Then Edward Lekhanyane headed his imposing corpulence towards the front door like a man-o'-war, his robes billowing sails from the age of wind-driven ships.

I grabbed the box of *glacé* fruits with such urgent fervour that several pieces jostled out onto the floor. Like a madman I was down on my knees gathering them up with fumbling fingers, scattering the spilled heroin powder as I did so. Then the silver sweetmeat sarcophagus was inside my loose shirt and I was off to the toilet like a man on an overdose of elephant laxative. The gurgling flood water sound of the lavatory flushing was sweet music in my ears, *but some of the incriminating torn-to-pieces evidence insisted on floating back up to the surface.* I piled torn-off wads of toilet paper on top of the offensive cardboard-and-fruit swimmers, waited for the cistern to refill and pushed the lever again. This time it all vanished without a trace.

Back to the kitchen I went, making a show of belting my trousers.

The gumshoe Goliaths were already there.

Reverend Bishop Lekhanyane was offering them coffee, the electric kettle on the boil.

One of the drug-squad duo dropped to his haunches and began dabbing a *boerewors*-sized finger at the brown spillage on the kitchen floor tiles.

I grasped the steam-spouting kettle, pretended to lose my grip and let it fall in a scalding splash of boiling hot water to the floor.

The finger dusted with heroin was severely blistered as its prying owner gave a Brobdingnagian yelp of surprise and pain and sprang to his feet.

Scattered little drifts of Burmese heroin turned to liquid nothing, vanished, *mfowethu*.

'Sorry! Christ, I'm sorry!' I apologised in a profusion of repentance. 'It slipped, it slipped! I don't know how it could've happened! You alright, detective? It is *detective*, isn't it? Can I get you some burn salve? There's a prescription tube of soothing *muti* in my medicine cabinet.'

He glared at me, while all of a sudden I'd become as cold and clear as distilled-water ice. Reverend Bishop Lekhanyane's face was impassive, but his eyes were alive with sarcastic amusement – or perhaps sympathy for the devil.

'Vuka Shabalala unfortunately died in his cell last night, *meneer* Bhekuzulu,' he said, sucking his damaged digit, his cornflower-blue eyes drilling deep into my own. 'He committed suicide.'

I wasn't to be trapped that easily, *mfowethu* – not by a big *apartheid*-blustering *bulongwe* bulldozer anyway.

Vuka had *committed suicide?*

That would be the day hell froze over. These drug-squad *gattes* guilt-determinators were *murderers*, torture-happy *murderers*, pure and simple, no arguments.

'Who did you say?'

'Vuka Shabalala, your homosexual friend.'

'I got gay friends, but whoever that poor dead *geeza* was, he sure wasn't one of them.'

'No more games, *meneer* Bhekuzulu. He gave us your name before he, ah, killed himself.'

'Rubbish. I never heard of the man before in my life.'

'Then how does you explain his confession, *meneer* Bhekuzulu?'

'Dhlamini Bhekuzulu is a well-known businessman in these parts, detective,' Edward Lekhanyane interrupted with dignified authority. 'His name is familiar to most folk here. Besides which glaring commonplace fact, are you two officers not out of your legal jurisdiction?'

'We has liased with the Swaziland police and we has investigative autonomy on this case, *meneer dominee.* You will speak only when you is spoken to from now on, are that clear?'

The Black Messiah was the wrong person to talk down to like that, *mfowethu.*

I held my breath.

'If you *gentlemen*,' Edward Lekhanyane roared like the lion of Zion that he was, 'wish to accuse a member of *my congregation* with a crime, then do it! I shall advise him in that case he need say nothing to you whatsoever and my lawyers will be here to protect his rights within the hour! *Is that understood, gentlemen?*'

The two brutal drug-squad barbarians turned more sheepish than sheep, although you could see they would like nothing better than to be able to pound the cheeky

kaffir Reverend Bishop to a bloody pulp with their ham-
like fists.

'Just doing our job, *meneer dominee*. Following a lead
that incriminates *meneer* Bhekuzulu with hard drugs.'

'*Then get on with it!*' the Reverend Bishop lashed them.
'*Or drop your innuendoes and leave here at once. This
poor man has a seriously ill child at the hospital this very
minute. I suggest you search for some shred of hidden
humanity within yourselves and allow him to be where
he rightfully belongs, at his boy's side where he is needed.
Good day to you!*'

So help me, *mfowethu*, it worked.

They shambled out backwards, dominated by the Black
Messiah's wrath, mumbling threats of an early return.

But they never came back.

I was off the hook.

With Vuka Shabalala dead, there were no gangland
links to me and the wasted heroin. *No worries, Bruce,*
as the Australians say. I was unprepared for the singeing
verbal heat Edward Lekhanyane now turned on me.

'Dhlamini, I hope and pray that poison that was so
carelessly hidden in your home has nothing to do with you
being directly involved. If I believed *for a moment* that was
the case, I would have let those two policemen find the
drugs and arrest you. I would be happy to see you jailed
and the key thrown away for your lifetime. Tell me I am
not wrong?'

'*Baba* Edward, I was used. I was blindly stupid and
foolish, I admit, but I was used. The drugs had nothing to
do with me. Thank you for your trust. I'm in your debt,
Baba Edward.'

'Your biblical allocation, your continued contribution
to our coffers, does much good for the children of Zion,
Dhlamini. Therefore there is no debt. *Now go to your wife*

and son!'

I showed the Reverend Bishop my back and put pedal to the metal heading for the hospital.

The nurse at the reception desk gave me the ward number as if she'd been expecting me.

Zsa-Zsa was in the corridor outside Vilakazi's private ward, sitting on one of those soulless moulded-plastic visitor's waiting chairs lining the wall. She wasn't the woman I had known yesterday or the day before. She looked haggard, like an ancient crone, withered by double the years that were her real age. Her breasts sagged beneath her creased blue-and-white ZCC robes and her shoulders were slumped forward without strength. She looked up at the clicking echo of my approaching footsteps.

'We can't see him yet,' she said hollowly. 'They have screens around him and they're finishing up with the stomach pump. We'll be allowed in give or take another twenty minutes, as soon as they've attached a cleansing intravenous drip.'

'Zsa-Zsa, if only I'd known,' I said, putting my arm around her shoulders. 'I should never have brought it into the house.'

'What are you talking about?' she said, her tear-stained face swollen and blank.

'The drugs in those fruit preserves. How was I to know?'

'There were *drugs* in there? And *you knew about that filthy poison?*'

'That's what I'm telling you. I *didn't* know. I thought the drugs were hidden safely underneath.'

'You brought gutter *drugs* into *our* home where *our* son could get hold of them? Are you *mad*, Dhlamini?'

'No, no, listen to me, it wasn't like that – it – it wasn't my fault –'

'*Then whose fucking fault was it?*' Zsa-Zsa *screamed* at me in a paroxysm of unfettered rage, her big brown eyes filled with a terrible hatred and using *that* swear word for the first time ever to my knowledge. '*You nearly killed your only son! There may be brain damage! You monster! Bastard! Bastard! Bastard!*'

I had to clamp her mouth hard with my hand.

She bit my fingers through to the bone.

But I rode the pain until her screams had turned to a bubbling hissing of unintelligible invective.

'Please, no more, Zsa-Zsa. You'll have us *both* end up in jail.'

'That's where you belong!'

'I'll die before I desert Vilakazi.'

'Then die, you bastard! Get your fucking filthy hands off me!'

I released her.

She got up and sat down several chairs away.

Her face was twisted into an expression that was barely human.

I clasped my bleeding hand between my knees and settled down to wait.

Midlife Crisis

The waiting was longer than expected.

A century seemed to pass before a doctor and a nurse appeared, seeming to materialise out of thin air.

'Your son will recover,' the doctor said. 'It was a near thing, but he has strength and youth's resilience and mercifully he is out of danger now. We have dosed him with a strong sedative and he is presently fast asleep, but you may go inside and sit with him if you wish.'

My wife looked awfully tired and spent, but her body straightened up and she held her head high. With the doctor's and the nurse's eyes on me, I got creakily to my feet, walked the few steps over to her and held out my hand.

'Don't try and touch me, you, you, you *tsotsi*!' she spat at me. 'Don't *ever* fucking touch me!'

The doctor and nurse politely averted their eyes and made their way elsewhere.

I sat with Vilakazi and Zsa-Zsa for an hour. My son's breathing was nice and regular, although he was the most dreadful colour. Then I left them, feeling numb and empty, every part of me. I had to get some sleep. I had a busy day ahead of me and somebody had to work to pay for the groceries and the hospital bills.

Later, I called the hospital from the restaurant, and an exceptionally cold and stern voice told me that Vilakazi wasn't allowed any calls, nor was he allowed any visitors for the next few days. That sounded unbelievable, but I accepted the word of what I presumed was a knowledgeable medical expert. When I went home, Zsa-Zsa was gone. She had taken all her clothes, all her personal possessions, the works. She left no note, *fokkol*, gone . . . just gone. With a sinking feeling growing in the pit of my stomach, I shot over to the hospital. His mother had collected Vilakazi that morning. *No, sir, she has not left us with a forwarding address, nor even a contactable telephone number.*

That night, Howard Postlethwaite and me, we got to be *driving goats* together when the last customers had left. *Driving goats* is an old Zulu saying that means you got drunk out of your tiny little alcohol-soaked mind, *mfowethu*.

Days later I worked up the courage to call on Reverend Bishop Edward Lekhanyane. He told me to pray. He also told me that my wife was determined not to see me again ever.

'Help me, *Baba* Edward,' I begged. 'Help me.'

'Pray with me, Dhlamini, my son. Patience might bring her back to you. Pray it is so.'

But he was wrong.

Nothing helped.

I was alone.

It was almost a decade before I saw my wife and son again.

Huge changes were brewing and fomenting within South Africa, with black voices, enjoined as one, becoming louder and louder, until the whole world could hear our cries of distress. But when those years were in the past, they added up to nothing much for me personally.

Business – *tsotsi* business that is – operated as usual. Things seemed to have been going the same way for a century. The restaurant ran with its customary efficiency and the profits grew every month. I dyed my hair platinum blond again and started up a whole new fashion trend for Africans living in Africa; soccer stars in particular took to the violent contrast between white hair and black skin colour.

I tried learning how to play the bulls and bears investment market for a while, anything to ease my lonely boredom, but I soon tired of it. Easier to let a broker do your thinking for you. Brokers did far better playing the market than I did anyway, and I finally concluded that one should leave a specialist's job to a specialist, be he creative dishonest con man or creative honest career man, or both.

I spent a lot of time at the restaurant with Howard. We had a regular bunch of diners who almost made the place their home. I became social-surface friendly with many of them. But that's as far as it went. Sometimes though, you'd become more *confidante* than friend, and then they'd tell you shocking things, things that could get them sent to either an insane asylum or a maximum-security jail, things that even their worst enemies wouldn't believe them capable of. What pissed me off, invoked my ire for their *bulongwe*, was that it never occurred to any of them to ever invite me back to *their* homes for a get-together. They'd drink your free booze when offered, be your biggest *bra*, but there was a line drawn that separated you as somehow inferior, because *they* paid *you* to feed their faces. *Apartheid* was

343

alive and well in the world's collective consciousness – know what I mean, *mfowethu*?

The law said I was a *gangsta*, a *tsotsi*, a bastard son of a bitch *skebengu* criminal.

Not the restaurant side of things, but the other business.

Maybe the smell of indulging in illegal activities permeated my pores to such a saturated extent that their noses could pick up on my taint? I don't know. But what about them, my sanctimonious critics? So many nine-to-five people masquerading as upright citizens who came to my restaurant were *proud* when they'd pulled off their sleazy little office scams, *proud* that they were clever enough to cover their cheating tracks. They broke the code of honesty a dozen different ways with monotonous regularity, and yet nobody so much as raised an eyebrow.

One of the hail-fellow-well-met big spenders who loved our restaurant and frequented it regularly whenever he came to Swaziland, told me of an *exposé* he'd seen on American television while he was overseas drumming up foreign investment – foreign investment which, I might add, was fighting shy of anything to do with South Africa.

This is what he told me.

A hidden camera followed a day in the life of an upper-echelon San Francisco advertising executive, who was a deacon at his Christ the King Church, a good family man and a solid, reliable tax-paying citizen. During this *one single day* he'd cash-notes paid off a traffic cop in lieu of a far larger fine, falsified his annual income returns with the help of another cash-grabbing Receiver of Revenue rat, treated his mistress to a bang-up lunch with catastrophically dear imported wines on his employer's company expense account, made another successful bribe to a zoning inspector to approve illegal building-extension plans so he could subdivide his personal property at enormous resale profit, accepted a 'gift' of a phenomenally expensive Bang & Olufsen superior hi-fi system for favours granted, and had blatantly stolen an office water-cooled fan unit to boot, with the pathetic excuse of 'taking it to be repaired' – it remained secreted in the boot of his car until he arrived home. If he could have somehow been prosecuted for his criminal activities, he'd sure-sure have done severe jail-time.

And this is what really gets my goat – he is *exactly* the same kind of *geeza* who'd turn his nose up at socialising with me outside of restaurant hours.

'*Fahk that fahkin shite fer a wankah's fahkin loony larf, me old sahn*,' was how Howard Postlethwaite put it with due Limey consideration. '*Bleedin' bollocks then, innit?*'

If I get caught, the public is outraged.

Outraged that I'm allowed to stroll the streets just like everybody else, breathe the same air.

Ask yourself, who is 'everybody else'?

I'll tell you who he is.

He's Sir Standard Citizen.

The *geeza* who buys a car radio plus CD player – or tyres, spare parts, domestic appliances, you name it – *that he knows is stolen*, for a tenth of its normal price. Amateur white-collar criminals: that's all *anybody* is who indulges in these drastic-discount shady deals. Their crimes, accumulated on a yearly basis, make professionals pale by comparison. Tell me I'm wrong, *mfowethu*? And these lily-white bubblegum *banditos* run no risks to speak of. Let's not get around to presidential-level perks that run into *hundreds* of millions because the old cavalcade limousine needs replacing, or the nearest African Head of State has a shinier, newer airborne glitterbug than you have.

Nobody's going to pull a gun and shoot *them* like they would a housebreaker or a hijacker, plus the *amapolisi* aren't after *them* twenty-four hours a day. These Sir Standard Citizen clowns rob their employers *and we the people* at every opportunity all their working lives; all that happens if they get caught is they get fired. Sometimes the consequence is something even less drastic, like apologising to the boss after an ear-busting lecture on civic, business and community responsibility – one of the community considerations that wrought my out-of-the-*tsotsi*-frying-pan-into-the-political-fire metamorphosis – but more of that later, *mfowethu*.

The insurance companies will tell you what the profile of Sir Standard Citizen appears to be.

He's frustrated. Life has been unkind to him because he hasn't become the adored emperor his mother told him was his inevitable destiny. Face facts: living ain't easy with so much everyday fierce competition. He'd prefer to screw his gorgeous young secretary rather than his domestic chore-worn wife (she's become hopelessly mundane, even in the boring-stakes) and, being married, he has a couple of average children who inexplicably think he is the biggest arsehole that has ever presented its anus at a porcelain toilet bowl. He lives in a nice, average neighbourhood (defined by how nice and average his contemporaries' neighbourhoods are) and is in the process of buying his own average home – if he's white, that is. He drives an average car, has an average income and has been somewhat vaingloriously employed by the same conservative firm or branch of ruling government for an average of six, seven, eight years. He has been stealing from his employers for an average of three, four, five years, and every year he sets his sights higher. On *average*, what he rips off conscience-free from the system that nurtures him one way or another *exceeds* his income by an *average* of one-fifth of his recorded salary.

That's a lot of averages.

Think of how many Sir Standard Citizens you know, now that you pause to think about it, *mfowethu.*

Thought so.

Lot of them around, aren't there?

The General asked me over for dinner whenever I was in his area.

He had an old *magogo* woman working for him who knew how to cook all the traditional country dishes using sweet potatoes, yams, corn, beans and wild spinach from where he'd grown up on the far reaches of Natal's inland borders. These were stodgy, leaden dishes to a restaurateur's faithfully fastidious consideration of appetite's delicate temptation. The platefuls she served up were huge, enough to daunt even Big Bang with a humungous hunger on him, but The General ploughed through them as if they were meagre appetisers, urging second helpings on me which I had to politely refuse.

We talked a lot during those evenings.

I got to know insightful things about politics and business I would never have learned any other way. The General was a gifted teacher. When he explained something, he made sure you understood what he was talking about, and he elucidated clearly and simply, so that you could always grasp the most complicated details.

Then Howard Postlethwaite went down with double pneumonia.

He nearly died from his illness. He spent months in hospital before he was strong enough to regain his feet.

I had to concentrate all my energies on the restaurant and I was glad to do just that. It got me away from the depression of introverted thinking and out of the ever-increasing fold of anti-*apartheid* politics that The General was embracing as a means to an end.

Reverend Bishop Lekhanyane came by whenever he was in Swaziland.

I found I now enjoyed him immensely, whereas before I'd merely tolerated him as an elderly religious whiz-kid. Whatever subject he chose to give his attention to, he'd draw you in on and drag out a response. He made me debate with him to such an involved-whether-I-liked-it-or-not extent, that I'd get outside myself and leave off brooding about my own troubles. He was so sharp, you had to be wide awake once you'd opened your mouth and thus trapped yourself, because otherwise he'd reduce you to admitting you possessed the intelligence of plant life. He'd stay at the restaurant until closing time, and then we'd play backgammon until the early hours.

That was when *Baba* Edward revealed his only vice.

He loved to gamble small amounts of money on the outcome of each fiercely contested game. As I've said before, *mfowethu*, he was no slouch at the addictive pastime and winning gave him an inordinate amount of innocent pleasure.

One night the Reverend Bishop came in with a white man whom he only introduced by his first name, which I immediately forgot.

A *strange* white man.

There was something about him – an aura if you will – that suggested power, not to mention the unmistakable fact that he was South African Afrikaans. Those rolling *rr*'s identified him the second he opened his mouth. Had to be an *Apartheid Baas*. You could always tell them. No matter how much they tried to arse creep you by giving you the status of a temporary human being, their distaste at your being black *always* came shining through like the whitelight of superior condescension.

This *mlungu* guy, middle-aged, as well-fleshed as the Black Messiah, sporting a goatee and wearing tortoiseshell bifocal spectacles, did not have that *bulongwe-baas* bearing in his make-up. You could tell by the eyes, the windows to the soul. They never lied – or rather, they *couldn't* lie. This *mlungu* categorised himself as just another upright biped, same as you and me, same as anybody. Only there was that succinct aura of power I've mentioned, *mfowethu*.

When the doors were closed on the last customer, we started a backgammon tournament, Howard joining in.

It was a lot of fun, and we passed several hours in fierce competition. According to our tournament rules, three losses in a row disqualified you from the final.

At last it looked like the Reverend Bishop was about to walk away with the extremely late evening's honours – Howard and me were long out of the stakes – when the Black Messiah passed some comment about the high incidence of car theft and hijacking in Jo'burg, and where did criminals dispose of all those thieved vehicles? Why were the police unable to combat such basic gutter-level crime, when the stolen goods were surely traceable through registration and serial numbers?

That got me going.

I'd always harboured strong opinions about *amapolisi* in general, why they are the way they are, and I plunged in headfirst, taking to the subject like a super critical duck to water. The way I phrased my feelings, I pulled no punches, I just let it all pour out.

'The reason the cars vanish over the border or end up in salvage spares is because investigative lawmen *do* collar the offenders, but then accept cash to turn a blind eye. I've heard it so many times from those in the know, I'm sick of hearing it. The biggest excuse for corrupt cops is that you'll always find a rotten apple in a big bag of edible beauties, but I say that's complete crap. You can spot a rotten apple the minute you see it *and* the minute you smell it – then you chuck the *vrot* thing away before its contagious mould contaminates the whole bag, don't you?'

'You got a *blêrrie* good point there,' André or whatever his name was said in an offhand non-committal manner.

'My point is this,' I rushed on regardless. 'It's the *whole bag* of apples that's actually rotten, with maybe one unspoiled beauty hiding in there. What chance has one untarnished apple got when his brother apples are going to make him just as rotten as they are by unavoidable contact? There must be cumulative millions and millions paid out in prearranged bribes to corrupt *amapolisi*. If you want police protection in some of the businesses I've known about, no details mind, the pay-off starts at the bottom and goes all the way to the top.'

'Is that so?' the big-belly Afrikaans *geeza* murmured, taking another of the Reverend Bishop's pieces and blocking off an additional landing area in his own home-base. 'What sort of no-names business?'

'Illegal trade, say. Let's call it the outlawed sale of internationally protected animal furs and ivory. The street cop gets his slice from the warehousers, and he picks up money for his sergeant who gets double so the street cop gets to keep his cushy beat, plus double at least again so the captain's kept happy by his sergeant, yet still has administrative control. You follow me? And we're talking basics here – people who pay off because it's a lot easier to part with some cash than to be dragged down to the station to answer questions that begin with the old *amapolisi* truth serum of clubs and fists and boots.'

'You're familiar with all these crooked *blêrrie* bribery techniques, are you?' And as that was said, the Reverend

Bishop was off the backgammon board again, needing a one or a five from the next throw of the dice.

'You'd have to be a blind man not to be. See, you have to be another kind to want to be a *gattes* anyway – '

'A *gattes?*' The eyebrows rose above the bifocals, which had slid down a rather thick, fleshy nose.

'Township *tsotsi-taal* for a policeman. As I was saying, maybe when most of these would-be protectors of the innocent and vulnerable sign up to be a guardian of the peace, they're honest and trustworthy, with stars in their eyes. But most *laatjie gattes* don't have a miniature midget's chance against a mountain-sized giant of staying that way, face it. Besides the stray off-chance that their *bra-amapolisi might* just let a stray bullet find them in the back if they prove too troublesome, you have the apathetic South African public – '

'Why doesn't the same *blêrrie* blanket of improvident reasoning apply then here in Swaziland, *jong?*' This was said with a small smile of amusement as the Reverend Bishop came back on the board and left him with a double six as his only option to escape defeat.

'I disagree with your use of the word "improvident", but that aside, this is a small country *and* it's a kingdom. King Sobhuza commands loyalty and respect from his subjects, unlike the prevailing attitude of the *majority* of South African citizens for the powers that callously arbitrate their lives. The King and his courtier henchmen have very old-fashioned methods of dealing with anything that makes waves to upset a fragile economy, tourism being a big part of it. Know how many tourists have been robbed or hijacked here? None. Says something, doesn't it?'

The Reverend Bishop and his Afrikaans antagonist were too busy with their game to answer or to look at me, but I could tell they were listening.

'Back to the bland South African public, black or white.' I was like a determined terrier shaking an already lifeless rat. 'They're responsible for turning cops into criminals. Almost every citizen, a voter or not, thinks the laws are made for somebody else. In the first place, your average *gattes* gets paid enough to feed an anorexic while useless government officials command huge salaries footed by the taxpayer, plus perks like luxury cars and subsidised free housing. Then public apathy shows the him-or-her-cops a sure way they can repair that breadline situation of theirs, the crumbs they're supposed to lay their lives on the line for. They're offered bribes to allow cars to be parked illegally and get the tickets unwritten, bribes to cancel speeding fines, bribes to ignore visa-unsanctioned immigrant vampires sucking the ordinary working man's blood, bribes so a *shebeen* can trade without a liquor licence, bribes to let whores work certain lucrative streets, bribes, bribes, bribes, bribes, bribes! The *amapolisi* don't have to go out looking for avenues to be dishonest; all roads lead to a Rome built out of cash notes, no receipts. How does mister or miss hungry *gattes* turn down that lovely money on offer every day of the year?'

The Afrikaans white *geeza* threw his double six. How lucky can you get?

Me, I carried on, carried away by the impetus of my scathing verbal monologue.

'You got to admit it doesn't take the average *gattes* long to understand what makes the wheels turn. Before you can draw a second breath, a creative cop is conjuring up ideas in his mind how he can make even *more* of somebody else's money line his pockets. These ideas are so intense and dedicated that his original purpose in joining the police force has long vanished in the shrouded mists of unimportance. Unimportance to him personally, that is. His job has become jut a dull routine to pass the time of day. No, the public have nobody to blame but themselves for the *gattes* they got. What I've got against most *amapolisi* is this. Fine, they're crooks, uniformed criminals, whatever, but it's not kosher if they're *dishonest* lawbreakers, you with me? They take a salary for enforcing the law, but they're taking big bucks more for *not enforcing it.* That makes them feel guilty, and that's why so many *gattes* are such mean paranoid motherfuckers. The *amapolisi* I've met are the most intractable human garbage I've ever known in any profession, bar none. Give me an even-keel, well adjusted, *rawurawu tsotsi* anytime when the chips are down.'

Reverend Bishop Edward Lekhanyane won the final game.

'Thank you, André, I enjoyed that,' he said to his equally corpulent Afrikaans friend.

So his name *was* André.

André who?

Who cared?

But André had turned his attention upon me. Those bifocal eyes of his were like a magnet, *mfowethu.*

'You have extraordinarily strong *blêrrie* opinions on much of law enforcement, Dhlamini,' he said nonchalantly enough, but there was something in his tone of voice that made *Baba* Edward's expression change to one of warning wariness. 'You seem to speak with the voice of experience.'

'That, in itself, is *your* opinion,' I answered. 'Where do you get your opinions?'

'André is an under-assistant to the Commissioner in the South African Police Force,' the Reverend Bishop said. 'He sees the Zion Christian Church as an immense power for good, a means to de-escalate crime amongst our youth and a bridge to promote racial harmony. He is an aware and concerned non-racist fellow countryman.'

That spun me out of orbit.

'Is he paying for the meal and drinks?'

'What do you mean, Dhlamini?'

'If he digs into his own pocket, then he can't possibly be a policeman,' I improvised. 'Stands to reason, doesn't it?'

That earned a good, hearty, boisterous laugh.

Howard had tears of mirth in his eyes.

It was late, time to say farewells, part company on an amicable note, keep the evening friendly.

'Nice to have met you, André,' I said at the door, holding out my hand to shake his.

'A pleasure, Dhlamini,' he returned, but not letting go my paw after grasping it. 'I enjoyed meeting you too. You see, I have known of you and your other interests for years and years.'

'You follow restaurant trends?'

'That is not what I meant at all, Shatterproof, and you *blêrriewell* know it, *jong*. Goodnight.'

I was floored once again. It was his use of '*Shatterproof*' that took my legs away. I was a little peeved that the Reverend Bishop, who incidentally hadn't a clue as to the origins of my unbreakable-glass nickname, had not informed me earlier who his unexpected guest was – ah, but that was all water under the bridge now, best to forget about it.

But the feeling persisted that André and Shatterproof would meet again – that his was a name to remember.

And so it was.

Meanwhile, things had turned a little haywire.

Television had just recently arrived in South Africa,

and if you had a strong enough antenna you could pick up SABC broadcasts across the Swaziland border. This local programming was generally poor quality stuff, but it was in its infancy and so forgivable. Single-channel lunchtime news plus evening news followed by mostly mediocre programmes that ended around ten at night were the viewing order of the day. The *World at War* series was my favourite, a black-and-white documentary narrated by Sir Laurence Olivier. But new wars were at hand, this time that of drugs, which showed another face on dynamic news broadcasts hungry for the outrageous and sensational that safely skirted anything to do with Nationalist Party politics.

Bengal Tiger got bust.

His splendidly moustached image regularly made its handsome appearance on the idiot box's addictive square screen.

He'd got greedy and was shipping in bushels of mandrax tablets from manufacture-anything pharmaceutical plants in India. What a furore that created, *mfowethu*! Mandrax hadn't been made illegal *yet*, so Bengal Tiger escaped jail – they could only fine him heavily for being in possession of unprescribed medicines – but the focus on him put the two-faced liquor operation in huge jeopardy.

Thank *Nkulunkulu* for the arrival of LSD.

The cops *hated* LSD, a psychedelic drug almost every young South African tried at one time or another. That synthetic magic-mushroom distillate took the focus from all other illegal substances on the turn. Or on the *turn-on*, so to speak.

I tried it myself.

Out Mantenga Falls way, to satisfy my own curiosity, I '*tuned in, turned on* and *dropped out*', to paraphrase Dr Timothy Leary, the high priest of acid and guru to millions of young anti-war Americans. What bullshit the hype of bureaucratic hate was. All the hallucinogenic drug did for me was show me the incredible natural beauty of the world we live in and ignore at our peril as a species. The 'hallucinations' were pretty good too, a massive awareness of vibrant colour, as well as experiencing the indescribable depth, harmony and poignancy of music. But enough of that valid hippie propaganda. The cops went *vreeslik mal bevok* over LSD. They saw it as the Evil That Would End The World.

One of the drug-squad dinosaur duo who had had a go at me over murdered Vuka Shabalala's forgotten heroin appeared on TV claiming he had taken the Dreaded Despicable Drug in the interests of Saving Our Youth.

Yes, *ja*, he said to a glued-to-the-screen audience, the horrors he had had to endure were unimaginable. He had turned on his radio while the hallucinogenic was turning his (already mushed) brains to mush, *and Donald Duck and Mickey Mouse had come waltzing out of the speaker and spoken to him, telling him the world of comics was the only world to inhabit, and ordering him to give up forever any notions of school or university or hard work and to take more career-wrecking LSD to fulfil his cartoon dreams.*

What patently fabricated lamebrain pigswill, *mfowethu*!

And to think unsuspecting people paid thousands and thousands of *amarands* to visit Disneyland, when all you had to do was buy a black-market budget-tour cap of acid for a mere ten bucks.

The investigative storm bombarding LSD continued unabated.

Our high-profile 'protection' went underground.

People got shot dead by over-enthusiastic narcotic *gattes* and too many experimentally minded young people went to jail to be anally *and* mentally raped by hardcore inmates while Flower Power waxed and waned.

But it all blew over eventually.

Business settled back down into a nice smooth hassle-free operation again.

Yet widespread drug use-and-abuse had gained its first toehold and, like everywhere else in the world, it just grew and grew and grew. When the people want something, they want it – price, physical damage and long-term mental-facility loss are secondary considerations.

Reverend Bishop Lekhanyane walked into the restaurant unannounced and suggested we go pay Vilakazi a visit at the University of the Witwatersrand. He had been one of the few black students accepted in those days – I'm sure Zsa-Zsa must have put the 'twist' in somewhere. My wife had *given permission* for me to see my own son now that he was well on his way to standing unaided on his own two feet and was beyond the insidious sphere of my dissipated *skebengu* influence.

I wasn't about to argue morality, the missing years, nothing. I just wanted to get there and be reunited with my boy while there was still a chance to make it all up to him.

I don't want to go into detail, but it went well.

We bonded as father and son in such a short time that it was almost as if no hurdles had been placed between us. After a few months of nothing but ongoing improvement, Vilakazi suggested we have lunch together – him, his mom and me.

That too went well.

Too well, *mfowethu*.

I wanted my wife back.

I wanted *that life* back.

I *had* to have that.

Baba Edward told me in no uncertain terms that it would be remotely possible *only if I was prepared to meet her conditions.* Which were? *She insists you change the life you lead.* What life? *More than just the life of yours we both know I am talking about. She wants you to cleanse yourself.* I have to bath twice a day? *That is not amusing, Dhlamini – clean in every sense of the word.* Be specific, *Baba* Edward, what does she want? *She wants you clean in the temple of your mind, your spiritual commitment if you will.* Spell it out, what do I have to do? *No one can spell it out for you, my son. Your only guide has to be* Nkulunkulu *and you have not had much practice at asking for His assistance, have you now?* What right do I have to ask Him for help? Surely He would only laugh in my heretic's face ? *You will never know until you ask, Dhlamini, my son.*

The answer came to me. But only after a great deal of introspective puzzling through a maze of convoluted doubts and self-deceptions.

My wife wanted a husband with no crimes at all hanging like a guillotine over his head. She wanted a husband independent of being future-guilty for past-offences that could snap at his heels like a pack of hunting dogs and bring him down to be torn and savaged when he least expected it. She wanted to look forward to a future where she knew her husband wouldn't be dragged from his bed in the middle of the night and she and their son reduced to visiting him once a week at some bleak prison for the rest of her life – a husband who'd never bounce his grandchildren on his knee.

That was what my wife wanted from me.

Just me, no baggage.

Just me.

How was I going to achieve that when I didn't know the rules? When I applied myself to any nebulous situation approximating a solution, I became more and more vexed, more and more confused, more and more mixed up as if a blender had chopped and scrambled my brains.

That was what my wife wanted from me.

Just me, no baggage.

Just me.

The first decision I'd have to make would be to get out of the sweet-as-distilled-honey homebrew alcohol operation that sold counterfeit labelled whisky, brandy, gin, vodka and the rest of it to the four corners of South Africa. But how would I ever escape from the years of crooked involvement which would stick to me like cow dung to a farmer's *veldskoen* if any of it ever came up before a 'twist-free' court of law?

That was what my wife wanted from me.

Just me, no baggage.

Just me.

The penny floated down from on high released by *Nkulunkulu*, as the Reverend Bishop would have it – and, not disputing or agreeing with that blind-faith belief, it dropped right into the awareness of that place which had my ears tuned like co-axial radar dishes on either side of my skull.

André.

The big nose who was close as a second skin (I hoped) to the Commissioner of Police and whom Baba Edward *had brought to the restaurant that after-hours backgammon night . . .*

That was . . . what my wife wanted . . . from me . . . just me . . . no baggage.

Just me.

I wasn't sure what my decision might have been right then, because bad things happened out of the blue and diverted my concentration.

Somebody tried to kill Bengal Tiger.

It was judged it had to be some other smart Big Indian Chief, who saw how much money the Asian Pussycat was making and figured with Bengal Tiger out the way he could take over and do the same thing. Bengal Tiger's massive Mercedes-Benz saved him. That solid metal body changed the trajectory of the AK-47 bullets, angled them just minimally enough away from true to crease him but not kill him.

First thing I knew about it was when I walked into The General's building.

Bengal Tiger was there swathed in bandages, heated up like a volcano about to spew out the molten innards of the earth, his clothes almost smouldering from his incandescent anger.

'I'll kill that bloody bastard *charra* an' all,' he was fuming. 'Him and his bloody wholesale family never mind!'

'You do not have evidence he was the one who tried to murder you.' The General did his best to calm him down. 'We must be certain before retribution, Bengal. Killing the wrong man makes enemies of friends. Publicity is very bad, sometimes fatal, for business.'

'Bugger that, I'm telling you an' all! I'll make bloody bunny-chow of that bastard, isn't it?'

Bengal Tiger looked up, saw me standing there and brusquely asked me to get him a packet of menthol cigarettes – he'd just run out.

When I returned, Bengal Tiger was gone.

'Some of these people are like babies,' The General said to me as if that explained it all. 'They fight over a packet of cheap sweets when there is a wheelbarrow of the finest imported chocolate right in front of them. Why does the first baby have to annihilate the second baby? Why can two babies not shake their rattles at each other and talk about who is going to get first suck at the teat of the feeder bottle? Especially when there are so many feeder bottles? Why murder each other? Every time another killing takes place it just makes it that much harder to operate. The mutual reality is that everybody loses a fortune of money. That is why we have our own rules, so that nothing is left to chance. Now homicidal maniacs want to make us as crazy as they are. Such a shame, Dhlamini, my boy, such a crying shame.'

The General was sure Bengal Tiger had seen reason and had calmed down.

He was wrong.

A prominent member of the Indian business community was slain, and Chatsworth erupted into a hotbed of reciprocal gangland-style murders.

Bengal Tiger was untouched.

The General blew his top.

He knew that once this venereal-vendetta killer-disease started suicide-syphilis in the human brain, there was no human antibiotic that could cure it and put a stop to the broadening bloodbath. He knew business would explode in his face. The residual wreckage could take long months, even years, to cart away and more years would be needed to rebuild what had been destroyed. If the lid came off Bengal Tiger's jar of tricks, then that was one of the biggest money-spinners ever gone down the tubes, goodbye, never to be seen again. And the black political heavies of The Struggle wouldn't like that at all.

I asked The General what we should do?

'We will do nothing, Dhlamini, my boy. We will keep operating as before with the cleared stocks we have on hand. Our side of the business will continue. But we shall keep our eyes peeled. We shall be ready to shut down overnight if we have to.'

The General looked as elegantly dapper as always with that jutting spade beard of his, but his face was visibly showing signs of terrible strain and downright exhausted tiredness. I registered something I had never seen before – that his hand trembled when he reached for his glass of French cognac and shivered all the way up to his lips.

I think it was that inevitable sign of age and corrosion I had observed that made me sit solo in my car for hours after saying goodnight to him. Encased by stationary metal and glass, I did some of the hardest no-illusions thinking I've ever done.

I decided after a marathon mulling to ask the Reverend Bishop to put me in contact with his contact – André, the under-assistant to the Police Commissioner, an Afrikaner who under normal circumstances was a natural-born enemy of all we *verdomde baster kaffirs*.

It had come to me, sitting alone and unmoving in that car, just *how* I could get out of the liquor-dominated pickle of my present embroilment that would cook my goose all the way up to my blistering eyeballs.

First, though, I wanted to be secure in the knowledge I could erase my past – and that meant making a deal with a representative of the law high up enough to carry clout, a big hitter.

André. It had to be André.

Sure-sure there were big risks involved, *mfowethu*, but my mind was made up. Come hell or high water, I was going to take my chances.

I was at The General's bright and early the next morning. There was an ominously cloud-locked grey sky overhead, but I was clear-headed and as determined as ever.

At first I hesitated. I made small talk over coffee and mounds of sweet Danish pastries with which The General loved to begin any day, but then I took the bull by the horns. I said that the threat of exposure to our finely structured national *tsotsi*'s liquor emporium, which balanced almost exclusively on Bengal Tiger as its fulcrum, had me worried sick. I was no longer up to it. There were other *geezas* who had worked alongside me smart enough to take my place. My mental stability was shot to pieces – and much, much more – but finally amongst this profuse verbal procrastination – I reached my objective.

I told The General I wanted to resign.

I wanted out.

I wanted no more of it.

I had expected practically anything but The General's quiet and considered response, and a searching look that pierced through to my shrivelling soul. I'd seen that look many times before, but it had never been directed at me. That look made you sweat ice-cold drops of perspiration. Then The General swung abruptly about in his enormous padded swivel-chair so that I could barely see only the top of his head as he faced the windows behind him, the venetian blinds drawn, light coming through the level slats.

'Dhlamini, my boy,' he said and I could hear his voice clearly even though it was projected away from me. 'You bring me an estimation on paper of what is owed for your splendid efforts. I will corroborate the figures with the others who are involved, get their approval and see to it that you get your due. I will take care of it all for you.'

I waited at least ten minutes in the following unbroken silence.

It appeared that The General had said all that he was going to say for now.

I got to my feet and exited as silently as any ghost who wore shoes.

Reverend Bishop Lekhanyane had set up my meeting with André for me.

Because of *apartheid* laws, there were very few places, public places that is, where a white man could meet with a black man. But the Oriental Plaza in Fordsburg was different. There was an Indian-cuisine restaurant with a full liquor licence, including a wonderful selection of wines, up on the second floor to which the authorities turned a blind eye. Where mixed couples met romantically and even openly held hands, and that was the rendezvous we decided upon.

André was dressed in a *fucking safari suit* – big belly to the fore in a short-sleeved hip-length open-necked jacket – short pants – matching pale-blue calf-length socks, one containing a silver-metal haircomb stuck halfway down the inside – hippo-wide feet jammed into shapeless *veldskoens*. Of all the things he could have worn, he *had* to don that Dutchman's Delight, the most desultory dress code ever created by Cactus Couture Calvinistic fashion gurus. He stuck out like a billboard-sized sore thumb daubed with dazzling Day-Glo. Just to be *seen* with this nightmare rock spider apparition would be enough to have me ostracised forever by some of the township bad boy *bras* I'd known in the past.

We shook hands in that peculiarly aggressive bone-crusher white-man-style, before being shown to a table by an Indian waiter who had so much Brylcreem in his thick, wavy black hair that it looked obscenely like an obsidian jellyfish made from grease was perched permanently atop his head.

The meal was a grand one of several courses. With each course, a three-tiered stainless-steel serving trolley was brought to our table with a stupendous spectrum of no-charge specialist Asian condiments, including pickled fruits and vegetables, all intended to complement, by your own pointed-out choice, whatever curried dish you were eating.

We got down to brass tacks over a selection of traditional Indian sweetmeat desserts.

No beating about the *bosveld*.

How little or how much was I going to have to tell André in order to walk away clean as a whistle? With no backlog of criminal indictment hanging like doomsday thunderclouds over my platinum woolly skull?

I explained to him what shouldn't have needed explaining – that I would be a top-ranking contender for the South African heavyweight death-sentence championships if even a mere whisper of my complicity ever leaked out. I *could definitely* give him inside turncoat information on a multimillion *amarands* illegal business that hopefully would not directly line me up as the prime suspect in its demise.

Would that be enough?

I was very cagey, *mfowethu*.

André listened to everything I had to say, then sat there turning things over in his mind, playing with his pointed piece of *bokbaard* chin fur for an eternity before he spoke.

'We in the administrative police force can only make

deals within a specified category, Dhlamini. Or shall I call you Shatterproof? No *blêrrie* matter anyways, *jong*, but you must understand that the size of your deal, *if I can arrange such a thing*, depends largely upon the size and quality of your information.'

'It's you who needs to be specific, André. Suppose I give you names, operating sites, methods of those same operations, times and schedules that will allow for arrests of split-second timing and guarantee red-handed guilt? Would that do the trick?'

'Perhaps,' he said, allowing himself to appear to be weighing up the pros and cons. 'That would be an excellent *blêrrie* beginning.'

'*Perhaps*? An *excellent beginning*? Are we speaking English or Martian here?'

'I do not follow.'

'You want what I've got to sell or don't you, André?'

'That sort of information would certainly earn you the Appellate Court's leniency, Dhlamini.'

'There you go again talking fucking Martian to an Earthman.'

'Strange *blêrrie* choice of comparisons, if I understand you.'

'They come from a Limey called Howard Postlethwaite, my partner at the restaurant. You and him both seem to share a love of science fiction, but in your case I'll just stick with the fiction.'

André shrugged and waited for me to continue.

'I need your "leniency" like I need a hail of AK-47 bullets. C'mon, André, suppose I gave you *all* the details on paper? From the tadpoles to the bullfrogs, plus every nut, bolt, screw and cog that turns the big criminal wheels? That do?'

'I can not make you any firm promises, Dhlamini,

jong,' André said lugubriously, but meanwhile I could see his investigative ship's deck was awash with barely hidden excitement. 'I am able, however, to take your same written proposition to the highest *blêrrie* authority and place it in hands capable of granting what you ask. You may be successful, but I personally cannot guarantee that.'

That simply wasn't good enough, *mfowethu*.

No ways was I going to risk my all for table scraps in return for being a good, traitorous lapdog Judas. But I judged we were now at least down to haggling ultimate price. They, his superiors, would be titillated and tempted enough to make some kind of concrete offer. Sooner or later. Meanwhile there was no point in my hanging around.

'Cheers, André,' I said, getting to my feet and leaving my garish shocking-pink and luminous-green coconut-sprinkled dessert unfinished. 'You can show good faith by paying for the meal. See what you can do in regard to digesting the rest of our shared evening together. *Hamba kahle, mlungu.*'

Just like that I walked out of there – down to the cool, tree-filled parking lot. I tipped the parking attendant and drove out into the night heading for Soweto and Sweet Cherry's *shebeen*, just for old times' sake, a visit down memory lane. There was a song playing in my head . . . *that was what my wife wanted . . . from me . . . just me . . . no baggage . . . just me . . . just me . . . just me . . . just me . . . just me . . . just me . . . just me . . .*

Not much later that same week, André made contact. Said I'd have to bring my documented list along with me, sit before a panel of law-inquisitors and undergo a truth-grilling on camera for their records.

Was I born yesterday, *mfowethu*?

Without giving myself away by howling with hysterical laughter down the telephone line, I kept my voice low, secretive and sincere, and told him I'd first have to search my conscience for any additional details his *amapolisi* Spanish Inquisition superiors could make use of in their proposed mental torture of heretic *tsotsi rawurawus*. I didn't quite put it like that, of course, but I knew I had André where I wanted him. And so I hung up without saying goodbye. Let him stew in his own *too clever* juices for awhile . . . *that was what my wife wanted . . . from me . . . just me . . . no baggage . . . just me . . . just me . . . just me . . . just me . . .*

Several weeks further down the timeline while I was still playing my cat-and-mouse game, Bengal Tiger was horribly slain.

His genitals were cut off and forced into the soft gap his battered, toothless mouth had become and his mutilated body was dumped in Durban's fairytale Blue Lagoon.

And that deed, *mfowethu*, was the deed that sang the funeral lament to our lovely liquor business.

Without Bengal Tiger, our illegal liquor operation was as extinct as the Mauritius Dodo *and that* put an entirely different slant on things.

That meant it was time to make my deal serious-style.

That meant it was time also therefore to woo Zsa-Zsa.

Serious-style, mfowethu.

I made a date with her and booked a table at the same multiracial Indian restaurant in the Oriental Plaza.

I got there early and, to steady my jitterbug nerves, knocked back way too many gulped drinks than were good for my sobriety. I found myself going over and over again in my mind what I was going to calmly and rationally say to her, but those *same* pounding revelation-headlines kept repeating themselves like a jackhammer gouging that *same* salvation song in my brain:

That was what my wife wanted from me . . .

Just me, no baggage . . .

Just me.

When she arrived, she looked like an African queen. She'd done her hair partially platinum, the same startlingly white-blond shade as mine, and added perfectly matching bead-and-glass interwoven hair extensions. Her dress was *Mame Afrika haute-couture* and I judged she was as stunning as any Black Is Beautiful darkie Hollywood movie star.

(*I had to have her back.*

I had to have her back or wither and shrivel, become a parody of the man I'd been or hoped to be.

I had to have her back. I had to have her back. I had to have her back . . .)

The meal of spicy curry dishes was perfect, culinary heaven.

Zsa-Zsa relaxed and enjoyed herself.

Electricity zithered between the two of us like gay Guy Fawkes sparklers, yet she kept casting her eyes down whenever I stargazed too intently into them.

(*That was what my wife wanted from me . . .*

Just me, no baggage . . .

Just me.)

I told her I was cutting myself off from all illegal activity.

It was all going to be buried in the past, nothing surer when I spilled the beans to the police authorities.

I wanted to come back, to have her back.

More than anything else in the world I wanted her back.

(That was what my wife wanted from me . . .
Just me, no baggage . . .
Just me.)

Looking at her, the tears she said I'd never cry started to well up painfully, forcefully inflating the back of my involuntarily expanding eye sockets.

The expression on her face was not what I'd anticipated, what I'd banked my everything on.

The expression on my wife's face was one of sceptical suspicion.

There wasn't anything further for me to say.

I sat there waiting for a response while centuries seemed to grind by.

Her hand moved across the starched linen of the table to hold mine.

She squeezed my fingers with warmth, with sympathy.

I believed I was home free.

Euphoria nearly lifted me off my chair to bounce up against the ceiling overhead.

(That was what my wife wanted from me . . .
Just me, no baggage . . .
Just me.)

Then Zsa-Zsa opened her gorgeous, desirable mouth.

'What will they do to you, Dhlamini?'

'That's the best part. Nothing. I'm making a deal. The *amapolisi* will grant me immunity from prosecution.'

'I am not talking about the police, my husband.'

'What are you talking about?'

My wife became a different woman in the blink of an eye.

She looked as if she'd been drained of all her blood and her emptiness seemed to echo a vacuum of loathing, *loathing for me.*

'Don't you see, Dhlamini? *Can't* you see?'

'What? What, Zsa-Zsa?'

'Your criminal associates. *They'll* kill you. Who'll give you immunity from their prosecution of death, their revenge? How can you ever hope to get away with what you're planning?'

'Let me worry about that.'

'I can't do that, Dhlamini. It's the same *you*. It will always be the same *you*. Now you want to sell out those you've called friends for *twenty years*? Just so you can get something for nothing, as always? How can I ever trust the word of a man who'd do that? A man who'd smile in the face of his own kind knowing he's sending them to prison's purgatory?'

'But it's all for *you*, don't you see th – '

'No, it's *not* all for me, Dlamini. It's all for *you*. It's *always* been all for you. You'll never know what it is to *earn* the God-given pleasures of life, never know suffering or anguish. You are an adolescent-minded adult *tsotsi*, a terrible teenage *tokoloshe*-man incapable of ever feeling penitence or contrition for the damage you have done to innocent human beings.'

'I can't believe my ears here. You know what I've been through. What more can I do?'

'No more, Dhlamini. You have done enough. How you can live with yourself is beyond me, but I can never live with you.'

An appalling frenzy of anger fell upon me, the mindless beast of madness descended with bared fangs into my bowels.

WHERE WAS I?

WHO WAS I?

A fetor of red-haze omnivorous rage, the spectrum of which included anything and anybody I'd ever come into contact with – my wife, my activities, the Black Messiah,

The General, even myself – swirled and solidified – and wrapped a pinpoint focus on the mother of my son.

I ground my teeth (**THAT WAS**) and my spittle seemed to turn to blood (**WHAT MY WIFE**) in my mouth, as my tendons stretched with agonising contained pain (**WANTED FROM ME**) and I crushed the wine glass (**JUST ME**) in my hand, the splintered shards biting deep (**NO BAGGAGE**) and the red blood gushing out, soaking falling spreading splashing stains stains stains (**JUST ME**) pooling onto and into the starched white tablecloth . . .

'You self-satisfied complacent cunt!'

(Was that a feral lion roaring, or was that me?)

'Does your fucking holy ghost god put a halo around your head so you can sit in judgement of others? How much that fucking halo cost you, you cunt? Don't answer, bitch, you shut your fucking mouth, you hear me? Me! Dhlamini Bhekuzulu! I paid for your fucking halo! Me! No me around, no *rawurawu* money, no fucking fucking fucking halo! Whose fucking cash allowed you to live like the pampered *poes* you are, huh? Shut your cunt mouth, shit's not allowed an opinion here! It was all my money! My money! Not your fucking father's money! My money! Fucking crucified bone-dry cunt, you won't dirty your religious fornicating son-of-God masturbating fingers on me, me, me who's sucked himself dry for you! Suck your fingers, you dried-up hag, get some juice into your life! But you don't mind taking a wet bath in my liquid cash, do you? My *amarands* deep inside your fanny, or your arsehole and your fucking mouth, eh? FUCK YOU! You want to see me suffer? RIGHT? Well you got your fucking wish, bitch cunt fucking church whore! Go fuck your God and suck his slimy fucking *umthondo*! I hope you fucking choke on it! I HOPE YOU FUCKING CHOKE ON IT!'

I rubbed her face with the copious blood pouring from

my palm . . . until . . . her . . . shocked . . . visage . . . was . . . . a . . . mask . . . of . . . red . . .

She made no move to stop me . . . doing . . . it . . .

Then I registered that most of the patrons in the multiracial restaurant were half-standing, chairs pushed back, looks of traumatised horror on their faces.

Two white-jacketed Indian waiters were holding meat cleavers in the present-arms position, but looking frightened out of their wits.

I booted my wife's table right over.

Plates, wine, utensils – everything went flying.

I stalked out of there gunfighter-style.

Nobody tried to touch me, or even call me back to settle the bill.

After binding my deeply cut hand with a handkerchief and some electrical tape I found in my car's cubbyhole, I headed for Sweet Cherry's *shebeen* in Soweto.

At least I'd be made welcome there.

Level Mette Gravel, Bra

Sweet Cherry laid it on.

I did cocaine in railway-track-sized lines, smoked 'buttons' or 'white pipes', (a mixture of mandrax and *insangu* in a broken-off bottle neck), took Obex amphetamines so I could keep going, drank spirits until I passed out, and reached for the half-empty bottle, appearing to my shattered senses to be at least half full, the minute I awoke. On top of all these lethal chemical cocktails, I ate morphine *pinks* for my splitting Armageddon hangovers – but there was still no ways I was going to cook up that death's delight surcease of all pain and spike it into my screaming veins. But I did *everything* else available, and I did it again and again, my underwear potently sour-smelly and stiff with dried crust from unwashed leftovers of leaking urine, faeces, and forgotten drug-world sex. I spooned down ice-cream and yoghurt when I remembered to keep my energy levels alive.

I was a very sick and totally disorientated *tsotsi geeza* by the time Big Bang drove down all the way from Swaziland at a worried Howard Postlethwaite's request to find me and bring me back to life.

Big Bang locked me up in the jailhouse room of some

strange house with sturdy burglar bars on the windows and began the thankless task of cleaning me up.

I couldn't have broken out if I'd wanted to – I was that wasted, dishwater weak.

He brought me food and forced me to eat, and *insisted* on making me swallow snooze sedatives like a contentious child when I'd eaten every last scrap of whatever it was he *insisted* I ate.

I slept a lot, and then after about a week and a twenty-four-hour dreamless snowballing of somnambulant zero, I woke up and seemed to be *compos mentis* again.

I was in control of my faculties.

Surprise, surprise, *mfowethu*.

I took a bath unaided, shaved away spiky sandpaper peppercorn stubble that had become a short beard, and dressed in the clean clothes Big Bang had brought me.

I was back on my feet, but somehow utterly divorced from myself.

It was as if I was perched in the air above my own body, disinterestedly detached and impartially looking down at everything I did. Weird, *mfowethu*, weird. I was observing a *geeza* I'd never seen before. How do you handle that?

I eventually got round to seeing The General.

'Time to close up shop now, Dhlamini, my boy,' he said gravely, spade beard tucked into his chest. 'You were right.'

Then he stood up.

I'd forgotten how small and slight he was.

He walked over to a wall-safe, clicked the tumblers and removed a compact but extremely deep-sided briefcase.

He handed it to me before seating himself in his enormous padded swivel-chair again.

'Count it,' he said, his lips smiling but not his raptor's eyes. 'You were asking a lot less than what is owed you. Not like you at all, if I may say so.'

I counted it.

It didn't take very long. Fat wads of high-denomination notes in banded lots of ten thousand are easy to assess.

It was more *amarands* than I'd ever held or even seen before, on my life, *mfowethu*. More than I'd fantasy-dreamed was coming to me. I was suddenly a cash-money multimillionaire, but I felt totally ambivalent about my new status.

I didn't know what to do or say, or how to express my thanks, and I left shortly afterwards.

It was years before I saw The General again.

But effectively, Zsa-Zsa's rejection of me at the closure of business after Bengal Tiger's death made any plans I'd conjectured taking further by staging a live production of *André and the Amazing Tsotsicolour Turncoat* suffer a severe dose of *rigor mortis*. My 'confession' was placed on a mortuary slab, slid into a cadaver-freezer and locked away, and the latch tool thrown into meltdown crematorium fires.

I spent more and more time with Howard at the Swaziland restaurant, doing more than my fair share, anything to pass over the suck-you-down-slowly quicksand morass of must-be-endured time. Doing the same thing, day after day, each day a replica of the last one, no knots in my guts about taking any risks.

Was this how life is supposed to be, *mfowethu*?

Was this the 'peace and contentment' that everybody craves?

Maybe so, but not for me.

I was like a skylark in a cage, a nice, secure, safe, comfortable cage, but my song had deserted me. The music was gone. Still, I needed the restaurant a lot more than it needed me, if you get what I mean, *mfowethu*.

I was surprised when The General dropped in out of the blue after much evaporated time, ordered himself several dishes of his usual phenomenally large amounts of food and polished off every morsel. I sat with him afterwards sipping *gratis* brandy liqueurs and we talked the hours away. I was happy to see him, had genuinely missed him. He was full of vim and vigour and complicated plans encompassing an absurdly lucrative future.

'I have big ideas for times ahead, Dhlamini, my boy. Our cities are growing, centralising the customer base. We will have diverse operations at work that will make past achievements seem like a drop in the ocean. We shall be moving into industry, electronics, areas where we will control a supply-and-demand monopoly that none dare stand against. Old methods will come into play to ensure new successes.'

He went on and on, and I wondered what exactly he meant by '*old methods will come into play to ensure new successes*', because that sounded to me like executioner's talk.

Suddenly those rose-coloured spectacles I'd always worn dropped away from my freed vision. Here was The General, well on his way to becoming a *madala*, an old man, but one with millions in the bank and no place to take his hunting shark's instinct other than into further devouring and filling a belly already bloated to bursting point. What was that about? He had no wife, no lovers that I knew of, no children, no friends, and no time in his single-minded albeit super-intelligent life for anything

377

other than this gluttonous procurement of the never never *never* enough.

The General had an IQ that could have had him attain anything earned through industrious merit. He could have been economics adviser to the non-racist Prime Minister of Great Britain, foreign attaché to the President of the United States, a scientist, a neurosurgeon, an aeronautics engineer, you name it. His addiction was being *The Man* who did things the law told him not to do, *ordered* him not to do. He risked life imprisonment and the death penalty for what? He had nobody to talk to except spiritually eviscerated me. Nobody loved him and *he loved nobody*. He didn't even *hate*. You see, *mfowethu*, the freakish ogre of *apartheid* and that bigoted monster's hand-in-hand permanent tenure on injustice were just old acquaintances to him, necessary annoyances that were to be tolerated by ignoring or manipulating them.

Suddenly I felt as if I was conversing with the living dead, an Einstein zombie, a shell of a man who perambulated with a by-rote remembrance of the past. Talk about me, *nothing* would ever change The General. Who'd lament his demise? Not me and nobody I knew of.

Then I saw myself, *mfowethu*.

No matter what, this was *not* going to happen to the summer of *my* life: it was *not* going to destroy *my* autumn years.

And in the space of a few minutes, while The General rambled incisively on, the answer I'd been searching so hard for came to me.

I didn't have to be the way I was.

I could change so much, not only me, *if I really wanted to*.

As easy as that.

Did I really *want* to change?

Yes, yes I did, *mfowethu*, and I could *allow* myself to ask for help. Something told me I would get all the help I needed *if I asked for it*.

My mind cleared, like it had been swept clean by the titan's broom of an August wind blowing away Jo'burg's foul factory smog. At last I knew what I was going to do – at long last, after all those empty, pointless years.

The next day in our cramped little restaurant office, I started adding up what I was worth. *Dadawethu!* That was a lot of *amarands* I'd piled up over the years! *Too much, mfowethu!*

Next, I called a lawyer Howard used and told him what I wanted to do.

From that lawyer's carefully phrased verbal-feedback legalese, I could tell he thought he was dealing with a prospective client who had clearly contracted Alzheimer's plus suicidal senility and infantile regression all in one go.

It had taken me just one fortnight to decide how to dispense with all the filthy lucre I'd taken more than two decades to accumulate.

I gave it all to the Reverend Bishop Lekhanyane and the Zionist Christian Church.

I judged that way the mountains of my money would go to good use.

That was a soaring feeling, a drug and alcohol-free high I'll never forget, one I still treasure.

There were reasons besides altruistic ones for my parting with a fortune, as I'll explain now.

What did I really and truly have that I owned, *mfowethu*? In the land of my birth, South Africa, a black man was allowed to own virtually nothing, and that's what I owned – *virtually nothing*. I had some treasured artworks, my own clothes, my hi-fi and my music, my own car, my own business; what more could I possibly want of material possessions?

Then I telephoned André, the goatee-bearded, safari suit-wearing under-assistant to the Commissioner of Police. I felt I owed him that call. He gave me a hard interrogative time on Alexander Graham Bell's invention.

'It's been years, Shatterproof! You let me down! You made an idiot of me, *jong*, led me like a *blêrrie* donkey along the garden path!'

'Calm down, André. You're the last rung in my upward climb on the ladder to redemption, hear me?'

'I hear you, *jong*.'

'My news is old now, but nevertheless I'm sure it'll be invaluable to you. I'll tell you everything. Every detail. Every name. Every address. But I want nothing in return. No deals, no nothing. You want to go for me, I'll have the best criminal lawyers keeping your *piranha* prosecutors at bay until the pall-bearers come to carry me to my final rest.'

'You mean it, Shatterproof? Especially the names and the crimes they were responsible for?'

'*Yebo*. You think I'm calling because I like the sound of your give-one-inch but take-ten-in-return voice?'

'When?'

'Soon. Patience is a virtue, *wena*. You'll have insight into a *tsotsi* empire that'll have your mind staggering. *Hamba kahle, mlungu*.'

That was André lined up.

Maybe next week.

Maybe even the week after.

Two nights later, Howard Postlethwaite came to call me urgently from the restaurant's kitchen where I was going head-to-head with the head chef about a massively important disputed something that has now lost all relevance entirely.

The General was at the bar.

'Nevvah seen such a mean lookin' little ponce cahnt in orl me born fahkin days, me old sahn,' Howard said in warning.

Thank *Nkulunkulu* the restaurant crowd was thinning out. There were just a few odd tables with a few diehard diners left.

The General was swaying ever so slightly, perched like a spade-bearded goblin on a high bar stool. He was always as balanced as a poised panther and I immediately realised he must be in that rare state for him: loaded and primed with liquor. I'd never seen him drunk. Just goes to show there's a first time for everything, *mfowethu*.

He turned around at my approach, his raptor's eyes half shut – but mean and nasty all the same.

'*Sawubona*, Dhlamini, my boy. How is my protégé that throws away all th' money I h've earned for him?'

How the fuck did he know that?

Warning bells should have gone off, but they didn't.

Right then, feeling the way I did after the heated tussle with the head chef, my chief and only worthwhile antagonist in the restaurant decision-making stakes, I was in no mood to further antagonise The General by asking him questions – the answers to which had already sneakily invaded my subconscious.

Anyway, prior to my giving that more pause for thought, The General was loosing off additional verbal broadsides. But before he did that, he downed two already-poured hefty glasses of brandy that had been waiting in front of him and then grabbed me by both arms and shook me like an errant child.

'Why, in th' name'f all tha's righteous, did you give our money away to *bulongwe* thieves, bogus savioursh, those *uthuvi* who play on the mental insecurities'f weaklings? Why, Dhlamini, my boy? Why? My *amarands* make y'feel dirty, my pretty little protégé with a white man's hair? Couldn't you h've asked me first was there not better way than th' way you h've chosen?'

The General nearly fell off his bar stool because the ague I'd witnessed once before was now so exacerbated that he was shaking violently with uncontrollable rage. I hung on to him, as he in turn grasped the edge of the bar to save himself from an ugly drunken plunge. I swear he was hissing like a hellishly amplified snake, *mfowethu*.

'You – you – you got funny way'f showing your loyalty, Dhlamini – Dhlamini, *my boy*, right? Ev'ything you have's come from me, me, me. Wha's the matter with people?'

'General, sir, you know I'm more than grateful for everything you've ever done for me and – '

'*Gratitude*, you say? Liar! I spit on your grat'tude!'

And so help me, *mfowethu*, the cool, calm and collected, always charismatic but low-profile behind-the-scenes leader of men it seemed I'd known forever hawked up an enormous ball of vile phlegm and spat it out before I could flinch. It struck with terrible accuracy like a slime sludge-post of *tsotsi* infidelity right over my traitor's heart and clung there, a horribly gleaming mucus oyster.

'Oi've fahkin 'ad enough orf this fahkin shite,' Howard growled under his breath, moving forward and embracing The General in what would have looked to a casual observer to be a farewell hug between two old male chums. But what Howard did was physically heft The General off his bar stool and swing him towards me, and together we half-carried, half-walked him to the restaurant's tiny but soundproofed office.

The General made no protest.

His small feet barely touched the floor.

We slumped him down in one of two squeezed-in armchairs. He immediately went totally slack, closed his eyes and appeared to have passed out, a dribble of bubbling spittle leaking from the corner of his mouth into his beard.

As we closed the door before heading back into the restaurant, we both heard him slur-mumbling, '. . . *eye for eye, tha's right, tooth for tooth, jus' like th' Bible* . . . jus' *like* . . . '

But as we paused to listen, turning back towards him, he began gently snoring, so we left him there to sleep it off.

Howard and I went back to the bar and had a stiff drink ourselves.

'Wot's up wif that geezer?' Howard asked me. 'Wot was orl that fahkin shite abaht, me old sahn?'

'Ghosts from my past come to haunt me, Howie, that's all.'

'Fahkin 'ell, fahkin vicious fahkin cahnt orf a fahkin evil fahkin ghost, innit?' Howard observed dryly, breaking his own record for the number of expletives used in any one short sentence. 'Yew sure evvything's kosher, me old sahn?'

'Nothing to worry about, Howie.'

'Oi believe yer, but fousands fahkin well wouldn't, mate. Yew watch yore fahkin back.'

'Relax, Howie,' I said. 'Let's have another drink.'

Howard Postlethwaite, I judged, was, besides Big Bang, the only real friend I'd ever had. The kind of friend you *know* will never let you down. The kind who'll be as constant as the northern star, no matter what. I longed to tell him all the details of my nefarious *tsotsi* past dealings, but I knew I couldn't. I'd save that for our old age or something.

Howard brought out the backgammon board and we played and drank pleasurably long after the last diner had departed.

Then the faint tinkle of the telephone ringing came vaguely through the closed office door.

Who could be calling at this time? It was after two in the morning.

Then the telephone ceased its muffled jangling.

It must have woken The General and he must have picked it up.

When I got to the office, The General was replacing the receiver. He looked a little dishevelled, but his fiery raptor's eyes said he was wide awake, his small body held militarily erect and no longer the least bit drunk.

'Everything okay, General, sir?' I asked. It was *my* phone and *my* office after all.

'Yes,' he answered, that single word seeming to contain a dictionary's worth of meanings.

'Any message for me or my partner?'

'No. All perverse situations are dealt with. I am content with future events, Dhlamini, my boy.'

That sounded like gibberish to me. *Perverse situations?* What was he talking about, *mfowethu*? What exchange had been made on that telephone? Again, surely *any* calls at the restaurant's number would have been for Howard or for me?

'Are you certain, General, sir? Nobody trying to reach the restaurant?'

'Of course. Why do you keep on and on repeating yourself, Dhlamini, my boy? I have answered you. What more do you want me to say? Are you concerned for *me*, Dhlamini, my boy? Surely not, after you have done everything you could do for my comfort and recuperation here tonight?'

He was being his plausible, dapper, diplomatic self once more. But beneath his outward armour of rigid self-control, I could judge he was seething like a nest of angry carnivorous worms dumped out of the carcass they'd been voraciously feeding upon. It was those raptor's eyes of his that gave him away. They would have cut through tungsten like lasers if they weren't deliberately shielded.

He was abruptly unsteady as he got himself around the desk and I made to assist him.

Then abruptly his legendary restraint shredded, tore itself into ragged flapping strips of insanely vindictive gangrenous venom.

'You dare to touch me? Keep your putrid polluted hands away from my body! You are a filthy disease!'

My legs nearly buckled under me at the sheer intensity, the tangible physical power of this unexpected verbal onslaught, and went into involuntary reverse.

Then The General metamorphosed, *right in front of me*, a change as mind-blowing and sense-encompassing as any witch doctor's sorcery, *visibly* switching bodies from hyena to human.

'Dhlamini, my boy, surely you know I am jesting with you?' he said, smiling genuinely at me with sincere warmth and suddenly being an inebriated old man again *in the space of a microsecond*. 'One cannot take drink the way one used to as a youngster. Not when you get to be my age. Drink meddles with the mind, my boy. Makes an astute man turn stupidly foolish without warning. Forgive my rudeness, Dhlamini. Take care of me now and call me a taxi. It is time for me to burden your hospitality no longer.'

'I'll take care of it, General, sir.'

'You always were a good boy, Dhlamini. You were always *my* boy, eh? I *always* reciprocate the care given to me by my friends, you know that. You have taken good care of me. I shall see to it that you are taken *good care* of in return. You have always been my favourite, my little helper with the white man's hair. Oh yes, Dhlamini, my boy, I shall take *good care* of you.'

The General was frivolously chortling and chuckling away to himself while he said this, and he continued to be as happy as a merry brown-skinned gnome, his spade beard nodding in syncopation with his mirth, until the taxi drove him off to I know not what destination.

It was getting close to four in the very early morning by the time I got home.

There was a message on one of those new answering machines I'd bought myself just a few months back, with Vilakazi especially in mind because my boy still meant the world to me.

The message was from safari-suit André of the *bokbaard* chin fur. He who drew a fat salary from the Police Commissioner's coffers.

The message said that his covert police electronics team had discovered there was a wire-tap on the restaurant's telephone line *and not to use it for anything under any circumstances except mundane and routine business exchanges*. End of message.

For me, it was like the scattered hundred pieces of a jigsaw puzzle had been thrown high into the air and mystically floated down with every little odd-shaped piece slotting *perfectly* together to form the complete picture. Now complete nonsense made *perfectly* complete sense to me.

I was up the creek without a paddle.

Small wonder The General's behaviour had seemed so aberrant and strange.

I had to think hard and fast.

There was no question of now going to André. Past *tsotsi*

secrets would remain past *tsotsi* secrets, because certain retribution would extend beyond me if I went ahead with my 'confession' – *they* would destroy my estranged wife, my son, Howard Postlethwaite, even Big Bang, just to let me suffer diabolically *before* the final ignominy of a brutal *coup de grâce*.

What The General said to me at the restaurant took on a radically different perspective in this new light.

What could I do?

What steps could I take to let *them* know that I was no longer a threat? And thus save my friends and loved ones from implacable vengeance?

There *had* to be an answer and it came to me like a bolt of lightning splitting the heavens.

I would join The Struggle.

My service as an MK soldier would stand me in good stead. As a reference demonstrating unshakable loyalty, my *Umkhonto we Sizwe* blood rites would be seen as staunch, resolute, unassailable and steadfast. The truth of that circumventive matter was neither here nor there. Under the protective wing of those fighting *apartheid* for change *that had to come in South Africa*, I would be untouchable, I would be safe.

Untouchable.

Safe.

Yes.

Yes, I could even become one of the future elite *if I gave it my all and proved myself invaluable*.

I felt changed by this decision from the man, or many men, I had been before. It came to me that this was the purpose in life for which I'd been continually searching.

I knew I was never going to be alone again – not ever again, *mfowethu*.

The next morning I was showered and dressed a half-hour earlier than usual and I walked to work instead of taking the car, making my legs work rhythmically, filling my lungs with exhilarating air.

As I stood at the crossing, waiting for the traffic lights we South Africans call 'robots' to change so that I could cross over to the restaurant's side of Mbabane's main road, a sleek barracuda of a car with darkened windows and an opaque windscreen pulled up further down, parking a few lengths beyond and parallel to the restaurant doors.

The driver wound down his window, fastidiously lit a cigarette and blew the projected tendrils of exhaled smoke pointedly in my direction. There was a crooked leering smile on his cruelly thick-lipped mouth, beneath pitch-black dark glasses.

He was not a man I'd seen before, but even with his eyes hidden I knew what he was. I'd spent too much time in the early days of township sudden death to ever forget, *mfowethu*. He was a hired killer, no doubts about that.

I wasn't apprehensive: no fear ran in my veins. He wasn't going to blow me away then and there, not with that traffic cop walking the pavement looking for the day's first four-wheeled recipients of pink parking tickets. Still, he wasn't there resting his hardbitten thug's *ezzies* because he was soaking up the sights. He was either coalescing my habits, collecting and marking them for a future decision of when and where to cancel me, or else he was advertising himself as a specific warning.

No way to read him, *mfowethu*.

So I just kept on walking.

Deliberately I took the restaurant keys from my pocket

and selected the two that would open the double-throw locks so I could get inside and start preparing early for the lunchtime trade . . .

. . .

Please pass me that jug of water, *mfowethu.*

I have a sudden cramp in my chest.

Most unusual and annoying.

Totally unexpected so soon after the last one that sneaked up on me . . . mild enough but . . . terribly uncomfortable . . .

We'll continue just as soon as I've swallowed these damned pills I have to live with . . . these days . . .

Can't live without them I suppose is what . . . it boils . . . down to . . .

No, no, I'll be alright . . . this happens to me now and . . . now and again, nothing to worry about, *mfowethu,* nothing . . . to worry . . . about . . .

My pills will soon . . . soon do the trick, you'll see, you'll see . . . there's a lifetime more . . . of my unfinished story to . . . tell you yet . . .

Walter . . . and Thabo that . . . that short arse and . . . Madiba and . . .

Why has it gone dark?

Mfowethu, please, why has it gone so . . . so *very very dark?*

I can't . . . see . . . properly . . .

Oh, *mfowethu,* the pain!

Why . . . not normal . . . inside my chest . . . this frightful . . . pain?

Help me, *mfowethu,* so weak . . .

Help me, I seem . . .

to . . . be . . .

blacking . . .

out . . .

 pain . . .
no . . .
no
. . . .
. . . .
. . . .
. . . .
. . . . .
. . .
.

EPILOGUE
The Present

'Help me! Guards! Somebody! The Minister has collapsed! Oh God, somebody help me!'

'What have you done to him?'

'Me? Nothing, nothing, I swear it!'

'What happened?'

'His face turned this horrible ashen colour! Then he fell off his chair!'

'He take his pills?'

'Yes, yes he swallowed some, he drank th – '

'Hey, wena!'

'Yebo, boss?'

'Leave the old man! Get on the phone and call an ambulance!'

'Ayikhona, boss, too late now. He's not breathing. There's no pulse, he's gone.'

'Do what I fucking tell you! Get that ambulance now! You want a job tomorrow?'

'Yebo, boss, I'm on it.'

'You!'

'Me?'

'Yes you, mister university boy. Give me that thick book you've been writing in.'

'But this's my personal notebook.'

'I won't repeat myself. Hand over.'

'When can I get it back? You see, it's my final-year work for my thesis and –'

'What's that?'

'This?'

'What you think, bright boy?'

'A micro-cassette to record interviews. It's my mom's actually and I need – '

'Give.'

'But it's not mine to give. It doesn't belong to me, I told you it's my – '

'No arguments.'

'Hey! You can't do that!'

'I just did. Now out that door, I want you gone.'

'I can't leave without my papers and my mom's recorder. Hey, take your hands off me!'

'Out, university boy. You want me to use this nightstick?'

'When can I get my things back?'

'Apply to the Minister's Office. Miss Khubeka will take care of all details.'

'But you have no right to – '

'Khuzwayo! Vulindlela! Get this young cockerel out of my sight! Put him in his scrap-heap car and make sure he's off of these grounds in two minutes flat! Get going! Hamba, wena!'

'Don't make it hard on yourself, laaitjie. You heard the boss.'

'You take his other arm, Vuli.'

'Got it, Khuzo.'

'Come along now, no fuss, it's all for the best.'

'Find those pills of his for me.'

'Here they are, boss.'

'Excellent. You didn't give them to me, you've never seen them.'

'Never saw them, boss.'

'Good man. Now let's get ready for the paramedics.'

'What you want me to do, boss?'

'Put him back in his chair. Make sure his head rests pillowed on his folded hands with his elbows splayed comfortably outward to either side, like he went to sleep at his desk.'

'Any reason, boss?'

'We want him looking natural. So it seems he passed away while taking a nap.'

'Okay, boss. Telephone's going, I got it. Yebo? I give him to you now. For you, boss.'

'Yes, General, sir? As planned, sir, to celebrate your ninety-eighth birthday. Yes we have all the relevant documents secured. Thank you, General, sir, you are more than generous, I am most grateful. Thank you very much once again. Until later then. Goodbye, General, sir.'

Glossary

All terms are translated from Zulu or Southern-African-Languages-based 'streetslang' (*tsotsitaal*) unless indicated otherwise.

Abbreviations: **Afr.** for Afrikaans

ama- the prefix indicating plural inclusive of 'adopted' English words

abantwana: young children (plural of ntwana)

AK-47: Kalashnikov semi-automatic assault rifle, standard infantry weapon of the East Bloc countries; most widely used criminal and guerrilla weapon in all Africa

amafutha: multiplied fat, excess (plural) fat

amaboere: derogatory *tsotsitaal* for the (then mostly white) apartheid police force

amabulldozer: a plethora of bulldozers

amacriminals: street patois for the plural of 'criminal'

amadoda: the men (olden times 'the warriors') – '*madoda*' also being ungrammatical slang for 'man' singular rather than the correct '*indoda*'

amapolisi: standard slang for the police (plural)

amarands: rands, South African currency

apartheid: (Afr.) 'separateness'; official government policy from 1948 to ensure racial separation at all levels of society

AWB: Afrikaans acronym for Afrikaner Weerstandsbeweging (Afrikaner Resistance Movement) – militant neo-Nazi organisation

ayikhona: no, not so – to disagree

baas: (Afr.) master, sir, boss. Former mode of address by non-whites to all whites

baba: father – also dignified term of respect used for older respected man

babalaza: atrocious hangover

bakkie: pick-up vehicle, small truck with or without canopy

Bantustan: see *homeland*

befok: (Afr. also spelt *bevok*) fucked up in the head, deranged

bhuti: brother

bioscope: outdated South African common-use term for 'the movies' back in the 50s and 60s

Blankes Aleenlik: bold sign of enforced segregation (on park benches, toilets etc.) denoting 'Whites Only' by apartheid law

boers: (Afr.) literally 'farmers' – derogatory reference to white ruling class, especially security forces and Afrikaners

boerewors: (Afr.) highly spiced pork and beef sausage, almost the national dish crossing ethnic and racial lines

bra: (via Afr.) township slang for 'mate' or 'black brother'

braaivleis: (Afr.) the cooking of meat on an outdoor barbecue

brandewyn: (Afr.) brandy

bulongwe: cattle-dung, bullshit

button: slang for mandrax tablet

bushveld: countryside dominated by thorn trees; usually cattle or game area

Coloured: (Cape Coloured) apartheid terminology for a person of mixed race, alternatively non-Bantu/non-white person

dadawethu!: literally 'by my sister!' ultimate declaration of what has or is being said to be true – in other words, 'may I sexually abuse and shame my own sister before I would lie to you!'

dagga: slang for marijuana, *Cannabis sativa*

die swart gevaar: (Afr.) 'the black danger' but particularly almost psychopathic Afrikaans paranoia of the time when *any* black person was considered a potential threat to the stability of tenuous white Afrikaans domination

dompas: slang for the detested reference or pass book, stamped weekly/monthly, which Africans were required to carry on their persons to prove they had permission to be in an urban or 'white' area

Durban Poisons: wonderfully potent marijuana grown in tropically humid KwaZulu-Natal and wrapped in brownpaper-sticks – also called, simply, 'Poisons'

'eat the earth': Zulu saying for death

ezzies: backside, bottom, *glutei maximus*, arse

eish!: term of exclamation, usually rueful and/or self-deprecating, sorrow, frustration

fokkoff: (Afr.) slang, fuck off

fokkol: (via Afr.) fuck all, i.e. nothing – also spelt *'vokkol'*

gangsta: style adopted by those blatantly flouting the law

gahle: take it easy, slowly, slow down

gal pil: detestable, beneath contempt, poisonous

gattes: tsotsitaal (derogatory) for the police

geeza/s: township version of Cockney English 'geezer/s'

gologo (u-): grog, booze, alcohol

guluva/s: those who do not work, but still (mysteriously!) manage to make a good living

hawu!: term of fierce exclamation, huge surprise

heytada: *tsotsitaal* township greeting, short for '*heytadadaso*'

highveld: high-altitude grassland on inland plateau where Johannesburg and the Reef are situated

homeland: one of ten areas set aside under apartheid for particular African tribes or language groups, earlier known as 'Bantustans,' to ensure Black South Africans were citizens of nominally self-governing or so-called independent territories thus leaving 'true' South Africa with its required white 'majority' – four opted for full independence in the 70s – Bophuthatswana, Ciskei, Transkei and Venda. All were reincorporated into South Africa in 1994

ikhanda: literally 'head' but also means intelligence, brains, power of reason

Immorality Act: sexual congress between a white and a person of another race, especially black or coloured, outlawed between 1950 and 1985 and punishable by a lengthy prison sentence

indaba: discussion, debate, council in search of rational answer

induna: (Nguni) headman

ingelozi: an angel – '*ingelozi yami*' 'my angel'

inja: dog

inkalakatha: see '*nkalakatha*'

ishongololo: millipede – in parts of KwaZulu-Natal these grow to enormous size

isibhamu: gun, firearm

izikhonyane: locusts

'Jewish': *tsotsitaal* which refers to exclusive tailor-made
  (and therefore exorbitantly expensive) stylish clothing
kaffir: offensive term for black people, much like the
  word 'nigger' used in Southern American States
  practising slavery – comes from Moslem term of abuse
  for non-Moslems
kaffirboetie: (Afr.) literally 'kaffir-brother' or 'niggerbrother' – offensive term for whites thought/assumed
  to be 'kaffir-lovers'
khaya: house, dwelling, place of abode
knobkerrie: (Afr.) also spelt '*knobkierie*,' a heavy, hefty
  stick with a large carved knob on the end used for
  hand-to-hand fighting or hunting; can be used as
  throwing missile
KwaZulu: self-governing territory of the Zulu people
  in Natal; officially KwaZulu never accepted full
  independence, but had its own administration, police
  force and parliament and was controlled by Inkatha.
  Now part of KwaZulu-Natal province
laaitjie/s: young guy/s still wet behind the ears
larney: very grand/attempting a social status way beyond
  one's status in society
lobolo: bride wealth/bride price
lungile: word of acceptance – okay, no problem
magistraat: (Afr.) magistrate
malgat: (Afr.) direct translation 'mad-arsed' – crazy,
  irresponsible, over-the-top
malpitte: (Afr.) direct translation 'mad-seeds/pips' – a
  seed from the *veld* when ingested gives violent and
  unpredictable hallucinations
mame: mother
mampara: brainless idiot
mampoer: (Afr.) illegal home-brewed peach-brandy, also
  called '*witblits*'

mandrax: hypnotic tranquilliser, sleeping tablet, banned as dangerous drug but still very much in ubiquitous illegal use – smoked in bottleneck 'pipes' mixed with dagga

madala: old man

mbaquanga: a rhythmic form of township music, fusing ethnic bass beat and melodies with jazz

mfaan: small boy

mfowethu: friend, usually used by or for younger persons

mielie meal: (Afr.) maize meal, staple food in South Africa

mjita: urban black slang for 'one of the boys' or friend – a supercool buddy

MK: nickname of Umkhonto we Sizwe, the military wing of the ANC

mlungu: (Nguni) mode of address to a white man, white person – use thereof, depending on inflection, can be derogatory

moegoe: tsotsitaal for dummy, nerd, deliberately stupid individual made so by his or her shortsighted convictions

muhle (i)nkalakatha: 'very-nice-big-thing'

National Party, NP, Nats: party formed in 1914 to represent white Afrikaner interests. Went through various splits, fusions and name changes until it came to power in 1948.

necklace: rubber tyre filled with petrol, forced over a victim's head and then set alight

ngonyama: lion, king of beasts

nkalakatha: huge, monstrous, unbelievably big

Nkulunkulu: Supreme Being, God

nkomo kanina: the bride's mother's slaughter beasts/cattle

nortch: streetslang for 'check that out' – to give a long, circumspect, analytical eyesearch

ntwana: young boy, more formal version of 'laaitjie'

nyaga-nyaga: tsotsitaal for 'endless ongoing trouble'

pap en vleis: (Afr.) maize porridge and meat

pass book: see *dompas*

pass laws: restricting black people's movements in the country of their birth; repealed in 1986

phatha-phatha: streetslang for sexual intercourse

phelile: finished, permanently over

picannins: young small boys

pink dollars: streetslang for a fifty-rand note, so named because of its colour

pinks: pure morphine capsules, prescribed as painkillers for severe pain – highly addictive – when 'cooked' and injected they are the poor man's heroin

phindaphinda: to do again, to fold, to return

rawurawu: callous robber – or to rob callously in true bandit-style

rondavel: (Afr.) simple, one room, circular thatched dwelling

sawubona: 'I see you' – much used Zulu form of greeting among many Africans

shebeen: (from Irish) in South Africa shebeens began as clandestine township taverns where blacks drank illegally obtained spirits such as brandy and gin which were *forbidden* to them by apartheid laws

sheshayo: hurry up – '*sheshayo wena!*' 'hurry up, you!'

sisi: sister

skebberesh: rubbish person, one without a vestige of morals, petty criminal

skebengu: a no-good, an opportunistic footpad, a ne'er do well, intrinsically bad felon

skellum: naughty bugger, often used affectionately

skokiaan: sometimes extremely dangerous alcoholic drink brewed away from prying eyes on hillsides or inaccessible places in tin drums using yeast (mainly) as base – 'extra' ingredients such as carbide are added to give it a 'kick'

skoroskoro: old car on its last breath, battered and/or in desperate need of repair

skollie: (Afr.) Afrikaans slang for a 'ducktail,' 'Teddy Boy,' dissipated hooligan

snowbound: 60s and 70s 'incrowd' reference to the cocaine trade

sonta: twist or 'the fix'

spaza: a small, rudimentary shop selling basic commodities in a township or poor suburb

State of Emergency: suspension of civil liberties during the years of apartheid to strengthen control of any perceived threat to the state; gave police and the military enormous extended powers which contravened basic human rights

strandlopers: (Afr.) 'beach-walkers' pre-colonial Khoi, original inhabitants of southern-most South African coastline

tokoloshe: supernatural creature in African folklore, powerful but of diminutive stature, capable of stealing one's soul while one sleeps – giving rise to the popular belief that a favourite lurking-place is under one's bed

tsotsi: township gangster

ugologo: see '*gologo*'

umdidi: arsehole

umdidi we mpisi: hyena's anus

uthuvi: excrement, shit

wena: you – as in '*Hey, wena!*' 'Hey, you!

bonsela editions

bonsela [ˌbʊnˈselə]
[Zulu: *ibhanselo* a gift]
An unexpected surprise

African Cookboy – author interview for Bonsela edition by Carien Els

***African Cookboy* is an explosive work of fiction – what kicked off this story that takes such a radically different stance on the usually tragic tsotsi life?**
The little explosive spark that sets the wheels in motion and drives you day and night to capture with words a story that unfolds only in your own head? More than one spark, I guess, a Guy Fawkes concatenation of unexpected events that combined, make you write those first tentative paragraphs. You put those few pages aside. Then you read them later. It next happens or it doesn't happen. If it does happen, the nucleus you've begun sinks its claws into you and there's only one escape. Forget eating, forget sleeping, forget the fragility of your financial complications – the blank paper draws your pen like a magnet, a magnet so strong that there is no release for the writer until that final page lets you know that you've got it *just right*, you simply can't do it any better and all that struggling was worth it.

You asked, 'What kicked off this story that takes such a radically different stance on the usually tragic tsotsi life?' Here are some of the ingredients: Joshua 'Joe' Sithole of early Kwela Kids fame died tragically and prematurely of pneumonia... Joe, godfather to my daughter Misty, in the days when *apartheid* was not just draconian, but ravenous with blind hungriness. Our connection was music and our open friendship quite frankly denied every tenet of enforced separatist ideology. Joe didn't moan, didn't weep, didn't wail, Joe simply adopted this attitude – F*ck You, *Apartheid!* What a man! He was the kernel of my protagonist, one for whom obstacles were to be overcome not overbearing. At this time, I'd gotten hold of a whole bunch of Dr Peter Bekker's (now forgotten and out of print) works on the beginnings of township life, tribal customs, tsotsi gangs and tsotsi-*taal*, afro-jazz, shebeens, the works . . . man, you mix gunpowder with heat, you gotta have an explosion. So, that's more or less how *African Cookboy* was conceived and executed (ha! ha!), and also, a very much also, to honour Joe's memory and indomitable spirit. (God's lucky up there, if there is an up there, to have Joe playing him his inimitable, heavenly guitar music).

Dhlamini 'Shatterproof' Bhekuzulu is a wildly authentic and astonishing character. How did you go about developing this remarkable personality?
You say Dhlamini 'Shatterproof' Bhekuzulu is a wildly authentic and astonishing character? Yes he is. Why? Because he's human. Totally human, vulnerable even, in

spite of, or even because of, his activities. As PJ O'Rourke, my favourite observer of the human race says; *Finally, people are all exactly alike. There's no such thing as a race and barely such thing as an ethnic group. If we were dogs, we'd be the same breed. George Bush and an Australian aborigine have fewer differences than an Ihaso apso and a toy fox terrier. A Japanese raised in Riyadh would be an Arab. A Zulu raised in New Rochelle would be an orthodontist. I wish I could say I learned this by spending arctic nights on ice floes with Inuit elders and by sitting with tribal medicine men over fires made of human bones in Madagascar. But actually, I found it out by sleeping around. People are all the same, though their circumstances differ terribly. Trouble doesn't come from Slopes, Kikes, Niggers, Spics or White Capitalist Pigs; it comes from the heart.* I think that says it all, don't you? Somewhere, deep inside of us all, lurks that authentic wildness just waiting for a stray catalyst to randomly ignite it – and then, hold onto your complacency, baby, a surprise awaits around every corner!

The main character is a criminal in virtually every sense of the word. Yet the reader is strangely drawn to him and I for one found myself wanting him to succeed in his criminal endeavours. Why do you think this is the case?

You found yourself somehow *wanting*

Shatterproof to *succeed* in his criminal activities? Not surprising! Firstly, there's the secretly empathic voyeur in all of us – go back to the huge success of Robert Louis Stevenson's *Dr Jekyll & Mr Hyde* during the ultra-strict morality of Victorian times, and you have your answer Yes, Shatterproof *is* a criminal, but as an imaginative, intelligent individual constricted by the barbed wire circumstances of his unasked-for birth, what true morality was available to be imparted to him apart from family values? In the sprawling and dirt-poor townships, only the successful were admired, the rich juice of tribal values long squeezed dry by those familiar companions of the terminally poor, hunger, no hope, constant fear and the pervading monster of sanctified inequality.

You seem to have a thorough knowledge of everything from petty crime in the townships to drug-smuggling and illegal alcohol brewing and bootlegging. How did you go about researching the criminal underworld?

You're asking me how I seem to have a *thorough* knowledge of everything from petty township crime to drug-smuggling and illegal alcohol brewing and bootlegging? Do you want an *honest* answer? This is like asking Archbishop Desmond Tutu if he's ever tried narcotic substances while 'converting' the courtesans of an Asian whorehouse to the faith, and you suddenly notice he's got his fingers firmly crossed as he beams you that fabulous smile and opens his mouth to answer. ('Come again?' as the Actress said to the Bishop!) 'Nuff, said, I think. Yes, ahem, quite so.

Shatterproof's flashback to his time in MK is horrifying and brutal. How did you gain insight and understanding regarding this period in his life?
You find Shatterproof's 'flashback to his time in MK' is horrifying and brutal? How did I gain insight? As a teenager I was compulsorily conscripted to the South African armed forces, on the 'other side' so to speak. There were a few revelations there, not many, just isolated and incredibly inhuman. But all we have to do (as creators of valid fiction) is think about the recent Hutsi & Tsutsi fracas, the Americans nosing into warlord-controlled regions of bleak northern Africa, our own groundless and horrific eruptions of racial prejudice against foreign refugees, Hitler and his fellow First World War Iron-Cross-awarded German Jews . . . and one doesn't need much graphic imagination to grasp the many pictures that roll onto the screen of one's inner vision.

Did you write this book purely for the enjoyment of storytelling or did you have a particular message that you wanted to convey?
Why did I write this book? Enjoyment of

storytelling or a particular message that I wanted to convey? The answer to that is both combined and yet more, much more. Apart from the enjoyment, that lovely, fiery, absolutely awesome experience of being somewhere else, in a different place with totally different people, and then the effort of swimming back to normal surroundings, is crushing in an unexplainably ecstatic way. It is always a shock. You walk out of your workroom in a daze. You want a drink. You need it. It happens to be a fact that nearly every writer of fiction in the world drinks more whisky than is good for them. You allow yourself at this stage of penned labour to drink whisky. Several large whiskies, in fact. You then search for the little spontaneous things your day's writing may have overlooked. When you have finished doing this, sometimes you eat, sometimes you don't, and then you go to sleep. Then, when you wake up, the first fastidious thing you do is go over it all one more painstaking time. Just so that you have made quite sure to remove the occasionally lurid and over-verbose trash the whisky might have added in its boundless enthusiasm. Then, and only then, do you plunge yourself into beginning again. There, those are most of the multiplied 'Why Did You Write This Book?' answers.

Excluding this: yes, there is a 'message' contained, one I personally consider to be essential. Here we are in the New Millennium in the New South Africa. Young adults of all races that I vibe with honestly and truly have no clue as to the realities of the ever-present past. Guitar students study me with wet-paint looks of hesitant astonishment on their faces when I tell them that a critically injured Black Person was not allowed-by-law to be rescued by a White Persons Only (on hand!) ambulance and that *nogal*, even should a Black Persons ambulance eventually arrive, it was not allowed-by-law to take said dying Black Person to the nearby White Persons Only Hospital, but had to travel miles away to where the Black Persons Hospital was situated in strict segregation. (I can see they don't really believe me, believe it or not!) Never mind that wonderful university academic, best buddy of Henry Verwoerd, who lectured publicly that Blacks were forbidden strong alcohol (by law), because the skulls beneath their wooly heads were smaller than a white man's, thus the ingestion of alcohol immediately swelled their tightly constricted brains causing instant dementia leading to rape, murder, robbing and general berserker madness. So, yes, I guess there *is a message* and this is it – To Understand The Present, You Must First Understand The Past.